CURVEBALL CURSED

FAIRIES AND FASTBALLS

BRIGID COLLINS

RON COLLINS

SKYFOX
PUBLISHING
Fantasy

SKYFOX
PUBLISHING
Fantasy

(In Trade Paperback)
ISBN-10: 1-946176-66-4
ISBN-13: 978-1-946176-66-0

(In Hardcover)
ISBN-10: 1-946176-67-7
ISBN-13: 978-1-946176-67-9

CONTENTS

To play or not to play, that is the question.

PROLOGUE

You will never be free of me, Adrien Thorn! the Unseelie Queen screamed.

Her use of his true name sent an agonizing ripple of power through his chest.

The roaring of the crowd echoed in his ears, too, a hollow cacophony of cheers, hoots, and snarls from the gathering of fairies who had sat in the stands of Unseelie Pitch, watching Fairy Realm history in the making.

He would remember her words forever.

Know this, boy! When next your mortal baseball team the Unicorns hold their tryouts, you will participate, and when you do — at that very instant! — you will return to my side. Do you hear me, Adrien Thorn? You will never be free of me! Never! Never! Nev—

"Adrien?"

Adrien gasped as the soft voice of Benji Amberman, sitting at the

1

desk across from him, arms folded and leaning on their elbow, snapped him out of the memory he had been reliving.

Adrien pressed his knees together and dried his sweating palms against his thighs.

He hated that memory. He hated, too, that even after months, the moment could still sweep over him with enough force to leave him trembling.

"You're thinking about the Fairy Realm again," Benji said in a voice soft enough to keep the pair of girls the row over from hearing. Benji's eyes sparkled with purple shadow, and the angle of their masculine flat cap gave them a conspiratorial air.

"No," Adrien replied after too much time. He hated the way Benji's face lit up whenever the topic of the Fairy Realm came up.

"Don't bluff with me."

"I'm not bluffing," Adrien said, holding onto his lie despite knowing it wasn't going to fly.

The memory flashed through him again.

But, breathing calmly, Adrien forced himself to hold on to the here-and-now: he wasn't on that accursed baseball field any longer, but in the mortal world, in the twenty-first century, attending his long-delayed senior year at Pattersonville West High School. Specifically, he was in English class, sitting across from Benji, his reading partner, as they worked through *Oedipus Rex*, the play Mrs. Rodriguez had assigned them.

He scowled at the text laid out on his desk.

Mrs. Rodriguez had described it as being about the inevitability of fate.

No wonder he'd relived that moment when, after a century of the Unseelie Queen's domination in the Fairy League, fate had intervened by sending another mortal player, Emily DeWitt, to the Small Folk. After a century of the queen holding on to the Web Gem, hence controlling all aspects of the Fairy Realm, her Unseelie Court baseball club had suffered the greatest upset in Fairy Realm history.

She had lost the Web Gem.

Perhaps as damaging, though, she had also lost Adrien, the mortal player she'd bound to herself that century before, beginning his long sentence as her Designated Hitter.

That was the thing about such fates and bindings.

As in *Oedipus Rex*, they had a way of twisting about themselves.

Miss Em, who had made the Small Folk victory possible, had also given Adrien the first glimmer of hope he'd had in a century. She, and Callie McMasters, another free agent mortal player, had conspired to save him. It took no effort to remember them both that fateful night, Callie standing firmly at home plate with Emily, Emily turning her beaming face on him, ready to cross with him back into the mortal world.

After a century of using his unworldly hitting to do the queen's bidding, he was finally going to be free of her. He was done with baseball, too, he had realized even as he approached Miss Em that day. Just the idea of holding a bat in his hand now turned his stomach with the sour residue of her indenture.

He was happy, though. He had missed so much. Lost so much.

What would be changed? What would still be the same?

For the first time, he had the ability to find out.

The idea of freedom felt like a fresh cloud of warm, popcorn-scented air, and home plate lay only a single step away.

Then, as he raised his foot to take his last step, the queen's voice crashed into his head like it had so many times before.

Never, though, so riven by fury as it had been then.

From the minute he'd stepped foot back in the mortal world, he'd worked hard to keep that memory and the curse the queen had laid upon him buried down deep. He had been certain of his distaste for baseball. He was free of the game, now. He had no intention of trying out for the Unicorns, which meant the curse would never be triggered, so there was no point in worrying about it.

He'd rather go out for theater, especially given how Mrs.

Rodriguez claimed his old-fashioned way of speaking made him a natural Shakespearean actor.

The question, though, was whether theater was interested in Adrien.

This play was testing his resolve. He'd prefer *A Midsummer Night's Dream,* even if that one *was* full of fairies. Or *Romeo and Juliet,* even if girls in this modern age made him feel awkward and out of touch. Maybe better *The Taming of the Shrew,* which was both funny and did not touch on the Fairy Realm at all.

"Are you thinking of going back?" Benji asked.

"Back to what?" Adrien responded before he understood what Benji meant, then followed up with an overly firm: "No!"

The girls across the row jumped. One let out a squeaky exclamation of surprise, and both glared at him.

Adrien hunched his shoulders and lowered his voice. It was as if his non-binary friend didn't realize how dangerous the fey folk were.

"No, Benji. I'm not going back."

"I would."

"Of all the people here, you should know better."

The Amberman family had an uncertain tie to the Realm, Adrien had learned. So, it was reasonable to say they should know how fraught such a transit would be—which made it that much more infuriating each time Benji tried to nudge Adrien into talking about it. But while Benji had been a help to Emily, they hadn't come into the Realm themself. That meant, for Benji, the idea was still cloaked in romance and fantasy. They didn't know.

Rather than get upset at Adrien's brash dismissal, Benji simply shrugged.

"It's a part of my heritage. I can't just close it off forever. That's not healthy."

"Yeah, well. Neither is doing nothing but hitting home runs for a hundred years. I'm shocked I didn't give myself scoliosis with all the twisting."

Benji laughed.

"Look," Adrien said. "Let's focus on this play. I need to get it right or I'll never get a part."

Benji leaned back. A smile tugging at the corners of their lips told Adrien he wasn't getting off the hook so easily. "You and I aren't so different, Adrien Thorn. This stuff gets into your blood, you know. Just like baseball. You can't deny that sort of pull, and trying to fight it only gets you right where you're already headed." Benji paused, then turned the screws by pointing to the manuscript on the desk. "That's what the play says, right?"

Adrien clamped his jaw and shook his head, hearing echoes of the queen's voice again: *You will never be free of me, Adrien Thorn!*

"I'm not stupid, all right?" Benji said, voice even lower. "I know you're all tangled up in stuff over there. I'm just saying, now that you're free and everything, a chance to go back, to see the good parts of the Realm, might do you better than a day at the spa, right? Besides, tryouts are coming up soon. You want to be at your best, physically and mentally, when that signup sheet goes up."

A flare of anger heated Adrien's cheeks.

"Stop it, Benji."

There was nothing good in the Fairy Realm. And even if Emily's friends among the Small Folk were a decent bunch, they weren't worth risking the dangers that lurked beyond their lands. There was no way Adrien Thorn would ever try out for the Unicorns.

The girls glanced at them again, then scooted their desks further away.

Benji, who had played third base for the Unicorns last year, and who had been on Adrien to try out for the team with as much vigor as they'd shown while giving Adrien the third degree about the Fairy Realm, gave a smile that said they had no clue how utterly horrifying everything they'd just said was.

"What part of 'I'm done with baseball,' did you not understand?" Adrien said, working to calm himself down.

"All of it," Benji said with a fresh wave of smugness. "I don't believe a word."

"Well, you're wrong."

Adrien folded his arms across his chest. He was not playing baseball ever again. Not in this century. Not in the next. And, most definitely, not in the Fairy Realm.

He was done with all of it.

GAME PLAN

CHAPTER
ONE

On a hot night on the cusp of true summer, when the sun had sunk well below the horizon and the tiny pixies were starting their lazy evening dance through air that hung thick like curtains amongst the tree trunks, when any reasonable gathering of fairy folk would be excitedly chattering about the new baseball season which would start with tomorrow's exhibition game between the Wild Hunt and the River Kin, the lords of the Seelie Court gathered in the darkened smoking room of the greatest among them: the Duke of the Silver Forest.

The room was dark not because of any purposefully set mood, but merely because nobody had yet lit the fire. Nobody had likewise laid out the smoking materials or properly filled the wine decanter on the sideboard. And though an intricately woven bell cord dangled gracefully from the wall with its fine golden threads sparkling invitingly with the pixie light from outside, if any of the lords were to pull it to request that the work be taken care of, nobody would answer the summoning chime.

Such was the sorry state of the Fairy Realm these days, these interminable days and nights that had followed the unexpected, unbelievable, unwanted victory of the Small Folk's baseball club over the reigning champions of the Realm, the Unseelie Court, that a lord of high birth and pure, noble blood, must sink to serve his own needs with his own two hands.

His Grace, the Duke of the Silver Forest, knelt to the task of lighting his own fire, and though he himself did not show any outward recognition of the great insult he was enduring, his guests felt no need to censor themselves.

"This madness must stop," said the Viscount of the Autumn Hills as the fire flared and a scent of hickory filled the chamber. "Not a single dwarf in my entire household to do the carpentry, nor a brownie to see to the mending and washing up. I've had enough of the feel of soot under my nails, not to mention how I am developing calluses. Mark me, my lords, the Small Folk must be brought back to heel."

The Countess of the Subterranean Castle gave a delicate, ladylike snort as she brought the tobacco box down from its shelf and set about preparing the Duke's exquisite array of pipes. Her sharp fey features glowed in the new firelight, drawn with anger and yet still smooth and beautiful. "As if the work is the worst of the indignities we've suffered of late. If I have to eat one more 'home-style dinner' or attend one more rustic country dance, I will become violently ill. This is not the Way Things Should Be."

In the middle of the room, the Earl of the Gray Moors fell grace-lessly into the largest, most overstuffed armchair among the duke's furniture and moaned. "How could the Unseelie Queen have allowed the Small Folk to win the Web Gem from her? She's held on to it for more than a century. Evil, yes, but running the Realm competently for all that. Nobody ever had anything to complain of under her rule. Except for the Small Folk."

He waved a single elegant hand to highlight the unimportance of such complaints.

The countess glided over to him and held out a pipe. "She lost, that's all there is to it. And, since she so admirably followed the rules of the game as well as those of her ridiculous bargain with the mortal players she and the Small Folk dragged into our affairs, our excellent Seelie King has declared there is nothing to be done about it. Everything about the ending of the last Fairy Season Series was by the book. Thus, we are stuck."

She grimaced, and her fine fey features turned dark and sinister, revealing her to be a creature of shadow and nightmare beneath her aristocratic exterior.

The Viscount of the Autumn Hills accepted his pipe from the countess's pale hand. "Stuck until the end of this next season, when the Web Gem might be won back from the Small Folk. They don't have their precious mortal with them this season, do they?"

"But the Wild Hunt have one!" The earl slammed both fists on the arms of his chair and bared his teeth in a snarl worthy of the hunters he spoke of. "Those filthy mongrels don't deserve the Web Gem any more than the Small Folk. I've seen the mortal in their ranks play in their scrimmage this pre-season. The girl is a real threat, make no mistake."

The countess whirled to face him again. "I will not wait until the completion of another season to have a properly cooked meal or a ball where the servants know their place amongst the décor!"

The duke, satisfied with his fire, rose from the hearth, brushed the soot from his hands, and turned to face his gathered guests. He graciously accepted a filled pipe from the still-seething countess and declined the space the earl made for him on his own armchair with an easy shake of his noble head.

"My lords, my lady," he said, nodding to each in turn. "Your complaints do not fall on deaf ears. But I must admit, even these problems pale in comparison to what I see happening in our fair Realm."

He stood before the fire, letting the flickering light outline him in the way he knew made him look his most powerful. As he expected, the eyes of all three of his guests remained upon him, glittering in rapt anticipation.

He took a puff from his pipe, and let the earthy flavor of the smoke linger in his mouth and nose a moment before blowing it out in a fine, silvery ring.

"The Small Folk have committed a grave crime since coming into power. This thing they've done threatens not merely our way of life or the richness of our meals. What we have to fear at their grubby little hands is far worse than all that."

He passed his gaze once more over each of his guests. The viscount, the countess, the earl. All three hung on his every word as they ought.

"The Small Folk have broken a piece from the Web Gem."

A stunned silence hung in the thick, humid summer air.

"Is that even possible?" the countess said. "The Web Gem is one of the ancient artifacts. It has withstood the churn of eons and witnessed the rise and fall of thousands of baseball teams within the Fairy Realm. Surely, such powerless creatures as the Small Folk couldn't even dream of breaking it?"

The duke let out another smoky breath. "My spies are reliable. The Web Gem has been divided into two pieces. But that's not the worst of it."

He waited another heartbeat.

"They have given the small piece to their mortal player, their Miss Em. It resides now well out of anyone's reach, safely tucked away within the mortal world. If we knew her true name, we might be able to simply call for her and pluck the piece right out of her unworthy hands. But as it stands, we do not have that knowledge, and the Small Folk guard it carefully. As long as she holds that piece for them, no matter who wins the Web Gem in this season or any other, the Small Folk will always maintain a meaningful hold on the power it grants."

"The little fools!" thundered the viscount, dropping a great clump of ash from his pipe as he leapt to his feet. "The little upstarts! They'll bring the wrath of the spiderkin down upon us all!"

The others voiced their dismay at this revelation. The spiderkin, having created many powerful artifacts, had left the Fairy Realm, and been gone from it or any other known world for so long that no one living today could know for sure how such beings would react to the destruction of one of their pieces. But it was a good bet they would be displeased to learn of the fate of their most powerful creation.

In the Seelie Court, it was a commonly accepted truth that the spiderkin held all the world's rules — all its natural and constructed laws — like so many flies suspended in the threads of their webs and that, when the spiderkin grew bored of toying with their prey, they had wrapped each individual edict up in their silken magic, thus creating a powerful artifact for the rest of the Fairy Realm to use as solid proof of the immutability of the Way Things Should Be.

Such law spinners would be within their rights to express their wrath at any puny fey who dared to break a rule, and the Duke of the Silver Forest believed the ancient weavers would be unconcerned with ensuring only the Small Folk got their punishment. He, and his guests, were all too aware that, to such old powers, there was little difference between the grubbing Small Folk and the fine, elite nobility of Seelie Court.

But while the viscount, the countess, and the earl vented their rage and fear in the flickering firelight and dancing shadows of the smoking room, the duke remained calm and composed. He took another pull from his pipe, savoring the evolution of the smoke as the embers burned through the dried leaves. A sweet aroma had emerged from the earthy beginnings. A flowery note that spoke of chances yet remaining.

It set his blood thrumming pleasantly within his veins.

"My lords," he said lightly over the grumbling. "My friends. Have no fear. I am not without resources, as you know." He let himself feel the resonance in his blood once more, verifying.

Yes. The results of his preliminary search still felt right.

Oh, little mortal Miss Em, he thought. *I may not know your name, but I have other means of reaching you.*

He smiled at his gathered friends, letting the fire and smoke mingle with the glow of his own power.

"My friends," he said once more, "I have a plan."

CHAPTER
TWO

T he illumination of the golden swirl of magic faded, leaving the Duke of the Silver Forest standing in a drab, muted place. He was no longer in the vibrant world of the Realm, but instead in the magicless plane that mortals called home. He almost choked on the empty air, and had to clutch the carefully wrapped Web Gem against his chest for a moment to regain his composure.

He pitied these mortals, truly. The poor wretches didn't even know what they were missing by living in such barren surroundings. The ones who lived today didn't know, at least. Some of them, though, came of fey stock. Descended from short-minded fairies who had thought life on the other side of the border might suit them better. The duke had no pity for them.

However, he couldn't deny that the poor decision of one of his own ancestors was coming in quite handy at this moment. A blood connection meant he didn't need to exert greater power to track down an adequate accomplice for his plan.

Once the spots in his vision dissipated, he relaxed his hold on the Web Gem and cast a glance around his new surroundings.

The room he'd pulled himself into was an office belonging to someone who, despite his poor situation here in the mortal world, appreciated the finer things in life. The carpet under the duke's feet was fabricated of something unnatural, but was plush enough that he could, if he closed his eyes, imagine he stood upon a thick bed of moss. The walls were paneled in dark-grained wood, and from the ceiling hung a modest, yet beautiful, set of witch-light globes. At least, the duke presumed they were witch-lights. A desk dominated the space, also made of fine, dark wood, and held a selection of leather-bound volumes and fancy styluses propped in readiness for their owner to begin writing his records of business.

The Duke of the Silver Forest approved. He approved quite heartily, in fact, and was chuckling in appreciation when the long-distant relative he'd come to call upon entered the office.

"What the hell are you doing in here?" said the mortal man. For a powerless human, he was robust, and his anger made his pale skin flush deep red. The antagonistic rounding of his shoulders had the gray suit jacket he wore creaking as if he were about to burst through the expertly tailored seams. "I'll call the police, sir!"

The Duke of the Silver Forest ignored this threat and peered around his relative. Beyond the open doorway was the showroom of a shop, one which appeared to be well-stocked with rather fine-quality baseball equipment. The duke's respect for the little mortal ticked up another notch.

However, a few mortal customers were milling about the showroom, and the proprietor's outburst was beginning to draw their attention away from their shopping.

The duke turned his attention to his relative directly. "I would recommend you close the door. What I have to propose does not bear scrutiny from the likes of them."

"Look, buddy, I don't know who you think you are, but I am Fred McMasters, and you'll get the hell out of my office before I call the police if you know what's good for you!"

McMasters poked his thumb at his own chest as he named

himself, baring his teeth as if he thought his identity would send any intruder scampering to obey.

The duke smiled in genuine pleasure. "I know who you are, though I appreciate you providing me with your name so... politely. Won't you close that door, Fred McMasters?"

His words sparked with a deft touch of magic, and McMasters closed his office door completely unaware he'd been controlled into doing so.

"Now, then," said the duke. "I hope you'll forgive my intrusion, especially once you hear the mutually beneficial deal I've come to propose."

McMasters' less-than-intimidating scowl transformed into a shrewd expression of interest. Still, he was no simple fool, a fact which the duke appreciated fully.

"A deal? Well, now, I'd be delighted to do business, of course. I'm afraid I'm rather busy at the moment but, if you'll just make an appointment with my secretary, we can go over your proposal. Now, if you'll excuse me—"

The duke put an arm out to halt McMasters' attempt to brush past him to his desk. McMasters bounced back comically, but to his credit, he did not splutter or gape. His eyes went wide, that was all.

The duke bent so his face hovered over McMasters, letting his fey essence shine through. "Fred McMasters. By authority of the noble blood we share, I claim an appointment with you right now."

He lifted one hand from the wrappings of the Web Gem and laid a single, long finger along McMasters' cheek. Where he touched, the light of the fey rippled and spread. The mortal man's eyes widened further as the light entered them, and he gasped a soft, almost inaudible sound of wonder.

"Our noble blood...," he murmured.

"Yes, ours. I am known as the Duke of the Silver Forest. And if your ancestors had stayed in the Fairy Realm instead of relocating to this drab world, you, too, could have claimed the title of duke. Your lands would have been adjacent to mine. You would have made a fine showing as the managing lord of the Seelie Court's baseball team, I'm sure." He pulled his touch away, but the light he'd awoken lingered for a few breaths before slowly fading. But the pinpricks of light that had brightened the mortal man's dull eyes remained.

McMasters coughed, then tugged at the bottom of his jacket to straighten it with a sharp snap. He stepped around the duke to his desk and touched one of the devices on it. "Carol, cancel the ten o'clock commercial shoot. Tell the boys we'll reschedule for … some other time."

A feminine voice started to reply, but she was cut off as McMasters removed his finger from the device. He lowered himself into the leather-covered throne and chuckled at its squeak of protest. "Long-lost fairy royalty, huh," he muttered, shaking his head.

Then he turned his attention back to the duke, all traces of levity replaced with a fiery drive the duke recognized innately.

"So, cousin. What is this business proposal you have for me?"

The duke approached his side of the desk, perfectly willing to let his mortal cousin claim that place of meager power for now. He removed the wrappings fully from the Web Gem and placed the trophy in all its glory on the desk, right in front of Fred McMasters.

Rays from the witch-light globes glinted off the artifact's crystal facets to run in rivulets down the golden body. That light scattered in rainbow prisms across McMasters' face as he gaped down at the treasure before him.

"This is a great and powerful artifact of our people, Fred McMasters. It is capable of granting the one who rightfully holds it immense power, so long as it is whole."

The duke's voice sank to darkness as he pointed at the one point of imperfection, the twisted, tarnished spot where a single crystal had been severed from the whole. Fury flared within him as he looked at the defilement.

McMasters' voice came as a low growl, too. "What happened to it?"

"What happened is that those who ought to know their place

thought they could win the right to control the Web Gem's power, and in so doing, nearly destroyed everything. My peers and I risked much to wrest it from their unworthy hands, but even I cannot keep it hidden from them for long, especially not while a piece of the Gem remains with one of them."

The duke splayed both hands upon the cool wood of the desk, one on each side of the Web Gem, and leaned forward so the artifact's light shone on his face. "Fred McMasters, I require the help of someone I can trust implicitly. Who better than one of my own blood, however diluted it may be by now? I see what you have made of yourself in this barren place. I see how you've risen above your meager beginnings. Will you help me?"

McMasters frowned down at the Web Gem. "I am a businessman, your grace. I'm all in to help you, of course. But time is money, as they say, and my time comes with a higher price tag than most."

"Oh, you will be compensated for your efforts, I assure you. And the efforts themselves are not so much to someone like you. All I require is that you keep this precious artifact safe for me while I deal with cleaning up the mess those miscreants have left behind in the Fairy Realm, and that you help discover who here holds the stolen piece of our treasure, then convince them to return to the Realm with it. For these acts, you will earn the right to use the Web Gem's power to enhance your business as you see fit."

The light glowing in McMasters' eyes told the duke he needn't bother exerting his will over the mortal. What little effort he'd already expended with the knowledge of Fred McMasters' true name was more than enough to convince him of the Web Gem's abilities. McMasters' ambition did the rest of the work for him.

"The missing piece is here, you say?" McMasters pressed the tip of one finger to his lips. His eyes never left the soft glow of the Web Gem.

"The Small Folk gave their piece to a mortal who played for their team last season. We are unable to track her ourselves. The lack of magic in this world blocks her from our sight."

That wasn't the full reason why the Duke couldn't find the one who went by Miss Em, of course, but he couldn't very well point out how he needed to know someone's true name in order to have any power over them. Not when their business was proceeding so well now.

Fred McMasters continued to stare at the Gem, his finger now tapping against his lip arrhythmically. "I have contacts I can use. But they won't be enough, not after that idiotic hoo-hah with my daughter at Unicorn Field last season. Do you have any leads I can follow? Anything I can get a start with?"

The duke paused, considering this worthy question. His power here in the magicless air of the mortal world was limited, and what little he had he needed to use to get himself back into the Fairy Realm. But the Web Gem did have power, even mutilated as it was.

"Perhaps a demonstration is in order," he said. He beckoned for McMasters to stand and join him in placing their hands on the crystal facets of the Web Gem.

Power flowed, ice-cold as a glacial river, red-hot as molten rock, smooth, harsh, and full of stars.

Fred McMasters screamed silently.

But he did not let go. The duke watched as the mortal held on to the rushing power with sheer force of will. A sensation of true admiration pulsed through him at the sight. This was his little cousin, distant and deprived, but making his birthright known.

Carefully, almost like a father teaching a child how to bat, the Duke of the Silver Forest showed Fred McMasters how to finesse the magic of the Web Gem, how to tame that raging river of power and bring it to his will.

When they were riding the power together, the duke finally put forth a command to it.

"Show us the mortal who last laid hands upon you," he said. His words reverberated against the crystals, setting them vibrating.

In their vibrations, an image appeared. A girl. A young woman, mortal, looking stern and commanding as she directed a field full of fantastical creatures with horns and hooves and sharp teeth through a series of baseball drills. She stood not in a baseball field, but in a small forest clearing, twinkling fairy lights filling the air around her.

McMasters choked in recognition.

"The Wild Hunt's newest recruit," said the Duke.

"My daughter," said McMasters, a cold emptiness to his voice as he turned away. "So that's where she ran off to, huh? Fitting that only a pack of monsters would let her play baseball after everything she's done."

The duke nudged his attention back to the image. "Now, now. That's no way for a father to speak of his children. Especially given that such a child is ideally placed to act as a conduit should that father require aid in his work."

"I won't need help," McMasters said. Then he relaxed his bunched shoulders and put on a thoughtful expression. "But a shrewd businessman never closes any opportunities off entirely."

His eyes, thin and snakelike, flicked back to the Web Gem itself.

"You say I can use this thing to enhance my business as I see fit. Could it restore my daughter's reputation among the athletic clubs here and make my flesh and blood a star player once again?"

Slowly, the duke removed his hold from the Web Gem, until only Fred McMasters was touching it. "It could, yes."

McMasters matched his grin of delight.

Then Fred McMasters' expression grew both firm and clouded. Resolved in a way the duke understood. Fred McMasters was holding something inside. And he had found a plan.

Fred McMasters' eyes glistened with the artifact's prismatic glow.

"It can do more, too, can't it?"

"Yes," the duke replied. "It can, indeed."

By the time the Duke of the Silver Forest drew himself back into the Fairy Realm, he knew that in his fierce little cousin, he had an ally he would be able to count on.

SUMMER SEASON

CHAPTER
THREE

After a tangle of misunderstandings, contract snafus, and plain old bureaucratic nonsense that was equally as asinine and convoluted here in the Fairy Realm as it was in the human world, baseball was finally happening in star player Callie McMasters' life once again.

The Summer Season in the Fairy Realm was ready to begin.

Not mere scrimmage, not simple games of catch, not the agonizing, painstaking work of coaching her new team into something resembling an enthusiastic group of players.

Real baseball.

The very air she breathed as she sat on the polished wooden bench in the dugout of the Other Field smelled of leather gloves, good, clean sweat, and maple resin ready to be lovingly rubbed into the grain of the bats.

Underlying it all was the unmistakable spice of magic.

Callie smirked as she laced up her cleats. She'd been looking forward to playing her first real game here at the main baseball diamond in the Fairy Realm. Hell, she would have jumped at the chance to play again even if the season-opening exhibition game was being held at the monstrously creepy Unseelie Pitch, instead.

She'd gone way, way too long without a real game, especially one that wouldn't end with dire consequences for herself or her friends.

The last time she'd played real baseball, she'd found herself kicked off the Bulldogs, her high school team, for cheating. She hadn't been cheating, not really. She'd been trying to rescue Emily DeWitt from this very place, thinking her rival had fallen into the clutches of some evil fey creatures. And she'd succeeded, sort of.

Then, when she and Emily had worked together to return to the Realm and tie up all of Emily's loose ends, Callie had been barred from playing in the final series games between the Small Folk and the Unseelie Court due to some of those notorious tangled-up contract shenanigans. The frustration she'd felt then still stung her at night sometimes, when she couldn't sleep for turning plays over in her head.

But in the process of helping Emily's team, the Small Folk, win their trophy and their freedom from the Unseelie Queen, Callie McMasters had found herself quite willingly agreeing to sign on with the Wild Hunt's team here in the Fairy Realm. Her blacklisted status back home meant the college scout who had been so excited about her earlier had gone sour. She had no hope of ever playing baseball again, not for real. But the fairies didn't care about any of that. In fact, rules being somewhat more malleable in the Fairy Realm, some of them looked upon her supposed "cheating" as being a sign of a good player.

Despite that last bit, Callie had found little to complain about during her time in the Fairy Realm so far. No fairy, no matter how malicious and greedy, could come close to touching the corrupting business practices of her dear old dad, who'd been all too happy when his star player daughter's only competition mysteriously disappeared.

Just being away from his toxic expectations was doing Callie a world of good.

She was taking a gap year — a common enough practice among kids her age. Trying to figure out what to do after graduating high school was rough for a lot of people, not just those whose parents were more concerned with them *winning* rather than *succeeding*. A chance to work out who Callie McMasters could be without her dad's influence was more than welcome.

Though most kids didn't run away to spend their gap year in the Fairy Realm.

That part was uniquely Callie.

But the place wasn't so bad, despite the warnings DeWitt had given her when she'd shared her plans. And it wasn't like Callie meant to stay here forever. Just for a season, long enough to figure out what she wanted to do with her life. That had been a part of the contract finagling she'd drawn the red line on. Once the Web Gem had been won, the contract was complete. Sure, the Hunt leader had tried to slip high-grade weasel wording into the deal that would have required the Wild Hunt to be the Web Gem winners before they considered her commitment fulfilled, but she'd squashed that clause right away. One and done. That was the deal. The fact that she'd be able to play baseball while she did her deep life thinking was the cherry on top of the ice cream.

Today, as the season's opening festivities were in full operation, instead of an air of oppression overlaying the excitements of this day, as would have happened in previous seasons as the Small Folk drudged to serve the other, more powerful factions of the fey folk, a happy buzz of camaraderie filled the stands. Fairies from all corners of the Realm had worked together to decorate the field and the stands for this festival game, and now took turns offering each other refreshments or getting up to move the awnings as the sun moved across the sky and the heat of the day built to uncomfortable levels.

She knew a lot of the current good atmosphere here in the Fairy Realm was due to the diligent work of Fennoc, the faun leader of the Small Folk, who had taken his new duties as ruler of the entire Realm quite seriously.

Everyone was ready to watch an exciting match, and nobody was going to have to suffer for anyone else's enjoyment.

Now if only Callie could guarantee her current teammates would make a good showing at this exhibition.

She glanced over at the cluster of pelt-draped centaurs, blood-encrusted Red Caps, and moss-covered rock trolls who filled the bench beside her, and pressed her lips together. One of the Red Caps was carefully skinning the baseball he held, a wide grin of utter glee stretching his little pink cheeks. The others were either watching with barely veiled interest or else outright egging him on.

"Hey," Callie said, clapping her hands sharply. The Red Cap squeaked, jumped, and looked up at her before guiltily hiding the half-skinned baseball behind his back.

Callie didn't give him any ground. Tightening her scowl, she snapped her fingers before holding her hand out, palm up, expectantly. "We don't do that to baseballs," she commanded, beckoning with her twitching fingertips.

A moment passed, one of the centaurs shifted his weight awkwardly onto one of his back hooves, and the Red Cap slumped his little shoulders while handing Callie the mutilated ball.

"And?" Callie said, hand still out.

The Red Cap sighed, his breath a faintly sour puff.

She didn't even wrinkle her nose, though. She was long past reacting to her teammates' attempts to unnerve her delicate mortal sensibilities.

Seeing she wasn't going to be swayed, the Red Cap finally set the flaying knife in Callie's hand alongside the ball.

"Very good, Thacker," she said, smoothly pocketing both items without looking at them closer. "I'm so glad to see your enthusiasm today, but let's focus more properly, yes?"

Thacker the Red Cap looked up at her through his grimy eyelashes, another grin curling across his lips. He was short, the top of his blood-colored baseball cap barely reaching Callie's hip, but where the gnomes of the Small Folk were squat, Thacker and his kind were gangly and knobby, looking a bit as if they were on the verge of dying of thirst. "Aye, Mistress Cal. D'you think we'll be able to carve some scales from yon River Kin today?"

Callie grinned herself. "Only if you can manage to make them slide home. You've been practicing your catches?"

In answer, Thacker sat back on his haunches and pounded his little fist into his other gloveless hand before raising both hands, talons crooked, in anticipation of a throw. He looked more like he was preparing to spring out of a bush at some unsuspecting prey than like a catcher squatting behind home plate, but Callie couldn't really fault his form.

"Nice," she said with a nod of approval. Over her month of training her wild teammates, she'd found that, varied though they appeared on the surface, they all shared a deep love of positive rein-forcement. From the littlest Red Cap to the biggest, strongest centaurs, they all loved earning Callie's approving nods.

The only one who appeared not to be so easily moved was the wolflike leader of the Wild Hunt. At every practice she'd held during their off-season training period, he'd kept himself apart from the rest of the pack and maintained a steady, slightly judgmental eye on her, as if waiting for the moment when she'd inevitably do something to void her contract.

She didn't understand that. He had been delighted to have her join his roster at the end of last season, and she had no desire to leave the team until this season was over. Frankly, creepy teammates aside, she was exactly where she wanted to be.

She let her gaze slide to the bullpen, where the leader was throwing his warmup pitches. As usual, he was throwing with full strength, a habit that had Callie biting her tongue against the admonishments that pressed against her lips. If a mortal player threw that hard before the game had even begun, she'd get a well-deserved reaming from her coach for jeopardizing her shoulder.

But one did not go around lecturing the leader of the Wild Hunt.

Not if one wanted to keep one's skin relatively free of arrow punctures.

"Mistress Cal," came a gravelly voice by her elbow. Callie turned to see one of the centaurs looking down at her, a keen light in his black eyes. He'd made the effort to comb his long black mane and beard, she noticed. And, while he hadn't *washed,* necessarily, he did seem to have applied a scent of some kind — something light and pleasantly floral — to cover his hunting odors.

When she met his eyes, a faint dusting of pink appeared on his wind-roughed cheeks.

"Trace," Callie said, fighting back her blush and straining to maintain her sense of authority over the team. She'd never had anyone back home show the kind of interest in her that the wiry centaur did. Most of the kids she interacted with were too intimidated to develop a crush, let alone act on it. But Trace had no scruples, it seemed, openly *courting* her — as the fairies called it.

She still hadn't decided what to think of his attentions. She liked him, certainly. And he was without question the most enthusiastic about baseball among the hunters. But they were hardly compatible. Right?

Out on the field, the River Kin's warmups sent the crack of a bat on a ball rippling through the Other Field, and Callie realized she'd been staring into Trace's face like an idiot for too long.

"Uh, yes. Trace. What, um, what can I do for you?" What was she doing with her hands? She never fluttered them like that. Quickly, she put both fists in her pockets, then immediately smothered a wince as her thumb brushed up against the edge of Thacker's knife.

Trace's smile turned fond. "I wondered which position I ought to play today. Perhaps left field?"

Finally, Callie managed to get herself under control enough to smile at him like a normal person. "You can check with Grangle. She's keeping the official lineup stone, remember?"

She pointed to the other end of the dugout, where the smallest of the Wild Hunt's rock trolls was hunching over a slab of marble. Grangle was in the middle of scratching a thick stylus across the pale gray surface, making a mark as easily as if the slab were regular paper.

"Ah," said Trace. "But I was hoping to discuss the subject with you."

He highlighted the riposte with a wider smile and the presentation of a single white daisy. Callie didn't want to know where he'd gotten it from.

"Plucked from the Other Field's third baseline itself, my sweet," Trace said as if she'd asked anyway. "A good luck charm for your work in the hot seat, as you called it."

"Hot corner, you mean?"

This time it was Trace who blushed. "Yes, Mistress Cal. The hot corner. That's what I meant."

"I don't need any charms or rituals to play good baseball," Callie said, but she didn't stop Trace from slipping the daisy between her ear and the brown fabric of her Wild Hunt ballcap.

"Of course, you don't," Trace agreed. "But the Wild Hunt doesn't bat until the bottom of the inning, so you won't be able to use my real pre-game gift right away."

He shrugged his well-muscled shoulders, and the oaken bat he'd slung over his back slid forward. It fell into his hands, almost glowing golden in the dimness of the dugout.

Callie knew she was gaping, but she couldn't help herself. It was a beautiful bat, the grain looping in gorgeous swirls, the smooth, satiny finish thirsty for a baseball's leather, the handle inlaid with the faintly glowing runes of Hunt cantrips.

"I tested it myself," he said. "I think you'll be pleased. It should even retain its magical properties when you carry it back to your home on the other side of the portal."

He dipped his head down, displaying a touch of shyness when Callie's fingers closed around the handle and brushed against his own.

Callie pulled the bat out of his grip and hefted it. "The weight is perfect," she whispered as she waggled it. The balance suited her measure exactly. She would know, too. She was Callie McMasters, daughter of the man who owned the premier sporting goods store in Pattersonville. She understood what it meant to have the best equipment.

But the stuff her dad provided was purchased, prepackaged, and machined to pinpoint perfection. Cold and impersonal.

This one smelled like the daisies Trace had sat amongst as he shaved the wood down and sanded it smooth. It had a pull to it, too, something that called to her inner self like a wolf in the night. Simply holding it made her blood thrum. She could do great things with this bat.

"I can't accept this," she said as every fiber of her being longed to keep holding it close. She tore her eyes away from it to meet his hopeful gaze. "It's too powerful for a nobody mortal like me. You should give it to someone who ... who can commit to it," she finished lamely.

Because she *couldn't* commit to it, or to *him,* no matter how much she liked him. She was leaving the Realm the moment this Summer Season ended, moving forward with her life back in the Real World where she belonged.

Trace snorted, a rather horsey sound. "'Twon't work for anyone else, mortal or fey. To all but you, that bat would only be a lovely bit of wood. And you look lovely with it over your shoulder."

The umpire's call to play ball cut off whatever reply she might have made, and Trace trotted away from her as if the matter was settled. Well, she supposed it was. She still felt the warmth his compliments had brought to her face.

She hated to have to set her gift amongst the other bats in the rack, but Trace was right. She couldn't very well bring it with her to play defense for the top of the inning.

But as she walked out to take her place at third, she couldn't stop herself from running her fingers over the soft edges of the daisy's petals. Even Thacker's open snickering didn't dampen the light, airy feeling growing inside her. Nothing would. *Baseball* was happening, and Trace's lovely gestures helped smooth over the last of her remaining disappointment at not being able to pitch.

She watched the rest of her team fan out across the field with a sense of satisfaction. Thacker squatting at home, Trace trotting out to center field, the other centaurs, satyrs, and Red Caps of the Wild Hunt all moving with purpose across the pristine grass.

Their leader stalked up to the mound, his eyes glowing as if the light of a full moon fell on them. As the first of the River Kin's hitters, a skittish little selkie, squelched up to the plate, the hunt leader tilted his head back and set up a howl.

On instinct, the rest of the Wild Hunt joined him. Their voices wove together into a haunting cacophony. It set Callie's teeth on edge, but each time she heard them do this, a small part of her almost wanted to join in.

Some of the spectators did join in, adding their shrill hollers in jubilation. The stands rumbled as fairies got to their feet for the opening pitch. Up in the highest box, the faun leader of the Small Folk, Fennoc, stood with a few of his teammates, all of them beaming down at the game that was about to begin. Behind them was a dark shape, a square covered with a thick velvet cloth: the display case where the Web Gem rested, waiting for its grand unveiling at the end of the season opener.

Callie clapped her hands as her teammates reached a crescendo. The very air vibrated with the sound.

Then, all at once, with a slight signal from the Hunt leader, the sound cut off.

A suspended moment of ringing silence enshrouded the Other Field.

Then, the cyclops who served as the field's umpire lifted one large hand.

"Play ball!"

THE WILD HUNT's intimidation tactics appeared to work for the first inning, with the River Kin getting only one runner onto first before the Wild Hunt registered their three outs. Callie never even touched the ball while she was out on the field. But she didn't fret too much. She knew the Wild Hunt lineup had her batting third.

And after Trace hit a sneaky slider out to left field good enough to make it to second, and a slim satyr who went by Pyrgin managed a sweet hit that skirted the foul line without ever crossing it, Callie knew she had the opportunity she'd been dying for — a chance to make a strong impression her first shot out the gate.

She curled her fingers around the bat, and the carved runes gave way to smooth oak wood against her hands. She grinned her fiercest out at the naiad who stood on the mound. The bat was humming softly, eager to get a taste of leather and sinew.

The naiad smiled coquettishly back, letting the sunlight flash off the scales that ran down her arms. But Callie wasn't fazed.

"C'mon, fish girl," she said. "Whatsamatter? Can't get your footing on land?"

The naiad smirked, shook her shimmery black hair out, and hurled the slickest fastball Callie had ever seen.

But Callie, starved for a challenge, lapped it right up.

The ball hit her bat precisely where she wanted it. She felt the impact race through the runes on the handle and crash up her arms like a tidal wave sweeping up the shore. She didn't need to watch as the ball rose on that wave and sailed up, up, and away.

She had more important things to focus on, like doing the running part of her first home run of the season. The first of many, she promised herself.

The commotion in the stands as she rounded first jived with her sense of accomplishment. And why not? The masses were here to be entertained, and she'd just shown them precisely how she meant to entertain them.

Behind her, Trace galloped across home plate. She heard his gravelly voice calling out to her as she kept running. She lifted one hand to acknowledge his cheers but did not look at him as she ran on to second. Ahead of her, though, Pyrgin had stopped running halfway between third and home. He was standing like he'd caught the scent of some sort of distant prey, head cocked, mouth slightly open.

Callie's irritation flared. "Get moving! I can't score if you're in my way!"

But Pyrgin didn't move, and now Callie realized the River Kin's fielders weren't moving, either.

They, too, were standing still and staring, though they looked less like hunters on the trail and more like so many fish gasping at the bottom of a boat.

Everyone was staring up at the stands.

Now that the rush of her victory was dying away, Callie realized the crowds had gone silent. Not the silence of reverence for a historic sporting moment, but the hushed silence of shock and confusion.

Callie came to a full stop right next to the selkie playing second base.

Up in the highest box, Fennoc and his Small Folk friends were no longer alone. A contingent of regal-looking fairies, all dressed in white and gold and wearing identical expressions of rage on their fine, pale faces, had joined them.

Callie had been here long enough to recognize members of the various fairy factions when she saw them. But what were a bunch of Seelie nobles doing disrupting the game? Wasn't that against everything the supposedly rule-loving Seelies believed in?

The truth was that the Seelies were notorious for being sticklers to the rules whenever they were in their favor, but open to interpretation when their application wasn't so clearly on their side.

She got the answer to her question as one of the Seelie men stepped forward to lean over the railing of the high box and address the crowd.

"Fairies of the Realm, know this: the Small Folk and their leader

Fennoc are in default of their solemn duty to protect the Web Gem, and thus are unfit to have the rule of our land!"

"That's preposterous," Fennoc said. He held his shoulders back and his spine ramrod straight, with no hint of prey behavior in his perfect posture. "The Web Gem is perfectly safe."

"If that's the case," sneered the Seelie man, "then unveil it now."

Now Fennoc looked nervous. He licked his lips, then clasped his hands behind his back. "Certainly, I have no issue with doing so. But it does go against tradition, you know, revealing it before the first exhibition game is finished."

"Some traditions are more important than others," said the Seelie through his teeth. Even from this distance, Callie could see how pointed they were.

He turned from the rail and nodded to the Seelie woman who stood beside the velvet-covered display case. "My lady, if you would."

With a smile that would fit right in amongst Callie's wildest teammates, the woman grasped the fabric and gave it a deft twist. It slid away to reveal the case beneath it.

It was empty.

Shock swept through the entirety of the Other Field in a palpable wave. Callie herself gasped as if she'd taken a slugger to the chest.

The Web Gem, the very thing that granted the right to rule the entirety of the Fairy Realm to the ones who held it, was gone.

"Stolen!" crowed the Seelie nobleman over the susurrus of dismay. "Taken from under their incompetent little noses! The Small Folk are unfit to rule, I tell you. But do not fear. The Seelie Court is fully prepared to step in during this emergency."

It certainly felt like an emergency. Shock and dismay were rapidly turning to panic, and the spectators drained out of the stands like someone had pulled a plug in a bathtub.

Fennoc looked as gray as if he'd seen a ghost. "But — How did — How could — I don't understand!"

Beside Callie, the selkie infielder let out a long sigh, stuck his gray-furred hands into his pockets, and strolled back towards his team's dugout. And across the whole field, everyone else seemed to be doing the same thing, shutting down and slinking away.

"Wait," Callie said. "What about the game?"

But she knew as the words left her mouth that the game was off. How could a frivolous, friendly game matter now in the face of such a disaster?

Then, a worse thought crashed into her.

What did baseball itself even matter to the people of the Fairy Realm if the very trophy they played for was gone?

As if in answer, the leader of the Wild Hunt stalked towards her where she still stood between second and third.

"Come," he growled, putting a heavy hand on her shoulder, not in comfort but in an attempt to steer her where he wanted her. "We leave this place of folly. We hunt."

Callie had enough presence of mind to struggle out of his hold. "I didn't join you to hunt. I joined to play baseball."

The growl became a snarl. "You joined us. We *hunt*."

Callie succumbed to his insistence. What else could she do? There was nobody else to play baseball with now.

But as she trudged into the dugout and flung her batting helmet to clatter against the bench, dread engulfed her.

CHAPTER
FOUR

Callie hardly knew what to do with herself anymore. Baseball in the Fairy Realm had all but dried up. With the fabulous prize of the Web Gem gone without a trace, nobody seemed to feel there was any reason to play.

Nobody except Callie, anyway. Much to her dismay, she'd discovered that the majority of fairies didn't play out of any love for the sport as she'd thought. They only played for what they could get out of it: power.

No Web Gem meant no power.

This ticked her off almost more than the constant, undeniable knowledge that she was well and truly trapped here in the Fairy Realm. A full-on damsel in distress. The very next Rip Van Winkle candidate, right after Adrien Thorn himself.

Her contract — the one she'd been so damn proud of negotiating for herself — stipulated that she had to remain in the Fairy Realm, playing for the Wild Hunt until the Web Gem was awarded. But if the season never even began, there was no way it was ever going to end. Thus, she was stuck.

She'd come to the Fairy Realm looking for a way to spend a gap year, but she'd always meant to go back home. Even if she couldn't play baseball, she wanted to go to college. If nothing else, she could walk on to a team. She wanted to make something of herself, something untouched by her father's influence. Staying here beyond one season meant stagnation and slowly falling behind as her own world churned on without her.

The thought, along with the myriad of noises that came from her beastly teammates, woke her up most nights.

Really, how could there not be a single fairy in the whole stupid Realm who didn't love baseball for its own sake? Even Trace, her best convert to the game, had indulged in only a few half-hearted bouts of catch with her these last few days, and even he'd seemed distracted by the antics of the others as they prepared for their next foray into the wilds.

True, she could join her teammates in their hunts. They were searching for the Web Gem, after all. Mostly because the Fairy Realm was all about Finders-Keepers, and if the Wild Hunt could come upon the trophy, things would get interesting. Their leader drove them hard and fast over rough terrain on each of their outings, sniffing for any scrap of a sign of where the coveted trophy had gone. Maybe that would even be a good thing to do. At least it might make her feel useful. But it made sense to her that whoever had heisted the Web Gem would have taken measures against the members of the Wild Hunt, who were the obvious search party, so she didn't hold out any expectation they would succeed.

Indeed, they always returned empty-handed and exhausted, reeking of mud, mold, sweat, and blood. Tensions were rising amongst the hunters, satyrs snapping at centaurs, Red Caps blunting their knives against the rock trolls' hides. And the night noises only got worse.

On top of that, the other fairy factions were taking matters into their own hands, as if the search for the missing artifact had become a competition itself. The Hag Sisters were casting spells of finding; the River Kin had run deep dives far out at sea; the Unseelie Queen was holed up in her dark castle, brooding over spells Callie didn't want to know anything about, but that sent alternate bolts of arcane fire and billowing black clouds spewing forth into the western sky; the Seelie Court was manning patrols across the whole of the Realm, and their troopers weren't being too subtle about nudging folk into line with what their nobles decreed during this time of emergency.

Not a single faction made any noise about playing the season, not even as a means of distraction from their troubles.

Callie could barely stand it.

Which was why she had called Trace to meet her by the granite standing stones that made up the center of the Wild Hunt's "village," for lack of a better term. None of the hunters had anything resembling even a bare shack for a home, all of them preferring to rough it out under the moon and stars, no matter whether the air was clear and fresh or drenched with torrential rainfall. Callie was the only one who regularly slept with a roof-like protrusion over her head, having taken her deer hide blankets into a tiny cave that burrowed into the side of a grassy hillock a short throw south of the stones.

Trace, to his credit, looked conflicted.

"Mistress Cal," he said in his soft, gravelly voice. "I understand your frustration. We're all running ragged these days. But what you're proposing is not going to sit well with our leader."

"That's only because our leader doesn't think baseball is more important than running his hunts," Callie said. She didn't bother to hide her disgust.

"We *are* the Wild Hunt," Trace said, smiling.

"People can be complex, you know. You can be more than one thing."

"*Humans* can be complex. Fairies are very straightforward."

"Trace," Callie said through gritted teeth. "I am asking you, very politely, to take me to see the Hag Sisters of the Wood. That's all."

But Trace was not mollified. "That is not all, and you know it, you vixen. If you get the Hags to agree to play a game, you'll need a team yourself. You'll need me to convince enough of our teammates to abandon the hunts and fill the field."

Callie forced the bubble of anger rising within her to back down. "Right. But if the Hags agree to play, surely that will make it easier to convince our players? Some of them genuinely liked playing, I know it. Hell, I'll even give Thacker a ball of his very own to skin as he likes if he'll just catch for us."

Trace shifted his weight to his back hooves, the motion setting the delicate rabbit bones in his black beard clicking in the otherwise quiet of the standing stones. A pained look crossed his face.

Callie stepped closer and put her hand on his elbow. His skin was rough, but warm. "Please, Trace. I can't wait for one fairy faction or another to figure out where the Web Gem went. I need the baseball season to go forward now. I can't stay here forever."

The pained expression didn't clear. "Maybe I don't want you to go home. Maybe I want to keep you here with me. I'll carry you on our hunts if that would be better. You could ride with me, feel the rush of wind in your hair, and sup on the fruits of our labors every night. I could teach you how to shoot, too. With your pitching skills, you'll be a deadeye. Your kills will never suffer unless you will it."

His voice rolled through Callie, and she felt the things he spoke of as if they were happening for real. Her muscles worked as if she were holding herself upright on his back as he galloped through the close-growing trees. She smelled blood on the air, not as a source of horror or disgust, but as a natural prelude to a well-earned feast. She heard the soft, sharp twang of her bowstring beside her ear and felt the ruffle of the arrow's fletching as it passed her cheek.

It could be good, she knew.

But it would never be baseball.

Trace was looking at her so intensely, his dark eyes burning with the light of enthusiasm as he watched her experience the phantom ride. His kin, the Centaurs, were known for their haunting bardic abilities, their skills as orators and story weavers, and Trace was a credit to his line.

Callie closed her eyes against the visions he was spinning for her. "Trace, I'm ... I'm not a hunter. I'm a baseball player. You knew that when you made that incredible bat for me."

The bat she'd stashed among her meager belongings ever since the abrupt closing of the season. Leaving it in its wrappings was killing her; she could still feel its pull, its desire to knock the stuffing out of a ball.

Though her eyes were still closed, she heard his harsh exhale loud and clear. "Now who isn't letting herself be complex? Ride with me, Mistress Cal. It's a good life here among the Hunt. We can be happy together, and when the urge strikes us, we can throw the baseball around in the shady glens."

Now Callie's anger was building again, the bubble she'd previously pushed down pressing back up to her chest. "No, Trace. You don't understand, or I guess you don't want to. The picture you paint is lovely, but even I know it'll never come true. Do you think I can't see how the huntmaster is working every one of you to the bone now? Your precious leader is hard set on sniffing out the Web Gem. And if he finds it, one of two things is going to happen. Either he'll do the right thing and hand it over to the Small Folk, and the season starts up again as it's supposed to, which will mean our team needs to be at the top of its game. Or he'll do the treacherous thing and keep the Web Gem for himself, which will plunge the Fairy Realm into the world of bloodshed and warfare you hunters have always dreamed of. Between baseball and war, I'd rather play baseball."

Callie stood before Trace, close enough to see the tiny shivers running across his muscles as she increased the pressure of her grip on his arm. She'd boxed him in against the granite face of the nearest standing stone like a racehorse before the race, something she knew he hated. But she had a point to drive home, damn it. If she pressed him far enough, let him in far enough, she felt certain Trace would come around to her views.

A light chuckle sounded behind her, and Trace stiffened like a child caught reaching for the cookie jar. Recovering, he tilted his head in a cramped bow.

Callie did not turn around right away, needing a moment to wipe away the derision she knew was all over her face. She had to bite her lip hard to manage it.

"Little mistress has strong convictions," said the leader of the Hunt. His words curled, and Callie could already picture the mocking smile he spoke them through.

She turned. "Just want to make sure I don't give you any reason to claim I'm in breach of contract."

Sure enough, the leader wore a derisive smirk on his lupine face. He looked as ragged as any of his riders, the billowing cloths of his multi-layered hunting cloaks showing more frayed edges than usual, the casual way he leaned against a standing stone betraying the exhaustion seeping from his bones.

But the tawny gold of his eyes still burned as fiercely as the day Callie had signed her contract with him.

"Our riders are meant to be resting now," he said, tilting his jaw forward to point at Trace. "Most of us have been working hard to right the wrong the Small Folk have done to our fair Realm. We do not have time or energy to waste on frivolities now, do we, Trace?"

Callie glanced at Trace on reflex. He looked abashed, and his cheeks flushed in shame. "No, my lord."

Callie gaped at him. "Trace!"

Trace looked at her, then instantly away. "I'm sorry, Mistress Cal. I really must rest before the next hunt."

He turned on one hoof, gravel crunching beneath its round sole, and cantered away into the trees.

Fury burned through Callie, and though she tried not to blame Trace, she couldn't help feeling abandoned.

"Fret not," said the leader. "You and our rider need not be apart. You could always ride with us as he proposed."

"Shut up," Callie spat, whirling to glare at the leader again. "You know I'm not going to do that. My contract says I go home once the season is over, so I'm devoting myself to making the season happen, one way or another."

"Ah, but is that truly the case, little mistress? We seem to recall another clause, what was it? Oh, yes. Not only must the season end, but the Web Gem must be awarded to the winner. Then you may return to your own land, and not before. But, oh, we seem to have misplaced the Web Gem, haven't we?"

The leader of the hunt stepped forward so quickly Callie almost didn't see him move. Now it was her turn to feel the barricading solidity of the standing stone against her back. She squirmed at the sensation, and at the burst of guilt at having done this to Trace.

His lips curled away from his teeth in a snarl that stank of old meat. "Until the Web Gem is returned, none of us has time to waste dallying about with the meaningless nature of baseball magic. You may do as you will, but our riders will *hunt*."

He snapped his teeth a hair's breadth from Callie's face on the final words, then pulled back to stalk away from the standing stones.

Callie struggled to calm her racing heart. Her palms scraped against the granite face of the standing stone, the rough grain leaving divots in her flesh. She told herself, as she'd done so many times already during her stay here, that the hunt leader wouldn't hurt her. That he needed her, in the end. That nobody else could manage the team's enthusiasm the way she had.

She was having a harder time believing that now.

Get it together, she admonished herself. *He's almost out of the circle!*

In all their snipping at one another throughout the preseason, she'd never let him get the last word in.

"You're wrong," was all she managed to say this time. But she said it loud enough so he could hear the conviction in her voice.

Because he *was* wrong, even if she couldn't convince him of it yet.

The leader of the Hunt, like so many of the residents of the Fairy Realm, didn't understand the baseball magic they used in all these squabbles over the Web Gem. But she did.

And, she recalled now, so did someone else.

"Go on your stupid hunts," she said, though the leader was long gone by now. "I've got baseball to play."

CHAPTER
FIVE

O ver the month or so of training prior to the start of the season, Callie had gotten familiar with the woods she and the Wild Hunt lived in. It was a tricksy place, make no mistake, full of snatching brambles and sucking bogs, as well as predators of every sort. But being a member of the Hunt gave her a degree of protection, and the tumbles of moss-encrusted stones gave her plenty of opportunities to work out like she used to at the rock-climbing gym. If she wasn't practicing with the team, she was scrambling about the forest, learning its twisting pathways as she stretched the muscles baseball left unworked.

The knowledge she'd gained of the lay of the land came in handy this morning, as she prepared to head away from the Hunt's camp on her own.

She wasn't running away or anything. She'd be back by nightfall. But she couldn't simply skulk about in the shadows of the trees all day while the rest of the Hunt went on their fruitless runs.

She had baseball to play, even if no one else would play with her.

She hitched her bag, a monstrous, leathery thing made from the stomach of a mud troll, higher on her shoulders. The things she'd packed — food for a day's outing, a bag of baseballs, a couple of gloves, and her wondrous bat, still wrapped in well-oiled calf skin — clunked together softly.

Her cleats whispered through the underbrush and fallen leaves as she set out.

She tried not to think of herself as alone. Being by herself had never bothered her before, so why should the fact that she was setting out unaccompanied be a source of frustration now?

She didn't need friends.

What she needed was to remember to turn left at the gnarled old oak tree, and to skirt widely around the large white boulder, which was in truth a nasty little goblin man lying in wait for someone to wander too close to his utterly still form. Then it was a dash through the deceptively serene open air of a little meadow full of yellow flowers, the petals of which hid such a vicious hive of minuscule pixies that Callie had yet to cross their field without obtaining at least one new tiny bite mark. After that would be a good old-fashioned bridge over a babbling brook, complete with a troll who eagerly awaited would-be crossers with a slew of mind-twisting riddles.

Or Callie could simply ford the brook where it bent a bit south from there, though taking that route meant she'd have to step carefully across the slick river stones so as not to tumble into the weedy embrace of the water hag who lived there.

Normally, she enjoyed running this little obstacle course. The Fairy Realm knew how to keep someone in prime shape, both physically and mentally. But today, the thought of jumping through all the hoops had her shoulders hunching in exhaustion.

They reminded her of the fact that, as things were now, she wasn't a temporary resident of the Fairy Realm any longer, and these trying little runs through the forest weren't merely a fun way to work out while she visited.

"I don't belong here," she mumbled to herself as she passed the gnarled oak. Its thick boughs curved strangely overhead, and dark shapes flitted about within the clumps of leaves, chittering menacingly.

Callie ignored their attempts at intimidation and walked on. The white boulder up ahead was going to need all of her concentration to get past. It was quivering, very slightly, in anticipation.

The path narrowed as it drew nearer to the false boulder. Steep walls of earth and thick, tangled tree roots conspired to drive a walker closer and closer to the predator lurking in plain sight. Callie knew from experience she'd need to jump to the side, use the bit of tree root sticking out from the earth as a brace, and then launch herself through the gap fast enough that the goblin couldn't get a grip on her.

She'd done it before, but never yet burdened with a heavy bag of baseball equipment.

If she'd asked Trace to come with her, if he'd agreed, they could have walked right by the goblin. If it tried to threaten them anyway, Trace's hooves would have left a sharp gouge in the thing's rocky flesh.

It didn't matter. She didn't need anyone on belay for her. She could do this alone, just like she could manage her own climbs at the gym.

She narrowed her eyes at the now perfectly still boulder and tensed her muscles.

Then, the boulder let out a thin squeak, and with a pop, became its mossy, gobliny self. A startled expression covered its stony face.

Callie, startled also, still managed to notice how the forest had gone completely silent.

A deep chuckle sounded from atop the lefthand rise. "Begone from here, lurking pebble. Your betters have come to speak."

Callie looked up. A figure stood there, not quite draped in shadow, but seeming to glow a bit, making it easy to pick out his ethereally handsome form. His dress was formal, not made for travel, and yet not a speck of dirt clung to his finery, nor did a single twig muss his long, pale hair. It was as if the forest didn't dare touch him.

Callie suppressed the flare of self-consciousness that rose in her. She recognized him now. He was the Seelie man who'd exposed the empty case where the Web Gem should have rested at the season opener.

He was the one who'd caused the season to end before it had even begun.

The boulder goblin scuttled away as if he feared being turned to gravel, leaving Callie and the Seelie lord alone in the still-silent forest.

The lord turned to her, an inviting smile curving his lips. "Mistress Cal, I believe. Or is it Miss Rival? I've been hoping to make your acquaintance these past few days."

On instinct, Callie stiffened. The soft breeze had carried a whiff of his scent to her, a mix of musky tobacco and sweet wine. It reminded her of her dad, though she didn't know why; her dad didn't smoke, and he preferred craft beer.

As if he'd noticed her defensive reaction, the lord adopted a more casual pose, leaning against a tree. But, she noticed, he didn't come down to the road to stand at a level with her.

"Forgive me my unannounced intrusion. I am the Duke of the Silver Forest."

He paused with an air of expectation.

Callie swallowed her annoyance and played nice. "How do you do, sir?"

"As well as can be expected given the recent follies. I know the situation has affected you, Mistress Cal, and I must say, it makes my heart cry to see so fine a player as you languishing. I come to offer you a reprieve, as it were."

Callie's heart gave a hopeful leap, but she squashed it down. She'd done intensive research on fairies before coming to rescue Emily DeWitt and even more before returning here to fulfill her contract for the Summer Season. She understood that nothing was ever given for free among the fey. Beyond that, she wasn't keen on the way the Seelie lords and ladies had been treating the Small Folk since their "emergency takeover."

Assessing the moment, she let herself drop her polite indifference in favor of a scowl. "I'm well enough here with the Wild Hunt."

"Of course, you are. Which is why I find you on your way elsewhere, all on your lonesome. One-woman baseball is so dull, don't you agree?"

Callie shrugged as if a fire wasn't burning inside her at his words. The bag slid off her shoulder, so she hitched it back into place. "Baseball's baseball. I'm not too fussed."

The duke laughed. "Come, now. You are an elite player. Even the most imbecile gnome can see it. You don't belong out here, scratching out a meager campsite, living rough among the pitiful creatures hunting for scraps among the tangled roots."

He waved a hand magnanimously around himself, indicating the space where the boulder goblin had sat until he'd sent it scampering off.

"You belong among more elevated company," the duke continued. "And you were meant to spend your days playing baseball."

Callie squeezed the strap of her bag until her fingers went numb.

"The season is dead," she said. "Don't tell me your team is still interested in playing."

"All I'm saying is, our players don't sit about idle all day, or run themselves ragged in futile pursuits. Their contracts are clear about their roles."

The dig at her negotiating skills sent a bolt of hot anger through her, but she simply shifted her weight, letting her cleats dig into the soft dirt of the trail rather than lash out. "That's great for them, then. At least my contract lets me go for a morning hike through the woods."

The duke laughed again, the sound deep and melodious among the quiet trees. "You misunderstand me, Mistress Cal. I don't mean to disparage your situation. On the contrary, I'm quite impressed with the skills you displayed in forging that contract. If the Web Gem had not been misplaced, the agreement between yourself and the leader of the Wild Hunt would have been a fine one. And how could you have foreseen such a turn of events? Even *full-blooded* Seelie mages cannot peer into the future so accurately."

The anger cooled enough, though Callie didn't let go of it entirely. She didn't like the way his warm, inviting smile never quite touched his ethereal eyes.

Then his words — and his implication — caught up to her.

"You ... You're saying I've got Seelie blood in me? That I'm, what, part fairy?"

The idea sent an entirely different emotion curling through her, one she couldn't name, but that left a strange, acrid taste in her mouth. Part fairy was one thing. She'd spent enough time here to see these strange creatures as people in their own right. But part Seelie?

Unfortunately, it made some kind of horrible sense. This duke did remind her of her dad in all the worst ways.

The duke's smile revealed a few more teeth.

"Your cousins would be delighted to have you among them. I believe they are particularly interested in learning your pitching techniques."

Callie's heart thundered in her chest. A part of her — a big part — was screaming inside, demanding she accept this offer. But another part felt the wrongness of it.

"My contract stipulates that I stay with the Hunt until the end of the Summer Season, and until the Web Gem is awarded. I can't break that —"

The duke waved one graceful hand as if shooing a fly. "That is hardly an issue. As a member of the emergency governing council, I have the power to break any contract made with *lesser* houses. Now, don't tell me I needn't go to the trouble. An elite like yourself deserves to live in proper housing for evermore, with proper servants to see to your needs as you ply your skills on the scrimmage fields. It is the Way Things Should Be. It would be a pleasure to do this for you."

He moved closer to the edge of the little cliff as if he might deign to lower himself to her level. His hand stretched towards her in an open invitation.

Callie's teeth had sunk so far into her bottom lip that she tasted blood. "Your offer is generous, and even pretty enticing." She would love to be able to sleep in a real bed, at the very least. And the other images dancing through her head now, of herself traveling about in fine carriages rather than tramping through the forest on foot and carefully avoiding the Fairy Realm pitfalls, or of fancy dinners held at a real table, with silverware and plates like civilized people used, even of pretty ball gowns or gorgeous, finely-made baseball uniforms, had her breathing hard with want.

But they were only images, not reality. And though this vision included a watered-down version of baseball, Callie realized it was otherwise no different than the lovely tale Trace had spun for her of how idyllic life in the Wild Hunt would be.

Both Trace and this Duke of the Silver Forest wanted to keep her here. And that was one thing Callie couldn't agree to, no matter how enticing the offer. She had a life to live back home, back in the Real World.

She met the duke's eyes firmly. "I'm sorry, but I'm going to have to turn your invitation down. Please tell my cousins I said hello, though."

The duke's smile did not shift even a millimeter, but somehow Callie knew it had become a grimace. "I think you will want to consider that choice a little more carefully."

Adrenaline pulsed through her veins, and her muscles tensed. Not to flee, or to attack, but to stand her ground. She knew she was making the right call.

In her bag, under all its wrappings, the bat Trace had given her hummed in agreement. It wanted real baseball, not scrimmage and stagnation.

"I wouldn't want to be called a contract-breaker," she said in a casual tone. "I'd rather see it out, you know?"

Now the duke truly did drop his smile. "You will regret this. The Seelie Court does not make a habit of inviting low-born mortals into its ranks."

Color Callie unsurprised. "I get it. Don't worry, if I change my mind later, I won't hold it against you if you don't renew your invitation."

She didn't think she'd be changing her mind, though.

She forced her sweetest smile at him as if to show she didn't see how upset her refusal had made him. "Anyway, I'd better be moving on, and I'm sure you've got important government stuff to do. Thanks for getting the boulder goblin out of my way."

With a deliberate step, she moved past the rise where the duke stood. She kept her shoulders back and her chin up, and she didn't give in to the incredible urge to glance back over her shoulder once she'd passed him.

The forest was still quiet enough that she could hear the soft, disdainful huff of his breath.

"So be it," he said.

A pair of fingers snapped, and a moment later, birdsong and pixie chirrups came flooding back.

Callie couldn't help herself. She looked back.

The Duke of the Silver Forest was gone, along with the opportunities he'd presented her.

She drew in a shuddering breath, then hitched her bag higher on her shoulders and set out to cross the meadow full of biting pixies, contemplating despite herself what it meant if a part of her was truly from the Fairy Realm.

CHAPTER
SIX

Callie stomped through the trees that surrounded the Other Field, the big mud troll stomach bag bouncing and jouncing against her spine. She'd walked through every dangerous obstacle between here and the Wild Hunt's encampment and was trying very, very hard not to begrudge every step.

She was also trying, and failing, to keep from replaying her conversation with the duke. The more she thought of his oily promises and too-smooth overtures, the more she thought of her dad.

She was glad she'd turned him down. But that didn't mean she didn't also yearn for the things he'd promised her. Baseball every day without having to go scrounging for other players? Even if it was only a scrimmage with no purpose, it would be something. Something more than she was getting now.

All it would cost was her self-respect. Baseball, real baseball, was something you worked for. Anything handed to you on a silver platter — by *servants*, for crying out loud — wasn't worth squat.

She heaved a sigh and hiked the stomach bag higher on her

shoulders. She'd never been so worn out after a run through the forest's deadly obstacles. Usually, the challenges made for a fantastic workout. But the run-in with the Seelie duke had sapped her strength. Throwing his offer back in his face so casually had taken more emotional effort than she'd realized.

For a fleeting moment, she wished again that she'd had Trace with her.

This morning, before heading out on her own, she'd asked Trace one more time to give her a ride. He'd asked her to go on the hunt with him.

They'd parted on something less than friendly terms. It made Callie want to knock the stuffing out of a fastball. She'd never had a fight like this with a friend before.

Then again, she'd never had a friend like Trace before, either. Ever since she'd joined Little League, she'd had teammates, and she'd had coaches. She'd had rivals. And, let's face it, even with teammates and rivals, she was always the best player around, which meant she was deferred to in everything. Until she got to know Emily DeWitt, she'd never hung out with a true equal on the field and off.

And with Trace, she had someone she could laugh over dumb jokes with. She missed the days in the preseason when she and Trace had tossed a ball back and forth after a strenuous session of corralling the feisty wildlings into actually running the bases. She would have appreciated having his warm sense of humor and support after the duke's intrusion.

Well, it didn't matter. Callie McMasters did just fine whether she had someone to giggle and make daisy chains with or not. All that mattered was baseball.

And to that end, here she was, sweaty and tired after a long hike through the perilous woods of the Fairy Realm, dragging her equipment bag with her so she could make certain that baseball. Freaking. Happened. The way it was supposed to.

Her cleats — the good ones she'd brought with her from home, not the shoddy things the Wild Hunt handed out for the few seasons they felt like fielding a team — whipped through the long grass of the meadows right outside the Other Field. She was coming in from behind the left-field stands, where the shadows were a little deeper this time of the morning.

A kind of silent awe hung like an invisible cloud over the main field of the Fairy Realm. Even now, when the fairies had abandoned the place, it still held that sense of power. Or maybe that aura was simply Callie's reverence for a good field with a solid set of bases.

Whichever it was, this power was not so tangible as whatever came from the Web Gem. She'd had her own experience touching the big trophy herself at the end of the last season, and she couldn't deny the crashing waves of power that rolled off the thing when it meant business. But just because the power of baseball's innate magic was less in-your-face than that didn't mean it was useless.

If her stint coaching the Unicorns last season had taught her anything, it was that even small talents could work big effects on the world. Especially if they were all pointed in the same direction.

She hitched her troll-stomach bag up from where it had slipped off her shoulder and stepped through the opening between the stands.

The Other Field spread out before her, a beautiful flat plane of bright green grass. Lines of pure white daisies grew between the bases, laying out perfectly straight paths for runners to follow. The mound at the center of the infield glowed like rich, melted chocolate. Tiny twinkling pixie lights dipped and bobbed over the field, leaving faint trails of sparkles behind them.

Callie drew a long breath in through her nose. The air tasted like cinnamon and vanilla, like seafoam and salt, like a warm welcome after a long day at school. It flowed through her lungs and out into her entire body, sending tingling lines of energy through her tired limbs until she felt she couldn't go another second without running, or throwing a hard curveball, or swinging a bat with all her strength.

A little imp of irritation threatened to dampen her surge of exhilaration — *it would be cool if you had anyone to play with, you idiot* — but she shoved that particular sensation down deep.

She strode out to the mound and stood there for a moment, feeling the beauty of the place from the perch of the pitching rubber, then she dropped her bag into the dirt with a heavy thump and kicked the leathery flap open to let her various gloves and balls spill out onto the ground. The wondrous bat Trace had given her rolled out of its wrappings. The sight of it brought a twinge that was equal parts loneliness and excitement to play. The runes etched into the bat's handle flared a faint blue.

Not just yet, she told it as it grumbled to itself about homers and the scent of an oncoming fastball. *Pitches first.*

She squatted and dug her favorite pitcher's glove from an inner pocket, then sorted the balls into a vague pile.

Selecting her first ball, she rose to her full height and felt the spark of real magic growing under her skin.

She'd felt it before, each time she'd worked to open the portal between this field and the Unicorns' home pitch back in the Real World. Back then, she hadn't known what she was doing, just that she needed something to help her accomplish her goals. This time, she meant to see exactly how much of this power she could amass all by herself. If she could make enough, she could refocus the attention of the entire Fairy Realm back to where it belonged: on the game.

She gripped a ball, toed the rubber, wound up, and — dialing in on the lights dancing in the air above home plate — threw.

Fastball, straight and hard.

The pixie lights scattered, but tiny, high-pitched giggles barely on the edge of audible tickled Callie's ears. She watched them dive and swoop and do delighted loop-de-loops around the bases, then she bent to grab another ball.

She let her fingers linger on the ridge of the red stitching, drinking in the comfort and confidence the texture lent her. Then she threw again, hand back, knee up, step forward, arm out!

Fastball, straighter, and harder. The pixie lights spun off in sparkling curlicues, and the ball slammed into the backstop with a strong *bam*.

Her bat made encouraging sounds in her head.

Her shoulder felt like it was on fire in the best of ways. Her muscles were bright, limber, and ready to do anything she asked of them.

Can you get me a team to play with?

No, no. She shook that off and focused again on the pure joy of her movement. Pitching was a special form of magic, she thought, remembering the way a high, rising fastball seemed to skip in mid-flight, thinking about the mystical movement of a screwball and the drop of a split-finger fastball. She scuffed her cleat against the rubber to get a better footing. Bent to pick up another ball. Three fastballs would make something happen here, right? Fairies loved the number three.

She straightened, holding the ball in her glove, her glove up to her chest. She breathed in deeply, eyes closed.

Then, in one motion, she opened her eyes and wound up for the third pitch.

Her arm was halfway through the throw when she realized home plate wasn't empty any longer. A gnome squatted there, his wicker catcher's mask pulled snug over his little face, his bulky padding strapped to his chest. He held his mitt out in eager readiness.

Callie could have pulled up and stopped her pitch. She was good enough an athlete to manage it. But she let herself follow through. Her fingertips gave the ball a tiny bit of extra spin, making it her hardest, fastest fastball of the three.

It hit the gnome catcher's mitt with a satisfying clap that echoed endlessly throughout the emptiness of the Other Field until Callie realized what she was hearing was no echo at all.

From out of the shadowy depths of the right field dugout emerged a faun. He walked with a casual gait, his little hooves swishing through the grass. His uniform was brown and somewhat shabby, and his cap set askew over his head of curls to let one stubby horn poke out. His mouth was turned up in a lopsided smile.

Callie recognized him. It wasn't Fennoc, the one who led the Small Folk, but his rougher, brasher brother. Maddoc. She remembered now.

"Nice pitching," he said as he approached the mound. "You almost made Nash fall over backward with that one."

Over at home plate, the gnome catcher rose from his squat and pulled his wicker mask up to rest on top of his head. He tossed the ball Callie had thrown up to himself, snatching it briskly from the air. His smile matched his faun teammate. "Nah, I had it. But I'll give you this, Miss Rival. You do throw harder than Miss Em ever did!"

Callie couldn't help herself. She let out a short bark of laughter. "I'd hope so. I couldn't stand it if a Unicorn could out-pitch me."

"Well, Miss Rival," Nash replied with a glint in his gaze. "Perhaps you throw harder than Miss Em, but she's a crafty one on the mound, she is. I'd be hard-pressed to say either one of you is the other's better."

"Well, blah de blah," Callie replied with a playful grin. "If you're not the little politician."

"It's a good catcher that can work with all his pitchers!"

Maddoc reached the bottom of the mound and stopped, folding his tanned arms over his chest as he looked up at her appraisingly. "We were going to use the field for a bit of practice today, but if you and the rest of your hunting hoard are planning to use it...?"

Callie snorted. "Hardly. Frankly, I wonder why you're even bothering. Nobody else wants to play. They'd all rather scramble around looking for the Web Gem, when really, it seems to me that ought to be your job, yeah?"

She nudged her collection of balls apart with the toe of her cleat.

Beside her, Maddoc made a dark sort of bleat in his throat.

"Aye, Miss Rival. But that's exactly why we have to bother. With the bulk of the Gem gone from our possession, our meager power isn't enough to cross through the portal to Miss Em."

Callie paused with her foot in the air, standing stock still as shock crashed over her.

A memory surfaced: Standing in Emily DeWitt's bedroom, handing her the folded parchment note that had appeared in Callie's own room that morning. The soft crinkle of DeWitt unfolding the letter. The spark of light from the bedside lamp caught a tiny, crystalline facet as DeWitt held it up in wonder.

Callie hadn't thought anything of the trinket at the time. She'd been too caught up in preparations for her journey back here, excited for her chance to play a Fairy Realm season.

Slowly, Callie lowered her foot and turned to face Maddoc full-on. "Miss Em has a piece of the Web Gem."

She said it quietly. You never knew who might be listening here in the Fairy Realm, and she was certain that this piece of intelligence could not be allowed to fall into the wrong hands.

Which encompassed most of the factions within the Fairy Realm, if she was being honest. She certainly wouldn't trust the leader of the Hunt with this.

Maddoc nodded once, his black eyes glimmering like two pieces of fired obsidian. "If we could get a message through to her, she could help us fight the Seelies' accusations and figure out what happened to the Gem. Alas, without the Web Gem, we are as weak and lowly as we ever were."

Movement in the dugout behind him caught Callie's eye, and her muscles tensed in anticipation of an attack.

But it was only Shady Marie, the dryad shortstop for the Small Folk. Her bark-like skin looked more rugged than Callie remembered, and her leafy hair was twisted around as if caught in a windstorm.

As Callie forced herself to relax, the rest of the Small Folk emerged from the dugout, too. They came onto the field in ones and twos, all kitted out for a full game. But their faces were harder than Callie remembered them from when she'd met them during the final games of the previous season.

The pixie trio, Mellica, Jessebel, and Izusa, fluttered their glowing wings in sharp, snapping rhythms. They floated so their toes skimmed the grass, leaving ugly lines that any hunter could follow with her eyes closed. The elves, Greeven and Delananey, stomped onto the field with no trace of merriment in their ruddy cheeks. Shayla and Twy looked ready to bite off the head of anyone who dared ask them to sing a nymph song.

The Small Folk players joined Maddoc and Nash, making a jagged circle around the mound, and around Callie.

Callie suppressed a shudder. The Wild Hunt was fierce, but right now, she'd bet a healthy pile of fairy gold that these guys would flush out any prey long before the hounds of the Hunt had even got a scent to follow. Where the Hunt was bloodthirsty, the Small Folk were *angry*.

Greeven spoke first. "What's the deal, Maddoc? Is she here as a Hunt agent, or what?"

A bolt of alarm crossed through Callie as she realized the Small Folk didn't trust her. Luckily, Maddoc was already answering.

"I don't think so. Miss Rival is different from our Miss Em in many ways, yes. Ruthless where Miss Em is driven, prickly where Miss Em is inviting. But they're exactly alike in one very important aspect." He tilted his head as he met Callie's eye again, and she caught the spark of mischief in his grin. "She loves baseball for baseball's sake."

He looked at her so intently that, for a sharp moment, Callie wondered if he knew what the Seelie duke had offered her, and that she'd turned it down.

Then he chuckled, and the brief spell was broken.

"I'd wager she's almost as put out about the season being canceled as we are, lads."

"Fat chance," said Jessebel in a rude tone that was entirely unfitting for her high pixie voice.

But the air of hostility diffused, and the gathered Small Folk shifted into easier stances. They still did not look joyful or merry, as they had during their celebratory feast near the end of last season, but at least they looked less ready to reveal that they, too, had fangs and claws.

Nash tossed Callie's ball to himself again, making it smack against his hand loudly. "Well, she's got the best fastball I've had the pleasure to catch since Miss Em went home. I'll not turn my nose up at that."

Callie laughed. And if it came out a little strained, nobody commented on it.

"Kiddos, I am desperate to play a good game of baseball. Hell, I'll take a crap game of baseball if it's all I can have. The way I figure, if everyone's so fussed about the power they can get from baseball, why not show them there's more to it than what the Web Gem can provide? I mean, come on. I managed to open this field's portal all by myself using the baseball magic, didn't I? I thought I was getting through to the Wild Hunt players about the potential of baseball magic, but..."

A lump clogged her throat as she pictured Trace galloping away from her this morning, and instead of finishing her thought, she simply shrugged.

Maddoc nodded. "That is what we think, as well. Well, most of us, anyway. My brother insists upon trying *diplomacy*." He said the word like it was something slimy he'd found on the bottom of his hoof. "He has gone, once again, to attempt to convince the Seelies to hear our voices in the ruling of the Realm."

Callie could guess exactly how that was going. Either Fennoc was admirable in his tenacity, or pitiable in his misguidedness.

Izusa stepped forward gracefully, his fine eyebrows pulled down into a deep vee. "Fennoc thinks we should tell them about Miss Em's piece, though we've convinced him to keep it a secret for the nonce. I don't trust the Seelies one bit. They weren't ever any sweeter to our people when we had to work for them than the Unseelies were. Too caught up in their rules and interpretations of the Way Things Should Be."

"At least with the Unseelie Queen in power, we were allowed to field a team," said Shayla. "Even if it was because we were supposed to be the punching bag for everyone else to gang up on. The Seelies never would have let us do that much."

Callie swallowed against a swell of nausea. "I definitely don't think you should tell them about that piece. I don't trust them, either, or anyone else in this crazy place. Except you guys. In fact, I trust you enough to be completely honest right now."

She paused, took a deep breath of grassy air, and clenched her hand inside her pitcher's mitt.

"I came here to build up baseball magic, just like you did. Because great minds think alike and all that, but also because with the way my contract with the Wild Hunt is written, I can't go home if I don't get the Web Gem back. If we work together, I think we can build enough baseball magic to show the Fairy Realm what can be done with it. You know, open the portal here and get that piece back from Miss Em? I've learned a thing or two even in my short time with the Hunt. I'm pretty sure if we get that piece, I could follow a trail to find where the rest of the Web Gem disappeared to. That would be good for us both, right?"

Maddoc nodded slowly. "Then the Seelies could shut their traps about the Way Things Should Be."

Nash clapped his fist into his catcher's mitt. "The season could resume."

Callie grinned. "And the Web Gem could be properly awarded at the end, letting me return home as I always planned to. Though, I'd transfer to your team if I thought I could break my contract with the Wild Hunt."

Maddoc leaned forward, arms crossed. "Oh, no. I think you're better placed as you are, Miss Rival. Why, you're the closest thing we've got to a second team in our little baseball rebellion!"

His words sparked the first bubble of genuine delight Callie had experienced since the aborted opening game. She glanced around at the gathered fairies, then focused in on herself.

Baseball rebels.

She almost giggled as her mind imitated the common movie trailer voice: *In a world where nobody wants to play baseball, one ragtag group of misfits will defy the odds to knock one out of the park.*

How ridiculous. She loved it.

Still ...

"One woman does not a team make, unfortunately," she said, scowling at the groove she'd dug in the mound with her cleat. "But we could split into two half-teams for scrimmage. Maybe ... if we can build enough baseball magic up, I might be able to convince a few hunters to come play when they're not running. Maybe."

It might take a powerful dose of baseball magic to get even one hunter to turn rebel against the leader, but the Small Folk were already looking brighter. The prospect that they might get to play baseball, even a modified version of it, was a powerful restorative.

Mellica flitted upwards so she stood higher than even Shady Marie and said "I'm on Miss Rival's team."

And as the rest sorted themselves out into Team Rival and Team Maddoc, Callie let herself breathe in that restorative power, too.

Baseball. Was freaking. Happening.

And his lordship the duke would never know what hit him.

CHAPTER
SEVEN

For three days, Callie snuck away from the Wild Hunt to join the Small Folk in their rebellious games of baseball at the Other Field. Though, calling them "games" was, as her father might say, more than a bit of a hard sell. They were hardly even scrimmages, really. A set of glorified drills arranged to feel like a real game.

It didn't matter, though.

Those gatherings, whatever she called them, were some of the most fun Callie had had since coming to the Fairy Realm.

She and the Small Folk players divided themselves up into Team Rival and Team Maddoc each day. Within a single cobbled-together inning, a friendly rivalry sprang up between the two teams. Using her bat with its ingrained Hunt magic, Callie hit what would have been two doubles and a lovely single, but with too few players to cover the outfield, they were all home runs. The bat yipped and yowled like any hunter as she ran the bases. Its satisfaction echoed the pulse of adrenaline flowing through her veins. It wasn't perfect, this game of baseball they were stitching together, but it was *real*.

Of course, Maddoc gave her a fair turnabout at the bottom of the inning with four miniature home runs of his own.

Three days of glorious baseball and joyful camaraderie later, they started to feel the effects of their work in the smooth flow of baseball magic over and around the Other Field.

It was a promising start, but nowhere near enough for what Callie and her fellow baseball rebels had planned.

And they were running out of time. She might be spending her days in a bliss of sporting happiness, but in the evenings she couldn't ignore the billowing dread that was rapidly spreading through the Fairy Realm. The Wild Hunt was running still, but the riders came back every night looking more pinched with hunger than they had the night before, and it had been many days now since they'd provided meat to the Realm. Rumors said the Unseelie Queen had erected bramble barriers to demark their territory, and the Seelie Court was enacting even firmer measures to keep the denizens of the Realm "in their places." One of the Hag Sisters had made a prognostication in the standing stones before the Hunt ran yesterday, lifting a boney finger in Callie's direction and spewing forth dark portents.

And Callie hadn't failed to notice that every day saw more and more Small Folk being made to do their old drudge work again.

Things were going downhill fast.

"We need more players," she said as she let the dugout's magical fountains sluice water over her grimy hands. They'd been playing all day now, and she'd just made a rough slide into home, taking a bit of skin off in the process, but she'd scored the run. The power of her success was still tingling across her skin and thrumming through the bat where it lay propped against her hip. "We've proved the concept here, but we'll never be able to build enough power for anything more than mending our own gloves if we keep playing by ourselves like this."

A disgruntled cough sounded from the bench by her knee. Essie, the brownie cheerleader for the Small Folk, sat there, nearly swamped over with the big leather mitt she was carefully stitching back together. The scowl she tilted up at Callie was fierce.

"Sorry, Ess," Callie said, coughing awkwardly. "You do great work."

"Hmph. Like to see you do any better," Essie grumbled. But she bent back to the glove cheerfully enough.

Maddoc stepped over to the fountain, nudging Callie aside with a friendly elbow. When she stepped away, he bent and ducked his whole head under the spray, then, when his fur was good and soaked, pulled it back and shook himself like a common barn animal.

"Ackpth," said Callie.

"Hey! Watch it!" said Essie.

Shady Marie, sitting on the other side of the fountain, giggled in delight as drops of water caught in her leaves.

Maddoc flashed a boyish grin at all of them. But as he met Callie's gaze, the grin turned into a more serious frown. "You're right. We don't have time to mess around like this much longer. Things are going to rot everywhere throughout the Realm, and the longer the Web Gem remains missing, the worse it's going to get. But I don't know how we can get more players without building up more power first."

He glanced out of the dugout into the bright blue sky overhead.

Callie followed his gaze.

A faint ripple hung above the field, not quite visible when looked at straight on. But the baseball magic was gathering, the small cloud of it slowly growing the more they played.

Callie pulled her attention back into the dugout. The rest of the Small Folk were coming in now, too, taking a bit of a break between plays and ready for their turns at the fountain.

"I've had an idea of who we could ask," she said, watching Nash simply sit under the fountain spray like it was a showerhead. "The River Kin. Those guys seem the least worked up about everything that's happening, and the most likely to believe we're just doing this to have fun. We don't want anyone to know we've got anything *planned* until we've got enough magic built up to accomplish something."

Maddoc nodded sagely, his hair curling as it dried in the warm air. "The River Kin could work. They're not the best baseball players, truth be told, but that's not so important right now. All that matters is a love of the game, and the Kin have that in spades."

Greeven dipped his fingertips daintily into the water still splashing over Nash's head. "Nobody loves a ball game like a selkie does, that's for sure."

"I do!" piped Essie in shrill anger.

Greeven, unperturbed by his little friend's grumpy mood, scooped her up, leaving the glove behind, and placed her in his breast pocket. "Nobody except Essie," he agreed.

Everyone liked the idea of inviting the River Kin to play, so, after everyone finished washing up, Callie carefully placed her bat among the others in the rack with a wistful little pat to its handle, and then she, Maddoc, Shady Marie, and Nash split off from the rest to head to the Riverfront.

The day was pleasant, if hot, and traveling across the rolling meadows between the Other Field and the Riverfront was easy. The four of them chatted as they walked, discussing pitching techniques and batting stances as if the world weren't falling apart around them.

Callie almost felt like she was back with her Bulldogs teammates, indulging in a mix of shop talk and banter. It was familiar and comforting.

It wasn't a bit like what she'd shared with Trace.

She was shoving that thought and the bitterness that came with it as deeply into the dark corners of her mind as she could, when the group rounded a hillock and collided with a pair of Seelie troopers.

"Whoa, there," said the first, clinging to his silver spear to keep his balance. His scowl pulled his beautiful fey face into an angled mask. "What business have you got here? I don't recall hearing of any travel for Small Folk being approved today."

His partner, who had fallen into the dirt, grumbled as he clambered back to his feet.

Callie rubbed at her shoulder where she'd forcefully bumped into the second trooper, scowling. His armor had probably left a bruise. "Since when does taking a walk need to be approved? I haven't heard anything about such a thing, and I guarantee the leader of the Wild Hunt would have told me, multiple times, with relish."

Beside her, Maddoc, bristling so hard that anger flowed off him like water, curled his hands into fists. "Your court doesn't hold that kind of power over these lands, last I checked."

The first Seelie trooper sniffed a haughty sound that emerged so forcefully it drove his nose right into the air. "Your information is out of date, then. The Duke of the Silver Forest has decreed that all Small Folk seeking to travel must do so under the supervision of one of their betters."

A spike of anger shot through Callie. She ought to have known the duke would be the sort to decree just such a thing.

"It's all to do with how untrustworthy the *lower* folk of the Realm have proven themselves to be," added the second trooper, standing straighter now. His voice was just as haughty as the first, but it was laced with more obvious hatred. "Someone needs to keep a sharp eye so they don't cause any more trouble than they already have."

Nash growled menacingly enough to put one of his Red Cap cousins to shame, and Shady Marie was already shivering so hard her leaves rustled against one another in an antagonistic hiss.

Maddoc took a forceful step towards the troopers, pointing one finger up at the closer one's nose. Callie felt his frustration coming to a head.

Inside, she agreed with him. If she'd had her bat with her, she'd have had a hard time keeping it from getting a taste of Seelie blood. But she knew that wasn't the way to come out on top with the Seelies. You had to do things their way, or they'd run to a higher authority.

She did *not* have the fortitude to deal with the Duke of the Silver Forest again.

She leapt in front of Maddoc, covering his hand with hers and forcing it down. "They're with me," she explained. "I'm their chaperone. So, your requirements are met. You can let us pass with your consciences satisfied."

The first trooper narrowed his eyes at her. "You are the mortal. The girl who signed on with the Wild Hunt."

"That's me," said Callie. She tightened her grip on Maddoc's fist. He was trying to pry himself loose from her.

"What business does the Hunt have in these parts?"

"Surely you know better than to trifle with me on matters of the Hunt. I am doing what we do. Following scents, chasing down prey." She paused to appraise the troopers before adding in a voice she hoped was threatening, "Reporting things that are out of order."

The trooper's eyes flicked up and over her shoulder, narrowing further. "And what purpose do the Small Folk here serve in your efforts?"

Callie laughed to change the mood. "Isn't it obvious, Sergeant? Or whatever your rank. I need someone to carry my prey back once I kill it. You don't expect *me* to cart my kill around like that, now, do you?"

For a moment, both troopers held their pointed stares on her. But then they glanced at one another. The second trooper shrugged one shoulder. The first let out a soft chuckle, shook his head so his wave of pale hair shimmered in the sunlight, and tilted a conspiratorial smirk at Callie.

"Of course, huntress, we'd never expect a thing like that. Forgive us, please. We're only doing our jobs, you know."

Callie nodded as if forgiveness was precisely what she had to give them. "I understand completely, gentlemen. It's hard these days, isn't it? Determining proper order?"

The troopers made sounds of agreement and commiseration.

Callie made the appropriate schmoozy noises back at them.

Maddoc, Nash, and Shady Marie stood in a tight knot behind her, still fuming, but holding themselves in check.

Inside, Callie fumed, too. A lump like bile had formed inside her chest. She hated playing this game. It made her feel too much like her dad.

At least this time she was using it to protect someone less powerful than herself.

"Well, gentlemen," she said when she could stand it no longer. "It's been lovely meeting you and hearing about your hard work keeping the Fairy Realm on the straight and narrow, but I'm afraid I really must be going. Hunt leader will bite my head off if I don't bring prey back in by sundown."

The two troopers laughed at her comment precisely the way Coach Jameson had when he'd met with her dad to ask for a McMasters' Ball and Glove sponsorship.

"Be on your way, then, mortal huntress!"

Callie made showy motions to the Small Folk, and together they continued down the road. Knowing it would spoil the effect, she never once looked back to see if the troopers had stayed where they were.

Besides, the Small Folk did it for her.

"They've gone off down the other fork in the road," said Shady Marie. Her voice held a hint of a quaver.

"Those rats," Maddoc snarled. He pounded one fist into his other hand and ground his teeth together. "Those *hobgoblins*. I can't believe my brother keeps trying to parlay with them. They'll never treat us like equals unless we force them to."

Callie knew he was right, which made it hard to say anything that would soothe him.

"Come on," she said. "It's not much farther to the Riverfront. The sooner we convince the River Kin to play with us, the sooner we can boot the Seelies out of their power trip."

Hopefully, the River Kin would be as easily swayed as those two Seelie goons had been.

THE RIVERFRONT WAS unlike any other place Callie had seen in the Fairy Realm thus far. It was a shimmering world of splashing water and sparkling light. Mossy rocks tumbled into the rapid flow, and sandy banks stretched the length of the river until it met the sea, where a salty tang joined the fresh air. Everywhere she looked, River Kin were enjoying themselves. Mermaids lay out on the beach, fanning their tails to cool their faces and maybe catch their lovers' eyes. Selkies dived and leapt into the water, swimming hard against the current before twirling on their flippers and riding the flow into the sea. Kelpies and sirens and water hags loitered in the rocky pools on the far bank like teenagers sneaking cigarettes behind the mostly abandoned malls back home.

An undine slithered up to meet them.

Callie, happy to let Maddoc take over now that the Seelie jerks were out of the way, marveled at the sights.

"We'd like to meet with Lady Marne if she's available," Maddoc said.

The greeter gave a moment's consideration. "I'm sure she will be interested in a session with the mortal," she said, then led them to a roaring waterfall upstream, and into a gorgeous little cavern behind it. Luckily, the rock muffled the sound of the crashing water to a dull radio-like static, so they were perfectly able to have a conversation without shouting themselves hoarse.

As they entered, Lady Marne, the mermaid leader of the River Kin and manager of their baseball team, was lounging on the edge of a large, still pool that filled her enormous cave. A scattering of stalactites that glowed with purple and blue water magic lit the space. A pearlescent plate full of spotless fish bones rested on the pool's lip beside her, reflecting back the eerie light.

Deeper in, a group of River Kin were batting a big pink bubble around in a game that Callie thought was something akin to volleyball, using noses, tails, fins, or tentacles to keep the bubble from touching the water.

The undine announced them, and as Lady Marne rose to climb from the pool, her multicolored mermaid's tail melted into a pair of scaled legs.

"What a wonderful surprise," she said, smiling widely enough that her small, sharp teeth showed. "Whatever brings you here during these troubled times? Do you seek to refresh yourselves in our pure waters?"

Maddoc bowed, a rather graceful motion for such a rough-around-the-edges guy, Callie thought. But when he straightened again, his customary lopsided grin was back in place and his eyes sparkled in ways that would have scandalized his brother.

"While I'm sure a bath in your pool would simply overflow with pleasures," he said, "I'm afraid we've come only to invite you and your players to have a bit of fun with us Small Folk. We're looking to banish our current woes with some good, plain baseball. What do you say, Lady Marne?"

Lady Marne was already nodding. "Oh, yes, yes! That is a lovely idea. Just what my poor players need. They've been so *depressed* ever since the Lords canceled the season."

She waved one delicate arm to indicate the River Kin sporting in the pool behind her. Callie squinted, trying to make out any sign of sadness in the lively group. There was a lot of splashing, anyway.

Maddoc stroked at his little goatee like a wise man. "I *thought* I'd noticed despondency in your folk as we passed through the River-front. So, you will come to play with us at the Other Field? It won't be much, just a few friendly faces gathered to make a day of it."

"We wouldn't miss such an opportunity for all the jewels in the sea," Lady Marne said. Her expression turned almost childish with hope as she leaned subtly closer to Maddoc. "Tonight?"

Callie's lungs finally relaxed enough to let her draw in a shaky breath. If the River Kin hadn't agreed to play, she didn't know what she would have done. The magic she and the Small Folk were building would never be enough to bring about the conditions that would let her go home.

But with Lady Marne's acceptance of their invitation, Callie had a chance again. She made a mental note to encourage Maddoc's flirtation with the mermaid leader every chance she got.

"Tonight," Callie said, coming to stand beside Maddoc. "Right as the sun sets."

She stuck out her hand to shake. By the time she realized she'd done it with the same little flick of the wrist her dad would have, Lady Marne was already pumping it up and down enthusiastically.

"Oh, Mistress Cal," said the mermaid. "We'll finally be able to settle up from that unfinished opening match, won't we?"

Callie found she didn't mind sharing her own shark-like grin with the sharp-toothed Lady Marne.

THE SKY WAS a blaze of orange and pink over the Other Field when the River Kin arrived. The sheer energy that vibrated from the watery team as they flowed through their warmups in the outfield showed Callie how the display she'd seen earlier constituted "depression."

She couldn't blame them. Her own heart was as a-flutter as if she were entering her freshman season again. A real baseball game was going to happen, and this time, nobody was going to stop it.

She'd make damn sure of it.

Joining the Small Folk to make a cohesive team, Callie took the mound.

Twy was an admirable replacement for DeWitt's pitching, but the nymph had happily given her position up to Callie, claiming she'd rather go back to cheerleading alongside little Essie for a while.

Callie's first pitch left a scintillating trail of baseball magic as it left her hand. And when the kelpie hitter connected for a line drive towards third, the scintillations flared like sunlight on water.

The cloud of baseball magic hovering over the Other Field

expanded a bit, a small bit, of course, but so powerful Callie couldn't stop her grin.

Back and forth the innings went as the sun sank below the western stands. The sky turned first violet then navy blue then midnight black, studded with stars. Maddoc orchestrated the Small Folk, touching the baseball magic so that each inning ended with the score tied, incrementing up one or two runs each time, the Small Folk constantly managing to scratch out an extra walk or double exactly as needed.

It didn't take long for the River Kin to notice what the Small Folk were doing.

"Hey, that's fun," said a selkie after diving to avoid a sparkling tag from Delananey at second. "How'd you make it do that?" he asked.

"The trick is in feeling *baseball*, you know?" Delananey explained. "It doesn't matter if you win or lose, so long as you let yourself be all-in on the game."

"Oh! I see," said the selkie, and he proceeded to send a spray of glistening magic up behind him on his dash for third.

Soon, all the River Kin were leaping and laughing at the glowing lines of baseball magic, hitting foul balls just to watch them fly in arcs of silver light and giggling over the muddy bronze color of sacrifice bunts. When one made a full puddle sliding into third base, the sky rippled in gleeful waves of energy.

Their laughter was infectious. First, Mellica started tittering along with the siren who'd just struck her out with a curveball that radiated a spiral of seafoam twinkles. Then Maddoc fumbled a catch at first and let out a guffaw so robust that emerald green light flowed from his glove to form a puddle at his hooves.

Finally, Callie herself simply fell over as she stumbled across home plate to even up the score once again, laughing so hard she couldn't draw breath.

The tumble made her ankle burn like fire inside her cleat, the pain throbbing all the way up her shin, but something about the way the cloud of baseball magic overhead distorted the stars in the midnight sky was just so funny.

She was dead tired, though.

Which was why she looked at the scorecard and realized they had played through thirty-three innings.

Thirty-three.

A glance at the horizon showed the sun making the eastern sky rosy, and for the first time, she felt like one of the characters from all the stories she'd read at the library back when she was researching how to rescue DeWitt from this place. She'd read about how hapless mortals who fell into the Fairy Realm often lost track of time, only realizing they'd been dancing for days on end when they noticed they'd danced their feet into bloody shreds.

She supposed it must be the same with playing baseball.

It was easy to forget how dangerous this place was when she was having so much fun.

Callie was still on the ground, lying on her back beside home plate. "All right, kiddos," she called out once her breathing was mostly under control. "I have to call a break, or my feet are gonna fall off, and if that happens the Hunt leader will gnaw my face to bits."

That sent everyone giggling again.

She watched the cloud of baseball magic ripple in response to the laughter, and she smiled.

Somehow, she pushed through the pain to stand up.

The kelpie who was playing catcher steadied her.

Lady Marne and Maddoc came to home plate together, both grinning fiercely, Maddoc dripping with sweat.

"Shall we pick up tomorrow evening where we've left off?" Lady Marne asked.

"Aye, lady, for sure," said Maddoc.

Callie nodded, too exhausted to speak, already dreading the long walk through the forest to reach her little cave near the Hunt's standing stones.

Maddoc and Lady Marne shook on it, and the River Kin flowed

into their dugout to pack up their things. The Small Folk did likewise, chattering and exclaiming to one another about plays they'd pulled off.

Callie grinned through it all.

She packed her equipment into the troll-stomach equipment bag, lovingly wrapping her bat in its calf-skin holder as it mumbled sleepily to her, then she said good night and started her trek through the forest.

She made it far enough that the Small Folk's voices had faded into the chirping of crickets and hooting of owls before a dark shadow moved to loom over her.

"Mistress Cal! Where have you been?" the shadow said in a gravelly voice.

Callie held a hand to her thundering heart. "Trace. Holy crap, you scared me."

The centaur stood in the darkness of the wooded canopy, the last rays of moonlight reflecting off his bare chest and glinting from his brown gaze.

"*You* scared *me*," said Trace. "I've been looking for you all evening. When we came back from the hunt today and you weren't in your cave, I thought some bloodsucker from the Unseelie Court had gotten you, or worse."

The catch in his voice made Callie's stomach twist with guilt. "Sorry. I didn't mean to make you worry. I've just been working with some friends who appreciate baseball. You know."

She shrugged one shoulder. The troll-stomach bag scraped against the small of her back.

Trace pawed at the underbrush with one of his front hooves. "It's nearly sunrise. You're lucky I covered for you with the leader. He's not happy you've been avoiding our runs. What were you thinking?"

Callie scoffed, though it came out more like a weak cough. She was tired right down to her bones. "What does he care? It's not like I've got the nose of a bloodhound or the hearing of a satyr. He doesn't lose anything by letting me do my own thing."

She hitched the bag back onto her shoulder and took a step along the trail.

The pain of her twisted ankle radiated up to her knee, and she stumbled.

"Whoa, now," said Trace. His hand was at her elbow instantly, warm and solid. "You're hurt."

"It's nothing." Callie tried to wave it off. "My feet are tired."

At least, that's what she tried to say. The back half of it got swallowed up in the most humongous, jaw-cracking yawn she'd ever yawned.

Trace *tsked* at her as well as any disapproving auntie ever had. "Get up here, then."

Callie tried to protest, but Trace easily overruled her arguments as, troll stomach bag and all, he pulled her up onto his broad horseback. Callie sighed, mumbled something about not needing help, and laid her head against his shoulder.

He moved through the forest in a smooth canter, barely jostling her.

"The hunts have been going poorly the last few days. I wish you'd come along with me. At least then I'd have someone to talk to. I've missed our discussions on the tactics of pinch running, you know?"

He glanced over his shoulder to see if she'd heard, but she hadn't. She was sound asleep, and snoring.

CHAPTER
EIGHT

A misting of rain began to fall as Callie entered the Other Field the next day, filling the air with the smell of fresh dampness. She drew a long breath of it in and held it, letting it drive off the last of her sleepiness.

She'd gotten amazing rest last night, and when she'd woken late this morning, the pain in her feet had all but disappeared. The baseball magic at work, she thought, feeling the tingle of it as she pulled a second lungful of rain-scented air through her nose.

The raindrops, falling faster now, barely stirred the cloud of baseball magic hovering over the field. The cloud was twice as large as it had been before the River Kin had joined her and the Small Folk. Callie knew it wasn't that the watery fey were any more powerful than the Small Folk; it was merely that real baseball was better than cobbled-together drills.

The River Kin were here already, and they were frolicking amongst the raindrops just as Callie had expected they would. And as Callie made her way into the Small Folk's dugout, Lady Marne emerged from the opposite one with a smug little smile of satisfaction on her face.

"I hope you don't mind I've whipped us up a little rain game," she called. "My players thought it might play nice with the baseball magic."

Callie lifted one hand in agreement. She didn't mind a little water. Not so long as the baseball kept flowing. "Just make sure we don't get a rainout!"

She stepped into the dugout, to find the Small Folk waiting with tangible anticipation. Izusa pirouetted in the corner as if he couldn't stop himself, while Shayla and Twy were busy on the benches braiding fresh flowers into each other's hair to keep it out of their eyes. "We're going to play in the outfield today," Shayla informed Callie. "That way Jessebel and Mellica can keep their delicate wings dry," added Twy with a smile Callie would have been able to see glowing from across the field.

"The rain throws my flying off too much," Jessebel said.

"And you drop the ball more often when it's wet," Mellica said with a teasing tug on Jessebel's braid in her hands. "Izusa doesn't mind the rain, though."

Izusa pulled out of his latest pirouette, gave Jessebel a jaunty bow, and started on a set of pliés. "I *love* a little rain!"

Mellica rolled her eyes at his antics. "We're perfectly happy to sit today out. Besides, Miss Em told us the spectators of a game can build baseball magic just as well as the players."

Callie nodded. "I'm sure that's true. And I've got high hopes for today."

"Yay, team!" Essie called from Greeven's shirt pocket as the elf stretched his arm.

A clopping of hooves announced Maddoc's arrival. "Are we ready to play? The River Kin have begun bouncing balls around out there, so I guess that means they're all warmed up."

He looked a bit miffed about the rain, rubbing his hands together and swiping at his reddened nose. But he still wore his customary grin as he grabbed a bat.

Callie hadn't done any warmups, but she knew she didn't need to, not with the way the baseball magic was already humming through her. Her bat, likewise, was practically vibrating as she set it in the rack with the others.

A booming voice echoed across the field. "Play ball!"

Callie peered out of the dugout in surprise. Sure enough, the cyclops who usually served as the umpire of the Other Field stood out there. Rivulets of rainwater ran down his craggy skin, soaking his loincloth and making him blink his single, massive eye.

"Hey, that's great," she said, pulling back into the shelter of the dugout. "Who managed to call in the ump?"

The rest of the Small Folk shrugged.

"I don't think anyone called him," said Greeven. "He just turned up. I think he missed the games, too."

"That makes sense," Callie said. "You've got to love the game to want to be an umpire."

The crack of Maddoc hitting the first pitch ricocheted over the field, and Callie joined the Small Folk in cheering as he dashed for first. The umpire swung his arms in the sign for "safe" with such obvious gusto that Callie had to agree with Greeven's assessment.

Izusa was next up. He held his bat daintily and fluttered his wings so the water flew off them in dazzling droplets as he waited for the pitch. When it came, he swung so hard he turned himself completely around, balancing on one pointed toe, then cartwheeled his way to first.

Nash waddled to the plate.

He never even swung his bat, instead letting his squat stance turn everything the siren pitcher threw at him into ball after ball. He walked to first, a wide grin on his face as he deliberately stomped in every muddy puddle along the baseline.

The River Kin seemed unconcerned to have Callie striding up to bat with the bases loaded. From the dugout, Lady Marne smiled as Callie waggled her bat over her shoulder. Callie smiled right back.

"C'mon, pitcher," she called. "Throw me the heater. Send me your best shot!" The baseball magic swirled through her, tingling in her fingers as they curled around the bat. They'd built so much of it already.

The siren wound up and threw. Fastball.

Callie swung.

"Strike one!" shouted the umpire.

Callie waggled the bat again, calming its dark muttering. She narrowed her eyes at the pitcher. "Well played, my friend." She chewed her lip, though, and pounded home plate with the end of her bat. She didn't like swinging and missing.

The siren on the mound shook out her hair, sending drops of water in a spray around her. Then she threw again. Changeup.

Callie swung.

"Strike two!"

Callie gritted her teeth. Rain dribbled down her face to drip off her chin, and she wiped it away absentmindedly. She hadn't struck out even once since coming to the Fairy Realm. She didn't mean to start now.

The bat agreed. It went utterly still in her grip, a predator waiting for its moment.

She tugged at the brim of her helmet. Then she readjusted her grip on the bat and aligned her fingers better with the carved runes. Straightening up and raising her eyes to recenter herself, Callie looked out at the mound.

Furtive movement in the dark trees beyond centerfield made a bolt of alarm shoot through her, and she stepped away from the batting box as if it were made of molten iron. "Someone's out there," she called.

The other players turned to look at the forest. Tension ran thick as the rain, now.

Was it the Seelies, come to stop their illicit play? Was it the Hunt leader on the prowl for blood?

Callie held herself taut as a bowstring as the dark shadow moved closer.

It emerged from the trees, and the shadow resolved itself into a familiar centaur shape.

"Trace," Callie muttered. "What's he doing here?"

Whatever he said, Callie wasn't going to ride the hunts with him.

Or was he here to bring her activities to the attention of the Hunt leader?

Her expression grew grim with the idea.

He looked nervous, though, glancing from side to side and letting one front hoof tap at the muddy ground as the gathered players stared at him. But as he came fully into view, Callie realized the thing slung across his back was not his usual hunting bow, but a sturdy oaken baseball bat.

"Is there room for one more player?" he called. His voice sounded small, like a mere skittering of pebbles among the hiss of the rain.

Callie let out a bark of laughter, more out of relief than humor.

She glanced over to third base, where Maddoc was crouched, to confirm. The faun gave a nod and a little two-fingered salute.

"The more the merrier," she called back.

Lady Marne, lounging outside the River Kin's dugout, lifted one scaled hand in greeting. "Join us, yes! The water's fine today."

The umpire, understanding that they were playing fast and loose with roster rules in this already two-day-long game, blinked his massive eye and waved at Trace to get into one of the dugouts.

A boyish smile spread across Trace's lips, and he trotted across the field to step into the Small Folk's dugout. The elves and Shady Marie scooted over to make room for him to join them at the benches, and he immediately brought his bat out and started some practice swings.

Callie's heart fluttered to see it. Not only was she happy to see him, she was glad to see his joy in getting back to the game. He *had* been the one who'd loved it the most among the Wild Hunt.

And now she had a chance to show him how she was putting his gift to use.

She watched him a moment longer, and when he looked up to

catch her eye, something passed between them. Something that tingled like the baseball magic, but was slightly warmer, a little cozier. Something that made the rain all but disappear in Callie's mind.

With a shake of her head and a smile on her face, she turned to see the siren on the mound looking at her, head tilted in a silent question.

Callie stepped back into the batter's box and waggled her bat.

"C'mon, pitcher," she said. "You haven't got rid of me yet."

LATER, after Callie's grand slam had brought their score up by four and after the River Kin had matched it in the bottom of the inning, Callie sat on the bench next to Maddoc as Trace went up to bat for the Small Folk at the start of the 58th inning.

"The baseball magic's getting stronger," Maddoc said. "Other fairies are starting to notice. We got the umpire, and now your Hunt friend. Though, maybe that one was less to do with the magic, huh?"

He dug his elbow into Callie's side, making her turn to see the teasing grin he wore.

Despite herself, Callie felt heat spread through her cheeks. "Trace likes baseball," she said matter-of-factly. "That's all."

"Sure, sure. Definitely nothing else going on there. And I'm just happy to see Lady Marne because I like the way she manages a team."

He dug his elbow in again, making sure she got the point.

"Yeah, yeah," Callie grumbled.

But she turned back to watch as Trace hit a solid double and galloped around to second. When he turned to grin at her across the distance, she couldn't help but grin back.

"Nice hit!" she shouted.

Maddoc chuckled, but he didn't press the issue any further than that. Instead, he leaned forward to look up at the now visibly shimmering cloud of magic overhead. "It's getting to be enough so we could call on Miss Em, don't you think?"

"Maybe so," she said, hearing the dark tone that had crept into his voice, a tinge that matched the thread of worry that Callie carried with her all the time now. She followed Maddoc's gaze to admire the maelstrom of power that circulated in the summer breeze over the Fairy realm. Without the Web Gem here to corral it, the baseball magic seemed to have nowhere else to go.

Though Callie agreed the amount of magic they'd built up was at least nearing enough to open the Other Field's portal and cross over into the Real World, she wasn't certain the time was right yet.

The Fairy Realm was becoming a less friendly place to be by the day, especially for the Small Folk.

Plus, she was feeling a little strange about the baseball magic. Before, when she'd opened the portal herself, all it had taken was three home runs as a Unicorn. Hell, she and DeWitt had done it a second time, just the two of them, with no other players around, let alone a full pair of teams. She didn't understand why the baseball magic had flowed so much more effectively back home, in a supposedly magicless world, than it did here in the Fairy Realm. Shouldn't it be the other way around?

It made her nervous, even while a part of her yammered at her to get a move on. Every day that she woke up in a Fairy Realm with no Web Gem in it was another day she technically had to spend as a damsel in distress.

"I'm not very experienced with magic on this side of the fairy ring, so I don't know what to expect. It feels like so much can go wrong if we move too soon," she said, watching as Greeven strode up to bat. "What if my contract with the Wild Hunt makes it so I can't go across with you?"

"That's a possibility," Maddoc said. "But if that's true it will occur despite any timing. And if that's the case, then I guess you'll just have to trust your teammates."

Callie's expression clouded.

"I've never been very good at sitting on the bench," she said.

"I understand that sentiment, Miss Rival," Maddoc continued. "But whether you go or not, if we get Miss Em to bring her piece of the Web Gem here, we might be able to use its power to alter your contract. We'd be able to with the whole trophy, anyway." He shrugged, then clapped as Greeven hit what looked like a smooth single, but the undine shortstop made a spectacular dive to stop it, then promptly tagged Trace out as he slipped in the mud on his way to third.

"I think we should at least wait until this game is over before we try anything," Callie said. "Who knows what the baseball magic or the River Kin might do if we stop mid-ga—"

The sky was split by a sudden lightning bolt, and a high cackle echoed across the field.

A tearing wind sprang up, whistling and screaming through the dugout.

The rain, which had previously been falling in gentle drops, whipped into slicing sheets.

Callie threw her arm up to shield her face and leapt from the bench to see what had happened. Maddoc joined her at the dugout fence, and Trace galloped over to grasp her hand tightly. She couldn't make anything out through the gray curtain of rain and mist, nothing except the silhouettes of the other players cowering in the onslaught. Even the River Kin looked unhappy about this turn of events.

But then, as quickly as it had started, the cackle cut off, and the wind drove itself up and away, drawing the rain with it. In the minia-ture storm's wake, sunlight streamed through the rippling cloud of baseball magic, glinting off the puddles on the field and making rainbows arch overhead.

A trio of women dressed in black baseball robes and pointed caps had appeared in the stands. Each one carried a knotted bat like a broomstick over her shoulder.

Callie gaped up at them. *Looks like the delegation from the Hag Sisters of the Wood has arrived,* she thought.

The tallest stepped forward and shouted down to the still bewildered Small Folk and River Kin.

"Sorry to alter your weather, but we hate rain games. Can we play?"

———————

THERE WERE SIMPLY TOO many players who wanted a chance to get on the field to remain as the Small Folk vs. the River Kin. So once again they split into Team Rival and Team Maddoc.

Callie had Trace, of course, as well as two of the three witches, a kelpie and an undine from the River Kin, and Delananey, Izusa, Nash, and Shady Marie. The rest of the Small Folk went with Maddoc and the third witch to take over the other dugout alongside Lady Marne.

The score was tied up twenty-seven to twenty-seven as the game entered its 64th inning.

Callie's team was defending first, and she stood on the mound turning the ball over in her hand. With so many players participating, baseball magic was tingling all around her. She hadn't even thrown a single pitch this inning, and already everyone in the dugouts was cheering, clapping, and having a good time through merely drinking in the atmosphere of the game.

Delananey had stepped away between the innings and reappeared groaning under the weight of a bona fide picnic basket. Now, the players who weren't going to see the field this inning were strolling through the stands, enjoying a hearty luncheon, and laughing amongst themselves.

Callie wondered if Delananey'd packed any orange slices.

She'd check after she'd pitched the inning. First, she had to strike Maddoc out.

He stood at home plate, the great log of his favorite bat swaying over his shoulder and a wide, lopsided grin on his face.

"Come on, Miss Rival," he called. "Betcha can't get one past me."

Callie smirked. "I haven't shown you all my tricks yet, goat-man."

Then she pitched him her favorite curveball, the one that waited until the very last second to spin away from the plate.

Maddoc swung and missed with an audible whiff.

The baseball magic zinged through her like a warm summer breeze, and she laughed as Nash tossed the ball back to her.

Trace called out from center field behind her. "Fancy pitching, Mistress Cal!"

Callie tossed a grin back at him.

Maddoc shook his head and brought the bat back up.

Callie wound up and threw again, sending her best changeup at him this time.

Maddoc whiffed again, hard enough this time he stumbled forward a step to keep his balance.

From the dugout, Lady Marne shouted encouragement. "Shake it off, Maddie. Like water off a selkie's back!"

Maddoc nodded at Callie. "You're good, I'll grant you. Won't get a third past me, though. I'm on to your tricks now."

But Callie only smiled as she switched the ball from her right hand to her left. She adjusted her stance to match.

"I'm ambidextrous," she said in response to Maddoc's widening eyes. Then she threw a fastball, straight down the middle.

Maddoc never even swung.

"Strike three!" cried the umpire. But nobody heard him, because Maddoc was laughing so hard that the loud brays echoed through the whole of the Other Field.

The cloud overhead pulsed with energy. Callie felt it down to her bones, down in her gut, down in her primal soul, and she gasped. Everyone else gasped along with her, and Callie felt that, too.

It was glorious. For one long, breathless moment, Callie knew she could do anything. *They* could do anything.

All of them together.

They were all connected as one via the cloud of baseball magic.

In the vibrating magic of that oneness, it crossed Callie's mind that she may never want to leave.

Then a loud crashing sound came from the woods, and the connection snapped.

Staggering at the sudden loss, Callie swung around to see what had happened.

Two figures stood at the tree line, but despite the distance, Callie had no trouble reading the matching fury on their otherwise unlike faces.

One was a faun, like Maddoc but standing taller, prouder, more like a proper butler than a baseball team manager.

And one was the leader of the Wild Hunt.

"What," growled the two unlike men in unison, "is going on here?"

CHAPTER
NINE

C allie stood frozen on the mound, feeling like she was caught in a scene from one of the old Clint Eastwood movies her dad liked so much. She could almost hear whistling over the wind as she stared down Fennoc and the Hunt leader from across the field.

Overhead, the shimmering cloud of baseball magic that she and her co-conspirators had built up convulsed. The other players, Small Folk, River Kin, Hag Sisters, and Trace, stood by in silent anticipation.

Someone had to break the tension. The only question was, who?

Well, Callie wasn't one to back down from a standoff. Her dad hadn't raised her to be any other way. The man might have been a crappy parent, but even Callie understood he knew how to do business.

Forcibly un-hunching her shoulders, she left the mound. Her cleats squished in the still-damp grass of the infield as she strode with wheeling-and-dealing purpose towards the trees beyond the outfield.

The Hunt leader snarled and stepped forward, his golden wolf eyes blazing with his fury.

Fennoc, with a deep scowl of his own, followed the leader and began to trek through the outfield.

As the three of them came within a few strides of one another, they all tried to speak at once.

"You're spoiling *everything* I've been working for —" from Fennoc.

"Of all the foolish wastes of energy —" from the leader of the Hunt.

But Callie made her voice cut above theirs with the precise pitch and tone her dad used on conference calls. She lifted her gloved hand and pointed it straight at the leader. "*You* have failed to uphold your end of our contract, buddy. You're lucky I don't go to the Seelies with my complaints."

Fennoc drew up short at that, but the Hunt leader growled low in his throat. His tattered cloak billowed around him as if caught in a high summer wind, though the air remained as still as the Hag Sisters had left it after they'd dispelled the rain.

"I have done no such thing," he hissed. He leveled on her the piercing gaze that conjured pure terror in his prey.

Callie didn't back down. "My contract states that I am here, in the Fairy Realm, on the Wild Hunt's team, to play baseball. Well, I tried to get you to field a team for the Summer Season, and when that fell apart, I tried to get you to help me convince the other factions to play. But you kept focusing on running your hunts, and that left me no choice but to find another way to fulfill my end of the deal. That's a clear breach of contract by you."

She capped off her delivery with a casual shrug.

"That is ridiculous," said the leader. He was so close to her now that she could smell the rankness of his breath like meat left too long in the sun, the staleness of his sweat after days of running fruitless hunts.

Callie raised one eyebrow. "Is it? Have you got the Web Gem scented, then?"

Another growl and the leader's claw-like fingers shivered as if he'd love nothing more than to wrap them around her throat.

She snickered. "Yeah, I thought not."

Fennoc broke in before the leader could leap upon her. He was shaking so hard that the point of his goatee quivered. "Contracts aside, this is utter madness. Do you comprehend what the Seelie Court will do if they find you shirking your duties to play in this kind of meaningless game? With the Web Gem gone, only the Unseelie Queen has the power to stop them from turning the Realm as they like, but she's walled herself up in her dark castle doing who knows what kinds of vile magic."

He stomped one pristine hoof in the grass, sending a great splotch of mud flying. "I have been feeding their haughty egos and ingratiating myself to their uncaring whims for weeks now, just to keep them from completely enslaving the Small Folk once again. And now I come back here to find you all, and *my own brother*, have been casually undoing all my hard work this whole time!"

The anger that rolled off the little faun was potent enough that Callie had to steel herself against taking a step backward. She couldn't afford to lose face in front of the leader.

The grass rustled behind her, and a moment later Maddoc and Lady Marne stood at Callie's side. Trace and the three Hag Sisters were close at their heels, arms crossed and wearing closed expressions on their faces.

Callie felt their support strengthen her spine. "Fennoc. I'm sorry you've had to kiss up to those Seelie asses. It's not fair. But I promise you, we're not trying to counteract what you're doing. We're just trying another approach."

Maddoc reached one muscled arm out to his brother. "We're trying the baseball magic, Fen. Don't you feel it?"

Fennoc's eyes flicked upwards, and a surprised spasm of pain, longing, and exasperation crossed his bearded face before he looked back at the gathered players. "The baseball magic isn't strong enough on its own, not without the Web Gem."

"That's not true," Callie said. "If it were, how could Miss Em and I have opened the portal in the Other Field before?"

Fennoc's expression turned thoughtful, but he didn't answer.

The Hunt leader did, though. "Sheer dumb luck," the leader said. "Which is also the only thing that has kept you from catching the attention of the Seelies, who would claim all this raw power you've so unthinkingly spun up. The baseball magic has never worked the way you claim before. There is no reason why it should start now."

Lady Marne made a watery noise of irritation. "Just like a Huntsman. What do you even know about the baseball magic, mister *we only field a team if we feel like it*? We've got a good thing flowing here."

With a snarl, the Hunt leader spun on her. "You, river dweller? You ask what the Wild Hunt knows about the baseball magic?"

"I'm glad to know your ears are in working order," Lady Marne responded, unintimidated.

"We know enough to say that if you seek to accomplish anything more with it than simple tricks within a game, you need a lot more of it than this."

"How much more?"

"Enough to cover more ground than the crow can fly over in three days! This piddling wisp won't do more than bruise yon Seelie lord's over-pale skin, and *that* is more easily accomplished with a solid cudgel."

Fennoc blanched. "Oh, my."

"Only if you can carry said cudgel past the lord's loyal guards," Lady Marne snipped. "Even you would have trouble with that maneuver, wouldn't you?"

"My lord," said Trace in a reasonable tone, cutting off the Hunt leader's snarled reply and bending his head toward the ground in deference. "With all respect due to you and your exalted position, without the Web Gem, the baseball magic is the only weapon we have against the oppression of the Seelies. And it is a truth we must admit. In all its runs these past weeks, the Wild Hunt has not managed to discover even a single whiff of the Web Gem's scent, just as the Hag Sisters' finding spells have turned up nothing, and the River Kin's deepest dives have returned equally empty-handed. It seems time we tried something other than our traditional tools."

The Hunt leader stood utterly silent, his hands clenching and unclenching until drops of crimson blood came trickling from his fists. The breeze picked up around them, creating a strangely mournful sound as it moved through the trees and over the grass of the Other Field.

Finally, the leader turned on Callie. "This changes nothing for you, little mistress. No matter how you might wish for the Realm to embrace the baseball magic for its own sake, your contract still says the Web Gem must be awarded before you can return home. You will be trapped here with us, playing your precious game for all eternity."

"No, I won't," said Callie.

She'd had an epiphany as the argument swirled around her. She had allies now. Allies who would stand with her if she pressed the leader of the Hunt to do the right thing. Which meant she could afford to lay her hand on the table.

"You might think the whole of the Web Gem is gone, but the truth is, the Small Folk managed to hold on to a single tiny piece of it."

"*Impossible,*" said the Hunt leader. "We've been all over the Small Folk's lands. We'd have picked up the scent if it were here."

"Ah, but did I say it was here?" Callie said. "Not all of the Small Folk are in residence this season, are they?"

The players around her whispered amongst themselves at her declaration, River Kin and Hag Sisters turning to the nearest Small Folk to confirm this information. Lady Marne flicked a questioning glance at Maddoc, who nodded curtly.

All the while, Callie continued to stare down the leader of the Hunt. She didn't dare even blink for fear he'd use the opportunity to rip her throat out.

A warm, solid hand pressed on her shoulder. Even though the revelation was as much a shock to Trace as it was to everyone else, he was still choosing to stand with her against his own lord.

Callie drew on his strength to lay down her ultimatum. "Thanks to Lord Fennoc's sense of loyalty and fair play, a shard of the Web Gem remains in play. If you and the Hunt help us build enough baseball magic, we'll let you use Miss Em's piece of the Web Gem to get a scent. But you're going to have to agree to a new contract stipulation. Once found, the Web Gem returns to the Small Folk immediately, and the summer baseball season recommences. No shenanigans with trying to keep the Gem for yourself or use its power to bring about your dream of war before handing it over. And everyone here will see to it that you keep your word."

Lady Marne slid forward to stand with Callie straight away, her scaled face hard as a thundering waterfall. The trio of Hag Sisters cackled in agreement. Trace stamped one hind hoof in the dirt as if planting a flag in the ground.

To Callie's surprise, the leader did not look as though he longed to murder her now. Instead, a pensive expression clouded his face and his head cocked as though he were listening for a rabbit softly scratching in the underbrush.

"Our Hunt has long found itself facing a fork in the trail, with many of our riders longing to follow one path, the rest straining at the bit towards the other. But you present us with an alternate route. Not simply hunting, nor simply baseball. A hunt run *by way* of baseball. It is an intriguing solution."

He lifted one hand to rub at his chin, and for a moment, Callie wondered if she hadn't given him more than she'd intended after all. But she couldn't figure out where she'd gone wrong, and so she chose not to worry about it.

The much, much more important thing to focus on was the fact that the leader of the Wild Hunt was going to agree to her terms and play baseball once again.

"Very well," he said.

Then he threw his head back and howled.

A moment passed, then another. Then, from the trees, more voices rose in answer, first one, then three, then a whole host of howlers, punctuated with sharp yips and the high, cold giggles of Red Caps. They melted out of the forest like a cloud of dark fog clinging to the ground.

The baseball players Callie had worked with back in the preseason stood at the front and formed a semi-circle around their leader.

"Come," he said, beckoning Callie and Trace to join their proper teammates. "We shall play by your rules if you play by ours."

Callie glanced over her shoulder at Trace. The centaur met her eye and held it, then nodded once. He slid his hand down from her shoulder and into her hand. Together, they stepped over to join their team.

Fennoc shook his head, but he, too, moved to stand with his brother. "I hope you all know what you're doing."

The leader of the Hunt laughed. "Of course, little faun. We *hunt*."

CHAPTER
TEN

For the second time, Callie stepped onto the Other Field to play for the Wild Hunt. The sky overhead was the color of slate, with flat clouds covering the sunny weather the trio of Hag Sisters had conjured. The rain from the earlier session with the River Kin made no return, but the air gained a metallic tang. It hung in the back of Callie's throat with every breath, a threat of lightning that made her blood tingle.

The feeling wasn't entirely born of the natural world, she could tell. Like the baseball magic, it came from somewhere else.

This was the innate power of the Wild Hunt, she realized, like what ran through the bat Trace had given her, but so much stronger. She would have felt it sooner than today if she'd ever agreed to accompany them on their runs.

And this time, as she straddled third base and tipped her cap back to let the windy gusts tangle her hair and cool her sweaty scalp, and when the leader of the Wild Hunt took the mound and set up his eerie howl, she didn't hold herself back from joining in.

She'd enjoyed playing with Maddoc and the Small Folk. They were a great bunch. Loved baseball.

But she'd signed on with the Hunt. This was her team.

The game began. No longer the unending roll of innings of a bunch of players out to have a good time for as long as possible, but a fresh, new game.

Real baseball. The Wild Hunt versus the Small Folk, with the River Kin and the Hag trio in the stands, pressing themselves right up against the fences to take it all in.

This game meant business.

Callie was in it to win it.

Greeven stepped up to bat first. A scowl of deep concentration screwed up his elfin face as he held the bat over his shoulder.

The Hunt leader threw him a curveball for a strike. But Greeven got the bat on the second curve, and he pelted a sharp grounder toward Callie at third base, then ran for first as little Essie's shrill cheers rose out of the Small Folk dugout.

Callie leapt forward, glove extended, as the ball bounced toward her. The scent of the leather-encased ball came to her, subtly different from the scent of her glove. As she snatched it up and hurled it towards Pyrgin at first, that smell lingered in her nostrils, setting her blood afire with Hunt magic.

It left her breathless.

Pyrgin caught her throw as neatly as catching a rabbit in a trap, and a split second later, Greeven crossed the base.

"Out!" called the umpire.

The River Kin made noises of upset, and the Hag Sisters cackled in delight as they clapped and whistled for the Hunt. Greeven turned and trotted back to the dugout, shaking his head.

Overhead, the cloud of baseball magic surged larger. It was as if, Callie thought, without the Web Gem here to bind it, the baseball magic was free to be itself, free to run free. That left it unfocused, which explained why they needed so much more of it to open the portal than she'd needed before, but the freedom gave it a certain crackle and zing that wasn't there earlier. The bounds of its shimmering form now sloshed over the edges of the Other

Field's stands and out into the wild lands of the Fairy Realm forests.

Her blood singing through her veins, Callie returned to her place at third.

BY THE BOTTOM of the third inning, Callie wasn't certain where the line between *playing baseball* and *hunting* was anymore. Everything was prey, every move was part of the chase. As she came to the plate, bat in hand, her focus dialed in on Twy so fully that she was able to shut out the chanting of the selkies and naiads in the stands. With an automatic part of her brain, she checked in on her packmates on base. Trace stood at third, hind muscles bunched and ready to burst forward the moment she hit. Thacker took a lead off first base, chittering softly to himself as he crooked his sharp little talons in readiness to leap.

But these details were the next thing to unimportant; her packmates could fend for themselves, as was expected of them.

There was only herself and her quarry: the ball currently turning over and over in Twy's delicate hand as the nymph shook off Nash's first two suggestions.

Callie ground her heel into the dirt and tightened her shoulders to just shy of a knot. *It doesn't matter what prey you throw, little Twy,* Callie thought with confidence born of certainty. And, in that moment, she knew it was true. Curveball, fastball, even the oft-magicked knuckler. The pitch would come. Callie would be ready. She and her bat, her trusty hunting dog, her closest partner in the chase.

A heartbeat later, it did come. A fastball close inside. Like a wildcat leaping from the brush, Callie pounced. The power of the bat flared so hard it left her gasping.

The crack of wood on the ball split the air.

A hit, a line drive sharp enough to rip the blood-red threads of the seam. She saw them fluttering in slow motion as the ball tore through the cloud of baseball magic, heading for the fence out in the deepest part of center field.

Then she was running. Breathing hard but smooth, conserving energy until the moment was right to spend it. Running, and running, and running.

The ball thundered as it crashed off the oaken planks of the fence.

With her peripheral vision, Callie saw Izusa's wings blur as he dashed to scoop it up. A smirk of satisfaction grew across her face as she pumped harder toward second base. The slate gray cloud cover had worked to her favor, obscuring the flight of her hit so the outfielders couldn't determine where it would come down until it was too late.

Baseball magic was on her side now!

Her breath flowed through her body as her foot pivoted around second base. Her heart beat a victory staccato as Trace scored his run. Thacker had done his part at third and was moving on, leaving the ravaged mess for her at third.

A glance to the outfield. Izusa had pulled the ball from his mitt. His arm was back, aiming for Greeven, who stood between Callie and her prey.

She narrowed her eyes, assessing at lightning speed.

At her fastest, she could beat Izusa's throw.

Blood roared in her ears as she sprinted full-bore, using that energy she'd stored up in the first part of her run. Her vision closed in until all she saw was the bulbous white rock that was third base, the grain of it standing out like neon lights in the dark of night. Adrenaline flooded her senses, power surged through her muscles. The aroma of blood intensified.

The ball was in the air, almost to Greeven's glove.

The base was two steps away.

Callie let instinct take over and followed it down into a slide. Dirt sprayed over the base, and her ankle jarred as the sole of her cleat struck the heavy stone. The smack of leather on leather told her Greeven had caught the ball.

The ball's unique scent filtered into her brain again as she sucked in a lungful of air to replenish her strength.

Golden magic glittered among the settling dust.

The umpire squinted his single huge eye.

"Safe!"

The cheers that descended over Callie as she clambered to her feet were stronger than three witches could accomplish on their own, even with their spells. And sure enough, as she looked into the stands she saw their little coven of supporters had grown. Ten or twelve ladies stood along the fence now, all clad in black robes and pointed caps, some hunched and wrinkled and others sparkling with their spells of eternal youth. They waved wands and raised gnarled hands in celebration, and the scoreboard changed to display the new score.

Wild Hunt 4, Small Folk 3.

Callie grinned and even knowing it was a wolfish grin did nothing to cut her fierce delight. She shook her arms out, then one leg and the other, dusting herself off. She removed her batting helmet, ran her dirty fingers through her hair, and then replaced the helmet.

The baseball magic thrummed so heavily she could taste it over the dirt that still hung in the air.

It's almost enough. I can almost get my grip on the portal.

The Web Gem's scent felt so close. Almost in her nose, the pulse of its power was only a tiny bit out of reach.

As soon as she won this game, she would have enough.

CHAPTER
ELEVEN

The game entered the bottom of the ninth. The score was 13-13.

If the Wild Hunt could score one run, they'd win.

Power whipped around the Other Field like a high wind on the moors. It wasn't just baseball magic, not anymore. It was the Wild Hunt's tracking spells tangled with Small Folk charms. River Kin enchantments interwoven with Hag Sister hexes. It was a humming, vibrating mesh of different styles of play, different ideals, and different dreams.

It was almost enough.

Callie reached her consciousness up to touch the swirling power. It tingled within her, so much like it had when she'd opened the portal from the other side, from the Real World.

She wanted to win so badly that her chest ached with it. She didn't know if a loss would affect the potency of the baseball magic, but she didn't want to take the chance. When the marbles were on the table, she had never played for anything less than to win. At the very least, she thought any disappointment she felt would surely sour her ability to work with the baseball magic. With the key to her freedom at stake, she couldn't play at anything less than her peak.

She was so focused she almost didn't notice Trace's attempts to get her attention. But when she went to grab up a bat in preparation for her turn at the plate, he took her cool hand in his two warm ones.

"Mistress Cal," he said. Though their other wildling teammates were making a racket in their excitement that echoed through the dugout, Callie picked up Trace's low voice perfectly.

He was looking at her with something that, on one of the kids she'd played with on the Bulldogs, might have been awe. But on him, it was something else. Something that made her blood grow warm, and not in a Hunt way.

"Trace," she said in barely more than a whisper. "I've got to get ready to bat. I'm next up."

At the plate, Pyrgin was currently turning Twy's first pitch into a strike.

Trace didn't let go of her hands. "I know it. And I know you'll get the run we need. But I wanted to say, well, to say I'm sorry. I acted a fool because I thought this Web Gem disaster had at least given me a bright opportunity, keeping you here in the Realm with me. But my refusal to help you make the baseball happen ended up keeping us apart, after all."

Callie knew she was gaping, but she couldn't help it. The unabashed sincerity shining out from his dark eyes left her speechless.

"I know you belong to a different world than I, but I would rather spend this little time we do have standing by your side, rather than trying to hold you back. You are magnificent on the field, my lovely. It is an honor to watch you work the baseball magic."

He lifted one hand to cup her cheek, and Callie felt her heart stir at the touch. The sensation was similar to the power of the Hunt magic that had been coursing through her all game but turned to a different purpose. The feel of it made her wonder if Trace wasn't entirely correct about which world she belonged to.

She was wondering about a lot of things, lately.

Silently, she pulled her hands from his hold, then reached up to wrap both arms around Trace's shoulders.

"Thank you," she said. "And I'm sorry, too. It's been a difficult time for everyone, and you deserved to have someone help shoulder your load with the Hunt. I missed you, Trace."

Her eyes stung with tears she refused to let herself shed. When this game was over, she'd go with him on a hunt. She wanted to see what he saw in it, to feel what he felt when he chased down his quarry. She wanted another thing to share with him, as he'd shared baseball with her.

Trace's arms closed around her, squeezing hard, which was just as well. She could handle his strength. She might have slugged him if she thought he was holding back.

When she pulled away, he grinned at her. The light of the Hunt blazed in his eyes, and Callie knew the same fire flickered in hers, too.

On the field, Pyrgin struck out and returned dejectedly to the dugout.

Callie bent to pick up her bat.

"Good hunting," Trace said.

Callie raised two fingers to her forehead in salute.

Then she stepped out of the dugout and up to the plate.

The chase was nearing its end, and she had her prey right where she wanted it.

From the mound, Twy narrowed her eyes as she peered at Nash. She shook his call off once. Twice. Then she gave a sharp nod, and a fierce grin curled over her pretty face.

Callie grinned back and waggled her bat. She was ready for anything.

Anything, that was, except for what actually happened.

Twy raised her arm for the pitch.

A thunderclap ripped at Callie's ears. The sonic pressure tossed players to the ground, and the gale wind tore at pennants that had been simply fluttering in the breeze before. The sudden black cloud smelled of harsh fire and woodsmoke as it funneled downward, the Unseelie Queen riding its slope like it was a stallion, flares of purple lightning forking from her raised hands.

She laughed as she descended to the Other Field, alighting on a patch of green between Callie at home plate and Twy on the pitcher's mound. Her high-pitched socialite's titter amplified to fill the entirety of the Other Field. The sound made Callie's ears throb painfully. The queen stood tall and dark in her midnight dress. Her blue-painted lips turned up in a wicked smile.

Callie, recovering from her shock, stood straight again, then adjusted her batting helmet. Trace's bat vibrated in her grip, tugging at the ends of her control like a dog on a leash.

The queen looked less poised and polished than she had at the end of the previous season. Her hair was disheveled, her dress a bit frayed along the hems. Her sharp nails showed chips here and there. But a dark, fey light was in her eyes as she surveyed the gathering. Her lips set. Her hands raised to cast magic. She tipped her head back to peer up at the roiling mass of baseball magic so strong it glowed and pulsed above them. Her lips parted in a gasp of visible hunger.

"Ahh," the queen said as the players and spectators recoiled from her might. "Such power you have gathered here. Such a delectable offering for your queen!"

Then, slowly, she lifted one graceful hand.

Callie's heart clenched, and her bat flared like fire.

"Stop her!" she shouted. "She's stealing the baseball magic!"

She leapt forward, feeling something uncoil deep within her bat, something intoxicating. It woke her blood like a song, an ancient chant of trees and the forest in a language she could feel more than understand. Fairy Realm history was as deep as the forest, immortal as the very trees from which this bat had been carved. Through it all

Callie felt a new sensation of bloodlust stronger than any she'd ever imagined.

She'd never intentionally bashed anyone with a bat before, but now seemed like an excellent time to give it a try.

The magic of the bat flared in violent agreement.

It was imbued with Hunt magic, after all, and Callie was a member of the Hunt.

The queen was within reach.

Callie swung, aiming for the shoulder of the upraised arm.

She and the bat both knew it was going to be a clean hit. Together, huntress and bat reveled in the anticipation of the crunch of bone.

Instead, though, the bat whiffed through empty air.

Off balance, Callie stumbled forward until she nearly collided with Twy, who'd come off the mound, her nymph song swelling wordlessly in her throat. Twy managed to cut her song off before it slammed into Callie, but Callie's blood was up now, and the bat was full of an unsated fury the likes of which Callie had never felt from it before.

She coiled, seeing Twy's prone form bared to her. The bat surged forward, whipping down toward Twy's delicate skull.

Twy's purple eyes grew wide and full of fear.

The thick part of the barrel swung downward.

"No!" Callie screamed, pulling so hard against the descending bat barrel that she thought her arms might rip apart. She couldn't stop the swing, but her pull was enough to alter its course. Enough. Barely enough. The bat snarled in empty hunger as it missed decapitating the defenseless nymph.

It wanted blood, though. It demanded sacrifice with the power grown over its long life. And Callie felt that call inside herself, too, felt the burn in that small part of her that carried Seelie blood, that piece of her that belonged to the Fairy Realm.

The queen stood now on second base, cackling in great humor.

"Yes!" she called. "Let it out, mortal! Feel the glory of battle rage inside as it is meant to do!"

The queen's splayed fingers cast purple tongues of lightning that sent poor Delananey and Shady Marie skittering away to keep from getting fried. A horde of Unseelie faithful, voices warbling with war cries, weapons gleaming in the macabre light of dark fey magic, stepped through the clouds to join the fray.

But by now, the rest of the Wild Hunt players were on the move, stalking out of the dugout and into formation at their leader's sign. Pyrgin and his satyrs brandished slings loaded with baseballs, while Trace led the centaurs in a charge straight for the queen.

The queen laughed as she simply teleported once again, reappearing behind the charge at third.

"Get them!" she called to her followers. "Sup on their bones tonight! Leave the insolent rebels with nothing!"

She'd forgotten that this wasn't the Wild Hunt's first run, though. The satyrs hadn't been aiming for where she was, and the moment she appeared on the base closest to them they let their slings fly. Baseballs filled the air, one striking the queen between the shoulder blades so firmly her magic sputtered. She let out an undignified yelp as she fell to one knee.

The satyrs sent up a keening cry of victory. But the queen whirled on them, her face twisted with murderous intent, the black folds of her dress whipping in fresh power. Black gobs of magic dripped from her hands, and where it splashed on the ground, the grass and flowers of the Other Field froze into stone.

A wave of cold horror engulfed Callie at the sight.

"Look out!" she cried.

Too late. The queen shoved her hands toward the satyrs, sending the magic spraying forward. In the space of one breath, Pyrgin and his two fellows became statues wearing slightly shocked faces.

"Fools," said the queen. "The Web Gem will be mine again. It belongs to me! Even the Seelie King would not deny it knows me best. And now that the Small Folk have shown it can be segmented, I will wield it with strength they cannot fathom. Fight me if you wish to expend your pitiful magics on futility, but know that in the end, you will feel the pain you are owed! The pain you deserve!"

Callie stared at the trio of statues the queen had just created. Bitter fear welled from the pit of her stomach. For an instant it felt as if she was the one who'd been turned to stone, her limbs frozen in place as she watched her teammates, her co-conspirators, and her friends rush towards the queen as one diverse mass, Trace leading the charge from the outfield, Maddoc astride his back, swinging his log bat in a downward arc towards the queen's head.

From the dugout, the leader of the Wild Hunt leaped forward, halfway through a monstrous transformation, his head, shoulders, and front limbs fully wolf, his back half still wrapped in his hunting clothes. His teeth were bared, though, and his golden-brown eyes burned with fire and determination. Hag Sisters and River Kin clambered over the fences, magic of their own flaring forth as they raised battle cries.

Beside Callie, Twy pulled in a lungful of air, preparing to sing. Shayla was coming up to join her sister, one hand reaching for Twy's.

They were all doomed, though.

Callie knew this in the way the ancient wood of her bat burned through her heart. She gripped the wood in both hands and felt its anger and its despair for the world, heard how it called to the powers of the Fairy Realm, and felt the pulse of the sap that had flowed through its woody core.

The queen lifted her arms. Her magic spattered outward in all directions, gobs of black oozy mana darkening the air, reeking and acrid like coal, striking the ground to turn patches of the Other Field into a stone-studded meadow.

Much of the Queen's magic found other targets, though.

A Hag Sister cried out as she, too, turned to stone. A kelpie froze while rearing, his forelegs pawing the air. Twy became a statue of a nymph on the cusp of a song.

And together, a single blast stopped Trace and Maddoc as a

horrific sculpture of centaur and rider captured in joint poses of attack.

Shayla screamed as she flung her arms around her sister's stony shoulders.

Fennoc bleated wordlessly and dashed into the outfield.

Lady Marne shed tears over a pair of selkies at the foul line.

Even the leader of the Hunt paced in wolf form between his satyr and centaur statues, alternately snarling and howling.

Others cried in dismay as they scampered for cover from the queen's ruthless onslaught.

Fury burned through Callie, turning the fear that had immobilized her to ash. With one hand she squeezed her bat so hard her fingers ached, drawing on the Hunt runes carved into the handle, feeling her blood surge. She raised the weapon, feeling its power swell inside her, and with the other hand, she reached up, blindly groping for the baseball magic.

It wobbled at her touch and slid out of her grasp.

The queen — grinning in wild-eyed delight — turned her full attention on Callie.

"Not so easy to wield the power of the Realm, is it, mortal? I told you once before, power like this isn't for the likes of you. You may have a drop of fey blood in your veins, but your mortal flesh weakens any claim you might lay on the baseball magic, either through the Web Gem or in its raw form as it is here. Now, see how a real sorceress handles her power!"

With a twist of her wrist, the Unseelie Queen commanded the cloud of baseball magic. It roiled with her touch, spun in a maelstrom of wind and rain, still glowing a celestial golden haze split with silver and green. Callie grabbed for it again. She raised her bat and tried to call to the cloud — and for a moment the wood took hold, and Callie sensed the bat wallowing in a satisfying sensation of home and beauty — but the queen deftly snapped the billowing cloud out of Callie's reach, laughing her horrible socialite's laugh.

Callie watched, powerless to stop her, as the queen pursed her lips and, with a great breath, inhaled every last drop of the magic Callie and her friends had worked so hard to accumulate.

When the queen was finished, her skin convulsed as though it couldn't contain so much power. She braced herself, breathing hard and deep as the power filled her.

In control again, the queen leveled her gaze at Callie, and her lips pulled back in a wicked smile.

"Let's see those infernal Seelies try to run my Realm now," she said.

The bat throbbed in Callie's grip. Callie rushed her. All her Wild Hunt gleanings fueled her, all her rage at the unfairness of being kicked off the Bulldogs, all her resentment for her father's inability to care about her. All her fears for her future, her worries about whether there was a place in any world for her.

The bat Trace had made for her was a rod of fire in her hands.

The queen's black clouds billowed around her once again when Callie swung.

She connected. The crunch of bone wasn't nearly satisfying enough.

Neither was the pained scowl the queen levied on her the final instant before the clouds whisked her away with all their baseball magic.

The silence that followed was deafening.

The queen was gone.

She'd taken the power to open the portal, and thus find DeWitt and her piece of the Web Gem, with her.

Slowly, dragging her bat behind her, Callie trudged to join Fennoc beside the statue of Maddoc and Trace. She slumped to her knees, looking up at the pair. The grass crunched as she settled on it.

"Trace," she whispered.

TRYOUTS

CHAPTER

TWELVE

T he tone indicating the end of class rang, and Adrien Thorn — eye already on the clock — shouldered his book bag, rocketed from his desk, and raced out of his history classroom so quickly his sneakers squeaked.

It wasn't his usual manner of escape. Normally, he was at least polite to his teacher, despite his dislike of the class. He liked to take his time packing up so he didn't have to fight through the crowded hallways at the end of the school day before dropping by the theater hall or the school library to meet up with his friends.

But today was not a normal day.

He shouldered his way out into the sea of kids already surging through the hallway, trying to ignore how their clamoring and yelling echoed off the linoleum tile floor and cinder block walls.

Lockers slammed. First-years thundered out to meet their buses. Kids of all years groaned about the homework loads they'd been saddled with.

Adrien grimaced at the press of bodies, then lowered his shoulder and pushed onward.

Wendy Thomas walked by, glancing at him with bright eyes, her cheerleader uniform swaying with her steps.

Adrien wrestled his grimace into something approximating a smile, then turned away from her.

He wasn't so stupid that he didn't understand the meaning under her glances. The Fairy Realm was nothing if not attraction-forward. And she was a perfectly nice girl, he was sure. But Wendy's lithe frame, crimson-tipped hair, and gemlike gaze reminded Adrien too much of the fey in general. There was no way for him to ever be comfortable around her.

He picked his way down the hallway.

He turned his steps not towards the dim corridor where the theater kids hung out, or towards the library (despite having a book or two he needed to return), but for the rear entrance of the school, the one that would let him out the closest to his house. He was in a rush to get home today, and he intended to avoid as many prying eyes on the way as possible.

Because today, the calendar said it was early February. It wasn't the annoying Valentine's Day flyers plastering the hallways that bothered him so much. People could celebrate their affections however they wanted, as far as he cared. Even Wendy Thomas, though he'd prefer if she turned her attentions elsewhere.

What had him ducking his head as he passed the gymnasium doors was only one simple, unassuming paper tacked up on the wall.

The signup sheet for the Unicorns' baseball team.

Coach Amabe had posted it early this morning, and the chat group all the players from last season used — which Emily had insisted on adding him to — had been blowing up ever since.

Benji had tagged him directly five times.

Adrien could pretend he hadn't looked at the app, but if Benji caught him in person, there would be no avoiding their enthusiasm.

The players weren't the only ones buzzing about the signups, either. Even though he was trying to keep his head down as he plowed unceremoniously through heaps of teenagers, he couldn't help picking up the excitement thrumming through the masses. Because, last season, for the first time in the one hundred years since Adrien himself had hit a championship-winning home run and gotten snatched up by the Unseelie Queen, the Pattersonville Unicorns had made a serious run at state. Success like that meant everyone was ready to be a Unicorns fan this season.

Whipping the excitement even higher, over the past week news had spread via every outlet in town that Fred McMasters, father of the Marion Bulldogs' disgraced and now-absent superstar Callie, was making amends for his daughter's attempt at cheating the Unicorns out of their chance at state by sponsoring the Unicorns this season. It was controversial, for sure, but the general population had settled into acceptance and was now eagerly speculating about the benefits such a financial backer could provide. Only the players themselves still discussed the cons of the situation — or, at least, they had until the signup sheets had gone up today.

The cherry on top of the whole shebang was Emily DeWitt.

Her brief stint in the Fairy Realm meant she'd missed too much of last year's schooling to graduate. Her disappearance and eventual reappearance was something the general population of Pattersonville had, after a furious few weeks' discussion, eventually chalked up to some weird, attempted kidnapping. But it meant their star player was back for her official senior year.

People in the modern age were like that, Adrien found. So much news flowed from every direction all at once that their attention spans stretched only so far. Whereas Grandma and Grandpa Thorn might have chewed on the goings-on around the city for months, the whole Emily DeWitt story had faded in barely two weeks.

Which was good for Emily, at least.

Simply put, with this perfect storm of opportunities, expectations were high for the team this season.

High enough that someone had started the rumor that *he*, Adrien Thorn, supposed descendant of the legendary *first* Adrien Thorn, might join the fray.

He didn't have to think too hard about who might have started that rumor. There were really only two suspects. Either Benji had been sharing their hopes too loudly, or Megan Moore had picked up her pen once again.

Megan Moore. The bane of his modern existence, better known as the Sports Editor for the *Unicorn Weekly Gazette.* She'd been all over him ever since he'd come back to town and seemed to have some kind of sixth sense that told her there was more to his story than he was saying. She'd already published too many pieces about him, running the gamut from flattering to scathing, and her constant attempts to get him to give her a proper interview had him slinking around like a thief in his own home trying to avoid her.

Her articles made it almost impossible to keep up his image as a normal, modern-day kid, an already mind-numbing chore given his learning curve with things everyone else took for granted. Earlier today someone had had to show him how to buy a candy bar with his cell phone — which was a piece of equipment more magical than just about anything in the Fairy Realm. The flat screen always boggled his mind, and his problems with it made the kid give him weird glances.

Even when he finally figured it out, he was still shocked at the price. Two dollars and fifty cents? When he worked at the general store, that was what he'd earn in a week.

Credit cards were easier to grasp, but still tripped him up.

No one in the Fairy Realm had to deal with banks, putting gas into cars, or pulling drinks from an automatic fountain dispenser kiosk.

But no matter how baffling these otherwise mundane things were to him, he had to keep his surprise and frustration firmly locked down. Keeping his story solid was important because he was certain that if he told anyone the truth, they'd send him to the nearest asylum faster than Emily could steal a base.

To the nearest hospital, he reminded himself harshly as a gap in the river of kids opened in front of him, letting him sprint down the open path. They didn't do asylums anymore in the modern age. Which was admittedly a relief, given how horrific such places had been in his day.

But still, if he ever claimed to be the hundred-year-old hero of the Unicorns, they'd take him to the nearest psychiatrist. Or dope him up on a pile of meds he didn't need. Of course, if Benji kept on him about visiting the Fairy Realm, he was going to go bonkers, so maybe the meds wouldn't be all bad.

Now, with baseball season approaching and this new rumor floating around, Megan Moore the relentless newshound was back on his case and causing him a never-ending stream of severe migraines.

So, yeah, Adrien had a whole boatload of reasons to go flying out of the schoolyard like a pixie out of the Unseelie Court today.

Because despite everyone's obvious hopes and dreams, Adrien was *not* going to join the Unicorns.

Even without the queen's curse ringing in his ears every quiet moment, the idea made his stomach churn.

He'd found the words to make that clear to Emily from the beginning, though even *she* still pushed him sometimes, saying that after playing for so long in the Fairy Realm he would dominate against normal high schoolers.

"I don't care," he'd explained back then. "I just want to focus on school."

Luckily, school was going well for him — discounting history. His grades were somewhere between good and excellent. Turns out a hundred years of learning certain basics about math and science in the Fairy Realm translated like a charm, and his ability to play the lute made music theory a breeze. Kids lined up in the hallway when he practiced, which was a bit annoying for a guy who wanted to keep a low profile, but he couldn't deny it was nice to have people recognize he had talent in something other than baseball.

And there was theater, which he was having enough fun with that he was reading parts for other actors. Even though he figured he would stick to understudy, or stay off the stage entirely, it gave him another reason to ditch baseball. He liked the plays a lot, but he liked building the sets even more.

Regret dogged his steps as he finally caught sight of the double doors that would lead him to freedom, standing open beyond the banked rows of lockers. His theater crew mates were meeting today to roll paint over the sets for their production of *Taming of the Shrew*. He'd rather be doing that, joking with the gang and getting paint splashes on his jeans, than slinking home like a weasel. Maybe he could double back and poke his head in, just to see how things were progressing.

"Adrien Thorn!" Megan Moore's unmistakable voice pierced the thrumming roar of post-school chaos. On reflex, he craned his head back to see her tall, gangly form pressing through the crowd, cell phone glowing in her raised hand, the record button certainly activated. "Can I have a word please!"

He dodged behind a bank of lockers so fast that the bookbag flopped off his shoulder, pulling his arm uncomfortably. He ignored the pain, though, and pressed on, fighting the current of students and wriggling in a serpentine fashion through the lockers. Megan's voice still rose above the clamor, but it came from at least two rows over, now. If he was quick enough, he'd lose her.

With another turn, he reached the double doors and dashed through them. Bursting into the open space, he let the brisk air fill his lungs. Despite the day being clear and sunny, with the faint scent of new grass growing green after this morning's rain, the early February wind was sharp on his cheeks.

When he was sure that he'd avoided the reporter, he slowed his pace (slightly) and shifted the book bag to a more comfortable position.

Blood flowed back into his arm, sending tingles down into his fingers.

Now in the open, Adrien sighed as he felt tendrils of pressure fade a little.

He zipped up his thin jacket to cut the chill, then set his course home.

Behind him, the end-of-day crowds spilled out of the blocky, yellow-brick building. Band kids lugged instruments. Athletes raced each other to the practice fields. Friends shouted at each other from opposite sides of the parking lot with youthful shamelessness.

Adrien put his head down and kept walking. Once he turned the corner onto Van Dyke, he'd get some shelter from the teenage maelstrom and, for the first time all day, he'd be able to hear himself think.

Not that his thoughts were going anywhere productive. He felt a need to vent about Benji and their incessant chatter about visiting the Fairy Realm themself. Adrien had begun to think he should make sure he and Emily were still together on Benji, and the rest of the world for that matter — as in, there was no way in all the Hells they would let Benji get close to the Fairy Realm, and it was still A Very Good Idea to keep the entirety of their time in the Fairy Realm an industrial-strength secret.

It was bad enough that Callie McMasters was still somewhere in the Fairy Realm, getting up to who knew what kind of mischief with the Wild Hunt. He wished her the best, he really did. But mostly he wished she hadn't taken such a risky step.

Because pain in the ass or not, Megan Moore was a surprisingly good investigator.

He was worried she would find something soon, and when she did, it was going to cause trouble for more than just himself. His friends among the Unicorns players already had enough on their plates what with the McMasters sponsorship and a high-pressure tryouts season without having to add "don't trip the Fairy Ring under Unicorn Field" to their checklist of things to do. Emily alone bore so much on her — admittedly capable — shoulders.

Of course, he was torn in two about Emily. On the one hand, she was one of the minuscule number of people with whom he could be his true self. On the other, she didn't know *everything,* and because of that, she had more power to hurt him than anyone else in the mortal world.

It was a good thing she wasn't here for him to vent at. With signups today, any conversation he had with her would probably wind up strained.

Home — the Thorns' place — was just around the corner and then down Bradford Street. If he could make the hedge row, he would be home free.

"Adrien!"

A step away from turning the corner, he heard Emily's voice call out.

Suddenly everything felt miles away.

He pressed his eyes tight, then sighed and turned to find her jogging toward him with her classic long, easy strides, her backpack swaying behind and one hand holding the Small Folk ball cap to her head. He had to admit he admired the way she wore her secret in such plain sight.

"Hi, Em."

"You're not getting away that easy, bud." She came to a halt beside him, then picked up her pace to stay close when he began to walk down the street.

"I told you, Emily, I'm not going to play," he said as he huffed down the street. "I just want to focus on other things. School. Theater."

She grabbed him by the arm. "I've seen your grades, Adrien. You're killing it so hard you might as well have been brought up in the modern school system."

Adrien swallowed his frustration. "That's not the issue. I don't want to play baseball."

Emily's lips screwed up as if she, too, were biting back bitter words. "That's fine, Adrien. You be you. If doing theater makes you happy, I say go for it. But you've got to tell me why you're pretending so hard to hate baseball when I know it's as much a part of your blood as it is mine. I promise you don't have to go so far just to fend Megan off."

Easy to say for someone who hadn't just practically army-crawled away from the tenacious reporter.

"I don't know how many times I have to tell you I'm not pretending," he said. "For someone from this era of modern medicine, you sure don't seem to grasp the concept of PTSD very well."

Emily scowled. "I get that what you went through in the Unseelie Court was traumatic. And if I thought it was truly hurting you, I'd back off. I promise. But I *know* you love baseball as much as I do. Maybe more. And I hate the thought that something as unfair as that is keeping you from joining the team. I guarantee you, if we get you on that field again, everything will be all right."

She wore that look of fierce determination she could get sometimes, as if this were a problem, like his anxiety over studying World War II, something she could fix through her not-insubstantial internal drive to help him.

It almost made Adrien laugh, but he twisted his lips into a grimace, feeling the chill of the breeze.

Emily's fingers tightened on his arm hard enough to make his fingers go numb again. "I'm deadly serious about this, Adrien. Tell me what's wrong. You owe me that much," she said with enough force it took Adrien aback.

His guilty gaze slipped away from hers.

She looked up at him and chewed her lips.

For a moment Adrien thought Emily might cry, but that dark cloud passed.

"I'm sorry, Emily. I ..."

He clenched his hands into fists, and his stomach gave a painful glurp as he recalled the words the Unseelie Queen had screamed into his head as he left the Fairy Realm.

Emily was right.

He did owe her an explanation. Without Emily's help, and

without Callie McMasters' help, he would never have escaped the Unseelie Queen's clutches at all. Such that he had, anyway.

More than that, it was time he told *someone*.

He'd carried the full weight of his situation on his own for as long as he'd been back in the Real World, and he was tired. And if he was going to have a real talk about Benji, it would be best to be transparent here, too.

He needed Emily DeWitt on his team. No one else would understand.

"All right," he said.

"Great!" Emily said. She let her hand slip away from his arm and turned so they walked side by side. When he didn't immediately say anything, she nudged him with her elbow and put on a sing-song voice. "I'm listening."

He met Emily's gaze, then pushed his balled fists into his jacket pockets and took one more breath before letting the story fall out.

"The queen had to honor the deal she made with Callie. When you fulfilled all three of her trials, she left me free to cross the portal."

"Of course."

"But we both know the fey are dangerous to deal with, Emily."

"Tell me about it." She shuddered, and Adrien knew Emily was thinking about her own contractual kerfuffle with the Small Folk.

"What you don't know is that the queen spoke to me just before we stepped on the plate together. A parting shot, as it were," he said, closing his eyes once more. "I can still hear her voice. The way she said the words."

Emily waited, still strolling beside him, her gait so smooth that her sneakers remained silent against the concrete sidewalk. But a taut thread of tension wove through her steps now, where she'd moved easily before.

His stomach twisted as he relived that moment back in the Fairy Realm again, the three of them — him, Emily DeWitt, and Callie McMasters — standing around home plate, clasping hands, and preparing to leave, taking a moment, then hearing the silken tone of the Unseelie Queen's voice as she cast her curse.

His voice twisted now as he mimicked the queen's.

"When next your mortal baseball team the Unicorns hold their tryouts, you will participate, and when you do — at that very instant! — you will return to my side."

The February wind whipped around them as they walked onward, reminding them that winter still had Pattersonville firmly in its grip, no matter how close to the warmth and light of springtime they might be.

"Oh my... she *cursed* you?" Emily said as she raised her thin fingers to her lips, understanding fully dawning. "Simply trying out ... "

"Would make me her servant forever."

The news hit her like he hoped it would.

Emily's expression darkened. She pressed her lips together and walked with him in silence as she contemplated his situation. His curse, as she'd put it.

"That witch," she finally said. She put a hand on his shoulder. "I see your problem. Thank you for telling me."

"You're welcome," he said, surprised to realize he genuinely meant it. "I ... feel better now that you know."

"At least that part makes me happy."

The breeze picked up again, this time bearing the scent of earth and trees.

"You can still be around baseball, though, right?" Emily said. "You could be Coach Amabe's assistant or the team manager. Or maybe you could run the stats department, or be a video guy. There are lots of ways to be part of the team."

Her suggestions hit him like a bat to the stomach, and he had to stop in the middle of the sidewalk to let them settle over him.

"No. Curse or not, I'm serious about being done with baseball, Emily. Listen, okay? This curse is really like a blessing in disguise. Because I don't want to play baseball anyway, and the very fact that trying out would land me back with her is almost like I've been given free rein to do literally anything else. I'm excited to finally have a chance to try other things, to see what I can be now that I don't have to be the Designated Hitter."

He stopped, turned to face Emily, and took hold of her shoulders to be sure she heard him.

"Baseball is ... it's great. I don't begrudge you or anyone else playing. But for me? It's ruined. I'd rather just move on."

Emily's face scrunched up under the bill of her Small Folk cap, but again she lightened up quickly enough.

"Can't blame a girl for trying, right?"

Adrien smiled. As they walked on enough tension ran out of him that his limbs began to feel loose. After a day of bracing for any number of axes to fall, it made him feel good. All in all, the conversation had gone better than he'd expected. It seemed like Emily was starting to understand his stance, at least.

By now, they were approaching his new home. He drew in a breath, about to invite Emily in for a glass of Aunt Peg's iced tea. He figured they could head up to his room and talk about the Benji problem. He wondered if he could convince her to come try out for *Taming of the Shrew*. He would love to see Emily DeWitt on stage.

Then they rounded the corner. The Thorn house came into view, and Adrien drew up sharply.

Sitting there on the front porch next to his ten-year-old "nephew" Sydney was none other than Megan Moore.

"Are you kidding me?" Adrien moaned. His buoyant happiness of a moment before ratcheted back up into a tangle of irritated tension. "Does she not know how to take a hint?"

Emily growled and took a protective stance between Adrien and the reporter.

Emily'd had run-ins with the self-styled journalist, too. She would probably gladly wring Megan Moore's neck for him.

"It's all right," Adrien said, holding Emily gently back. He'd already gathered himself. "No reason to hurt the team by giving her anything to spin a story around."

Emily's shoulders relaxed, though her gaze remained sharply pointed at the reporter. "I guess there are worse things to deal with than a snot-nosed sophomore who thinks everyone's business is her business, but I can't think of too many."

"Yeah," Adrien said, laughing as he watched Sydney demonstrate to the reporter how to throw a slider. "Like dealing with a snot-nosed ten-year-old who wants to play baseball all the time."

Emily laughed then, too.

"All right," she said, touching the brim of her Small Folk cap before she went on her way. "I'll leave you your space to deal with her on your own. But I promise you we're not done here. I get your whole thing, but I'm going to keep working on this. I know I can help you, Adrien, and I'll find a way. We'll get your love of baseball back somehow."

"Emily..."

She was already walking away, repositioning her book bag against her back. "See you tomorrow! We can chat about Benji then. I know you've been worrying about them."

Adrien pressed his lips together and breathed in the chilled air until he felt his lungs might burst. Then he let it out in a long, slow flow.

How much worse could his day get?

He turned back to the patio where Sydney and Megan were sitting, and prepared to find out.

CHAPTER
THIRTEEN

"What do you think you're doing here?" Adrien said as he approached the porch. Sydney and the reporter sat side-by-side on the steps, mostly blocking the path to the front door.

The reporter stood.

She was tall and gawky — the kind of kid Adrien knew was going to grow into her body sometime later. With one hand she pulled at the hem of her Red Sox sweatshirt to straighten it. She wore her hair cut short, razored on the sides, now with a curly-cue pattern cut into the left side — which showed through the mesh side of a white *Unicorn Gazette* baseball cap she wore backward. Freckles covered one cheekbone, making her face seem out of balance.

"She's interviewing me!" Sydney said with his normal buoyant lilt.

"You don't say," Adrien replied.

In any other situation, Adrien might have loved having little Sydney Thorn as a family member, but as it was the kid was a rambunctious pain in the butt.

Sydney wore his favorite Unicorns sweatshirt, a godawful thing that had needed to be laundered last week, along with a pair of jeans with dirt stains on each knee. His Unicorns cap, perched on his forehead, was also sweat-stained. The baseball mitt that seemed superglued to his left hand was, well, superglued to his left hand. Brown hair poked from under the cap, as disheveled as ever.

Adrien didn't have to ask whether Sydney had been regaling the reporter with his stories about "A1" and "A2" as he called the original Adrien Thorn of Pattersonville legend (of whom Sydney was the foremost authority in the city), and the current Adrien Thorn, who would never even deign to throw a baseball, better yet lead a team to anything remotely like a championship.

A2 — a nickname Adrien despised — was the ultimate bummer as far as Sydney was concerned.

"We were just having a chat," Megan said, palming her phone, which Adrien noted was clearly on full record mode.

"Likely story."

Sydney stood up then, too, revealing a second glove sitting on the porch step behind him.

"Let's play catch, A2! It's a brilliant day for a game of catch, isn't it? Maybe Megan can get some good action shots for her article!"

Though the sun was technically out, it was *not* a brilliant day to play catch. It was cold and still overcast from the rain earlier. There was, however, no such thing in Sydney's vocabulary as a bad day to play catch.

"Sorry, Little Dude," Adrien replied, trying to mimic the advice Jamal Douglass, one of the Unicorns players, had given him earlier today on dealing with over-enthusiastic kid siblings. "I've got lines to memorize. And Megan can get better action shots over at Unicorn Field." He added that last part with a pointed glare in Megan's direction.

Megan just smiled at him and held her phone a little closer, soaking up all the drama.

"Just a few minutes!" Sydney said, lifting the second glove. A worn baseball peeked from the webbing of the glove Sydney was wearing.

The sight of the ball and both gloves made Adrien's stomach clench. He turned his head away so Megan and her stupid phone couldn't capture whatever might be written too plainly on his face.

He didn't need her to publish another opinion column on his *inability to humor his kid nephew's pure-hearted request* or some such.

He forced himself to put on a wistful smile before he turned back to his nephew.

"I'm sorry, Syd. I just can't."

"It's Sydney, thank you very much." Trust a ten-year-old to answer a polite rebuff with his snottiest tone.

"Right, and it's Adrien, thank you very much," Adrien shot back. *Two can play that game.*

It was one of his dad's favorite sayings back in the day. His real dad, not the fictional version he'd made up for his false cover story. Adrien fought another pang of loss. He could never explain that pain to anyone, not even Emily DeWitt. She still had her dad, after all. But spending a hundred years in the Fairy Realm meant everything Adrien knew about the mortal realm had been washed away on a river of time.

It was a big part of why he was failing history class so badly.

His real dad had died fighting in France just before the Great War ended, which had been bad enough. But since returning to the Real World, he had discovered his little brother, Oliver, had been killed in the Pacific Theatre of World War II. The last time Adrien saw him, Ollie had been a little younger than Sydney.

A dour expression crossed Sydney's face. "It's just a nickname."

Adrien fought an urge to admonish the kid for his loose rendering of names. There was power in names. Even here in the Real World. Naming a thing with precision gave someone power over it if only a little bit. But he didn't want to give the reporter anything more to work with than she had already finagled.

Instead, Adrien hitched his book bag higher onto his shoulder and pushed past the two of them, reaching toward the door.

"The little guy was telling me he wanted you to sign up for the Unicorns ball club, but that you wouldn't do that. Care to comment?"

Adrien turned back to find the reporter braced defiantly on the first porch step. She held the phone to his face, obviously trying to intimidate him.

He managed not to snort at her ridiculous attempt. For as much of an annoyance Megan might be, she was no Unseelie Queen.

"Comment?" he said.

"Yeah. Comment," Megan said. "You know? Tell the world just why you refuse to follow in the footsteps of Good Old A1? Is it nerves? Are you afraid you won't live up to your namesake's legend? Or is it plain old daddy issues? I presume your dad's the one who saddled you with the name 'Adrien.' Must've been a huge Unicorns fan. And where is he, by the way? Back in the mountains?"

Adrien stifled a grimace.

He should have just pushed through when he had a chance. Now his stomach clenched at the idea of what kind of headline he would see in next week's Gazette. "I have no comment other than to say I'll be cheering the team along as they try to make the tournament again."

"And just what is your relationship to Emily DeWitt? I saw you two strolling together over there, arm in arm, on the street corner, even. You looked very cozy together."

Now Adrien did snort. "Emily and I are very good friends."

"Ah," Megan said, nodding knowingly. She raised the phone to her mouth and said, "*Very* good friends."

"Just good friends. Really. Please leave her out of this. Emily has enough to deal with just trying to pitch."

"I'm sure that's true. I never *did* get your take on DeWitt's big disappearance last year. Everyone says the Unicorns would have taken state if she'd been able to play the whole season. And I'm not the only one who noticed you turned up shortly after she reappeared from being quote-unquote kidnapped. What's the connection there?"

Heat rose to his cheeks. He'd gotten himself bamboozled and now was officially in too deep. A wave of exhaustion swept over him, but he managed to paste a ghost of a smile across his face.

"Ever heard of a coincidence?" he muttered.

Megan's smirk told him she wouldn't be dismissed so easily.

"There is no connection, Megan. Give it a rest. Come on, Sydney. Aunt Peg and Uncle Gary are going to want you to wash up before dinner."

He pulled open the door and held it for Sydney, then stepped in himself, wincing as the screen door slammed shut behind him.

He should have caught it, but he couldn't deny the brief flash of satisfaction letting it crash in Megan Moore's face gave him.

He hung there for a moment, listening. When he heard the dull thuds of footsteps leaving the porch, he drew a deep breath through his nose. The warm, homey smells of his aunt and uncle's house settled his spinning thoughts enough to let him breathe in another.

Aunt Peg and Uncle Gary had insisted he stay with them last fall after they'd heard his manufactured cover story: that he'd slipped away from his backward parents and their sheltered cabin in the mountains and come to Pattersonville all on his own to finally get a proper education.

In reality, he'd appeared on their doorstep unannounced only a day after breaking free of the Fairy Realm and the Unseelie Queen, looking as bedraggled as he felt. He'd stayed with Emily and her dad that first night, but he knew he couldn't impose on their generous hospitality any longer than that. Emily had already sacrificed more than enough for his sake. Benji had pushed him to stay with them, but even though Mrs. Amberman had *tsk-tsked* his thin frame and promised to fatten him up on her homemade potato kugel and *matzah* ball soup, he knew they didn't have space. Not to mention

Benji's enthusiasm to pick his brain about the Fairy Realm had been just as strong even back then.

Besides, he still had family in town, even if they weren't the family he'd left behind when he'd first fallen into the Fairy Realm.

Aunt Peg had taken one look at him, listened to half his story, and opened her heart.

"No relative of ours is going to stay in a shelter, no matter how distant they might be!" she'd said as she dragged him by the biceps over the threshold and into an enveloping hug.

And that had been that.

Several weeks of home-cooked meals later, and as many long sleeps in a real bed, Adrien had to admit things were good here. Both his aunt and his uncle were kindhearted people — always available to talk to and never disposed to judge him for not understanding things everyone else around him took for granted, like computers and the internet. On his bad days, they gave him space without prying and even helped him fill in the gaps on what he'd missed during his "absence from the family," sharing stories and introducing him to relatives that had come after his time.

It was Uncle Gary who had told him about Ollie's fate on an island called Okinawa.

Though figuring out life in the bafflingly futuristic *twenty*-twenties was draining, he shouldn't complain.

At least he had someplace he could call home.

He took another deep breath. A glance out the front window confirmed Megan Moore was nowhere to be found.

With the immediate threat gone, Adrien realized he was hungry. Again.

He'd never gotten so ravenously hungry while he was in the Unseelie Court, though to be fair, the revolting fare his captors preferred had as much to do with that than any change in himself. Regardless of the cause, though, he was, once again, a growing boy.

"Dinner in an hour," Aunt Peg called from the kitchen as if she'd picked up on his empty stomach from across the entire house.

"Burgers on the grill," Uncle Gary added from his office. He was an architect who worked from home. Aunt Peg ran a boutique but opened it mostly in the mornings.

"Hot dogs for me!" Sydney yelled back. "With ecks-tra mustard!"

"The one true way," Uncle Gary replied.

Adrien couldn't help the grin spreading across his face. With an hour until dinner, might as well get a snack to tide him over.

He extracted an arm from his book bag and started toward the kitchen.

Sydney, already sitting on one of the stools at the breakfast bar, kicked his legs out. "I got interviewed for the Pattersonville West High School paper, Mom! D'you think they'll make it seem like I live with the real Adrien Thorn?"

Aunt Peg tossed an exasperated look over her shoulder at him. She wore jeans and an orange top, her dark hair pulled back in a simple ponytail as she worked to clean grilling utensils with great enthusiasm. "Not if they have any journalistic integrity, they won't. And your cousin is just as real as your hero. It's not nice to behave otherwise."

Adrien slid onto a stool with a thin smile. He let his book bag slide to the floor as he took an apple from the bowl on the counter. He may have let out the smallest of sighs. Apples reminded him of the Fairy Realm, in a good way. Apples, and the copses of oak and sycamore trees that separated Pattersonville West High School's campus from Unicorn Field. There was something wonderful about them that brought out the best of those memories.

The apple's fresh-tart flavor combination made him slow down to savor it.

Sydney took an apple from the bowl, too, and polished it up against his shirtsleeve just like Adrien had. He took a monstrous bite, chewing it with his mouth slightly open.

"How's the play shaping up?" Aunt Peg asked, tilting a smile at Adrien over her shoulder.

"Pretty good so far. I've been reading lines for Lucentio. Hoping to get understudy so I can keep working on the set construction, too."

"Sounds like fun. Just don't forget to study for that history test you've got coming up."

Adrien's fingers tightened around his apple, and his chewing became mechanical.

Aunt Peg's smile softened, her brows slanting down in concern.

"Still struggling with World War II?"

"Among other things," Adrien replied warily as he bit into the crisp fruit with slightly less gusto.

Aunt Peg's expression got as dour as Sydney's had been a moment ago.

"I really am going to have to find your parents and give them a piece of my mind."

Adrien swallowed his bite of apple too quickly.

"You, too?" he whined. Was everyone a detective these days?

"I'm sorry, hon."

"It's all right," he said. "I'm sorry, too. It's been a long day."

Even Emily's last words to him had been wearying. He didn't want help. He didn't want to play ball. He didn't want to answer the school reporter's nosey questions, and he didn't want anyone fiddling around with his past.

Emily and the Unicorns knew at least some of his truth, but the rest ...

Adrien's stomach churned with dread. With people like Megan Moore prying at even the tiniest loose threads, he wasn't sure how much longer his cover would last.

At least she was just a stupid high school reporter.

All the real reporters had cooled on his story as soon as the inevitable new disturbance popped up. These days, they were turning their attention to Callie McMasters' dad making a big show of his sponsorship of the Unicorns. The newspapers were lapping up his story about "making up for his daughter's disgusting show of poor sportsmanship," even if the Unicorns players weren't buying it.

At least that was something that hadn't changed in his century away.

Rich people still tried to make themselves look good by purchasing forgiveness.

If Adrien let himself think about Unicorn Field – his old home field, the one where he'd learned to love the game before it had been tarnished by the Unseelie Queen – bearing the McMasters Ball and Glove logo, he'd be in danger of bringing the half an apple he'd eaten so far back up.

All the scuttlebutt around town was that Callie, after being expelled and kicked off the Bulldogs, had hooked up with an independent traveling baseball team and was out playing the towns.

Of course, Adrien knew better.

He hoped Callie was faring all right with the Wild Hunt. Time moved strangely in the Fairy Realm — he'd be the first to know that — and there was no telling if her Summer Season had even started, or if it was nearly over. She was a strong person, and if anyone was going to withstand the Fairy Realm's darker influences, it would be her. Still, he worried.

Beside him, Sydney took a loud, crunchy bite of his apple and spun on his stool so he was facing Adrien.

"So, you're really not gonna try out?"

"No, Sydney."

"That reporter would write a story about you if you did!" He talked with his mouth full, which earned him a disapproving stare from Aunt Peg.

"I don't want her to write a story about me. Besides, I told you. I'm not very good at baseball."

"You play basketball! I'm sure you would be just as good on the baseball field."

Adrien dipped his head in acknowledgment. He had started playing "hoops" after being introduced to the modern version in gym class. It surprised him how much the game had changed since he'd been gone. There was more running today. And a lot more contact. When he was a kid, everyone shot two-handed and didn't jump much.

"Different thing. And besides, I can't shoot very well now, can I?"

"You'll get better, though."

Adrien shrugged. That much was true. "I'm just not a baseball guy."

Sydney deflated.

The expression reminded Adrien of Ollie, his little brother from a century ago, and a strange sensation that was equal parts joy and loss washed over him. The kid's shoulders rounded exactly like Ollie's used to in his disappointments. He hated the thought of causing Sydney that kind of pain.

At the same time, Adrien thought about Emily's suggestion that he help the Coach.

That wouldn't play at all, but a new feeling grew that almost felt right.

He'd been past Unicorn Field several times in the past few months. It could use a good sprucing up, and his time on the theater crew reminded him that he liked building things and working with his hands. Maybe the coach would let him do some work on the grandstands and reposition the chain link fences down the lines.

The fences could use a fresh coat of paint.

Now that Megan Moore wasn't shoving her questions in his face, he had space to get excited. A little, anyway. Working on the field would be different from being on the team itself. He could be with his friends, too.

Then came the idea that if he had to paint on the McMasters logo, he could add a little flare of his own. Something small enough that only an outfielder could read it. His heart swelled in sardonic glee.

He swiveled his seat to face Sydney.

"I tell you what, Squirt. I'm not going to play, but if you'd like we can go to the tryouts anyway. Even if I can't play, I do like the

Unicorns. And I want to talk to Coach Amabe. I bet one of the players would love to play catch with you."

Sydney's eyes got as bright and twinkly as fairy lights dancing over a field at night.

"Really? You'll take *me* to tryouts?"

"Sure. Why not?"

Sydney nearly peeled out of his skin. He whipped his baseball cap off and threw it in the air.

"Mom! Did you hear that? A2's taking me to tryouts!"

Aunt Peg chuckled. "I heard."

Adrien couldn't help but smile. Sydney was a good kid. It was just that he had only one speed. From the corner of his eye, he saw Aunt Peg give a contented smile as she dried her spatula. She clearly liked when Adrien helped Sydney. He'd once overheard her talking to Uncle Gary about how great it was that Adrien was becoming like a big brother to the kid.

He ruffled Sydney's newly exposed hair.

"You have to eat all your dinner tonight, though, all right?"

"Hot dogs on the grill with ecks-tra mustard? No problemo!"

"Yeah, probably not."

"Oh, man, what if I get scouted for the team?"

"You're not in high school yet, Sydney. And you're only ten."

"Ten-and-a-quarter. And I've been practicing my curveball, super hard." He held up his baseball, placing his fingers in an approximation of a pitcher's grip to throw a curve. "See?"

"Yes, I see," Adrien said, barely managing not to ruin his cover story in one swoop by giving pointers.

"I better go practice it some more, just in case." Taking his half-eaten apple with him, Sydney scooted out of the kitchen and into the living room.

With a chuckle, Adrien tossed his apple core into the bag the family used to gather backyard compost.

Aunt Peg finished arranging the utensils.

"You're so good with him, Adrien. I know he can be a load, some-times. But he idolizes you."

Adrien gave his aunt a half smile, flashing on Ollie once again. "Yeah. Thanks. It's good though. The squirt's fun."

"Well, go on up and study, then. I'll call you when the burgers are ready."

"Thanks," Adrien said again, picking his book bag up.

He climbed the stairs quickly, thinking he'd spend time studying for that history test before practicing lines and working out more details on his ideas for renovating Unicorn Field. Once he got to his room, though, he was too exhausted to do anything but collapse into bed.

CHAPTER
FOURTEEN

Rather than reading, as she had planned, Emily DeWitt paced the six steps from her dresser to her desk, glanced at the corner of the shelf where her mom's baseball sat — as if that ball would somehow magically provide her the answers she needed — then turned on her heel and paced the six steps back.

She'd been doing this ever since her walk home with Adrien. That had been almost half an hour ago now.

Taking senior year over due to her disappearance last spring meant she was supposed to be reading *Wuthering Heights*, but instead, she'd been rereading *The Art of Fielding*, which was just as good and had more baseball. When she'd left off last night, Henry Skrimshander had just made his bad throw.

But right now, not even *The Art of Fielding* was enough to distract her.

Her e-reader lay abandoned on her bedspread, the screen dimmed into sleep mode.

As she paced, she fidgeted with the shard of crystal that usually sat on the trophy shelf beside her mom's ball.

The shard was part of the Web Gem, the Fairy Realm's championship trophy. Just holding it could give her the sensation of being at the Other Field, surrounded by her Small Folk teammates. A sense that she could accomplish anything if she believed in the baseball magic hard enough. She'd worked hard to regain her belief in the baseball magic after her mom's death, and she knew nothing would ever shake that belief again. Today the crystal was quiet, though, like any other chunk of glass.

It, like her mom's baseball, was no help. Neither had answers for the problems she couldn't stop mulling over.

Things were not good.

She'd already been worried about Callie, who had been gone for months. Even though Emily, of all people, knew that time worked in warped ways between the mortal world and the Fairy Realm, that still felt like too long. She'd long ago stopped looking at Unicorn Field so closely in hopes she'd catch Callie on her triumphant return. It was bad enough that Emily had been debating the wisdom of using her shard of the Web Gem to find her.

Now everything was worse.

The Unseelie Queen, the closest thing Emily had to an outright enemy, had cursed Adrien.

No wonder Adrien was convinced he hated baseball now. If just the act of trying out for the Unicorns meant she had to live beside the queen forever, Emily would quit cold turkey, too.

It was enough to make her stomach roil.

There was no question in Emily's heart that she would do anything to break that curse. She even knew how it could be done. She had the shard, and since she and her Small Folk team had rightfully won it during the last season in the Fairy Realm, it gave her the right to demand a boon of any fairy leader. All she had to do was open the portal under Unicorn Field, shove the shard in the Unseelie Queen's snooty nose, and demand she break the curse.

The real problem there, though, was how to get Adrien to let her help him.

He was such a *boy* sometimes.

It had taken her three months of wheedling to get him to even divulge this curse in the first place. And with Benji pestering him all the time about visiting the Fairy Realm – which she knew was annoying because they'd put the pressure on her sometimes, too, something she thought was essentially harmless – Adrien had his hackles up regarding the danger of going to the Realm at all. He was a hundred percent right, of course. Nobody could be allowed to go traipsing off to the Fairy Realm whenever they wanted.

Another pang of worry over Callie pierced her heart.

She and Adrien had agreed months ago that it was safest to keep the whole thing as secret as they could, and so far, so good.

But, *of course,* Benji wanted to see the place.

It was Amberman ancestry, after all. But Benji didn't know how to work the baseball magic, which meant they couldn't get in without either Emily's or Adrien's help. So long as she and Adrien kept cool and brushed them off until the tryouts were over, Benji would calm down once the baseball season started and everyone got too busy playing ball.

Of course, once tryouts hit, Emily herself would be too busy to do any rescuing or curse-breaking. And the signup sheet had gone up today, a fact which, until right this moment, had caused her nothing but joy.

Maybe she should go back, just for a day. Check on Callie just to be sure she was all right, and then use the Web Gem to save Adrien. With luck, she could be back home before anyone noticed she'd gone again.

Outside, the sound of Dad's car wheels crunching on the driveway came through her partially cracked window. He was home early today. Probably wanted to get a good start on making the season's first batch of Victory Lasagna after signup day. He'd talked about it this morning before they left the house. *Just to get into shape,* he'd said with a gleam in his eye. *I need to make sure I've got it down this year.*

Likely story.

Her dad was a big lasagna fan.

Emily laid even chances he would suggest a post-lasagna run to Ratner's Ice Creamery, too.

Sure enough, the door to Emily's room gave a soft sigh as it cracked open. Dad stuck his head through the doorway. He looked her up and down, then put on an exaggerated expression of deduction.

"Hmmm," he said. "Pacing the room? E-reader asleep on the bed? Intense dissatisfaction in your posture? Signups were today, right?"

"Yeah," Emily replied, palming the shard as she turned to start another set of six steps.

"Then why the sour face? I thought you'd be bouncing off the walls."

"It's nothing," she said. She didn't want to get into it now.

"Problems with Rip?" His goofy smile was borderline sheepish.

"Dad!"

"What?" he said as he stepped farther into her room, then leaned against the doorframe, arms crossed over his striped, button-down shirt.

"First, stop calling Adrien Rip van Winkle. And second, we're not anything special."

Dad gave her that look that said *Oh, really?* "It's only elementary, dear Emily. An old-fashioned gentleman *and* the only guy who poses a challenge to you on the field? What's not to like?"

"Dad, I swear."

"You swear I'm right?"

Emily glared. Ever since she and Adrien had returned from the Fairy Realm together, people seemed to think they were an item. And she had to admit, Adrien Thorn could be plenty charming. The light of the Fairy Realm still clung to him, making him shine in ways only a few people could see, but that everyone responded to. On his good days, anyway. On his grumpy days, not so much. Lately, there had been more grumpy days than charming ones.

But now Emily knew why he'd been so taciturn, and it just made her heart hurt for him even more.

That was what solidified her feelings about him. She just didn't see him as someone to get together with; she saw him more as a long-lost brother who needed a helping hand from a caring sister – whether he admitted to needing that help or not.

Dad gave up making doofy faces at her. "So, I'm guessing he didn't sign up, eh?"

Emily gave a half sigh. She felt different about Adrien playing baseball after their talk, but it was still confusing.

"No," she said. "He didn't."

"I'm sorry to hear that. I know it's important to you that he plays."

"It's okay. He's got some other problems to deal with."

Dad knew parts of their story but not all of it. And Adrien's revelations felt too raw inside her right now. Sharing it felt wrong, and even if it wasn't, she didn't want to worry her dad right now.

Unlike Adrien, Dad had been nothing but happy ever since she'd returned from the Fairy Realm for good. He hummed while he cooked their breakfast of champions every morning, and he smiled while they watched basketball on television in the evenings, even if the Bulls were losing. He even barely grumbled as he headed off to work every day. And he gave Emily the tightest hugs his teenaged daughter could stand as often as he thought he could get away with them.

Of course, some of his happy glow might also have been because, after several years now, he'd finally decided to date again. Emily wasn't sure Elaine was the perfect fit for him, but she was nice and cute in that "always put together" way that real estate agents had. She liked baseball, too.

Sometimes, when Emily held Mom's ball, she got the impression Mom liked Elaine, too.

The last thing Emily wanted was to reintroduce Fairy Realm troubles into Dad's rediscovered domestic bliss. But as he leaned against her doorframe the look on his face said he was worried. He'd expected her to be bursting with excitement at the start of a new season.

"Well, Emily. Maybe you just need to give him more time. You said he's been getting big into theater?"

"Yeah. He's always talking about the progress the crew's making on building the sets, and I think he's reading lines now."

"Good for him," Dad said.

They shared a quiet moment.

"Maybe he's just worried about getting back onto Unicorn Field," Dad said, eyebrows raised. "After all, the last time he played there changed his life forever."

"Maybe."

"Or maybe it's just a bout of teenage mayonnaise?"

Emily rolled her eyes. "Better than old man-aise."

"Ouch."

The sound of another car rolling up the driveway came through the window.

Dad's gaze flickered in that direction, and a frown lined his face. "What's Fred McMasters doing here?"

Emily sat up, clenching her hand more tightly around her piece of the Web Gem. "Callie's dad?"

"The one and only."

She twisted to look out the window. Sure enough, Mr. McMasters, wearing gray business slacks, a pair of shaded sunglasses, and a dark satin sports jacket with his store logo embroidered on one breast, got out of his shiny Mercedes, and made his way toward the front door. His sandy-gray hair caught the last rays of the sun.

Dad pursed his lips, then left to go to the door.

Alone for the moment, and watching Mr. McMasters approach, Emily felt a harsh, unsettling buzz come from the crystal shard.

A warning?

Silly, right?

But her stomach did a flipflop anyway. Callie and her dad were never on the best of terms with each other, and Emily was inclined to side with her rival on the matter. And that was well before Mr. McMasters simply settled deeper into his business when Callie had "left town."

The fact that he was giving money and equipment to sponsor the Unicorns didn't make her feel any better.

The sound of the front door swinging open filtered up to her and, after amenities were exchanged, Dad called Emily down to the living room. With a cleansing breath, she got off her bed, and on a whim, rather than put the Web Gem crystal on the trophy shelf next to Mom's baseball, she slid it into the little side pocket of her jeans.

"Mr. McMasters says he wanted to have a chat with you," Dad said after she'd made her way to the top of the stairs.

"I've already said that I don't know where Callie is," Emily replied, connecting her gaze with Mr. McMasters'. He was standing beside the upholstered guest chair that sat to one side of the television screen, looking just as over-polished as he did in his commercials.

"I'm not here to talk about Callie," the businessman said.

"Mr. McMasters says he has a proposal for you," Dad added. Emily heard the air of concern layered into his voice.

"Oh."

Emily padded down the stairs, suddenly conscious of her socked feet and the feeling of discomfort coming from her pocket. She felt like she might need a double shot of Pepto Bismol soon.

Mr. McMasters sat down, perched forward, with elbows on knees and hands rubbing together. The cloying aroma of cologne wafted from him. Something woody, but plastic at the same time. Emily took a seat on the sofa a short distance across from him. Dad took the other side of the sofa.

"Thank you so much for your time, Emily," McMasters said with a smile that looked like he was gunning for "relaxed." He'd got "annoying" instead.

"Sure, I guess. But what kind of business proposal can you have for me?"

"You might remember that McMasters Ball and Glove took an unfortunate beating due to its ... association ... with Callie after she pulled her unsportsmanlike behavior against your Unicorns. I know you returned from your unfortunate absence around that time, so I wouldn't blame you for being a bit in the dark on the details."

"I remember," Emily said. The look on his face, like he pitied her mental deficiencies, made Emily grit her teeth against a more biting reply.

As if she would ever forget a single, minute detail of the moment when Callie McMasters, her bitter rival since Little League, had risked everything to pull her from the Fairy Realm. Besides, given the way the whole town had gotten behind the Unicorns when they became the city's feel-good story of the summer, there had been talk that Fred McMasters might even go out of business. Those rumors hadn't come true, of course. And today Fred McMasters spoke and held himself with the confidence of a Fairy Realm lord.

Which didn't make her trust him any further.

"This year I've devoted myself to making sure everyone knows there's no hard feelings and that the Ball and Glove does not condone that kind of behavior," McMasters said.

"Yeah. I heard you were giving a bunch of money to the Pattersonville West athletic program this year. That's really great, I suppose."

"It is! It is! And I'm happy to do it, too. More than happy."

Emily waited. When he didn't do anything more than continue to smile at her, she reached to fill the odd lull. "I'm not sure what part of all that brings you here."

McMasters peered at her intently, and a thin needle of fear shivered along her spine. She thought the temperature dropped ten degrees.

"Where else would I turn to but you, Emily? Miss DeWitt, I should say. I don't do things by halves, as you may have heard me mention a time or two when I'm getting the word out about the old shop." He chuckled, and waved a hand at the television behind him, even though the screen was black. "I know that if I want Patterson-ville to believe that I truly do regret the unfortunate events of last season, I've got to make a big splash. This year, I'm not only spon-soring the Unicorns — I'm also going all-in on the best player in the city. And that just happens to be you."

McMasters' grin force-fed her the aura of win-win.

From anyone else, the compliment would be flattering, but the sharpness of McMasters' too-wide smile and the perfect shine of his teeth made her stomach want to curl in on itself. She found herself wishing she was seeing him via one of his crummy advertisements. At least then she'd be able to mute him with the touch of a button.

Emily may only have been a teenager, but the heavy weight of the shard in her pocket reminded her she'd already seen more back-office contract negotiations than she ever cared to see. The memory of the Seelie King pontificating with the cyclops umpire over the enforcement of a particularly strange Fairy Realm rule played through her mind, and for an instant, she smelled the sweat and mud of the Wild Hunt on a chase.

Was she going crazy?

She didn't think so.

"You," Emily finally said. "Callie McMasters' dad. Want to sponsor me?"

"You got it," he said, his weird, fairy-like smile turning fatherly. He even reached one hand out as if to pat her knee, though he pulled it back before he touched her. Her relief at that averted disaster nearly kept her from noticing the way the shard had flared hot against her leg at his approach.

McMasters recovered instantly, opening his hands in an expan-sive gesture. "It's a fine coincidence that you've been my daughter's rival for so long. All the way since Little League. Tee ball, even! Christ, Arthur. Do you remember watching this fine young lady swinging her tiny bat at that tee back when she was just a little thing? Took her a good year or two to grow into even the smallest batting helmet we stocked, eh? And now look at her. Best player in the whole damn city, right here." He turned his grinning face up at Emily's dad, looking for backup.

Emily's dad, however, wasn't so easily distracted. "What exactly does sponsorship mean?"

"Exactly what it sounds like. I'll provide any equipment Emily needs. All branded with both that adorable Pattersonville Unicorn logo and my own Ball and Glove. I'll make sure she has special transportation to and from games, and all the sports drinks and nutrition that the best player in the city should be entitled to. All I'd need Emily to do is to be her usual self, and to pitch and hit the Unicorns to win after win."

"That's all?"

"Well, she would get a stipend, too, of course. The sporting rules are clear that a young lady's image is hers to control, so I would need to pay her for that. And I'd expect her to do a few little promotional things."

"What kind of little promotional things?" Emily said, wrestling the moment back. She didn't like being left out of conversations that were all about her.

McMasters gave what he clearly hoped was an impish smile.

"Oh ... a few commercials, you know? Little bits. I'm thinking we arrange to do them right there on Unicorn Field." McMasters' voice caught a small hitch there, tiny enough to miss if she hadn't been paying attention.

The flare of her Web Gem shard burned against her hip. Her stomach turned on itself again, and her hair stood on end.

McMasters continued, oblivious to her discomfort. "I'm sure the school will be happy to let us use the field. They'd better be, after all the money I've given them."

He laughed and winked like it was a joke.

She didn't think he was truly kidding, though.

"I'm not sure I like that idea," Emily muttered.

The whole thing felt sleazy.

The bigger problem, though, was Unicorn Field itself. And Callie, she realized.

While she'd scoffed at her dad's suggestion that Adrien could be afraid of Unicorn Field, the place wasn't anything that should be messed around with. A fairy ring lay under its dirt. Who knew what could trigger a transfer?

The image of the field swallowing Benji up hit her hard.

For the first time, she felt the same anxiety Adrien must have been experiencing ever since he'd gotten his freedom.

The strange behavior of the Web Gem shard wasn't helping, either. When Callie's dad mentioned doing special events at Unicorn Field, the shard started pulsing heat against her thigh. It was hot enough that she felt the urge to squirm away from it, but she forced herself to keep still, not wanting to prompt any inopportune questions. She felt physically ill.

She couldn't imagine doing Callie such a disservice as aligning with her dad.

The moment when Mr. McMasters' voice had caught, Emily had felt a sharp wave of Callie's unique form of snark. It made the worry about her rival turn in horrible new directions. Could the shard be tied to Callie? Could its proximity to Mr. McMasters be allowing Callie to talk to her through it?

Was Callie calling for help?

There was so much she didn't understand, but one thing she did grasp firmly.

She couldn't betray her friend.

"I'm not the best player in the city," Emily said, loud enough to finally cut McMasters off from his ramble, which had somehow moved from buying advertising slots in the Virtual Reality worlds where all the kids were hanging out these days to dropping cash into the pockets of all the biggest retailers in the country.

McMasters hesitated. "Of course, you are."

"Your daughter is better than me, and you know it."

McMasters' expression grew conflicted with well-practiced ease. "My daughter is old news now, Emily. Last I checked, she's no longer even in the city, better yet its best player. As a father, it pains me to say that, but, as a businessman, I need to base decisions on facts, not emotions. This year, my money is on you."

"No," Emily said, standing up and feeling a firm truth settle down on her. "Sorry, but I don't want your money."

The moment she stood, the shard cooled. Her relief was as multifaceted as the small hunk of crystal.

Now McMasters' dark expression looked more genuine. "You can't turn this offer down. Besides all that, Callie isn't even here."

"Yes, I can turn this offer down, and you should be ashamed of yourself for not putting that money toward finding your daughter. For all you know, she could be dead on the side of the road somewhere!"

With that, Emily got up and stomped back toward the stairs.

McMasters turned to her dad as she left.

"Arthur? Are you going to let your daughter lose the opportunity of a lifetime?"

Emily could almost hear her dad's deceptively noncommittal shrug. "She has a point, Fred."

Emily gave a private smirk as she retreated to her room. Score another one for Dad.

LATER, after showing Mr. McMasters the door, Dad poked his head around Emily's bedroom door again.

"Sorry about that," he said. "I should have vetted his intentions better."

"It's not a problem," she replied.

Emily fell back on her bed. She held the Web Gem shard between her fingers again, twiddling it from hand to hand.

An odd power came from it now. A sense of calmness, though she had absolutely zero clues about what that meant in the wake of all that had just happened.

Was Callie in trouble?

Could something be happening in the Fairy Realm? Something bad?

All she knew for certain was that the shard was quiet now.

That silence made her want to be there, to know what was happening.

Movement at her bedroom door reminded her that Dad was still there.

He reached Mom's baseball off the shelf and gripped it like he was going to throw a forkball. Then he relaxed his hold and tossed it softly to her. Emily caught it with her free hand.

"Are you okay?" Dad said.

"Yeah. I guess."

"You guess?"

"There's just a lot going on right now."

"I see."

Problems never came in an orderly one-at-a-time fashion. Her worries for Callie bumped up against Adrien's problem, and Mr. McMasters' unnerving proposal tangled around the two like a thick cobweb. And hovering in the near distance was tryouts.

Should she go back all by herself? Would Adrien forgive her if she did – even if she did manage to break the Unseelie Queen's final curse?

Probably not.

She turned the crystal over in her fingers, mildly aware of a headache growing from frowning at it too hard.

"Maybe you should go over there and talk to him?" Dad said.

"What?" Emily said. Hypnotized by the shard and her churning thoughts, she'd already forgotten he was still here.

"Adrien. I know you want to talk to him." Dad put the ball back. "Maybe convince him to play a little game of catch or something?"

"He doesn't play catch, Dad. He's a *theater kid* now." She gave a comical roll of her eyes to show she meant it as a joke, but she didn't think she'd managed to cover the tinge of bitterness in her tone.

"Well, then" — his eyebrow waggled — "maybe use your feminine wiles."

"Dad."

Dad raised his hands in surrender. "I know, I know. Sorry. Maybe use your *nothing special, just friends* wiles?"

Emily sighed desperately and then grumbled.

"Seriously, Dad. It's okay if Adrien doesn't want to play. Everyone should make their own choices in life, right?"

He smiled. "That's my girl."

She returned the smile, but inside her anger grew. Adrien wasn't getting to choose, was he? The Unseelie Queen had stolen the choice from him as cruelly as plucking the wings off a pixie.

"My Victory Lasagna will take a while to bake, so there's still enough light left in the day to do some damage if you wanted to go over there anyway."

She twisted her lips up, thinking.

Dad was right, even if he didn't know why. She needed to talk to Adrien and get his opinion before she jumped into something rash.

She twirled the ball between the fingers of one hand, feeling something of her mom in the raised seams while clutching the crystal in the palm of the other.

"Maybe I should," she said. "Ratner's later?" she asked in a casual tone.

The lines on Dad's face grew dark with his put-upon grimace. "Well, if we have to," he said with a smile.

"I hear ice cream heals old man-aise."

"I may be too young to be a valid test subject."

"Oh, I promise you are not."

"In that case, I'm willing to be a guinea pig."

"You've always been ready to take one for the team."

"It's a true burden."

Emily smiled and turned Mom's ball on its seams. She already felt better. "Thanks, Dad."

His expression curled to a slanted smile, and his eyes glittered, then he turned to leave her room.

"Dinner in an hour," he said as he walked down the hall. "Don't be late!"

CHAPTER

FIFTEEN

"He's up in his room," Mrs. Thorn said, waving Emily to the stairs.

"Thanks, Mrs. T," Emily replied.

Climbing them one at a time, Emily felt calmer now that her Web Gem shard was quiet, wedged in the pocket of her jeans where she had left it. She didn't like to carry it around while in public, but the thought of leaving it alone after McMasters had gone made her feel queasy. She didn't exactly love the way the sudden need to keep it close by made her feel like some kind of Gollum clone, though. Every time she touched her side pocket, she heard his voice whispering *my precious*.

She found Adrien seated at his desk, chin in hand and staring out the window as the sun dropped toward the horizon. His shadowed expression seemed almost dazed. He'd let the shock of dark hair falling over his forehead grow shaggier than she'd seen it in the Fairy Realm, which certainly added to his melancholy actor vibe.

The window overlooked the fenced backyard, where Sydney was busy throwing a baseball against the concrete garage wall. He'd drawn a blue chalk square to represent a strike zone. Sydney's voice rose like he was broadcasting a game. Emily couldn't suppress a smile as she remembered doing the same thing with her mom in their backyard.

"Hi," Emily said. She threw herself into the hardback chair beside Adrien's desk, then ran a hand over her hair to push it off her forehead.

"Hello," he replied.

His voice was drained, but he seemed happy to see her this time. His demeanor was a pleasant change from the past couple of weeks. The glowing phone on his desk told her that he'd been trying to practice the nuances of modern-day communications. The exhausted slump of his shoulders told her he'd met with the expected result.

She'd have to check if he'd posted anything in the group chat later.

He pushed the phone away with relieved disdain.

"You didn't have to come all the way to convince me any further," he said as if capitulating. "I've decided to see if Coach Amabe will let me work on the field. I got some ideas this afternoon. I was trying to run them by the rest of the players, but …" He waved a couple of limp fingers at his phone, then gave a one-shoulder shrug.

"That's great," Emily said. "I'm sure he'll be thrilled to have the help. But I didn't come here to pester you about signups or to help you figure out texting, Old Timer."

He did a subtle doubletake at that. The chair squeaked as he sat back, twisting toward her, arms on the rests. "Lay on, Macduff."

"Shakespeare becomes you."

"Well, I have been practicing." He nodded at the pile of papers on the corner of his desk. It was the script he'd been lugging about for the past few weeks.

"Did you know there were two baseball players named Shakespeare?" Adrien said, a quick gleam coming to his dark eyes.

"Really?"

The depth in his gaze showed how old he really was. He'd been studying in the library every day, and part of that study had focused on baseball — as if, deep down, some unconscious part of him knew he couldn't keep completely away from baseball, no matter how much the Unseelie Queen had warped the game for him.

"Yeah. A long time ago. Though, as I recall, it was their middle names."

Emily hesitated, uncertain whether she should ask her next question. Adrien turned his head inquisitively, so she decided to go ahead. "Did you know them?"

This time it was Adrien who laughed. "No. They were before my time. Played before the 1900s."

"Ah," Emily said. Sometimes it was hard to place him.

"So, seriously, if you're not here to twist my arm about those signups, what brings you here so late? We finished up dinner a little bit ago."

"Two things," she said. Her fingers ran unconsciously across her side pocket. The edge of the shard was hard against her hip bone and fingertip. "First, Mr. McMasters. He came to my house and offered me a sponsorship contract this season."

"A sponsorship?" Adrien's eyes slit and his arms crossed. "What kind of sponsorship?"

"It sounded standard, I guess. He gives me money, I wear Ball and Glove brands and agree to do advertising for him."

"But?" He drew the question out.

"I despise the idea of working for Fred McMasters. It's bad enough he's sponsoring the team as a whole," Emily said.

"Right. It's a bad look. If nothing else, what would Callie think?"

"Nothing good, that's for sure." Emily nodded. "I turned him down, of course."

"That's good."

"I mean, I know I need to get used to the business side of baseball if I'm going to play in the colleges or the pros, but signing on with Mr. McMasters? I can't even. He's up to something with all this, I just don't know what. It makes me worried about Callie."

Adrien tilted his head to one side. "How so?"

"I was already worried about her, you know. She's been gone for so long. But this afternoon I had my piece of the Web Gem in my pocket while Mr. McMasters laid out his plan, and the whole time he was blabbering, I kept getting flares from it."

"Flares?"

"I don't know what else to call them. Flashes? Jolts? Like magic, but not. Whatever they were, I'm shocked I didn't come away with blisters on my thigh."

Adrien scratched his chin. "That's not good."

"Ya think?"

She twisted in her seat. "It was really uncomfortable. I wondered if it might be Callie trying to contact me. Do you think she could be in trouble?"

"It's possible, I suppose. But I doubt those flares were her calling for help."

"Why?"

"Well," Adrien said as he sat up in his chair. "Callie is a big girl. Given what I saw of her with the queen and the way she negotiated her contract with the Wild Hunt, I'd say she can handle herself. She's about the only person, other than you, that I'd trust to be in the Realm at all. Not to mention, she hardly struck me as the 'call for help' sort."

Emily nodded, despite herself. "Yeah, but I'm still worried. She's mortal in a fairy world."

"That's true enough." Adrien shivered. "But in addition to her being a strong person, there's the whole shard vs. Web Gem thing."

"What do you mean?"

"I mean that since the shard is tied to the Web Gem, any strangeness happening around it could be tied to the bigger trophy somehow, too. And while about anything is *possible* when it comes to politics in the Fairy Realm, Callie doesn't have a direct link to the Web Gem." He shook his head. "It just doesn't feel right that she'd be able to channel anything through its magic. Well, unless she and the

Wild Hunt won it. But in that case, she definitely wouldn't need to call for help getting home. She'd have all the power of the Web Gem at her fingertips."

"That makes sense." Emily crossed her arms, feeling better, but still thinking. "Could it be the Small Folk? Maybe calling me back?"

"I suppose it could be. I'm not sure why they would do that, though. And the timing seems like too much of a coincidence. How likely is it that Fennoc just happened to call you exactly when Mr. McMasters was in the middle of doing his spiel? I assume it stopped when he left?"

"Yeah. It did. Right when I told him 'no,' in fact."

"There you go, then. More likely it was just reacting to your dislike of the guy. Some kind of feedback loop. Not that I blame you. Sleaze hasn't evolved much in the past century."

Emily smiled weakly, but her heart remained unsettled. She contemplated telling him she had the shard with her right now, but she got the feeling that if she brought it out for a detailed inspection, Adrien would get exasperated with her.

"Maybe you're right about Callie, but I can't break the feeling that something is going on in the Fairy Realm," Emily said. "Something not good."

Adrien shrugged. "We can't know without going there, and we both know that's a bad idea."

Outside the window, a baseball rose and fell through the clouded sky — Sydney tossing a popup into the air. It was growing darker.

Emily checked the clock for the time, pressed her dampening palms down her jean legs to dry off her anxious sweat, then pressed on, looking Adrien purposefully in the eye.

"About that," she said.

Adrien's shoulders stiffened, and his gaze turned sharp as the thorns his family was named for.

Emily pressed on before he could interrupt. "After our talk ... after what you told me about the Unseelie Queen, I know what I want to do with the boon I'm due."

Adrien was already shaking his head.

"No," he said. "It's too dangerous. And you've done too much for me already. I can't let you waste a boon on me. Besides—"

"It wouldn't be a waste, Adrien," she replied, words spewing out of her like water from a geyser. "And I can do it, too. If we work the baseball magic, I can go back to the Fairy Realm and use my boon to make the queen take her claws out of you. She wouldn't have a choice. Then you could play baseball again."

"I told you, Emily. I don't want to play anyway, and—"

"I could be in and out quickly. Maybe even get back so soon you could play with the Unicorns this year. Wouldn't that be great? You would be free to be part of the team, and I would gain the best player in the history of the Unicorns as my teammate."

She ignored the rawness of the anger building in his gaze.

"What if that's what the Web Gem was telling me to do while Mr. McMasters was talking to me? Go back, check on Callie, and break your curse so we can save Unicorn Field from having him plaster it over with the Ball and Glove logo. He's already got his hooks far enough into it, right?"

Adrien held up a hand.

"Stop it, Emily. Just stop it." The cold edge of his voice made her do just that. "You and Benji. Geez. You both give me the heebie-jeebies. I thought we were on the same side, Emily. As far as I'm concerned, no one is going back to the Fairy Realm, ever."

"But—"

"There's no reason for you to do that. None at all. Honestly, I don't *want* to try out. I'm not *going* to try out no matter what you do. So, there is no reason for anyone to ever go to the Fairy Realm."

"Even to see what's up with the shard and Mr. McMasters?"

"Nothing is up with the shard and Mr. McMasters," Adrien snapped too quickly.

They sat in the heat of the moment.

Adrien shook his head again.

"Trust me, Emily. You don't know her the way I do. I spent a hundred years trapped with her. What if she doesn't comply? Or what if she can't comply? Fairy magic is impossible to predict, and the Unseelie Queen doesn't play fair. I've seen her cast rings around other brilliant spellcasters. You don't want to take that kind of chance with her. It's too risky, Emily. I can't let you go back. Not for me. Not for anyone."

Emily crossed her arms in defiance. "I'm not here to ask your permission, Adrien."

A cold, bitter silence hung between them, thick as fog and just as unpleasant to swallow.

"I see," Adrien replied. His voice was whisper-soft. He turned away from her, letting his desk chair spin slowly towards the window.

Grappling with her own anger, she let him stew.

Finally, he made the chair turn back to face her.

"I won't help you," he said. "I owe you my life, Emily. But I won't repay you by helping you throw yours away."

Emily set her jaw and felt the pit of her stomach gnaw at her.

"Good to know," she said.

She got up to leave then, the Web Gem shard weighing heavy in her pocket.

Adrien grabbed her by the forearm, his grip firm enough that she stopped in her tracks.

"Promise me you won't do this," Adrien said, looking up at her with a sharpness to his gaze she couldn't remember seeing before. "Or I'll tell Megan Moore you don't intend to join the Unicorns this year."

"You wouldn't."

"Watch me. She'll follow you around forever, then. So much for building baseball magic on the sly."

Emily gave a soft shudder. The threat wasn't an empty one. Megan Moore was like a bloodhound.

She blew a breath out through her lips and let her shoulders curl in on her.

"I understand," she said.

She was almost ashamed of the relief that crossed Adrien's face.

"Thank you," he said. He let his grip soften, and she slipped her arm free.

Emily left then, walking down the stairs, saying goodbye to Mr. and Mrs. Thorn. Then she walked briskly back towards her own house.

She needed to go to the Fairy Realm now. She'd come here looking to get talked off the ledge, and Adrien had delivered that in spades. But the visceral reaction she'd had at his refusal to take the risk and help Callie had simply solidified her decision to jump.

Adrien's analysis was right enough, of course. Callie would never ask for help. That didn't mean she didn't need it.

And, yes, despite his impassioned statements otherwise, she suspected — strongly suspected — that Adrien Thorn was still a baseball player. No one could love the game that much for that long, and simply turn off the spigot.

If she had a chance to take away the Unseelie Queen's influence from him for good, he might finally be able to see it himself.

She rubbed her palm over her piece of the Web Gem and felt nothing.

It would be difficult to manage a transition without Adrien's help, and nearly impossible if he was going to put barriers in her way. And Megan Moore was another big barrier.

Above her, the first stars peeked through the darkness in the east.

"I'm not sure it's going to work out, Mom," she said into the sky. "But this feels right."

The sky wasn't talking, though.

She picked up her pace.

At least she knew Dad's Victory Lasagna wouldn't let her down.

CHAPTER
SIXTEEN

As expected, Dad's Victory Lasagna was in full regular-season form.

After they wrapped the last two pieces for the freezer and cleaned the dishes, they met up with Elaine, Dad's new girlfriend, for Ratner's ice cream. It was good to see her dad relax with another adult again, and when Elaine asked about Emily's mom's favorite flavor, the answer had come out easily.

"Butter pecan. She always got two scoops, too, even if she was *so full* after dinner."

"I've always been a strawberry girl, myself," Elaine had said as she sat on the plastic seat across from them and spooned a banana split. "But my dad was all about the butter pecan. Going past it in the grocery store always makes me think of him."

At first, Emily thought Elaine was just trying to find common ground with her new boyfriend's teenage daughter, but the warm curl at the corner of Elaine's lips and the distant gaze in her eyes spoke of real happiness, so Emily felt better about that, too.

It was impossible not to feel good at Ratner's.

The drive home was nice, too. Quiet and easy.

She'd almost forgotten to be miffed at Adrien.

Maybe that wasn't so bad, though. Adrien was probably right. Callie was probably fine, and even though he pissed her off sometimes, Adrien was more than an adult. If he didn't want to play, he didn't want to play. In that case, it would be better if she stayed in her lane and played ball.

"Good night, kiddo," Dad said as she padded up the stairs to her room. "Sleep well."

"Good night, Dad," she said, rounding the hall corner.

She froze.

The door to her room was left ajar — something she never did.

Though it was dark in the room, from the angle, she could see things were wrong, too. Something had moved her bed away from the wall. The window curtain waved gently in the breeze from outside.

"Dad?" she said, stepping forward, her piece of the Web Gem pounding urgently in her hip pocket, and her heart beating in time with it.

"What's wrong?" Dad called. His voice had that tightness to it that said he was alert for trouble. Footsteps rumbled like thunder on the steps.

She stepped closer and pushed the door open.

Yes, the bed was cattywampus, but it was too dark to make out more details. Edging her hand along the wall, she flipped the light switch.

She wanted to scream, but it got stuck in her throat.

The place was a wreck. Books and pictures lay scattered across the floor. Her laptop had been cracked open and left on the edge of her dresser, which had had its drawers pulled out and emptied onto the floor. Her diary? Its security lock had been cut open, and the diary itself was now splayed on her desk, pages side down. Trophies from her shelf lay tossed onto the bed, which was, in turn, stripped of its sheets and comforter, both wadded in piles at the bed's center.

Instinctively, her gaze flitted around the room until she found her mom's baseball bumped up against the wall in the far corner. A cold wave of relief flooded over her at the sight of its pale white cover.

Across the room, her closet doors had been pulled back to reveal all her clothes, including dresses she hadn't worn since her mother had died. Her Small Folk uniform dangled limply from its hanger, a large, flapping strip of the front of the jersey drooping toward the floor.

The heat of her piece of the Web Gem radiated through her body.

A scent lingered in the air. Something that first reminded her of the Fairy Realm but then went flat.

Woodsy, she thought. But artificial. Familiar, though.

"What the hell?" Dad said, standing behind her and breathing heavily from his run up the stairs. He rarely swore around her. She didn't blame him for doing it now.

"Someone broke into my room, I guess," Emily said. She was missing something important. Until she knew something more, she didn't want to scare him.

"I'm calling the police," he said. "Don't touch anything."

"I won't." She nodded, taking in more details around the room as he pulled out his phone and began to report a burglary.

Emily's mind caught up to her.

She knew where she'd smelled that scent before. It was cologne, the kind only a certain type of person would wear.

Mr. McMasters.

She drew in another breath of the cologne, knowing it would disappear into the fresh chill in a moment. She went to the window and looked out. She was sure she heard a car engine start around the street corner, then the tires of a car pulling away.

She grabbed her bit of the Web Gem from her pocket and stared at its golden glow in her cupped palm.

The shard.

Fred McMasters had ransacked her room, and he'd been looking for her part of the Web Gem.

CHAPTER

SEVENTEEN

Sitting on the hard bench in front of his gray gym locker, Adrien crumpled a copy of the Extra Edition! of the *Unicorns Weekly Gazette* that Megan Moore had pushed out this morning, 10:13 this morning, to be precise, if you could trust the time stamp for when his phone had blown up.

Voices echoed. Lockers clanked. The cloud of disinfectant that permeated the locker room bit at him. The white noise of the showers added to his mounting sense of despair.

Adrien's Cincinnati Reds T-shirt, which had been a present from Aunt Peg after she heard him chattering about how the Reds were the first real baseball team, was drenched with enough sweat that it pasted itself over his back. When the ventilation kicked in, he got a chill that was as bad as the headline.

Tuesday afternoon, and already the week was horrible.

Then Benji Amberman plopped down unexpectedly beside him, making him jump like a terrified pixie.

"Hey there," Benji said.

Great. Just what Adrien needed.

"Hello, Benji," he replied.

"Sorry to startle you."

"It's all right."

Benji had already changed into street clothes. Today's outfit consisted of a black, sharply pleated skirt and equally black leggings to ward against the chill. Their button-down shirt was pale gold and decorated with a pattern of clock faces. The military-sharp shoulder pads gave a snappy aura of discipline. A soft leather vest and a black-brimmed White Sox hat topped off the ensemble. Their shoes were a comfortable pair of red sneakers. A slight touch of earthy rouge sharpened their cheekbones, and eyeliner added to the black trim everywhere else.

As an openly out non-binary, Benji represented another difference between the Real World Adrien had grown up in and the one he found himself in now. Enbies, like other gender-queer people, were never openly enby when he was a kid. Admittedly, this was a positive change. If nothing else, a century in the Fairy Realm had made Adrien open to all sorts of genders, species, and sexualities, and had proven that he liked living in a more inclusive world.

"You feeling okay?" Benji said.

"Totally fine."

Benji's expression said he didn't look fine.

Adrien looked at the paper again. He was going to kill Sydney.

Cursed Pitcher From Fairy Realm Roams Halls of Pattersonville High Today.

What a headline.

The story that followed was worse, laying out a string of events and "facts" that were, unfortunately, more truthful than he'd like — though no one at Pattersonville West, beyond himself and Emily, had any chance of separating the truths from Megan Moore's Google-rific fabrications. Her article also flat-out stated that Adrien Thorn *was* the kid from a hundred years ago and said that he'd been playing baseball late at night, then asked straight-out why Adrien wouldn't deign to play for the Unicorns when he knew full well that his presence would bring an automatic championship.

How selfish does a Fairy Lord have to be to keep from helping his teammates?

The line struck him straight in the heart.

Someone had taped the article to his locker, which also just happened to be right next to the baseball team signup sheet. When he first heard the story had dropped, Adrien had hoped beyond hope that – like Moore's first hit piece last fall – it would be too weird for even this stupid paper to feature. Alas, "if it bleeds it leads" remained true even a century after the yellow journalism of his time had run rampant. The whole school had been joking about it, a few going so far as to ask him how Narnia had been before scampering off down the hall in peals of laughter. Others were not so kind. When Ms. Dinkins called on him in calculus, for example, he was so focused elsewhere that he jumped. Once Ms. Dinkins had calmed everyone down, Peri Yanar asked if an elf had his tongue, and everyone laughed again.

And, of course, they started bugging him to play baseball again. He'd seen Coach Amabe coming down the hallway just before lunch, clearly intent on cornering him. He'd had to duck into the chorus room stairwell to avoid the conversation.

The effort it took to avoid people had left Adrien drained.

Except for Emily, of course. Emily, being mad at his dismissal last night, was easy to avoid. She might never talk to him again.

Her demeanor annoyed him, partially because her reasons made the anger justified. But they had agreements, right? And now, despite those agreements, Emily had made it clear that she wanted to step back into the Fairy Realm. He felt like the rug had been pulled from underneath him — like he'd gotten the old switcheroo. The idea of her in the Fairy Realm made him mad. Combined with the article, he was now officially steeped in a weird sense of forlorn doom.

Why couldn't people just leave well enough alone?

Even if Emily pulled off the triple-headed feat of helping Callie McMasters with whatever she needed, figuring out what was going on with the Web Gem, *and* giving him back his freedom, Adrien knew *he* was still screwed.

The article guaranteed that people would be talking about him, and not because of his burgeoning theater career.

He grimaced, then threw the balled-up article across the room, bouncing it off the wall and into the garbage container.

Crumpling the page made him feel better but didn't change anything. Calvin Obekwe, for example, sat a bench away, scrolling through the edition on his phone and glancing at Adrien with anxious animation every so often. Several others were doing the same. Having fun at his expense.

"Good job out there today," Benji said.

Adrien laughed. "Right. I'm a real triple threat, aren't I? Can't pass, can't dribble, and can't shoot."

He was tired now, which was a good thing. Hard exercise calmed his thoughts. After so long in the Fairy Realm, he'd forgotten the deep burn of a good workout.

"Don't run yourself down. You play great defense, and your passing is magical. The rest just takes practice."

He tried to ignore Benji's Fairy Realm flare as it glowed around the edges of their toothy smile.

To normal people, Benji's glow simply drew attention when they walked into a room, attention that went beyond Benji's penchant for daring fashion. Normal people could not see Fairy Glow for what it was, but subconsciously they knew it was there, just like it was there for Adrien, too.

"At least I didn't embarrass myself totally. I can safely leave that chore to Megan Moore and her bleeding pen."

Benji scowled but didn't pursue the conversation. "So, are you gonna sign up?" they said instead. "There's still time. Tryouts are this afternoon, you know?"

"Please don't do this right now," Adrien said, pulling on pants and a shirt.

Those damned signup sheets. Despite everything, they called to him with the power of the Unseelie Queen. He'd felt the weight of her curse on his shoulders since he'd woken up this morning, and the pull had gotten nothing but worse as the day went on.

He hated that feeling.

The sensation brought memories of the queen's starry gaze as she sat on the bench and stroked the Web Gem with her long, spidery fingers. The feeling welled so strongly that he half expected to find her leaning against the wall, proffering a poisoned pen, her night-black dress billowing around her in the stale, sweat-scented gymnasium air.

He shuddered.

"I'm not signing up, Benji. Believe me, I know better than anyone else that tryouts are today."

Benji waited to talk until Adrien caught their gaze.

"You can't fool me, you know?" Benji said. "I saw you staring at the signup list after rehearsal this morning. I don't care about that stupid article. I know who you are, and I know you want to play."

Adrien gave a manic laugh.

Benji glanced at the wadded article.

"If the truth of the Fairy Realm is out there, whether or not people believe it, there's no reason not to try out, right?"

"Benji."

"Don't fight this, Adrien. Holding yourself inside is bad for your health."

"I know you're trying to help, but please stop."

Benji hesitated, then continued. "It's all right, though. Take the time you need. We'd all love to have you with the team no matter what you want to do."

"I seriously doubt that."

"Well. I know *I'd* be thrilled to have you in the dugout. And I know I'm not alone."

Adrien glowered.

"At least Emily says you're going to be the team manager or something?"

"Grounds crew. But now I'm thinking that would be a bad idea, too."

It was worse than bad, Adrien thought. The idea of mending fences and fertilizing the outfield, or whatever, felt horrible now. Every time someone looked at him, they would snicker. Or the ones who believed this article would look at him like he was the worst kind of traitor, which could be even more disastrous.

Simply being around Unicorn Field might be dangerous.

Benji leaned in closer, though, and whispered.

"Like it or not, Adrien Thorn, we are more alike than you think. We both have fairy magic in our blood now. And we've both got the game running through our veins, too. So, there's something else going on, isn't there? I feel it in you." Benji gave the other kids a sideways glance, then returned their gaze to Adrien's. "Whatever that something else might be, just know it doesn't matter at all. Not to me, anyway."

Adrien clenched both fists but then pressed them into the hardwood of the plank bench. Benji's words burned into his marrow.

There's something else going on, isn't there, he thought.

Even though Benji was wrong about Adrien's love of the game, the Unicorns' third baseperson was astute, and now they were getting too close to the truth.

If something horrible happened to Benji because Adrien had let them fall into the clutches of the Fairy Realm, he knew he could never look the Amberman family in the eyes again.

Rising, Adrien grabbed his book bag and slammed his cubby shut. "I need to get to history," he said. "But if you really want to help me, go tell Megan Moore to print the truth for once, instead of spinning yarns that only get people's hopes up."

Before Benji could reply, he was already gone.

He walked with a hard pace out of the locker room. Maybe it would work. Maybe Benji would take the hint and finally leave him alone. All he knew for sure was that the pressure of the gazes and whispers following him as he made his way out of the gymnasium was driving him batty. He heard the whispers of "Fairy Lord" a million times in his head, and when even Wendy Thomas hid a furtive chuckle as he passed, he realized he'd had enough.

Instead of history class, Adrien made for the double doors at the rear of the building and headed off, away from school and into the city.

He needed to be alone, and he needed to walk.

If nothing else, if he stayed away from school all day, he'd miss tryouts for sure.

CHAPTER

EIGHTEEN

S tanding at her open locker, Emily slid her book bag off her shoulder and reached in to switch out her books.

She just had to get through two more class periods without exploding at someone.

If it weren't for the fact that tryouts were later that afternoon, Emily might not have tried so hard to make it through the school day. Maybe she would have let her dad keep her at home, soothing her jumpy nerves with hot cocoa and ESPN's speculations for this year's spring training.

Heck, maybe she even would have spent the morning reading the chapters of *Wuthering Heights* she was supposed to have gotten through for class today.

But tryouts *were* today, and she wasn't going to let Mr. McMasters scare her away.

But dealing with the break-in — talking with the police, explaining that no, nothing had been taken, standing back while they'd taken pictures of every angle of her room for hours — had been so draining. She was flagging by fifth period. It wasn't even so much that she was tired. On the contrary, she was buzzing with the frizzy kind of energy that came from being wired. She'd brought the Web Gem shard to school with her, tucked safely in the depths of her pocket, and she brushed her hand over the slight bulge of it often, reassuring herself that it was there. Each time, it gave her a little spark, and her focus sharpened a little more.

She didn't know why he was looking for her piece of the Web Gem, or how he'd come to know about its existence in the first place, but his attack last night had only solidified her decision to become a Unicorn again.

She had to get back into the Fairy Realm.

It wasn't just about helping Callie, or breaking Adrien's curse, or checking in on her Small Folk friends anymore. At the very least, she knew she had to get the shard out of Mr. McMasters' reach. Whatever he wanted with it, however he'd heard about it, she knew he couldn't be trusted.

"Emily!"

Emily turned to see Benji striding towards her, gliding easily through the throng of students. Their hair, still damp from the showers after gym class, shone as if it were full of pixie dust.

"Hey, Benji," Emily said, clutching her copy of *Wuthering Heights*. She tried not to sound strained, but the quirk of Benji's fine eyebrow told her she'd failed. "What's up?"

Benji leaned against the locker next to Emily's and crossed their arms over their chest. "Well, I was hoping you could tell me something about Adrien, you know, this whole article and the tryouts and everything. But that response says you've got your own things going on. What gives?"

Her sleep-denied brain flashed on telling Benji about everything. How nice if things were that simple. But she couldn't bring Benji in on her problems, which were all entirely tangled up in the Fairy Realm. She and Adrien had agreed.

"No time," she said. "I've got Mrs. Pitcairn next."

Mrs. Pitcairn's classroom was all the way on the opposite side of the building.

Benji laughed. "No loss, right? You've been posting so much in the group chat about *The Art of Fielding*, I figure you haven't even done the reading."

They nodded towards the book in Emily's hands, which did, in fact, sport a baseball card acting as bookmark not quite deep enough along the spine for adequate participation in today's class discussion.

Emily dropped the book into her bag with a half smile. "What can I say? Skrimshander is way more interesting than Heathcliff."

She zipped the bag closed and slung it over her shoulder, then slammed her locker door shut. But when she looked back up, she found Benji frowning at her. Not with an angry frown, but with one that showed curiosity or sudden inquisitiveness.

Their finely penciled brows furrowed as their gaze focused on Emily's pocket.

The Web Gem shard flared with the same heat that bloomed across Emily's face. Her fingers squeezed tight around the straps of her bag.

Slowly, Benji brought their gaze back up to meet Emily's.

"You'd better hope Megan Moore doesn't pick up on whatever *that* is," they said, their voice so soft Emily ought to have needed to lean in to hear it over the noise of the hallway.

She didn't need to, though. As always, Benji's ability to hold a person's focus on them was magical.

All at once, Emily's exhaustion caught up with her. Mr. McMasters' break-in, her worries over Callie and the Small Folk, Adrien's curse and his refusal to help her, the baseball magic. McMasters and his sponsorships and whatever dark secrets they were covering up.

On top of that came Megan Moore's idiotic article this morning. Every word made her want to wring the sophomore journalist's neck. It didn't matter that everyone else was laughing at the article — and at poor Adrien. Megan didn't understand the powers she was playing with. The things she had printed were varying shades of the truth, and if anyone took it into their minds to play at fairy baseball, it could lead to real trouble.

It all added up to put everything on Emily's shoulders, and it was just too much.

Her only plan was as dangerous as Megan's article — use today's tryouts to build the baseball magic necessary to make the transfer, use her part of the Web Gem to store it for use later that night, and hope no one at tryouts noticed any of it. It seemed as likely to succeed as a squeeze bunt, but it was the only idea she had.

The piercing intensity in Benji's gaze told her how fat her chances were.

How had she thought she could do this alone?

Adrien wouldn't help her. She didn't blame him. Not really. He'd already been through so much.

But Benji was here, and they...

They would understand. Even without having been to the Fairy Realm themself, Benji still had the tie, the family history. What pieces they didn't know, Emily could provide. Benji would pick those pieces up quickly enough to share her burden.

She brushed her hand over the shard again, letting its solid presence drown out the sounds of kids shouting down the halls. She took a deep breath and, as the tardy bell rang, made her decision.

"Is your next class important?" she asked.

Benji grinned, and their eyes twinkled with mischief. "In senior year?"

"Then come out to the field with me so we can be alone. I think I do want to talk about it, after all."

"Wow," Benji said after Emily had finished telling them everything. "That's a lot, Em. I see why you're so worried."

Suddenly emptied, Emily simply nodded. She felt like a deflated balloon. After months of stretching herself to keep everything contained, the relief of letting it all go was incredible. She should have shared everything with Benji ages ago.

Emily and Benji sat together on the bleachers – new ones that Mr. McMasters had paid to have installed, but as far as Emily could tell, the only difference was that they were shinier than the old ones. They weren't any easier on the butt, that was for sure. The open space of Unicorn Field lay still and quiet around the two of them, a faint breeze carrying a few tendrils of February's chill, but no bite. A scent of spring greenery lurked below those tendrils, biding its time.

The infield dirt had been freshly raked, the lines newly chalked, the bases pristinely arranged. The outfield grass didn't need mowing yet, but the chain link fences had been replaced with – surprise – shiny new ones. Emily supposed the old ones had sported a few flecks of rust, maybe. These sported banners full of tacky advertisements for McMasters Ball and Glove as well as several others.

She wondered now if Adrien would have had any work to do if he'd ever spoken to Coach Amabe about joining the grounds crew. Everything looked so professionally done, so precise and error-free, that it was obvious no highschooler had had a hand in any of the work. So much for charm, then, or letting the kids take pride in work they'd done themselves.

Worst of all was the concession stand, which had been repainted in Unicorn blue and teal as well as having new windows installed. Both windows sported decals, one the Unicorns logo, the other a McMasters Ball and Glove logo so big the window was practically opaque.

Emily scowled at the logo as if it were McMasters himself.

"I hate that," Benji said, following her eye line.

"It takes away all the magic of the place."

"No, it doesn't. But it does taint it."

Benji's words hung in the cold air, their truth ringing on the edge of hearing.

Emily shivered and hunched her shoulders around her ears, balling her fists in her pockets. The Web Gem shard dug into the flesh of her palm. Its heat did little to cut through the chill she felt now.

"I have to keep the shard away from McMasters. I can't let his touch taint it or the baseball magic."

"Definitely not," said Benji. They turned their knees toward Emily's. "So, what's the plan?"

Emily sighed out a puff of wispy white. "Build up baseball magic during tryouts, I guess, and see if I can store that power in the shard until I can come back here when no one's around and open the portal. Callie and I managed to do it with only the two of us, so it should be easy enough to manage on my own."

Saying it out loud sounded worse than it had in her head. It all depended on if she could work the shard like that, but she had no idea if that was even possible. She'd never tried using it for anything.

Benji frowned out at third base and tapped their fingers against their thighs.

Emily watched them for a moment.

When they turned their eyes back on her, they wore the most serious expression she'd ever seen on them.

"Why not do it right now, you and me? I'll pitch, you'll score your home runs. We've got three hours until tryouts start, which given the way you said time works in the Realm might be enough for you to pop in, make your boon request to break Adrien's curse, check in on Callie, and get back with none the wiser."

Emily opened her mouth, but Benji held up one hand as if to forestall any protestation. "I know you and Adrien have your reasons for trying to keep me out of the Realm, and now that you've told me about all this stuff I understand that even more than I did before. I'm not saying I promise never to touch the Fairy Realm, because I can't promise that. It's part of my heritage. But I am saying I'll do what I can to help you deal with this problem, and I won't get in your way. Please, *please* let me help you."

Finished with their pitch, they folded their hands in their lap, fingers laced tight, and stared at Emily with eyes wide as saucers. Their fairy glow shimmered hopefully around their edges.

Emily laughed. The sound echoed among the bleachers. "Benji, I appreciate what you've just said so much more than I can say. But you've got me wrong."

"What's that?"

"I am so far from telling you not to help me now. And you doing the pitching is a brilliant idea. Coach Amabe even has the equipment all laid out in the dugout for tryouts."

Benji's light flared strong enough even those not attuned to the Fairy Realm might have been able to see it, had anyone like that been around. They stood, brushing non-existent dirt from their pants, and held a hand out to Emily. "Let's do this."

The breeze swirled up suddenly, and the smell of infield dirt mixed with the new growth around them. The air grew warmer, just a bit, but enough to carry the hope of spring rather than the dreariness of lingering winter. Heat from the Web Gem shard flared against Emily's hip.

She took Benji's hand and stood. "Fairy Realm, here I come."

A few minutes later, Benji stood on the pitcher's mound, rubbing up a baseball while Emily stepped into the batter's box. Benji had left their jacket lying across the dugout bench and undone the top button of their shirt. A dozen new balls lay on the infield grass around Benji. The sun was just past its peak, and as Emily swung the bat, her muscles stretched against themselves with that lovely burn. She would have liked to change into some baseball pants, but at least her jeans were comfortable. The corner of her lip tweaked sideways at the sight of the McMasters Ball and Glove advertisements hanging on the left field, right field, and center field fences that stood before the copses of trees behind them. She did her best to ignore the ads and pulled on a batting helmet to get herself ready.

"All right, Meathead," Emily called out to Benji. "Let's see what you've got. Remember, you've got to be trying to get me out."

"Got it," Benji replied. "Let's get this party started!"

Their tongue peeked out from the corner of their lips, and an expression of concentration crossed their face as they went into a windup that made them look like Satchel Paige.

The pitch was a mile wide.

"Sorry," Benji said. "Nervous, I guess."

"No problem," Emily said with only a touch of snark. "We've got a whole three hours to waste."

She stood at the plate, bat up in readiness.

Benji toed the rubber, then peered into the plate as if getting a sign. They shook off the catcher once, then gave an exaggerated nod.

Emily loosened her shoulders and took one last practice swing.

Benji pitched. Curveball.

Emily waited, then turned on it.

The crack of the bat was sweet. The ball rose into the blue, almost cloudless sky, flying over the fence and beyond the lights to disappear into the woods.

"Good pitch," Emily said while trotting the bases.

Benji beamed.

Their second pitch was a fastball with oomph, which made sense because Benji had an arm good enough to play third. Emily drilled it into the woods behind the left field fence.

A round trip later, Emily touched the plate for her second run, then picked up her bat. She could almost feel a vibration through the lumber as power ran in the bat's grain. In her pocket, her piece of the Web Gem seemed quiet, but a sense of confidence radiated from it.

She looked to the mound.

Benji gave a hearty symbol for "okay."

Two homers. The time was here.

Emily breathed in the scent of the soil that came on the gentle breeze. She thought of Fennoc and Mellica and Jessebel. Shayla and Twy, and Greeven and Essie. The image of Izusa pixie-cartwheeling around the base paths made her smile. The memories merged with the jaunty piping of a flute and a collective clamor of little voices calling to her, chattering like infielders. A sense of happiness came over her.

Baseball magic, she thought. It would be great to see her teammates again.

She gripped the bat more firmly and readied herself.

Benji's pitch was a curveball that flew, then dipped.

The bat cracked again.

The ball rose majestically, and it felt to Emily like the entire field pulsed with an invisible wave of energy. She ran, doing her best to maintain a proper pace rather than sprinting around the bases.

She rounded third base to find Benji standing beside home plate, waiting for her as waves of magic wafted in the air.

"What are you doing?" she shouted at them, though the obvious answer made her throat squeeze tight.

Benji waved her in. "Don't worry, Em. I promised I wouldn't get in your way and I'm not going to. I'm just seeing you off properly."

Emily began her jog again.

As she neared the plate, Benji continued the chatter.

"Go tell that Unseelie Queen who's boss, and let Callie know we'd all love to see her again even if her dad is stinking up our field. Oh, and say hi to that little brownie cheerleader you told me about. She sounds like a lot of fun."

Emily laughed. "Will do."

Her steps had slowed, though she felt as if she were still running at full pace. The thickening magic in the air made her move like she was enveloped in molasses.

Then she was there, at home plate with the magic swirling around her.

"See you soon," she said. Then Emily stepped on home plate.

Nothing happened.

No magic. No flow. No welling of power or thick scent of the realm.

No anything.

The power she thought she'd felt collapsed into her breathing. A deathly silence rode on the cool breeze. Had the magic ever been there at all? Had she imagined that molasses feel and the wisps of power in the air?

"Is that it?" Benji said with a confused glance. "Are you back already?"

Emily shook her head slowly, her hand already dipping into her pocket to touch the Web Gem shard. "Something's wrong. I don't understand."

"The baseball magic didn't work?" Benji asked.

"It should have. Thrice on the bone-white plate," she added absently, frowning down at the white shape under her foot.

"Bring home some bloodthirsty fate," Benji replied, which brought a quick and questioning glance from Emily. "Hey," they said, holding both hands up in surrender. "I know my fairy lore."

Emily sighed, punching her toe on the plate again but getting no better result.

"I was so sure I understood how things worked."

"Maybe the timing was wrong? My great-grandma Amberman always said fairies like rituals and such done under the light of the moon. We could try again at midnight?"

"Maybe. Yeah. That could be it."

But Emily was sure that wasn't it. She *had* felt the beginnings of the power building inside the baseball magic. She couldn't have imagined all that. Something else was wrong. Something missing, maybe? Or maybe it was Benji, their own fairy lineage unconsciously messing with the flow of the magic?

That didn't make sense, either. But whatever the issue was, the result was the same.

Emily was stuck on this side of the fairy ring, and the Web Gem shard was still in Mr. McMasters' reach.

"I guess we should get everything ready for tryouts again," Benji said with a little too much pep as they stepped toward the mound to pick up the extra baseballs.

Emily frowned at home plate once more, then sighed. "Yeah. We don't want to let anyone know we were out here doing anything. McMasters might hear about it, and he can put two and two together. The fewer questions, the better."

She picked up the bat and put it back into the bag. Team tryouts, still coming up in a couple of hours, were going to be weird now. She wasn't sure if she'd be able to keep her head in the game, as it were, with this new problem fogging up her brain.

A fence gate rattled from down the third-base line.

The sound, common enough during a game or practice when the field was full of players, made Emily freeze up like a sighted rabbit. A sense of dread engulfed her.

Sure enough, as she whipped her head around to look, she saw Megan Moore striding rapidly away from Unicorn Field. The reporter held her phone in one hand.

"Are you kidding me?" Emily muttered. The dread twisted into a sick fear and settled deep in her stomach.

What had Megan seen? What had she *heard?*

Whatever the answers, given the subject matter of the article she'd already published this morning, it was a worst-case scenario.

The next special edition of the *Unicorn Weekly Gazette* was going to be, as Fennoc would call it, *Adoo Zee.*

CHAPTER
NINETEEN

Adrien skipped school for the rest of the afternoon.

He didn't head straight home, though. Didn't want to raise suspicions by showing up where he wasn't supposed to be. And wonder of wonders, he managed to set the alarm on his phone to remind him when school let out for the day — a small miracle, there.

Instead, he spent the extra free time walking around the Little League fields where Sydney had played last summer, thinking about baseball and the Fairy Realm. The fields were empty now, the grass of the outfields still a bit brown, the dirt hard and cold under his sneakers. The forlorn wind whistled through the chain link fences, making the loose sign on the currently abandoned snack bar smack dully against the siding.

The tiny little ballparks were perfect just as they were. No fairy rings. No weirdness. Just baseball played by kids. Sure, Emily was right to worry about Callie. And the Web Gem flipping out on her was a good indication that *something* was weird in the Fairy Realm. But something was always going to be weird in the Fairy Realm. That was its whole definition. No reason to bring it here.

Seeing these small baseball diamonds empty and free like this was just what he needed.

He felt thoroughly better when he got home, and even more so when he realized Aunt Peg was still out at the boutique dealing with some last-minute issue. Given it was likely she'd already heard about that stupid article, he would take any delay to the inevitable conversation he could get.

Uncle Gary was in the living room, watching a hockey game and doing paperwork. The crowd was a dull roar in the background as Adrien slipped into the kitchen and rummaged through the fridge.

He'd gotten halfway through an egg salad sandwich and a glass of milk when Sydney thundered down the stairs and into the kitchen.

"Okay, A2. I am *ready*. Let's get going!"

The squirt crashed to a halt beside the kitchen table, one hand covered with his leather baseball glove and his cheekbones lined with semi-professionally applied eye black. Aunt Peg had freshly laundered his Unicorns' sweatshirt for the special occasion.

Adrien swallowed the bite of the sandwich he'd just taken, then chased it with a swig of milk. Both tasted like glue. Tryouts. He'd forgotten he'd all but promised Sydney he'd take him. All the inner quiet he'd found at the empty Little League fields drained away, leaving him feeling heavy and dull.

"I'm sorry, squirt, but it's been a long day. I don't think I'm feeling up to tryouts."

He felt like a jerk even as the words left his mouth.

If it weren't for that stupid article.

Damn you, Megan Moore.

Sydney narrowed his eyes like Adrien was a catcher trying to signal a screwball.

"My friend Patrick's older brother texted him about the stuff that reporter lady posted," he said from the side of his mouth. "I'm *really, really, really* sorry I talked to her. I told everyone all that fairy stuff was dumb and that I'd definitely know if you were the real Adrien

Thorn. I think that convinced a lot of kids, right? And this would be a great chance to talk to the coach about your ideas for the grounds crew! I could volunteer, too! We'd make a great team, wouldn't we?"

The puppy-dog softness in Sydney's gaze made Adrien sigh. He knew the kid was just being his normal enthusiastic self. But it wasn't easy to brush aside the fact that the article had *hurt*.

His truth was out there now, even if it was a distorted version of the truth, and everyone had laughed at it. Adrien the wannabe theater kid, the secret alter ego of Adrien Thorn, legendary hero of the Unicorns? Ridiculous.

"It would have been better if you hadn't told the reporter your stories in the first place, Syd."

"I know," Sydney said. He kicked one cleated toe at the floor, shoulders slumped. Then, at whiplash speed, he brightened. "When we get to the tryouts, we can tell everyone how wrong the article got everything. That'll put things right!"

Adrien chuckled despite himself, then frowned down at his half-eaten sandwich.

He really should go.

If nothing else, he should support Emily, who had taken such huge chances to retrieve him from the Fairy Realm, then given up her summer to help him learn the remedial history he needed just to barely skim by Pattersonville High's admission testing. She was a good friend. He wished he hadn't gotten so mad at her, even if she had been talking about opening the fairy ring again.

She would understand if he didn't turn up, but she deserved his presence. And it would be fun to do something with Sydney.

Get over yourself, man, he whispered to himself.

At that moment, the front door chime rang.

"Who's that?" Uncle Gary called from his recliner.

"I'll get it," Adrien replied. He put a brotherly hand on Sydney's shoulder as he passed him, then went to the door.

He didn't know who he expected to find standing on the doorstep, but it wasn't Mr. McMasters, owner of McMasters' Ball and Glove and now the principal sponsor of the Unicorns baseball team.

Adrien could not reconcile this man with Callie McMasters, the other girl who'd helped pull him out of the Fairy Realm. The man's toothy smile gleamed an unworldly white, and his eyes sparkled like brown crystals. He wore khaki business slacks and a dark blue golf shirt that peeked out from his springtime jacket, also a shade of navy blue with white and sky-blue piping. Its left shoulder was stitched with a McMasters' Ball and Glove logo. Something about the man gave Adrien a sense of foreboding but, at the same time, drew his attention in a way he couldn't ignore.

His hackles rose in defense.

"Adrien Thorn!" McMasters said. "Just the man I was hoping to find."

"Hello?" Adrien said through the screen once he realized he was staring rudely.

Uncle Gary's heavy footsteps came from behind, and little Sydney seemed to push up against Adrien's side as if he'd appeared from nowhere.

"Wow!" Sydney said. His gloved hand shot out like it was a beacon. "How are you, Mr. McMasters? I'm wearing the glove you helped me pick out last season!"

"I see that," McMasters said. "Are you keeping it good and oiled up?"

Sydney's cheeks beamed from under the eye black. "Every month, just like you said!"

"That's great, kid. Keep it up, and you'll be an All-Star in no time."

Uncle Gary pulled the door open further. "Good to see you, Fred. What can we do for you today?" He said it with enough energy that Adrien realized Uncle Gary was putting on airs. He ran his hand through his hair as if straightening it out or tamping down a wild stray that might make him unpresentable. What was it about Callie McMasters' dad that brought this out in people?

"I just thought I'd come by and have a word with Adrien about a little business venture I had in mind."

Adrien turned cold. Emily's story from last night replayed itself through his mind. This man had offered her a sponsorship, and she'd turned him down. She'd claimed the Web Gem shard had flared hot enough to burn her the whole time he'd been at her house.

Now he was here to talk to Adrien.

"A business venture, you say?" Uncle Gary responded. He opened the screen door, and Adrien picked up a faint odor of old blood wafting in on the breeze.

"I'm not interested in a business venture, Mr. McMasters," Adrien said, stepping to block McMasters' path into the house.

Uncle Gary made a low noise in his throat that meant he thought someone was being rude. "Come on now, Adrien. Where are your manners? Let Mr. McMasters in. We can at least hear him out."

"Thank you, Gary."

The door shut behind them, and Mr. McMasters followed Uncle Gary down the short hallway that opened to the living room.

As their guest crossed into the house, Adrien felt a familiar pull deep inside his chest.

The Web Gem. It was impossible not to remember how it used to speak directly to him as the Unseelie Queen caressed it between innings. Its voice was something between a song and a thought.

His heart froze with the sensation.

Emily had been right. Something was absolutely going on with the Fairy Realm artifact.

But why would he be getting this surge from McMasters? He had to be imagining things. Per law, the Web Gem was in the hands of the Small Folk, or whoever might have won it since.

A sliver of fear for Callie grew deep inside Adrien. For the first time, he thought she might really be in trouble. He wished he hadn't brushed Emily off so callously last night.

Bloodlines made fey sorcery stronger. Adrien knew that much.

If Callie had gotten herself connected to the Web Gem, maybe she could use it to reach out to the mortal world through her father. Adrien didn't know Callie very well, but he knew her enough to confidently say she would never contact her dad unless she had to.

Uncle Gary turned down the sound to his game, swept his spread of paperwork into a loose pile, and motioned Fred McMasters to take one of the recliners that sat angled toward the big screen. McMasters took it, then sat up toward its edge.

"Can I get you something, Fred? A soft drink or a beer? It's nearly evening, right?"

McMasters looked at his watch, which Adrien saw carried an Angels logo. "No, thank you. But maybe *I* have something for the little guy — if you don't mind?"

"Something for me?" Sydney called brightly, his funk over missing tryouts forgotten.

McMasters flashed all his teeth, leaned back, then pulled a card from his jacket pocket. He handed it to Sydney.

"I figure an advanced athlete like you could use a bat, or some extra balls and caps, to keep you on the field a bit longer," he said.

"Oh, wow!" Sydney exclaimed, peering at the card as he held it in his bare hand. It was a gift card. Adrien saw it was for a not-insignificant amount of money.

McMasters beamed with a tone that matched Sydney's. "Come down to the store later and pick out whatever you want."

"Really?"

Then the man reached into his other jacket pocket and pulled out a pair of small batting gloves, handing them over, too. "I figured you'd best get decked out like the pros, too. You'll want to protect those hands, and I happened to stumble on these earlier this morning."

"Oh, cool! Mookie Betts's signature, too!"

"Aw, Fred. That's too kind," Uncle Gary said, smiling as if he, too, couldn't believe his son's luck.

Sydney threw his baseball glove down.

The sound of Velcro clasps tore through the air as Sydney immediately donned the gloves.

"We'll probably never get them off him, now," Uncle Gary said.

"Happy to help," McMasters said. "Glad the little guy appreciates them."

Watching them, Adrien understood.

Uncle Gary and little Sydney were starstruck.

He'd seen it a million times before in the Fairy Realm — a place where social rank was everything. Callie's father was a rich man around the city, which meant he had a position of power.

As these thoughts flashed through Adrien's head, McMasters sat back in his chair and turned to Adrien.

The temperature in the room dropped ten degrees.

"So, Adrien Thorn, *direct descendant* of the greatest player in Unicorns history. I have some ideas I hope you'll appreciate as much as your little cousin there."

"Emily DeWitt is the greatest player in Unicorns history," Adrien replied, feeling the truth in that statement. Adrien had been good while he was in school, but the game around him had been so different. Emily was far better today than he'd been when he was her age.

McMasters' eyebrows ticked upward with an almost imperceptible rise.

The corners of his lips moved, and his eyes grew sharp under a veneer of amusement.

"Gary," McMasters said so abruptly it felt like a spell had been snapped. "I'm wondering if Adrien might be more comfortable with this conversation if we could have a few moments alone. Just him and me. That way, he can turn me down without any pressure from outside." As Uncle Gary began to argue, McMasters added, "I promise we won't enter any deal without your blessing. I'm not here to rip Adrien off."

Uncle Gary seemed perplexed, but Adrien saw the value of McMasters' suggestion. He didn't trust Callie's dad as far as he could throw the Unseelie Queen, but if nothing else, dealing with this by himself would keep the rest of his family from being exposed to whatever illicit doings McMasters had up his sleeve.

"He's right," Adrien said to Uncle Gary. "I'd like to hear what he has to say alone. I promise I know better than to sign anything stupid."

Uncle Gary frowned, obviously disappointed and wanting to be in the loop. But Sydney got his gloves on and stood up. "Maybe we could go out and play some catch, Dad?"

Uncle Gary saw the writing on the wall.

"All right," he said, answering Sydney and McMasters in one breath.

A moment later, they were out the door.

Adrien and McMasters were alone.

Neither of them said anything until the sound of a ball smacking into a glove came from the front yard.

"That was some article in the little ol' *Gazette* today, wasn't it?" McMasters said coyly.

That Web Gem sensation pulsed against Adrien's skin again, making the hairs on the back of his neck stand up.

"I don't know what you mean, Mr. McMasters. That rag's not much more than a tabloid at this point."

McMasters sat forward with his elbows on his knees. He rubbed his hands together so they rasped like a dry winter's wind over an empty diamond. The glitter in his eyes turned into a sharp gleam, so forceful that Adrien's entire body froze under his stare.

"Let's not beat around the bases, all right, *Adrien Thorn?*"

His pause was perfect Fairy Realm drama.

"I know exactly who you are. And I've come to make you the deal of a hundred-year-old lifetime."

CHAPTER
TWENTY

S taring into Mr. McMasters' dark gaze, Adrien felt as tense as he ever had sitting beside the Unseelie Queen. He sat now, frozen in place as McMasters edged forward in the recliner with anticipation oozing from him. McMasters' hands spread over his knees. The tips of his fingers brushed the fabric of his pants with the same absentminded sense of satisfaction the queen had shown as she caressed the Web Gem.

The queen, Adrien thought.

Had the queen sent McMasters to meddle with the mortal world? To mess with Emily and torment Adrien? Another surge of fairy magic came over Adrien, less intense than before but definitely flavored with the familiar scent of the Web Gem. The queen could do it. She was powerful enough to work her will over the Web Gem, even if it was no longer in her hands. She'd held it for so long, after all. She'd used Adrien's batting skills to keep it in her clutches for a full century, which was long enough to have imprinted parts of herself onto it.

Like a ripple on the water that betrays the predator lurking below, the queen's curse rolled deep within Adrien's gut.

"Just what is it that you think you know about me?" he finally replied, stalling.

McMasters gave a soft *hmm.*

"All right." He raised his hands and spread them wide. At that moment, he stopped emanating the control that reminded Adrien of the queen and instead radiated the Wild Hunt's leader's cold confidence as he toyed with his cornered prey. "I mean. I guess we can do it like that if you want. Works out the same to me."

The wry clarity of Mr. McMasters' smile was all Adrien needed to confirm that the man knew beyond any doubt that Megan Moore's article was right about him — that Adrien was *not* simply a long-distant descendent of the legendary baseball player who had disappeared from Unicorn Field a century before. Somehow, Mr. McMasters *knew* that the Adrien Thorn sitting in this modern-day living room was that same baseball player.

"How?" Adrien said softly. "How do you know anything?"

"I have my connections," McMasters said as if that was only natural.

Adrien sneered at McMasters' attempt at coyness. "You can tell her it's no use. I'm not giving her squat. No tryouts. Not ever."

McMasters' smile was oily. "Yeah. That's a nasty little curse you've got there, isn't it? Your queen must have been a real pain in the backside."

Adrien hesitated, and McMasters pressed on.

"Look, kid. Here's the deal straight up. I'm building the greatest high school baseball team that has ever existed, and you're going to be on it."

"I'm never playing baseball again, Mr. McMasters. And if you know about my queen's curse, you'll understand why I say that."

McMasters flicked his fingers dismissively. "Forget about that. I'll take care of it."

Adrien scoffed. "Just how are you going to do that?"

If the man thought he was going to make a slick deal with the

Unseelie Queen and come out with the upper hand, he was in for a nasty surprise.

"You don't need to worry about it," McMasters said, snapping his fingers. "Let's just say things are happening. You can trust me on this, Adrien. I'm a businessman. And a good businessman never overruns his headlights. Under-promise, over-deliver, I always say."

The man's tone reminded Adrien of countless court sessions he'd attended at the Unseelie Queen's side. From listening to those, he understood politics was a game of shifting sands and sleight of hand. He'd never grown comfortable with it, but he knew it was happening when he heard it. Being in the middle of it now, though, he wished he understood more details.

McMasters continued. "I've just come from signing the papers on *another* big deal with the Pattersonville High School baseball club. A real win-win. Everyone's gonna love it."

"I don't care about your business deals."

McMasters laughed. "You'll care about this one."

"I seriously doubt that."

McMasters still smiled like he'd just sunk the hook.

"I've just acquired naming rights to the field and bought out the best seats in the house. That means I'll have a representative at every one of those kids' games to see that things go well. You name it, the Unicorns are going to get it."

"Naming rights?" Adrien felt like he was missing something.

"I'm thinking 'McMasters Park' has a nice ring to it."

McMasters sank back into the chair.

Adrien was puzzled for a moment, then he understood.

"You own Unicorn Field."

"It's prime property, isn't it?"

The skin on Adrien's forearms crawled. He was still missing something. Something important.

"That first cash outlay was quite a hefty chunk of my capital. More than hefty, to be honest. So I decided it would be wise to take on a bit of insurance. Call it another future revenue stream. But once your girlfriend turned me down, I had to go another way."

"Emily DeWitt is not my girlfriend."

"Whatever," McMasters said. He wiped away the difference with a nonchalant wave of his hand.

Adrien swallowed the anger that was climbing up his throat.

"So," he said. "After Emily refused to sign, you went bigger."

McMasters beamed. "Let's just say the DeWitt girl had her chance and whiffed. I'm here to sign you to an even bigger deal than I offered her. The whole thing. A complete management package. You play ball, and I see to it that your finances are always in top shape. Full ride scholarship, room and board, and a small living allowance until you're, um," McMasters gave a sly smile, then cleared his throat with a fake cough, "twenty-one. Plus, since you'll be a huge winner, there will be advertisement deals. The sky's the limit, Adrien. Write your meal ticket, right? Nothing but the best for my client. And for you, I'd take a pay cut. Only twenty-five percent."

"No, thank you," Adrien said, feeling a rancid growth building in his gut. "I'm serious. I don't want to play baseball ever again. And even if I was interested, since you know about my curse, you know why I'll never be able to play for the Unicorns anyway. Trying out will send me right back to the queen."

"Oh, you'll play," McMasters said, chuckling. "Haven't you ever heard of a loophole? I'm not asking you to try out. You're already on the team."

Adrien gaped.

A chill crossed his spine.

McMasters sat on Uncle Gary's chair, gloating.

This horrible, self-serving businessman had, with a simple twist of the rules, caught Adrien in so tight a trap he could hardly breathe. But he saw it now, saw with clear sight what the connection must be.

This kind of evil wasn't of the Unseelie type. They cared nothing for rules and spared no effort in sniffing out *loopholes*.

Mr. McMasters wasn't with the queen at all.

Fred McMasters had Seelie blood ties.

He saw it in the precise curve of McMasters' thin jawline and the deep glitter embedded in his gaze. He felt it in the man's upright posture and heard it in the commanding tone of his voice.

More pieces of the pie fell into place then, too.

The essence of the Web Gem reeked with too much new power for it to be seepage from the Fairy Realm itself.

"You've got the Web Gem," Adrien said before he could hold the words in. "The Seelies gave it to you."

"Of course I do, you fool," McMasters said. "And I'll have the whole thing soon, too. They showed me how to use this power – my birthright! – and I'm committed to using it to build my baseball empire. I'll be able to break your queen's simple little curse for good, and you and I will make beautiful mountains of cash together."

Adrien ignored the promise of riches, too busy snapping even more pieces into place. "You made that deal with Pattersonville High School so you could manage the link between Unicorn Field and its fairy ring."

McMasters reveled in the moment.

"Well, now that you mention it, that little fairy ring would come along with the package, wouldn't it? Though, I hope I don't need to remind you that it's called 'McMasters Park,' now. Either way, I'll control Emily DeWitt's destiny, too, once she officially becomes a Unicorns player again. Just like the rest."

The fullness of McMasters' plan formed in Adrien's mind. He could see it now. Somehow the Seelies had acquired the Web Gem from the Small Folk and had given it to McMasters. The only reason they would have done that was if they'd gotten the trophy without properly winning it first, which would necessitate finding a hiding spot where the rest of the Fairy Realm wouldn't be able to find it. They wouldn't care about anything on the mortal side of the fairy ring, so they'd give McMasters whatever he wanted for as long as he kept the Web Gem safe.

But they didn't have the whole thing. Emily still had her tiny piece, the shard the Small Folk had broken off and sent across the worlds to thank her. Whatever the Seelies were planning, they needed that piece.

"You're going to force her to give you the shard."

A wall of magic washed over Adrien. He braced against it but couldn't ignore it.

"I need the Unicorns to win big now, you see?" McMasters' smile widened into a Cheshire Cat–like crescent. "Now is the moment to strike, while everyone's all hot and bothered about all the money I've been dropping on these kids. And with you and Emily DeWitt on the team, winning big would be guaranteed."

McMasters shifted his weight forward until he was barely balancing on the edge of the recliner. His voice took on a chanting lilt. "Wouldn't it be great to be able to play ball again? Full bore? Wearing that bright new Ball and Glove Unicorns uniform? Blasting balls out of the park like you were shooting a Gatling gun? That's what you were born to be, Adrien. A star player. That's who you *are*. You're better than all these kids put together. Better than Emily DeWitt. Better than my daughter. Hell. You, Adrien Thorn, are the best baseball player who has ever been on a Unicorns roster, or a Bulldogs roster, for that matter."

He paused for a breath. Then he pulled his phone out of his breast pocket.

"All I need is to have you sign this little contract, and we'll be cooking with nitroglycerin."

He placed the phone between them on the coffee table. The screen glowed like pixie light.

Adrien couldn't stop his heart from thundering in his chest.

It was as if Mr. McMasters had ripped open his soul and seen the depths of reality inside him. He wanted to play baseball more than anything. He wanted to breathe in that thing he and Emily DeWitt called the baseball magic. He wanted to feel the weight of a swinging bat and hear the grunt of effort disappear into the crack of a baseball on a bat.

He gazed — slack-jawed — into Mr. McMasters' eyes and saw everything he wanted written inside them.

That dream felt so close he could taste it.

A sparkle flickered on the edge of his vision, and he flinched.

No!

It was a lie. He felt that in the flow around him.

All those desires. They were simply waves of fairy magic telling him things the magic needed him to hear.

All that baseball could bring him now was the memory of the Unseelie Queen's cackling laugh and the bitterness of being a slave to that magic.

He drew a cleansing breath, and as he wrenched his mind free of the illusions, the small sounds of the house and the lilting warble of Sydney's voice as he and Uncle Gary played catch outside seeped back into existence.

"No." Adrien's eyes narrowed as he spoke. "I don't want to play anymore. I know the difference between a true desire and one brought on by the hollowness of magic. I'm done with baseball. And if I ever did play again, it sure as hell wouldn't be for you."

"I'm disappointed to hear you say that, Adrien," McMasters said, sitting back with a resigned expression. "Not that it puts that much of a dent in my plans. Every good businessman has a backup."

He left the phone on the coffee table between them, glancing at the time.

"I'd bet your Unseelie Queen would love to have another mortal tied to her. I'll have a whole dugout full of bright-eyed kids on my roster. I wonder what she'd give for one of them?"

Adrien's heart pounded. *Benji.*

"You wouldn't."

"It's just business, Adrien. You know that now, don't you?"

Adrien stared at McMasters. The choice pulsed in his temple, growing clearer and harsher with every breath. Sign the deal, and lock both him and Emily — not to mention the rest of the Unicorns — into arrangements to play baseball for McMasters, or don't sign the deal and let McMasters use the power of the full Web Gem to hand any number of the kids who made the team to the Unseelie Queen.

He was a loser either way.

McMasters' smile grew even oilier than before. "So, what do you say, Mr. Thorn? Do we have a deal?"

Adrien's glance ping-ponged between McMasters and the glowing face of the phone. The clock in the upper corner of the screen read 4:19. Eleven minutes until tryouts started.

As he watched, the clock ticked off another minute.

And, in the face of the oncoming deadline, a third option opened itself in his mind.

He could keep McMasters from getting the shard and take himself neatly out of reach. It would be easy. It wouldn't stop McMasters entirely, but it would buy Emily time. Time she could use to stop him for good.

Ten minutes. A sharp blast of adrenaline flooded through him. A powerful force welled up.

His heart lurched. The curse writhed.

Fairy magic, Adrien knew. Pure fairy magic.

Adrien launched himself from the sofa and, in a rush, ran for Unicorn Field.

CHAPTER
TWENTY-ONE

The screen door slammed shut behind him.

Sydney yelled something, but Adrien didn't hear it. The squirt's voice wasn't sharp enough to overcome the sound of the rage building inside him.

He knew what he had to do. Stop her from trying out, keep her off the team, save her from the clutching grasp of Fred McMasters. Simple.

But there was no time.

So Adrien ran.

Hard.

He was already a fast guy, and playing basketball all winter had kept him in good condition. His chest pumped. His arms and legs churned in rhythm as his stride ate up the sidewalk.

Somewhere, he heard distant drumming and the melody of a flute. He'd missed those parts of the Fairy Realm, the beautiful parts that made it alluring despite its deadly danger. He hoped they'd be a balm to him once again.

He crossed Valiant Street and made his way over Turner Boulevard, settling from his sprint into a distance pace.

He let the ephemeral music carry him forward, remembering the smells of the woods that had been so prevalent in the Fairy Realm. But the music inevitably twisted into the panting and yipping of the Wild Hunt as they raced for blood, and the rasp of the breeze through the bare branches of the trees became the haggard whispers of the Hag Sisters of the Wood. He tried to bend his thoughts towards the good things in the Realm, the Small Folk, the way the light of a pixie could transform a glade draped in midnight into someplace warm and inviting. But then the image of the Unseelie Queen would break in, or of the Seelie King — who was as unbending and as brutal in his pursuit of power as the next Fairy leader.

Emily had the shard of the Web Gem.

And now the Fairy Realm was looking for it.

The blocky, yellow brick outline of the school loomed ahead, and the urge to check his phone clock tugged at him.

But even a second's hesitation could mean the end of Emily's freedom.

He ran harder, his blood pumping.

Unicorn Field was in the back of the school grounds.

Grass whipped against his sneakers as he cut through campus. He shouldered around the corner like one of the downhill skiers he and Emily had watched during the Olympics earlier this winter.

There. Ahead.

The light stands around Unicorn Field loomed above the field like skeletal vultures.

Voices rose in an unsteady roar of mingled sports chants and fey songs.

The fairy ring sang in a tone too low for mere mortals to hear. But Adrien felt it.

Coach Amabe stood in the dugout wearing his new golden Ball and Glove Unicorns hat with its McMasters logo stitched into the side. Kids scattered across the field.

And Emily DeWitt?

There she was. Bat in hand. Stepping out of the dugout with her helmet on and her dark #11 bold against her old Unicorn uniform.

Adrien's lungs nearly seized.

"Emily!" he yelled, but his voice was winded, and Emily didn't react.

He put on a burst of speed and crashed through a group of spectators who had come to see the next State Champions begin their quest.

People scattered like bowling pins, Mr. DeWitt being one of them, yelling at him as they hit the ground.

Adrien didn't take the time to apologize.

He focused on Emily as she stepped up to the plate.

"Slow down there, Thorn!" Coach Amabe yelled.

Without thinking, Adrien grabbed one of the bats leaning against the chain link fence. He felt the smooth surface of the wood in his hands as, still running, he clutched it with practiced ease.

His muscles sang with recognition of the grip. His heart soared with anticipation of the pitch.

Emily had entered the batter's box. The pitcher was preparing to wind up.

Power rose around him. The fresh smell of the forest wafted in the ether.

He didn't want to hurt Emily, but there was no time to be gentle. The pitcher had already thrown.

She turned to him, confusion crossing her lightly freckled cheeks. But she had no time to do anything before Adrien crashed into her. She grunted as she tumbled into the dirt. And, as Emily fell, Adrien's instincts kicked into the highest gear.

He couldn't stop himself.

The ball was already in flight, spinning through the air.

He stepped into her place in the batter's box.

He could make out every detail: The logo, rotating, the seams spinning red threads as the fastball came in.

His swing was smooth and clean, full of the simple grace of pure talent honed by a hundred years of practice. The bat flashed through the strike zone, impacting the ball with the purest of sounds known to the game.

Thunder crackled on the horizon. Lightning flashed.

The ball rose like a rocket under full power, and Adrien nearly cried to watch the brilliant white sphere arc through the springtime sky before disappearing into the wooded park well beyond the fence.

His heart pounded with an essence of light and beauty.

There would be time to hate the Unseelie Queen later, but for now, Adrien Thorn basked in the simple glory of what it meant to be able to play a game at the peak of his ability.

He turned to Emily, wanting to help her up.

"Adrien? What are you – Are you okay?" she said.

"I'm fine," he replied.

He wasn't fine, though.

His legs buckled.

He pressed the bat to the ground, trying to stay upright, but he had no strength. His fingers went numb, then his hands and arms. He slumped so hard against the bat that he figured he'd be bruised for days.

His vision warped as a hurricane force crashed in on him.

The world twisted around him, and it was as if time itself had caught up with him.

He felt the familiar power that had controlled him for a hundred years taking hold once again.

He fell.

Flat on his back, Emily DeWitt's concerned gaze floated overhead.

"Adrien? Adrien, what are you doing? Adrien!" Emily called, shaking him, putting her arm around his shoulders, and trying to lift him. "Adrien!"

Then came Benji Amberman's face, Coach Amabe's, and others.

"Give him air," the coach yelled, holding back the mob.

But Adrien was already so far distant from the surge of onlookers.

He could barely feel the dirt below, or Emily's arms as they tried to hold him in this world.

"Emily," he said. "Emily."

"I'm here, Adrien."

"Callie's dad has the Web Gem," he whispered.

"What?"

"*Don't become a Unicorn.*"

"Adrien!"

But Adrien couldn't hear her over the Unseelie Queen's soft, satisfied snicker.

The wind of the world roared in his ears.

Then everything went black.

HIT AND RUN

TWENTY-TWO

McMasters burst into the front office waiting area.

"Well, hi there, Fred!" Carol, Fred McMasters' office manager, said. "I thought you were going to the baseball field?"

"Did that," McMasters said, pushing the door to his private office open, then letting it slam shut behind him.

She had been pouring water on the bristly green plant that sat on the wide coffee table for guests to look at while they chilled their heels. The clock said it was past the time she was due to leave for the day — though McMasters knew Carol tended to put time in off the clock so she could stay ahead of the game. Usually, that was more than fine. Now, though, he just wanted to be alone.

He was panting now. Angry and wheezing from his exertion as well as from lacking anything resembling a plan.

The air conditioning was going full force.

He wrenched the thermostat down.

Damned system. Chilling in the winter, heating all summer. Cost him a fortune.

"Damnit," he whispered to himself. "Can nothing just *work* anymore?"

A big breath calmed him to the point where at least his distraught thoughts weren't ping-ponging off each other. He'd tried to play the game nicely, hadn't he? Tried to buy off the DeWitt girl. Tried to find the missing bit of the Web Gem by slipping into her room so no one would get hurt. He'd even tried then to get the old-time teenager to play ball.

But nothing doing.

He stepped to his desk and took his chair, swiveling it to face the lead-lined safe that lay behind the full-sized painting of himself.

Blood drummed at his manic temples. His fingers itched with anticipation.

From inside that safe the presence of the Web Gem pulsed, and the quicksilver electric taste of lightning coated his mouth. Every hair on his arms rose. He'd used the artifact several times now, just like the Duke of the Silver Forest had said he should. Always just before going to make his business deals. Always just before expanding his circle of power around the city of Pattersonville. The Web Gem pulled at him. Reminded him of the duke's steely gaze as they made their pact. Reminded him of the Seelie heritage born in his blood.

He had promised the Seelie lord he would keep the Web Gem safe — just as he'd promised, too, to gain the last piece of the trophy so that it could regain its full powers. But his feeling now was bigger than any simple commitment. He'd tasted what it was like to have the Web Gem on his side. He wasn't going to lose it now.

He had tried it the easy way, but Emily DeWitt and Adrien Thorn had kept that shard from him anyway. Now the Thorn boy had gone and done something so preposterous it had nearly given McMasters a heart attack.

He'd triggered his own damned curse.

Seemed a hell of a step to take just to keep himself out of McMasters' reach. And somehow, in getting himself ripped back to the

Unseelie Queen's side, the kid had convinced the DeWitt girl not to join the Unicorns.

McMasters had to take a moment to forcibly relax his fingers from their white-knuckle grip on the arms of his chair.

As his thoughts calmed, resolve settled.

It was time to get serious.

A shadowed movement against the frosted glass of his door drew a flicker of ire.

Carol, he saw, standing tentatively at the door as if pondering if she should check in on him.

"Have a good night, Carol," he said too quickly.

Even given the anxiety that rose at the idea of Carol catching him meddling with the Web Gem, he thought it might be fun to have a fling with her. His gaze narrowed at the gauzy shape of her figure on the glass. She was attractive enough to gain his attention, which he admitted to himself was the reason he'd hired her in the first place. But, like every other time the daydream flashed through his mind, he knew somewhere deep that the only thing that would come from making an advance was that he'd lose her. Carol Demeter was a top-notch worker. He'd be lost without her. And the truth was that mostly she laughed at him for his exploits outside the office. Carol had turned out to be as good at her job as she was precisely because he couldn't bullshit her.

The shadow of her hand pressed against the frosted glass for an instant, but instead of cracking open the door, she stepped back.

"Thanks, Fred. You have a good night, too."

Then she was gone and McMasters was alone in the office area, feeling once again the pounding of the Web Gem at his temples. At least the Thorn boy's disappearance cleaned things up by leaving him only a single target. Emily DeWitt.

He clenched his jaw.

The chair gave a soft squeal as he rolled it to the wall.

A firm pull levered the picture frame around to reveal the safe.

Entering the lock code made the door pop open with the mechanical precision he'd come to admire from it.

Top dollar.

Worth every penny.

In the dark chasm of the safe, the amazing presence of the Web Gem pulsed with kaleidoscopic colors. His fingers burned with cool power as he hefted the trophy, and he nearly wept at the gaping hole where the shard belonged. The low throb of something that might have been a wolf's growl rose in the back of his mind. Smokey tendrils of magic drifted around him. Heat from the trophy warmed his cheekbones.

He turned and placed the gleaming artifact from the Fairy Realm squarely on his desktop, then bent to stare into its crystals. There, focusing on his daughter, Callie, he saw what he knew he'd see, what the Duke of the Silver Forest had told him he could see if only he'd wanted to.

Callie was with the Wild Hunt, the duke had said with a *tsk*ing shake of his head — had signed her life away to play a frivolous game when she could have done so much more.

But the Hunt had its values.

McMasters knew that even before the duke's half-hearted training.

Fred McMasters had been a boy at one time, and as a boy, he'd loved the darker tales of the fey. The tricky nature of fairy magic and the fluid way rules worked in the realms he'd read about gave him heady dreams. Those dreams had dulled as he'd moved into adulthood, but never completely left him alone.

Now, the image of his daughter in the Fairy Realm filled his mind.

The smell of the Hunt wafted over him. The braying sounds of their hunger echoed in his mind.

Emily DeWitt was alone now. He had his prey in his grasp.

Reaching into the Web Gem as the duke had taught him was easy. Molding the bloodhound essence of the Wild Hunt was harder, but the presence of his daughter among that slavering horde gave him a pathway in. Using that line — that connection to his own bloodline — he pulled hard on the power of the Hunt.

"Tie me to Emily DeWitt," he whispered, feeling lighter now, as if he was floating in the wafting coils of the magic that emanated from the Web Gem. His voice gained power. "Make it such that she can never be out of my sight."

The Web Gem pulsed.

Light flashed in McMasters' eyes. Muscles clenched. His throat caught with power.

Then, finally, a most delicious essence washed through him.

There she was, in his thoughts.

Walking home from tryouts, the scent of misery and fear rolling off her in curls. Someone else was with her, one of the other Unicorns kids, he supposed, offering comfort, or begging her to come back to the field. McMasters didn't care either way. He had no interest in any of those kids.

He only cared about Emily DeWitt.

Slowly, then all at once, the image of her faded from his mind. When the magic receded fully, Fred McMasters caught his breath, then put the Web Gem back into the safe. It wouldn't do to be careless with it now, he thought, as he straightened his jacket and ran a hand through hair that had gone disheveled.

He sat in his chair then, just breathing, fingers lightly grasping the chair's armrests, and closed his eyes.

There she was, still, as visible to him as if he stood on the street she was hurrying along. Her scent floated through his memory, making his nostrils twitch.

He smiled, feeling the points of his canines brush his lips with wolf-like sharpness.

"You can run, Emily DeWitt," he said to the walls. "But you cannot hide."

TWENTY-THREE

E merging from the dark tangle of the curse's grasp, Adrien fell
to the stone floor.

His cheek pressed against the dark flagstone.

His muscles burned with invisible flames. His breath came in
gasps.

Swallowing against his panic, he forced himself to open his eyes.

Around him, the familiar shadowed depths of the queen's private
meeting hall coalesced. Cold, just as he recalled it. At five points
around the chamber, fairy lamps gleamed with fresh power —
dimly, though, always dimly. The scent was the exact tinge of
lavender the queen was fond of, and that always reminded him of
the rosin bags that were stored in a nook of the dugout at Unseelie
Pitch.

He raised himself to his hands and knees, and then up to fully
kneeling.

Desperation came over him at that moment, as the hard stone bit
into his knee.

He was dressed, once again, in his Unseelie Court uniform, its
retro style a throwback to Olden Times, which, too, was embedded in

the nature of his curse. While others on the Unseelie Queen's team updated their apparel as time progressed, the Designated Hitter wore the fashion of his arrival. Hence, the uniform was baggy, and its colors muted. Its pinstripes were brown and blue rather than the black of his more modern-day teammates.

The number thirteen was stitched onto his vest.

"My Queen," he said meekly as his senses returned fully. He hadn't meant to say it. He'd rather scream until his throat tore. He hadn't had a choice, though. He'd known that from the moment he'd first grabbed the bat.

"My Designated Hitter," she said, cackling with delight. "I knew you wouldn't be long."

He raised his head to find the Unseelie Queen standing on her dais. Around her, silver and gold flashes of raw baseball magic danced and dipped, the cloud of it pulsing as if it was filled with thunder and summer rain. Waves of its pressure buffeted Adrien with such strength he put a hand up to shield his eyes.

"Did you enjoy your little fancy, Adrien Thorn?" she continued, using her tone of superiority as a cudgel, and his true name as a stiletto that let him know the extent to which she commanded him.

"My fancy?"

She leveled gleaming black eyes on him.

"It was fanciful for you to think you could have gone forever without playing. You are too weak, and baseball is in your blood."

Rage and shame swirled through Adrien's heart. He'd tried so hard to do something different with his life, to be something different than what she'd twisted him to be. And yet, despite every-thing, here he was. Did it make a difference that he'd had no other way to keep Emily out of McMasters' grip?

He wasn't certain it did.

And he couldn't deny how good the baseball bat had felt in his hands.

"I cannot fight that truth," he said. Then he looked up at her and clenched his jaw. "But I can fight you."

With a herculean effort, he rose until he stood on both feet before her.

The queen watched him with narrowed eyes. Then, she spoke the words of her arcane magic, and the cloud of baseball magic gave a new pulse.

Wind swirled. A howl rose like a troupe of banshees. Adrien's hair whipped over his forehead. His body ached like a rock troll was trying to pin him.

Adrien fought the elemental magic, gritting his teeth and grimacing into the gale, but it was no use. The wind buffeted him, staggering him backward step by step until he struck the hard black stone of the far wall, and pain exploded at the back of his skull, his shoulders, and his tailbone.

There he stayed, splayed defenselessly against the wall, fighting until he could fight no more.

The storm died to a whisper then, and Adrien crumpled to the floor.

"You will kneel to me, Adrien Thorn."

He struggled to a standing position, wavering in his fatigue, but still, standing. "I will not," he replied.

The queen's fingers twitched, and the baseball magic crackled in her hand again.

As before, the wind rose.

With one arm shielding his face, Adrien tasted infield dirt in the whipping currents. The crying groans of spectators gathered from across a century of games wove through the maelstrom like forlorn wraiths. Wraiths who, like him, couldn't leave the ballpark no matter how they tried. Wraiths who had become nothing more than the spirits of baseball itself, bent now to the will of the strongest player in the Realm.

Their buffeting pressed him down, toward the floor.

The Unseelie Queen's voice echoed with vivid delight.

"I said you will kneel to your queen."

An understanding dawned inside him.

Fairy Realm history said that baseball magic had overwritten the innate magic of the Fairy Realm, that the Web Gem had birthed baseball magic, and that this new form of power was stronger and more formidable than the raw essence of the Fairy Realm's magic. But the wrongness of this story was strong enough to have come from the pages of the *Unicorn Weekly Gazette*. There was no "baseball magic" or "fairy magic." There was only magic, much of it fueled by poor mortals like himself who got themselves tangled up in fairy bewitchery.

But now the Web Gem was gone from the Fairy Realm, placed instead with Mr. McMasters in the mortal world. Without the Web Gem to manage the flow and direct it through the channels of baseball, the world had once again gone to chaos.

The fairy lords were free to gather every element of power as they could. They were free to lie, cheat, or steal — and when they did so, they could use those ill-gotten powers however they wanted.

Magic, Adrien realized, was like money in the mortal world.

The currency of the land.

Like his father had said back in the day, the price of poker had just gone up.

And now the Unseelie Queen, surrounded by a massive cloud of this magic, stood before him in her most stately grace, her eyes hooded, and her head tilted back in bloated satisfaction.

She was in control.

The sight chilled him far more than the wailing wind she'd called up. The all-encompassing certainty of her power cut him right to the bone. Try as he might to fight her, he'd accomplish nothing but to exhaust himself.

He bit his cheeks against indignity until he tasted copper, but having no other choice, he finally allowed the wind to force him back down to one knee.

"What is your command, my Lady?" Adrien said, bowing his head.

Instantly, the wind evaporated. In its absence, the meeting hall rang with a throbbing silence.

The queen's smile was predatory. She plucked a phantom baseball from midair and tossed it lightly to Adrien.

"Your first task, my Designated Hitter, is to round up the remains of the Small Folk baseball club and command them to Unseelie Pitch."

"What for, my Lady?" He turned the ball in his hand. It was pure and white on the outside, but from inside he felt its poisoned magic seeping through the red seams.

He loathed the way his heart yearned to hit a pitch thrown with this ball.

"For their freedom," the queen said with such deadness that the hairs on the back of Adrien's neck rose. "It is time they learned a lesson about their place, don't you think?"

Dread and loathing swept over him as forcefully as the magical winds had done. Her intent shone clear in her eyes.

Without Emily DeWitt or the Web Gem, the Small Folk stood no chance to beat the Unseelie Court. The queen was going to use a game against them as a form of blood sacrifice to generate more magic for herself. Then she'd use that power to ensure the Small Folk would be enslaved to her for eternity.

And with her Designated Hitter returned to her, each game she forced her victims to play would be a bloodbath.

I won't do it, he told himself. *I won't be her instrument.*

But he'd given in to her demand to kneel. His body was not his to command.

Such was his bond. Such was the magic of the Fairy Realm.

He bowed low, a sweeping gesture that would have fit perfectly into a performance of any of Shakespeare's plays. Mrs. Rodriguez would have been delighted. Adrien would have wept if he could.

"It will be done, my Queen."

"Go," she said, dismissing him with a wave of her long-nailed fingers. "Let me know when the tilt is scheduled."

With that, Adrien turned to leave the meeting hall, stealing away like a runner edging off first base and eyeing second, dreading the long walk through the familiar, darkly shadowed halls of her ancient home.

A rattling *whump* in the distance made him draw up short.

An explosion, Adrien thought. An explosion that vibrated the floor at the same time as it sounded.

The queen's expression darkened, and her cloud of magic faded for an instant before she reacted.

Voices rose beyond the meeting hall's door.

Then, before Adrien could move, the door burst open in a flare of silvery white light.

Seelies!

SEELIES AND UNSEELIES, already locked in combat, slashing with claws, and bashing with club-like bats, biting, and tearing, and casting spells wrapped around baseballs in a cacophony of fury.

Behind him, the queen gave a hiss of fury. On instinct, Adrien sank into a crouch, hands hovering at his sides in readiness for a fight.

They poured through the door and filled the meeting hall in the space of a single fastball.

Adrien grabbed the bat away from one attacker, and with an instinctive pirouette and an elegant swing, crashed it first against that attacker's knees, and then into a second Seelie Court barbarian's arm.

The Unseelie Queen wasn't one to keep out of the game, though, nor would she command her troops from a place of safety. She had already joined the fray, and her spellcasting burned with the sharp scents of wood and fire.

The Seelie Court marauders brought their mages, too, however, and despite the cloud of baseball magic at the queen's command,

Adrien could tell that their triangulated power would soon overwhelm her. She knew it too. Adrien saw that in her posture. He heard it in her spell song, which had turned toward dirge.

Even as Adrien fought on, the Seelies were quickly dispatching the Unseelie fighters. They fought with a fierceness Adrien had never seen before in all their skirmishes over the century of his service to the queen, as if some great cause drove their attack this time. Blood as black as pitch coated the floor, the walls, and the pure white armor of the Seelies as they cut their way toward the queen.

"Kill the queen!" one Seelie Courter yelled, brandishing his bat like a battle standard. "Seize the baseball magic! For the glory of the Seelie Court!"

The queen cried out. Desperation stained her voice.

Magic flared.

Thunder roared.

Like a whirling cyclone, Adrien fought to protect his liege — to protect the baseball magic. He rode a flare of power. He couldn't tell anymore whether the queen was willing his actions, or if he was acting on reflex. But he knew he couldn't let the Seelies — just as dangerous as the Unseelies, only more particular about how they worked their evil — have the power contained in that still-pulsing cloud.

A spell song of his own spun up in his head.

Take me out to the ball game! he sang.

Take me out with the crowd! He batted another Seelie attacker unconscious, then pulverized a second's knee.

Buy me some peanuts and Cracker Jack! He disarmed a mage who had been readying a killing bolt, then destroyed the crossbow that had been targeted point blank at the queen's chest.

I don't care if I never get back! An extra flip of the bat crunched the attacker's jaw and dropped him cold.

And, for the eternal moment of bloodshed and battle, he truly didn't care.

The Real World and all its modern frustrations were but a dream, distant and fading.

Via his queen or not, the baseball magic was here, immediate, and pulsing through him in ways that theater and grounds work never had.

And then, suddenly, violently, it wasn't.

He staggered.

Gasping, he fell to the hard stone.

His lungs collapsed.

The baseball magic! Where had it gone?

He groped blindly for it, and nearly got his head bashed in by a Seelie Courter's bat.

He dropped to the floor in time to avoid the swing. Black blood from a puddle slicked his hands.

A rough hand clamped on the back of his collar.

"To the victor go the spoils," said the Seelie Courter gleefully in his ear.

Adrien jammed his elbow up and back, catching the Seelie in the ribs. As the Seelie coughed and staggered, Adrien swept up his bat and spun around to bring it down on the Seelie's head.

The Seelie crumpled to the floor, dead.

Breathing harshly and tasting grime and the sweat of his exertion, Adrien regripped his weapon. He whipped around, searching.

The only Seelies he found were the — *very* few — dead and wounded ones.

The queen, bloodied and lying prone on the dais, glanced up at him. Her usually composed self-assurance was as demolished as the furnishing of her once-stately room. Her gaze was now glassy in the way only a first taste of mortality could achieve.

Still, she was alive. There was, at least, that much.

But the cloud of baseball magic that had been feeding her was gone.

The Seelie Court had taken it.

CHAPTER
TWENTY-FOUR

"*You're a winner, Callie McMasters.*"

If she'd heard it once she'd heard it a million times.

Every day. Multiple times each. In the morning at breakfast. On the way to school as Dad dropped her off. Weekends on a "lunch date" that always happened to include a trip to the store to *just take care of one thing*, and then led to a three-hour stop. She heard it on her birthday and on the day her dad *celebrated* to denote the anniversary of her mom leaving him.

"*You're a winner, Callie McMasters. Not like your deadbeat mother.*"

Everything about her dad — even his push to keep custody of his daughter — was formed by the idea of winning over everything else.

Winning was everything she'd known.

Which meant Callie had never felt this kind of defeat.

Each day she would go out to the Other Field and sit silently, taking in the rows of stone statues. Sometimes she'd caress her bat with an absent-minded touch, listening to its aggravated whispers and feeling it seethe. The bat's vengeful surges of ancient power gave her what little comfort she could scrounge these days.

But the bat's power couldn't do anything about putting the statues to right, and neither could Callie.

Sitting at the Other Field helped in a torturous kind of way, but it was thin gruel. Inevitably, she finished her daily pilgrimage to the Field of Statues by standing before the frozen countenance of Trace, the centaur caught in mid-stride, carrying Maddoc on his back — the faun's face pulled back in a distraught grimace as he held his Small Folk hat on his head.

She missed them both.

Most days she found others had come here, too. Shayla would sometimes kneel at Twy's stony feet, sniffling as she pressed her clenched fists into the dirt. The trio of Hag Sisters who'd first come to play in the rebel games came each time the moon was "in a good phase," forming a triangle around their coven mother, each time chanting new ineffective spells.

Most heart-wrenching was Essie, who climbed the stilled statue of Greeven, the elf, every single day. She refused everyone's help in her endeavor, and, once she reached his shoulder, proceeded to press her face against his granite neck and sob her tiny heart out.

The loss was deafening.

So many of her friends.

Callie had never had friends before. Only teammates and rivals. Emily DeWitt had loomed monolithic in her life, the one to beat, the one to push all her aggression towards.

Then she'd met Emily for real. And the rest of the Unicorns.

Then the people here in the Fairy Realm. The Small Folk and the River Kin. Even the Hunt, her own team, while abrasive, could be good friends. Callie had grown up around abrasive people. She could handle herself around them.

But now, staring at Trace again, putting her hand on the stone of his bare chest and letting the sun's heat radiate from his firm surface into her bones, she could almost feel him breathing.

For the first time in her life, Callie realized she didn't care about winning and losing.

For the first time, Callie missed someone with such intensity that she found it almost impossible to sleep at night.

She gripped the bat handle tightly as the barrel levered over her shoulder.

Its energy filled her.

We will claim our vengeance, it told her, its voice the rasp of freshly cut lumber.

How? Callie shot back. Her mental voice burned with raw bitterness at how powerless she felt.

No one was playing baseball now. Not even for the pure joy of it. The Unseelie Queen's play to steal all their baseball magic had broken the games up.

"Why play if we're just going to make the queen stronger?" Fennoc said.

And the rest agreed, even Izusa, the irrepressible pixie, and Shady Marie, the dryad who lived for moments when she could leave her tree and play ball.

Over the passing days, though, the bat's whispers emboldened her. She knew they had to push back against the despair that choked them, had to act to fix this awful situation. If the whole of the Fairy Realm didn't come together to fight back, the queen would simply ride roughshod over them all.

It was up to her now.

She had to get a game going. She knew that.

She just didn't know how to get it to happen.

How could she when her own heart wanted to wail just as loudly as little Essie?

"I'm going to get you back," she whispered to Trace, standing there in the open afternoon sky. "I promise you, Trace. I'm going to get you back if it's the last thing I do."

When she walked away, the same wind that dried the tear from her cheek ruffled the petals of the tiny white flower she'd tucked behind his stony ear.

"I'M GOING to the Unseelie Court," Callie said to the leader of the Wild Hunt.

It was mid-morning, and he was lying on an expansive, flat rock that jutted out over the cold-running stream below, sunning himself and catching a few brief winks of sleep. The Hunt last night had been a long run, and a hard one, too. Yet, as unfulfilling as all the rest.

Callie didn't think the leader was providing his riders with real targets anymore. By now he had to know they weren't going to find the Web Gem, but the Hunt was the only thing her teammates knew, and when all you've got is a hammer you imagine a lot of nails. The question she'd been fighting was why the leader was imagining them. Was he truly deluded, or was he simply at a loss for what else to tell his constituency? The thought made her veins burn, and the bat she now wore slung across her back fed that feeling.

"We think that is unwise, Mistress Cal." He yawned, then shifted so he was flat on his stomach.

"*I* can't sit here anymore and do nothing," she continued. "Not when my friends are sitting in the Field of Statues like a collection of Michelangelo's discarded still life projects."

"Michael who?"

Callie ignored him. "I want your help."

"It was bad business to confront the queen even before. But now that she has all our baseball magic, it's closer to suicide. We do not think you're going to get any takers."

"I'm asking *you*," Callie said.

A Red Cap, fishing knee-deep in the shallows, snickered as he concentrated on a dark shape just under the stream's surface. "You won't make it a quarter step into Unseelie land if the queen doesn't want you there. Not even with the leader's help." His hand shot out, and a moment later a pair of silver-scaled fish landed on the stream bank. "Dinner!" the Red Cap called as he danced back up the streambed.

"I'll make it there," Callie muttered.

"No, you will not," the leader said. He rolled to his side. The sun illuminated the matt of dark hair that grew on his chest, and his sharp eyes pierced her. "And you get no points for false bravado here, Mistress Cal of the Wild Hunt. You have not seen this land for the harsh terror it can be. The queen is no longer fettered by the Web Gem. We cannot predict what she will do. But if you persist and press forward with your single-hearted attempt to destroy your mortal soul, we're afraid we can't stop you."

"You know what I think?" Callie snapped. She stepped onto the leader's rock, letting the toes of her cleats brush up against his side as if she meant to nudge him into the water. "I think you got a taste of that world of war and bloodshed you say you want so badly, and you realized you couldn't handle it. It sucks when it's your folks who are doing all the dying, doesn't it?"

In a flash, the Hunt leader was on his feet, snarling in her face. Saliva dripped from his bared teeth to splatter on Callie's shirt.

"You dare to insult my courage, mortal?" he spat.

Callie wasn't cowed. Jaw forward, she braced herself. "Yes. I do so freaking dare. I know what you're doing here, lounging by the riverside every day, and running yourself in circles every night. You're *sulking* because you lost. You lost at the only thing you really care about, and you don't know what you're going to do when the rest of the Hunt realizes it."

Silence had fallen over the riverside, only the chattering of the water droning on. The Hunt leader's snarl deepened. He was flexing his hands, and Callie noticed his fingers had sprouted talons.

"You want to die so badly, mortal?" he finally said in a deadly soft voice. "I can do the job for you. No need to travel so far as the Unseelie Court."

Callie, bolstered by the pulsing of the bat against her spine, laughed. "I'm going, whether I get you to accompany me or someone else. And I have no intention of dying."

"No one will accompany you, you fool. I told you, what you propose is a suicide mission."

"I'll go with you," a tiny voice said.

"Essie?" Callie made a quarter turn to see the brownie clinging to the stem of a thick water reed as it bent and rotated under her weight. She had been climbing, Callie assumed, so she could gain both height and visibility in their conversation.

Callie reached her hand down and lifted the brownie to her shoulder.

The Hunt leader snapped his jaws. "What are you doing here, little crawler?"

Essie turned a furious scowl on him. "I came here to see what plans you Hunters were cooking up to help our friends. I'll do anything to help my poor Greeven, even go on missions you big folk are too cowardly to try."

Callie smirked at the gob-smacked expression on the leader's face. "Thank you, Essie. I'm sure you will be a great help."

"I'll be better than a help. I know how to sneak you in," Essie squeaked.

"You do?" Callie stopped, remembering. "Oh, right. You were the one who made it possible for the Small Folk to call Miss Em in the first place."

Essie nearly glowed in pride.

"There's a little hole in the barrier," she said, holding her hands one of her shoulder widths apart. "It'd be a tight fit for you, but I can squeeze through fine. Then I can open a bigger door from the inside."

Callie nodded, letting her hand drift up to the handle of the bat over her other shoulder. As her fingertips brushed the smooth-polished wood, a hum of anticipation built along its length. It wanted to taste the queen's blood again.

"All I need is a way to talk to the queen, then," Callie said.

Rustling footsteps came from the glade behind her.

Before she could turn to face them, the leader's expression

turned from surprise to bewilderment to fear. He sprang to a defensive pose, back arched and hands forward to attack.

"Ask and ye shall receive," he said in a dark tone.

Callie's heart flooded with adrenaline. She didn't have to turn around to know what she'd find behind her. And sure enough, when she did turn around, the Unseelie Queen was there.

What surprised Callie, however, was the way her enemy lay draped over Adrien Thorn's shoulders.

He was dressed again in Unseelie colors.

Callie gaped at him, not knowing if she ought to exclaim at his predicament or scream at him for turning traitor.

The two came to a halt at the tree line.

"My queen seeks an audience," Adrien said, shrugging awkwardly against the weight of the queen. He sounded exhausted, but he met Callie's eye with no trace of guilt. "I am hers to command, whether I will it or not," he explained.

The Unseelie Queen lifted her head from where it lay against her Designated Hitter's shoulder. "I'm here ... to parlay," she said, breathing hard with the effort.

She looked sick. Her skin was pallid. Her cheekbones were gaunt to the point of making her seem hollow. Her fingers were reed-thin now. Her arms, lithe to begin with, looked as brittle as glass. Callie remembered what it had felt like to bash the woman with her baseball bat. She heard the bone break in her memory. Baseball magic had healed the queen in the moment, but maybe the healing hadn't stuck. Maybe that's why she was here? Maybe the wound Callie had inflicted had drained her so far, she couldn't operate.

Score one for Callie's bat. It buzzed against her back now with a thirsty energy that she had to fight to keep from letting it pummel the queen to finish the job.

Not yet, she told it, feeling pleased seeing the Unseelie Queen shy away, regardless.

"Parlay?" she said. "After what you've done you expect us to *negotiate* anything?"

"We have mutual interests."

"Yeah, right," Callie said, drawing the bat forward. "We'll talk after you un-stone all our friends."

"I — can't," the queen replied, grimacing as if the word were a razor blade. "I couldn't even if I wanted to," the queen replied.

Callie steadied little Essie as the brownie tried to lunge for the queen. "What do you mean? You had an easy enough time doing it in the first place."

"The Seelie Court made an unprovoked attack," Adrien said. "They stole all the magic my queen had gathered."

"The magic *she* gathered?" Essie screeched. "Isn't that just like her? The high-and-mighty lady! Let the Small Folk do all the work, then claim the spoils for herself! And turning my Greeven to granite, to boot!"

Callie shushed the brownie, though she fully agreed with everything Essie said.

The Hunt leader turned to face the queen. "You mean they did to you what you did to us?"

The queen shifted her gaze away, hatred burning like coals in her eyes. "Yes."

"And that should matter to us because?"

Adrien replied. "Because I think the Seelies know where the Web Gem is. And worse" — his eyes searched out Callie's gaze — "I think they are hunting for Miss Em."

Slowly, Callie let her eyes close.

It was too much. Everything.

No baseball season, her friends turned to stone, and now Adrien Thorn, back with the Unseelie Queen and reporting that Emily DeWitt was in the crosshairs of yet another dangerous bunch of fairies.

Everything was going to hell.

But Callie McMasters was no quitter.

"So," she said, her hands tightening around her bat. "What are we gonna do about it? Muster a militia and storm the Seelie palace?"

Her bat pulsed in eagerness.

The queen spread her lips to show her teeth in a mirthless grin. "Yes. It will take all our powers together, but with all the Realm under my command—"

"Under *your* command?" growled the Hunt leader. "As if we could trust you. I will lead the charge on the palace—"

A furious burbling rose from the river, and a moment later, spray erupted like a geyser as Lady Marne emerged from the water. Her scales had crept up to cover her face, looking like a knight's helmet fashioned after an ancient aquatic nightmare. Her sharp teeth and bright scales sparkled in the sunlight.

"No military action is moving forward without my naval expertise," she said, levering her frigid gaze upon the queen. "And I refuse to follow the one who petrified my people and my dearest friends. I can lead the charge through the caverns below the palace."

Callie wiped river water from her face with a grimace. The stuff reeked of rotten vegetation. "That won't do for us land-based troops. We need to hit them hard and fast, and I say—"

"Stop!"

A startled silence fell over the riverside as Adrien dragged the queen forward with him.

"We can't beat the Seelies with brute strength," he said. "I'm sorry to have to point it out, but my queen and her Court were the strongest of the entire Realm. If we couldn't fend off the Seelies when she had the baseball magic you whipped up, then we simply don't stand a chance facing them head-on."

Callie ground her teeth so hard they squeaked. "What do you suggest we do? Roll over and let the Seelies have their way? That's not my style."

Adrien shook his head. "Hardly. I never said we were without an advantage of our own. But we need to move fast."

The queen sneered at him, though the effect was spoiled by her need to be carried over his shoulder. "Tell us this advantage, and I may forget you withheld the information in the first place."

Adrien pressed his lips into a thin line. "I know where the Web Gem is. We simply have to get to it before they do. And," he said, raising his voice above the clamor of his audience, "with the Web Gem back in the hands of its *proper caretakers*, the deterioration the Fairy Realm is dealing with should go back to normal."

The Hunt leader snorted. "Meaning you won't tell us unless we all agree to hand the Web Gem over to the Small Folk."

The queen tittered. "I can make you tell me, my dear."

But Adrien shook his head. "In front of everyone? Then they'll have just as good a chance to get it as you, my queen. And I bet a sack of fairy gold they'll not be inclined to let you or me out of their sight for a private conference now that we've put ourselves into it. I am, after all, the one carrying you now."

The queen scowled and said nothing more.

Callie winced. Adrien was playing with fire, flaunting the queen's orders like that. "I wholeheartedly agree to return the Web Gem to the Small Folk," she said quickly.

Lady Marne surged forward. "I agree as well."

The Hunt leader snarled, then nodded his agreement. "The Web Gem goes to the Small Folk."

Callie watched the Unseelie Queen bite back anger as she made her calculations. The bat squirmed anxiously in her grip. "You said you wanted to parlay. I'd say you'd best get to it."

The queen, seeing herself outnumbered and at a disadvantage, made a noise of disgust. "Very well. I swear on the First Blood, the Web Gem shall go to the Small Folk."

"All right, then," the Hunt leader said. "Where is the Web Gem?"

Adrien cast one last look around the gathering. His gaze ended on Callie.

A split second before he spoke, the wash of tingling numbness that overtook Callie made it impossible to deny what was coming.

"It's with your dad. In the mortal realm."

Her ears rang. Blood pumped through her veins in harsh, hot

bursts. A need to run, to bite, to tear her prey to bits coursed through every fiber of her body.

Her father. Her damned father!

The bat in her hands called her back. *Listen to your teammates,* it said.

She did listen.

"That puts us in exactly the same predicament we were in before," Lady Marne was saying. "Opening the portal in the Other Field requires more baseball magic than we can accumulate in the time we have."

"And that's assuming someone doesn't come and rip it all away before we can use it," said the Hunt leader. He snapped his teeth at the Unseelie Queen.

But the queen did not respond to his goad. Instead, a thoughtful, almost querulous expression worked its way across her pointed face. "In magic," she said. "Like calls to like. Why would such a powerful artifact fall into the hands of a powerless mortal? These things do not simply happen. No, it does not make sense."

Adrien frowned. "I'm not lying. He's got it, no question about that."

The queen's lips quirked in a crafty smile. "Oh, no. You misunderstand, my Designated Hitter. I know you wouldn't dare lie to me. I mean to say this girl's father could not have reached into our Realm and plucked the Web Gem away all by himself. Not even the Small Folk are incompetent enough to let that happen."

"Someone gave it to him," Lady Marne said.

"The Seelies," Callie hissed, recalling her conversation with the Duke of the Silver Forest. Her skin crawled. The Seelies, like her dad, loved coloring up to the lines and beyond where they could, thumbing their noses at the people who tried to call foul on them. She could see her dad making a slick deal with the jerks.

The queen smiled in earnest, even holding some of her own weight in her wicked delight. "And now, I must ask myself, why would the Seelies do that? Why give it to a nobody human with no magic to speak of? Unless…"

Her smile curved right at Callie. A bolt of pure fear shot through Callie's chest.

"Unless they found a blood connection," the queen continued. "Why, if they found that, they could use the other way of crossing the Realms."

The Hunt leader let out a bark of laughter. "There is no other way of crossing the Realms, only the Other Field."

"Maybe not for the *lesser* houses," said the queen with a sweet smile. "For the Courts, however, a blood connection makes things, oh, *so* much easier. You don't even need the old portal."

She lifted one beckoning hand to Callie.

"All I need is a drop of blood from the line we wish to follow, and a little baseball magic to give the spell its proper structure. We could generate that in a single game."

A moment of uncomfortable silence passed as everyone contemplated this proposal.

The queen's eyes sparkled, and Adrien bit his lip so hard he was likely to add more than a few drops of his own blood to the mix.

Callie didn't know what to think.

Give her blood to the Unseelie Queen? Willingly?

That seemed a fool's choice. But if it could help her friends …

With that, Callie's mind was set. With a tight band around her heart, she slid her bat into the holster against her back and stepped up to the queen.

"I'll do it. One drop. After the game."

Finally, Lady Marne spoke. "Where would we play the game? The Other Field is *occupied,* and I will never agree to play at Unseelie Pitch, no matter how many promises you make, your Majesty."

It was Essie who piped up. "We can use the practice field in the glens. It's where Miss Em taught us Small Folk to play and to love the game. It's just as good for building baseball magic as the fancy fields are. Maybe even better!"

"If practice there resulted in your miraculous upset last season, it must be powerful, indeed," said the Hunt leader. "So be it. Tomorrow. At dawn. Gather your best players from among those who remain. The Wild Hunt will face the Small Folk on the field of baseball."

"And the Unseelie Queen shall open a path into the mortal realm," said Lady Marne.

Callie's blood prickled.

The queen smiled.

But the Hunt leader wasn't finished. He stalked forward until his snout pressed a hair's breadth away from the queen's nose. "If the Unseelie Queen betrays us," he said, his voice a dangerous whisper, "the Wild Hunt will put her to the chase until the Fairy Realm crumbles to dust."

The queen's smile only grew.

CHAPTER
TWENTY-FIVE

To some, perhaps, it would have been seen as audacious of the Duke of the Silver Forest to host this meeting. Or at least presumptuous. Yet as the duke settled into his smoking chair and tamped out the dead embers from his last pipe, then meticulously filled it again, he felt nothing but the opposite.

He was the one with the power.

Leave it to the king to travel to him.

And when the bellpull chimed, the Duke of the Silver Forest did not budge, waiting instead for the faun butler to lead the royal subject into the room. Completely at his leisure, the duke pulled a burning straw of kindling from the flames and lit his pipe as the king removed and folded his riding jacket, then took a seat across the fire.

"Would you care for a smoke, your Majesty?" the duke said after the king was finally settled. "Perhaps a snifter?"

"Brandy?" the Seelie King replied hopefully.

"Apple brandy from the high orchards," the duke assured him.

"That sounds too good to pass up after such a journey."

"Archibald," the duke said to his faun. "See the king's desires are met."

The Small Folk scurried to his task.

"It is good to have the world righted, is it not?" the Seelie King said. He sighed as he settled deeper into his plush armchair. "Good job I got the fields to working again when I did."

The Duke of the Silver Forest nearly gave in to the urge to set his king straight on the matter. It had been both the Earl of the Gray Moors and the Viscount of the Autumn Hills who had collaborated to bring workers back to the production-starved fields — and, indeed, the viscount's actions were the very steps that had been needed to make the brandy that Archibald the faun was now serving to him so intently.

The duke pulled on his pipe again, instead.

Including the Countess of the Subterranean Castle, they had all agreed that there was value to the cover that such a figurehead as the Seelie King brought — and supporting the king's assessment of himself meant it was more likely that the bumbling fairy lord would indeed spend more time managing his little baseball club than meddling in affairs that mattered. If giving the king a sense of importance was required as upkeep, that was of no import.

The king sipped, then murmured with proper appreciation, licking his lips greedily as he set the drink on the tabletop beside him. "I'm glad you asked for this meeting," he said then, his voice growing artificially cold as he sat back to give the impression that he was in control of their conversation. "I am assuming this is in regard to the raid your council authorized without my review."

The duke paused for long enough that the cloud of smoke he let seep from his lips came with a sense of anticipation. "It is, my King."

"That's good, because I wanted to have a word with you on that subject, myself."

"A word, my Lord?"

"I have to say, I do not appreciate being informed of such activities only after the fact, Duke."

The duke dismissed the king's concern with a wave of his hand. "It was a simple precaution, your Majesty. We all knew you would approve of such bold actions, but there was the chance of backlash from the other houses of the Realm, however slim. We authorized the attack on the Unseelie Queen to avoid you getting your hands sullied in the whole affair."

"I see," the king said, taken aback. After another moment, he adjusted the cuffs of his sleeve to ensure the silver beetles showed prominently. "Then please do pass on my appreciation to your co-conspirators."

"I will," the duke said, tamping down his pipe.

The action would still reflect on the king rather than the council, though the duke doubted any repercussions could come from it that would matter. Or, to put it in more proper terms, there were many other things happening today, and all of them mattered considerably more than any complaints from the Unseelie Court. Still, whatever those repercussions were would fall on the king's shoulders rather than theirs. That the king could not see this was part of the satisfaction of the plan.

Exhaling a thin stream of smoke, the duke considered the king's smug expression and relegated him, once again, into the slot of a fairy lord far more suited to a bench in the dugout than a seat at the court.

"The reason I asked you here was to report that our actions have significantly disabled the Unseelie Queen. Not only that, but we have also absorbed considerable quantities of the baseball magic, which she had earlier purloined from the other families."

"That's what she gets for playing a closed game," the king said, sipping again from his brandy. He had obviously heard reports of the queen's raid of the other houses. "What's good for the wing is good for the hoof," he said, sitting back again, clearly pleased with the sophistication of his language.

"Yes, yes. But I need you to look at the bigger tapestry here. With the power of the queen's baseball magic in our hands, we have the means to unlock the next stage in our plans. Meaning that, as we speak, there are actions underway that will acquire the full and unmitigated use of the Web Gem for the Seelie Court."

"The Web Gem?" said the Seelie King, sitting up so quickly he sloshed his brandy over the rim of his snifter. "Do we even know where it is?"

Even in the moment, the duke gave himself proper accolades for refraining from giving the king a scornful scoff. "The council has our thoughts," he said instead.

The king sighed and leaned back into his cushions again. "I would so love to get my hands on the Web Gem."

"Assuming the artifact falls to the Seelies," the duke said, again enacting strength, "it is the council's ruling that *we* will hold its chains."

The king's chest puffed to twice its normal size. "I am the king. I get the Web Gem."

"No. We are not going to squander control in the same fashion as the wretched Queen of the Unseelie Court has done. There will be no parading of it out in public, no sitting with it in the dugout. Such displays are simply asking for trouble. The Web Gem will stay in the council's control, under lock, key, and every protective spell our magic can devise. If you don't agree with that, then we can find another king."

The Seelie King glared into the amber in his snifter, his brows forming a deep, dark vee of consideration. Likely, the duke thought, he was replaying the events that had earned him his crown all those seasons ago.

Finally, the king let out a blustery breath and drained his glass. "Very well. The Web Gem goes to the council."

The duke, having finished his smoking, tamped ash from his pipe, then set it aside.

"We don't mean to shut you out entirely, my King. There is something we need you to do, something only you can accomplish for us," he said.

The king leaned forward.

"You have always been the manager of the baseball club. And as our manager, you have guided the Seelie Court through many a very good season. But you have never won a championship, my good King. And championships are the currency of the baseball world. After all the work we've done untangling the mess of the Unseelie Court's loss and the Small Folks' unaccountable win, the council has determined that we cannot afford to give up any more championships."

"I see," the king replied, though it seemed clear he didn't. "You want me to step up our game. I can assure you, once the Web Gem is in place my players will be ready for the new Fairy League sea—"

The duke cut him off with a sharp gesture. "No, my King. We're done with the traditional league. Why risk the Realm falling under the governance of imbeciles once again? We want you to make a baseball league of our own, with teams that consist of nothing but subjects of the Seelie Court. They will entertain us as well as power the Web Gem. That way, we expect to be able to keep the artifact in our ranks where it belongs, in perpetuity."

"But, Duke…" The king seemed to ponder several options before settling on: "What if we cannot find enough to play? And even if we do, the quality of that league will be suspect. How will that affect the baseball magic? The rules state—"

"When we have the Web Gem and the power of the baseball magic, *we* make the rules," said the duke. "And quality will not be a problem, will it? So long as *you* are good enough to train your contributors."

The king rubbed his chin, contemplating the threat not so hidden in the duke's admonition. His eyes glittered in the firelight. "There are actions already underway to obtain the Web Gem?" he finally asked.

"There are, my King. But I will not say what they are. There are Small ears about, after all." He cast a glance at Archibald, who shifted on his hooves where he stood in the shadowed corner with the brandy decanter.

The king stood. This time, the duke paid him the respect of rising with him.

"A league of our own is a brilliant maneuver," said the king as he held his snifter out for a refill. "And me at the head of it! Yes, this is a fine refreshment you have here, Duke. I will begin to arrange it."

TWENTY-SIX

Instead of throwing herself onto the comfortable mattress of her bed, Emily sat in the hard chair in her room and fretted. The hard corners of the chair pressed against her legs in a way that made everything more real. The slats of its back felt like bars when she leaned back to stare, unfocused, into the unfathomable depths of the ceiling. Outside her window, the world pretended to move along like nothing horrible had happened, but Emily knew that was a facade.

The Web Gem shard in her hand was giving off an intense aura of unease, whispering to her frantically of the danger the Realm was in, of the trouble hounding Callie McMasters, of the plight of her teammates among the Small Folk.

Emily tried to shut it all out. The shard's portents of doom were too vague to be useful to her now. She was already keyed up to the max, anyway.

Enough light remained of the day that rows of houses were easily visible. And inside those houses, families were trying to go about their everyday lives. At one point Emily and Adrien had agreed they would keep all they knew of the Fairy Realm under wraps. Keep it quiet to save them all. It had seemed so proper and so right. But now she doubted why they ever thought that.

Now, everything had changed.

Adrien was gone.

Disappeared out in the public eye in such a way that no one could possibly miss.

And the look. Emily shuddered.

The look on his face as he'd turned to her after blasting the pitch that had been meant for her into orbit was forever seared into her eyeballs. A mixture of horror, ecstasy, and resignation had shaped the lines of his jaw and the shadows around his cheeks. She squeezed her eyes shut and recalled the desperate light in his eyes as he'd delivered his final message.

Don't become a Unicorn. Mr. McMasters has the Web Gem.

The truth of the situation was clear as a perfect Opening Day. Adrien had sacrificed himself for the sole purpose of protecting Emily.

The thought made Emily's heart clench so hard she thought she might vomit.

At least she knew now why Mr. McMasters had gone to such lengths to try and get her piece. Her memory flashed on the night he'd ransacked her room, and she felt a shiver of cold.

A soft clatter from her bookshelf snapped her out of her dire thoughts, and she jumped.

Benji Amberman stood across the bedroom, holding her copy of *Wuthering Heights* in one hand. They still wore their workout uniform from tryouts. A third base mitt dangled from a belt loop at their side.

"Sorry to sneak up on you," Benji said. "Figured I'd find you here."

"Go away, Benji. I need to be alone."

"Right now I think that's the last thing you need."

Coach Amabe had canceled tryouts the moment Adrien had vanished in plain sight. While most of the participants had lingered to exclaim and jabber on and recite breathless stories about the shocking occurrence amongst themselves, Emily had slunk away. Apparently not before catching Benji's eyes, though.

Benji slid *Wuthering Heights* back into place on the bookshelf, then took a seat at the corner edge of Emily's bed, right in front of Emily. "Talk to me," they said.

"What good will talking do now?"

"Maybe save the world?"

The earnestness of Benji's tone and the flare of fairy glow in their eyes made Emily give a strained chuckle.

"Yeah, right."

"You'll need to get your story down."

Emily sighed and slumped. The hard edge of the chair's back pressed against the base of her skull. She ground her neck against it, giving herself a much-needed massage. "Everyone will know everything, Benji. This is going to be so bad. When I fell through the fairy ring last year, the whole city was willing to be convinced of mundane explanations, even if those explanations made no real sense. But this ... Adrien disappearing out in the open like that, I mean ... it was real, you know? Real magic out in the open. And everyone chattering ... I just ..."

"Yeah," Benji replied. "Everyone's gonna be lining up to read Megan Moore's next article, that's for sure."

Trouble, said the Web Gem shard in its desperate whisper. *You have to do something!*

In a surge of frustration, Emily squeezed the shard tight enough to cut her palm, and pounded her fist on her desk, making the trophies on the shelf above rattle.

"I *know* I have to do something. I just don't know what! The baseball magic didn't *work* for me."

Her eyes burned. Her throat went tight.

"I think that part makes sense, now," said Benji. "Why the baseball magic didn't work, I mean."

"Oh, yeah? Enlighten me, then. Because it's all a murky mess as far as I can see."

Benji quirked an eyebrow at her tone but carried on. "Adrien said Mr. McMasters has the Web Gem. If that's the case, it makes sense that he can control the flow of baseball magic at a field he basically owns now."

Emily nodded. "You've got a point. The place is more Ball and Glove than Unicorn Field at this point."

Their shared disgust was palpable in her quiet little room.

Emily considered Benji's theory.

With Unicorn Field as tangled up in Fairy Realm magic as it was, she didn't want to think about the power Mr. McMasters could gain if he owned the place. And Adrien's warning meant that, with the Web Gem in his hands, McMasters had the ability to wield that power in ways that went far, far beyond simple business leverage. She thought back to the moment when he'd proposed sponsoring her. At the time the offer made her angry, but now it made her want to hurl. She'd said no, of course, but if he owned the field as well as the whole team, he'd have control over anyone who joined the Unicorns, herself included.

Adrien truly had saved her.

"Okay," she said. Her competitive nature was spinning up again. She sat up straight, then leaned forward, elbows on knees. "So McMasters stopped us from using the baseball magic. If we assume he can do that any time he wants, what options do we have? I have to get to the Fairy Realm *now* — before things get any worse, and our only way in is blocked."

Benji was already shaking their head. "Unicorn Field isn't the only place in the world with a fairy ring."

Hope welled so quickly Emily had to gasp for breath. "And you're here to tell me where to find one, right? You and your Amberman family history?"

Now it was Benji's turn to look dejected. "Sorry, Em, but no. I don't know why, but our fairy ancestors didn't pass that information down."

"Maybe they didn't want you going back."

"I hope that's not it." Benji sounded unnerved at the thought, though, as if it had never occurred to them before. "Anyway, I only knew about the one under Unicorn Field because I sensed it the moment I tried out for the team as a first-year. But I think that effect ought to be the same at any fairy ring, right?"

Benji's eager expression made their intent clear.

Emily sat back in her chair. "You're saying you can help me find another one?"

Benji's smug smile was all the answer she needed.

"Like some kind of radar," she whispered. "Or a divining rod?"

Benji's sharp brows tweaked, and their shoulders gave a shrug. "It's worth a try, isn't it?"

"How far out will we have to go, you think? And how will we even begin? Given the tsunami of attention we're going to be getting any time now, I don't think we'll be able to just walk around scanning every square inch of Pattersonville to see if one place or another could serve as a doorway into the Fairy Realm."

Besides, she thought, anxiety rising, every moment that passed here could be another hundred years for poor Adrien.

On top of that, Mr. McMasters was already on her trail. She felt as if he were stalking up behind her right now, his hot breath misting in the cool air like a wolf's.

She swallowed against the panic that rose in her throat. It didn't help that, after all her questions, Benji looked as uncertain and frightened as she felt.

It was just the two of them, a pair of teenagers against the world.

The sound of a car pulling into the driveway broke through their shared funk. Both of them went on alert. It was just Dad, though. A rattle of keys and the opening of the front door followed, and Dad's voice filtered up the stairs.

At first, Emily thought he was on the phone, but a second pair of footsteps said someone else was with him.

"Yes, I think she's here," he said. "Her bag is on the table."

Whoever was with him answered too quietly to make out a voice.

Emily tightened her grip on the shard and rose from her chair. Her dad wouldn't let Mr. McMasters back in again, but that didn't mean the tenacious businessman hadn't sent a flunky.

She nodded at Benji, who nodded back. As footsteps sounded on the stairs — both her dad's and the mystery person's — Emily edged toward the window, and Benji blocked the door. Outside, the gable roof was dry and would be easy to traverse if she needed to clamber out. She'd done it when she was younger.

The footsteps reached the top of the landing.

"Emily? You in here?" Dad called. "I found one of your school-mates standing on the porch when I pulled up. She wants to ask about tryouts?"

Dad appeared in the doorway, a vaguely concerned look on his face. Behind him was none other than Megan Moore, looking deadly serious as she tapped her phone against her hip.

"I think it's about time you finally gave me that interview, Emily DeWitt, don't you?"

An urge to bolt out the window crashed over Emily. She put her hand on the sill.

Benji stood transfixed, too.

Telling Benji her story in full had been a relief. But the idea of telling this sophomore reporter anything about the Fairy Realm made her heart lurch. Megan had been little better than a gossip columnist until now, for crying out loud, though the bits of the truth her articles did hit on were sharp as barbs.

But there was more at stake now.

Come nightfall, everyone in Pattersonville was going to know some version of the truth. This was Emily's chance to make that version hers. And standing like a deer in Megan Moore's headlights, Emily saw something else in the reporter now, too, as Megan stood there, so awkwardly tall and gangly with her giraffe legs and scarecrow arms that jutted from a Pattersonville West T-shirt and worn jeans. Megan was actually concerned. To a degree, anyway. To whatever degree she could be, Emily supposed.

"Promise me you'll get this right?" Emily said to Megan. "No hit piece. No underhanded digs."

"All I want is the truth," Megan said. "Like a real journalist."

Emily glanced at Benji. "What do you think?"

They clenched their teeth, then shrugged. "Story's coming out anyway. Best you own it, right?"

Emily nodded, letting go of the windowsill. "All right, Megan. Let's do this."

EMILY SAT across the kitchen table from Megan, watching her fiddle with her phone recorder settings. The sophomore had a kind of glow to her now. Not like Benji's, nothing so magical as that, but more like she knew she had a real lead this time, and it was time to get down to business. It was a sensation that Emily found, for lack of a better word, comforting.

Megan clicked a final button, gave a satisfied little nod, and placed the phone directly in the middle of the table, microphone facing Emily. She flicked her gaze first to Emily's dad sitting on the left, then to Benji sitting on the right, before settling it on Emily. She placed both elbows on the table and curled her opposite hands around them to support herself as she leaned her thin frame forward. She led off by giving the time and date, and the fact that this was an interview between her and senior baseball star Emily DeWitt.

Preliminaries finished, she nodded sharply to Emily.

"All I want from you, Miss DeWitt, is the truth. Everyone at Unicorn Field today saw Adrien Thorn disappear in plain daylight. I think there's something in this town that takes people, and I believe that every single citizen of Pattersonville deserves to know what it is. What do you have to tell me about what happened today?"

Emily wiped sweaty palms down her thigh. "It's a long story."

"I've been chasing this story since seventh grade journalism class. Believe me, I've got time."

"Seventh-grade journalism class?"

"I did a project on the Adrien Thorn legend. The star player of the Unicorns disappearing after hitting his championship-winning home run, yeah?"

"I see."

"So, what do you have to say about what happened today?"

Emily drew a long breath, knowing that this was the moment when everything was going to change. "Well, you see, the story of what happened today started for me last year."

"When you disappeared."

"Right." Emily took a sip of water from the bottle Dad had given her. "When I fell out of the world, I found myself on the other side. In the Fairy Realm."

From there, Emily let the details pour out of her.

It was different from telling Benji. That conversation had been like an extension of the conversations she and Adrien had had, two people sharing a thing that had happened to them. Benji, with their family connection, already knew enough background to make Emily's telling feel smooth and easy.

Megan knew only what she had managed to piece together, and most of that was hearsay mixed with storybook tales. Megan's background seemed deeper, though. She'd been doing her homework, and her questions were often more insightful than Emily expected, which made her feel like Megan was on her side.

There were stops and starts, interruptions and requests for clarification, and even interjections from Benji as Emily had to explain just what baseball magic was, to start with. So the conversation was convoluted.

Plus, Dad was listening, which was a different kind of embarrassing.

She'd told him the basic story before, but not everything. Some things she'd kept back because she hadn't wanted to worry him more than necessary, others because they had felt too personal. But now everything was different. Now, Adrien was gone. And Emily wanted to make sure the people responsible for that got what was coming to them.

If putting everything on the table for Megan to print helped make that happen, Emily was more than willing.

By the time she'd explained about the Unseelie Queen, the Web Gem, the Small Folk, Mr. McMasters, and absolutely everything to do with the Fairy Realm, night had fallen, and her voice was hoarse with exhaustion and emotion. Dad had gotten her a second bottle of water a while ago. She drained the last of it as Megan tapped her phone to stop the recording.

"You've helped me so much tonight, Emily," she said. Her voice was rough, too, tight even though she hadn't been talking as much as Emily. "I can write a solid article based on what you've given me. I've still got a bit more research to do, but now I know what direction to go with that."

"Great," Emily croaked.

She looked at the journalist and felt something had changed in her. Megan sat upright but radiated a sense of something that might have been relief. She seemed happy, yet, at the same time, as if she wanted to cry. Her whole body seemed to be struggling to stay together as she leaned over to slide her phone into her pocket.

"Are you all right?" Emily said.

Megan gave a wistful smile. "Yes. Yeah, I'm fine."

Emily narrowed her gaze. Megan was not fine. "You asked some really interesting questions tonight."

"Thank you."

"You said you've been working on this story for four years. Adrien's story?"

"That's right. Yeah. I have."

Emily saw it then, in the rapid-fire way those words came out. Megan was worried. Afraid.

Emily's tale tonight had filled in gaps, but the important thing here was that for Megan, those *were* gaps. More of them than Emily knew. She reached out and touched Megan softly on the shoulder. She saw that she was right in the way Megan's eyes grew bigger. "What else is there?" Emily said. "Tell me what you know."

"Turning the tables on me?" Megan said.

"Call it that if you want. Or just call it a friend wanting to help."

Megan chuffed. "I don't have any friends."

Emily wanted to say that writing sharp-tongued editorials in the school paper was not a great way to endear hearts, but instead took a page from Dad's playbook and sat back silently instead. In the moment that followed, Emily linked gazes with Megan.

The journalist seemed to weigh options.

"Let me guess," Emily said. "You've got a story to tell, but no one will print it?"

Megan gave a fuller laugh then. "Kind of."

"The story about Adrien Thorn you said you researched? I thought you already printed everything you could about him?"

"And more," Benji quipped.

Megan ignored Benji. "Bigger than that."

Emily sat back and crossed her arms contemplatively. At her periphery, she felt Benji and her dad lean forward. "Bigger than Adrien Thorn?"

Having made up her mind, Megan continued. "Everyone knows Adrien's story now, of course, or at least the legend. But I got excited as I was doing research for the project: looking into missing person reports, and digging through old newspapers at the library. Did you know there have been other disappearances between then and now?"

"Others?" Emily said.

"How many?" her dad added, his voice prickling with parental alarm.

"Eight. Pattersonville has racked up eight unsolved missing persons reports in the past hundred years, and they're all connected to one place."

Emily wet her lips. "Unicorn Field."

Megan smirked. "I thought it was funny how nobody seems to have put that detail together except for me. I took it to the police first, but they kept shrugging off the baseball field thing as if it had no bearing. Like what happened with you last year, yeah? You vanish right from home plate, and yet everyone is perfectly happy to accept that some creeper came onto the field and kidnapped you right from under that pile of players." Megan tipped her head towards Benji. "I dunno, did *you* see any creepy kidnappers that day? You were part of the pile. Did anyone even ask you if you saw said creeper?"

Benji gave a wry smile and shrugged one shoulder. "Only you."

Emily made a noise of frustration. "So? The authorities are bad at their jobs. That's not news."

"True enough," Megan agreed. "But what made it news was that *you came back.* You were the first person I knew of who disappeared from Unicorn Field and then returned. I was so excited when that happened. Finally, I thought, there's going to be a real lead on this thing. Someone who can give me a firsthand account of what's going on with that field. Someone who can confirm my suspicions of a supernatural influence over this town. But you brushed me off along with every other reporter."

The bitterness in her voice made Emily cringe despite herself.

Megan continued, visibly setting her resentment aside. "The police did their bumbling thing, so at least I got to see that in action. That was valuable. But then something even more interesting happened. A new kid enrolled at school, and he was going by the name Adrien Thorn. I just knew. I knew it was him. I had to get his story. But he wouldn't talk to me, either, no matter how I tried to approach him."

Emily scoffed, her earlier guilt melting. "Well, yeah. Nobody's going to want to talk to someone who prints the kinds of things you have about him."

Megan slumped a little. "Look, I'm not proud of everything I've written so far, but I'm getting frustrated. There's a real danger right in our communal backyard, as it were, and I'm trying to warn people about it. But every step of the way, the people who can help me are shutting me out instead! I know everyone thinks my articles are stupid nonsense. I see everyone laughing about them in the halls after I post. But at least I've put the idea in their heads that there's a fairy ring under that field, and with this latest thing about Adrien Thorn disappearing — again — this time in plain sight, I've got a chance to make this story public." She punctuated her words by tapping one pointed finger on the table. "This fairy ring. It's taking people."

Emily nodded. "You've certainly got people talking."

Benji reached across the table and put one hand on Megan's. "I know your articles aren't nonsense. Mean-spirited, yes, and written sometimes without all the information. But you do hit on the truth. And I agree with you. Everyone deserves to know about our town's connection with the Fairy Realm. It's part of our history, and it shapes who we are, even if we don't know about it."

Emily wished she could put her head down on the table, either to cry or to sleep. Instead, she rubbed the heels of her palms into her eyes, then blinked blearily at Benji and Megan. Their blurred forms brought her decision into crystal clarity.

"There's too much at stake now to have misinformation swirling around out there," she said. "Maybe you're right, Megan. If Adrien and I had gotten the real story out there to the masses earlier, maybe Mr. McMasters wouldn't have been able to get up to his dirty business with the Web Gem, and Adrien wouldn't have had to ... to ..."

She drew in a shuddering breath. In her pocket, the Web Gem shard pulsed softly, its message still urgent, but dimmed for the moment. It sensed she was moving along the path to right the wrongs it spoke of.

She nearly laughed. The idea that working with Megan Moore, of all people, would help her deal with Fairy Realm problems was too surreal. If Adrien were here, he'd throw a fit.

But Adrien wasn't here.

Megan, perhaps not so oblivious to Emily's internal conflicts, raised one eyebrow and seemed to catch a second wind. "You said Mr. McMasters has this Web Gem. And that he's up to some dirty business. Do you think it has anything to do with Callie McMasters' mysterious disappearance?"

"Callie's not involved with anything her father's doing," Emily said instantly. The heat of anger built in her, no product of the Web Gem shard this time, but instead, her own sense of righteousness. "Here's another story for you. Callie's playing baseball in the Fairy Realm because it's the only place that will let her play after what happened the day she pulled me back into the Real World."

"Wow," Megan said, goggling from across the table, completely devoid of her journalistic doggedness for a blissful moment. "That is a story."

"She gave up everything to help me, including turning her back on her toxic father. Frankly, I'm sick of listening to everyone badmouth her all the time, especially when I'm worried that something's gone wrong for her on the other side."

"I see," Megan said. "I'm sorry I asked, but it was a natural question. Everyone's going to jump to that conclusion."

Emily put her head into her hands and pressed in on her throbbing temples. "I know. I'm sorry, too."

"This story you're writing," Benji interjected, tired too, propping their cheek on their hand. "Will it make it to print for tomorrow's *Unicorn Gazette*?"

"Oh, no," said Megan. "I've learned my lesson. This isn't high-school gossip fluff. I'm not putting this in the *Gazette*. If we want to get McMasters under the gun here, we've got to put this in a real newspaper, someplace with legitimacy. I'm thinking the *Patterson-ville Times.*"

Emily frowned. "Will they accept a piece that's basically a fairy tale?"

"Adrien did just disappear in front of everybody," Benji said.

"Right. The *PT* will drool over an exclusive interview with you, Emily. Give me a couple more days to gather my research and interview a couple more people, and I know they'll take it."

"I can see that," Emily said, "but still. I'd like to get McMasters feeling the pressure sooner than later. He's already too close for comfort."

"I'm not going to let that monster anywhere close to you," Emily's dad said. He clenched the edge of the kitchen counter he'd been leaning against. "I'll call the police if I have to."

"Thanks, Dad. And I love you and all that. But really, you haven't seen what fairy magic is capable of. McMasters on his own might be enough of an imbecile that I can keep away from him for a while, but if a lord from the Fairy Realm figures out he's got the Web Gem and decides to come get it, and my piece, too, there's nothing you can do."

"Still," her dad said, eyes harder than she'd ever seen them. "I'll do whatever I can."

Emily smiled, knowing there was nothing she could say to dissuade him.

"Thanks, Dad," she said, letting it lie.

Megan raised her hand as if to request the floor. "I'll go as fast as I can. I'll give it a human-interest angle, and that'll get it past the biggest stumbling blocks. But it strikes me that there's something else you might want to look into."

"What's that?"

"You said you need to find another fairy ring ASAP, right? That it might be the key to being able to use the baseball magic again so you can rescue Adrien?"

Emily blinked at her. "Yeah. Are you saying you know about one?" Was Megan blushing?

"Not directly. But see, there *was* actually one more person who disappeared, but it didn't happen at Unicorn Field so I didn't add it in. There wasn't any info about him because he was Black, and you know how that sort of thing went back then."

"A Black kid?" Benji said.

"Tommy Mathison, in 1917, so before Adrien. I found a tiny scrap of an article about him that said his friends reported him missing after playing a game together."

"I see," Benji said. "Back then, Black kids weren't allowed to play with white kids, so they wouldn't have been at Unicorn Field. Or, like, anywhere white kids normally played."

The shard in Emily's pocket pulsed once, then settled. "An old field," she mumbled. "That makes sense."

"I never looked for it because I assumed Tommy's story wasn't tied to the others," Megan said apologetically. "But now I'm wondering if I was wrong."

"It's a place to start," Benji said. "And I'm pretty sure I know someone who can work with that to home in on what we're looking for."

Emily glanced up at them. "Who?"

They grinned. "No one works a pair of dowsing rods like Patsy Pell, let me tell you."

"Dowsing rods?"

"She says she can find anything. It's like her superpower or something."

"Interesting," Emily replied.

"She says all she needs is something she can use to get the scent."

The image of her Mom's baseball filled Emily's mind. "I've got just the thing," she said.

"It's a plan, then," Benji said. "I'll call her on my way home. Ten o'clock tomorrow morning? School parking lot?"

"Ten o'clock," Emily said. "I'll be there."

A smile spread across her lips, and for the first time all day, Emily felt a spark of true, substantial hope.

CHAPTER

TWENTY-SEVEN

Megan Moore liked to think of herself as a terrier. She could get sharp and yappy when she needed to, but when the trail was hot and her target was in her sight, her focus locked in. Once she got her teeth into a story, she never let go, no matter how hard the thing thrashed to get away. Her tenacity was a quality her mom often praised, and it was how she intended to build her career as a reporter.

She'd finally gotten Emily DeWitt to talk. Usually, the high of that success would keep her floating two feet off the sidewalk for a while.

This evening had been the rawest, roughest interview Megan had ever conducted. Emily hadn't kept anything back. She'd laid everything out there, and Megan had happily lapped it all up, while at the same time suppressing the shudders that threatened to undo her journalistic poise. It was a strange feeling, being both excited and horrified by the story she'd chased down. As she'd suspected since her first tentative investigations into this story in middle school, the Fairy Realm was no place to mess around with haphazardly. It left people messed up, even the ones like Emily, who clearly had mixed emotions regarding her experiences.

Basking in the post-interview afterglow, Megan was already writing snippets of her article in her head, trying opening lines and scathing quips to see how they felt.

But she was too good a reporter to think she was finished. There was still pavement to pound. If she wanted to get the big fish, a real exposé printed in the *Pattersonville Times* — one that revealed not just the dangers of the fairy ring, but also Mr. McMasters using forbidden fairy magic in an attempt to control it for himself — she had to get the story perfect.

And while Emily's interview had been an incredible treasure trove, it wasn't the whole picture.

As fraught as the interview on deck might be, she needed to talk with the Thorns.

Which was why she was walking the neighborhood where the Thorns lived.

It was getting on towards nine o'clock, now, and as the nighttime cold of February bit deep, she pulled her coat tighter around her shoulders. Luckily, she was close to her destination. Only one more turn would put her on Bradford Street.

Pattersonville West High School was on her right. Even though Unicorn Field was on the opposite side of the campus, she could still see the glow of the big field lights haloed against the night sky. That radiance was a white aura, the kind of will-o-wisp the baseball-rabid citizens of Pattersonville were most susceptible to. People were still there. Probably talking about the abrupt end of tryouts.

Knowing what she knew of fairy rings, she hoped nothing was lurking there, waiting to feed on such a feast.

She shivered and hunched her shoulders and pressed onward.

When she made the turn, she zeroed in on the house. Every light in the place was on as if the family was trying to remove any places where someone could hide.

The sight made her heart squeeze in a way she'd never felt before, and for a moment, she considered turning away and just going home. She could just hit up the library tomorrow, and do some follow-up interviews with kids at school.

No.

That wouldn't do.

She shook the cowardice off. She was a terrier, and her teeth were in the meat of this story. She wasn't letting go now.

The porch steps creaked as she climbed them. Her fist trembled, but her knock was as sharp as ever.

A moment later, the door opened. A woman stood in the framework, silhouetted against the lights of the living room behind her. Her shadowed face showed a strained, fearful expression of faint hope.

Megan took a deep breath. "Hello, Mrs. Thorn. I'm Megan Moore, a reporter for the *Unicorn Gazette*. I'm sorry to turn up so late, but I was hoping I could talk with you and Mr. Thorn. About Adrien."

"Do you know where he is?" Mrs. Thorn asked. Her hair was in a hastily made bun. The wispy net of falling strands floating in her backlit haze made her look a little like a frazzled witch. "Gary says he ran off like a bolt this afternoon, and people are saying the strangest things about seeing him at tryouts ..."

Megan bit her lip. "Could I come in? I walked all the way here from Emily DeWitt's place."

"Oh, of ... of course. Please." Mrs. Thorn stepped aside and held the door open.

Megan, a little ashamed to have used the woman's well-known big heart to gain entrance, stepped in and slid her bag off her shoulder. The warmth of the place enveloped her, though, and she didn't have to fake the sigh of relief that came as the cold melted away and her muscles unclenched.

The carpet was spotless, and the furniture shone from recent polishing. But the coffee table was littered with paper plates full of crumbs and half-empty mugs of various brown liquids, all mismatched. An honest-to-god phone book lay open amongst the cups, its yellow pages flopping over the edge of the table. The TV was running the local news channel, the volume on low, and closed captioning activated.

Mr. Thorn sat on the sofa, elbows on his knees, and fingers laced in front of his mouth, staring at the set as if it might soon reveal the secrets of the universe. He made a grunt of acknowledgment as Megan came in.

"Would you like a cup of tea?" Mrs. Thorn said as she closed the front door, fidgeting. "We're having tea tonight. Or coffee. Or hot cocoa. I made cocoa for Sydney, but he went up to his room a bit ago in a huff when I told him the police wouldn't look for someone until they've been gone twenty-four hours."

Oh, hell, Megan thought, realizing she was officially in over her head. *This sucks.* The helplessness in Mrs. Thorn's voice was making Megan's stomach roil.

"I don't need anything, thanks." Feeling that amazing sense of confidence that seemed to always come over her when she just needed to power through, she stepped decisively into the room and sat on the loveseat, setting her bag beside her. As she dug for her phone, she glanced up at Mr. Thorn. She chewed at her lip for a moment, then said, "I don't think you're going to hear anything on the news tonight, sir."

Mrs. Thorn lowered herself onto the sofa beside her husband. "If you know anything, please tell us. We're worried about him. He comes from a strained family background, you know? We've tried so hard to give him the home he deserves, but he's always held parts of himself back from us, I can tell."

Megan swiped to her phone's recorder app. The coffee table was too full to place it neatly between herself and her interviewees as she had with Emily DeWitt. She'd have to balance it on her knee. "I have some things to share with you, yes. I'm hoping you can also shed some light for me on some others, too. You see, I'm writing an article about—"

"Hey!"

The voice came from the top of the stairs, and Megan looked up to see the kid she'd interviewed earlier this week — Sydney — standing at the landing, scowling down at her with an expression far too dark for a ten-year-old as he came stomping down the stairs.

"You're that reporter lady. You wrote that dumb article about my cousin."

Megan didn't flinch at his accusation. *Terrier,* she thought. "Yeah, I did. I was trying to get him to tell me about something important, and when he wouldn't talk to me, I got petty, I guess. But I didn't lie. I wrote the truth as I knew it."

"You made it sound like he was really A1. He hates it when people do that. Now he's gone, and if it's not your fault, you had a big hand in it!"

Mrs. Thorn turned a stern glare on her son. "Sweetheart, you apologize. This girl had nothing to do with it, I'm sure."

Sydney's face screwed up even tighter as he pressed his lips into a thin line.

Megan held her ground. "You heard what happened at tryouts today?"

Mr. Thorn never took his eyes from the TV, and his words came out muffled around the fingers still pressed to his lips, but for the first time, he spoke. "People don't just vanish out of thin air. Someone will have seen where he went."

"Someone did see where he went," Megan said, stretching the truth a little to get her point across. "Emily DeWitt was front and center, and she just now told me everything."

She swiped through her recent recordings, then searched through the interview she'd just finished. A moment later, Emily DeWitt's voice crackled out of the speaker.

"—Adrien's had a hard time adjusting to living in the modern world, but he was trying, you know? Trying to make something new of himself after a hundred years trapped in the Fairy Realm. We'd talk about it. When we were alone, you know? Our experiences with the fairies, how we felt about having escaped. I guess Adrien wanted to make sure he'd really gotten away, since he didn't even want to play baseball anymore. But it turns out Adrien hadn't escaped. The Unseelie Queen kept her claws in him from the moment I pulled him back through the fairy ring, and now she's either manipulated things or taken advantage of the chaos Mr. McMasters has stirred up to yank Adrien back into her clutches. He ... He did that for me. He sacrificed himself so I wouldn't—"

Megan hit pause and looked up into the wide eyes of the Thorn family. Emily's tearful tone was reflected in their faces and the slump of their shoulders.

"Holy...," Mr. Thorn said. "That's hard to believe."

"The Fairy Realm?" Mrs. Thorn said, lifting one hand to touch her lips.

"It's real," Megan said. "I know how hard it is to accept, but once you start to see the patterns, it's hard to believe anything else. I've been researching it for four years now. There's a fairy ring, a portal to the Fairy Realm, under Unicorn Field."

"And Adrien? He's ... is he ..." Mr. Thorn trailed off. He looked bewildered but driven to act, to do something to make sense of what he'd been told.

Megan wished she could make it easy for him, but the situation was dire. "Mr. Thorn, I need your help. I need all of your help," she said, sweeping her gaze to include Mrs. Thorn and Sydney. "Mr. McMasters is trying to make a power grab to control that fairy ring. Like you heard Emily say on this recording, he's stirring up the pot, and that's letting the fairies reach even further into our world than they've been able to before. And Adrien is a hero. He shouldn't have to be, you know? He's already lost over a hundred years to them, but Adrien has willingly given up more of himself to stop them from hurting anyone else. That's what I've come here tonight to try and help fix. I might not be much more than an awkward teenager, but I can write a killer article exposing everything so all of Pattersonville knows what's going on and who's stepped up to protect them."

Sydney, who had been standing this whole time, sat down on the coffee table hard enough to rattle the mugs there. His mother didn't even reprimand him.

"You're saying A2 really has been A1 this whole time?" he said. "But, why wouldn't he tell us?"

Megan shrugged one shoulder. "Would you have believed him?"

Mr. and Mrs. Thorn shared a glance full of dismay, but Sydney's face screwed up in frustration. "I would have!"

Megan let herself smile at his vehemence. "I guess that makes two of us, then. But most people wouldn't have. They'd have thought he was trying to get attention, or that he needed, like, mental help. And, I mean, who even really knows who Adrien Thorn was as a person? As a normal kid playing baseball a hundred years ago? He was my age when he was snatched away, right? I can't imagine how much that would mess with me. And now, all anyone remembers about him is the legend. According to Emily, he's spent the last hundred years being forced to play as Designated Hitter for the Unseelie Queen. I think he wanted a chance to be himself for once."

Sydney frowned. "I guess ... I guess if he'd told us who he was ... maybe we wouldn't have let him get into the school plays and everything else he likes so much."

Megan nodded, feeling a pang of guilt of her own. She was the one who had tried to pin down Adrien Thorn, Unicorns Legend. She hadn't wanted anything to do with Adrien the aspiring Thespian. But Adrien Thorn, baseball player, was a story. "Yeah, that could be, squirt. But we have a chance now to show the world who he is, in multiple senses of that phrase. It's time we show people how much of a hero your great cousin really is."

Mr. Thorn sat up straighter. "That's why you want to interview us. You want to get our picture of what Adrien is really like."

"I think it's important," Megan said. "And not just because it will help Emily DeWitt fight back against what Mr. McMasters is trying to do."

Mrs. Thorn balled her fists against her jean-clad thighs and nodded sharply. "I think you're right. Adrien deserves to be known and to be able to be himself, whatever that means to him."

"And Mr. McMasters deserves to go down!" Sydney chimed in. "If he's made the best big brother anyone's ever had get sent back to the Fairy Realm, he's gonna be sorry!"

Megan stifled the urge to grin.

"When should we start?" Mrs. Thorn asked.

Megan swiped to a fresh audio file and hit record.

IT WAS past midnight by the time they wrapped up. Mr. Thorn insisted on driving Megan home. Gratefully, she accepted. It wasn't a long drive to her house, but the walk would have been difficult even on a warm night.

She was in a strange state between exhausted and exhilarated, too. Exhaustilated.

She knew she wasn't going to sleep tonight, even though she needed it. Her article was spinning through her head now, full sentences glomming together into full paragraphs just waiting for her to put her fingers to the keyboard and let them spill out.

She had almost everything she needed.

All she was missing was the *pièce de résistance*.

But she had enough to let the words onto the page tonight. Enough to build the framework and put most of the flesh on the skeleton, so that when she crashed tomorrow morning, she'd have the bulk of her work finished.

It wouldn't be the first time she'd pulled a frenzied all-nighter.

She thanked Mr. Thorn for the ride, then quietly let herself into the house. Her mom was used to her keeping late hours, so though the place was mostly dark, the kitchen light was on for her, a point of warmth and welcome on a cold night.

She waved through the window at Mr. Thorn, who'd waited idling at the curb until she made it inside.

Then she marched up to her room and opened her laptop.

Tonight, the words.

Tomorrow, the hunt.

Because she was a terrier, and once she'd got a story in her sights, she never let it go.

Mr. McMasters was about to learn that the hard way.

TWENTY-EIGHT

E mily shivered as a sharp breeze picked up.

They were in a park now, mostly alone, but even so, she couldn't help feeling uncomfortable. Even here, under the open springtime sky, she felt like she was being watched. Or if not watched, hunted.

Paranoid much? she thought to herself.

But, as the old saying went, it wasn't being paranoid if something was really out to get her.

"Dowsing is like hitting," Patsy rambled on, oblivious to Emily's discomfort as she, Benji, and Emily ambled down Tansy Park's grass-lined, hard dirt path. "It's all in the hands."

Patsy walked slowly, palms up and fingers wrapped around the custom handles of her handmade dowsing rods — a pair of thin copper tubes bent with her own hands. She'd painted her nails with an alternating color pattern of indigo and turquoise today, which matched the colored fabrics she'd decorated the handles of the rods with. Currently, the rods were balanced and dangling to either side of her.

She had explained the process in the car on the way to the park.

"Pick the right tools, give them the respect they deserve, and they help you find the thing you're looking for," Patsy had said. "With the right training and the right mindset, *anyone* could do it." Her tone had suggested strongly, though, that no one else in their circle had enough dedication to make it work like she could. Seeing Emily's skeptical glance, Patsy had told a story about finding her phone once. "I thought it was a goner for sure," she said, hefting her flexible copper dowsing wires. "But these babies found it in nothing flat. Outside in the garden. Probably slipped out when I was planting the radishes."

"Cool," Emily had said.

"Don't worry, Em. I come from a long line of dowsers. I've got your back here," Patsy said. "Finding things is my superpower."

Tansy Park was a small plot of land the city had made into a pleasant enough play area. The park wasn't getting much use yet in the still-clinging cold of February, which meant they had the place themselves. Its grassy mound, public picnic tables, and barbecue pits were to their left. A jungle gym and set of swings for the kids stood to their right. The open field was covered in grass that was beginning to green up.

Emily should feel better about things. Really, she should.

She couldn't help it though.

She hadn't slept much, constantly turning in bed and dreaming about eyeballs focusing on her.

Now even the sight of three kids off in the distance made her feel jumpy.

At least Emily and her friends were doing something, though. In the past, that had always been enough. Taking action usually made her feel better. Under the gray hoodie she'd borrowed from Patsy, she wore her lucky Chicago Cubs T-shirt untucked. She also nervously tossed her mom's baseball to herself as they walked.

Once Patsy was ready to start, she rubbed her dowsing tools against the baseball, saying that doing so was like priming a bloodhound.

When she was finished, Emily shoved her ball into the hoodie's pocket. Then since they were by themselves, she held the shard of the Web Gem in her open palm, hoping it would pick up any vibrations from the Fairy Realm that even Benji might miss.

Intently listening with all her senses, she swung the shard in a sweeping arc widdershins — like running the bases — starting from east and turning as they walked.

She felt nothing.

Closing her fist around the shard, she shoved it into her pocket and let her shoulders slump in dejection.

Nothing helped.

Part of the problem, of course, had to do with this dowsing. She didn't believe in it.

Benji said it was good and, really, what was the harm?

Until now, she hadn't been able to answer that question directly. Now, though, traipsing through the park and watching Patsy turn in different directions, seemingly at random, Emily was embarrassed. Dowsing was ridiculous. She hoped no one would see her.

She swallowed a grumble of frustration.

She hated not having control over things.

A new wind made leaves skitter across the path, and she again felt the ominous presence of people watching. She scanned the area and found only those same kids loitering off in the far distance.

"All right," Benji said with an essence of glee in their voice as they walked. The discordance of their bubbliness against Emily's dour mood nearly made her stumble. "I can't help myself any longer!"

Breaking away, Benji loped freely to the swing sets, threw their lanky frame into the closest sling of a seat, and pushed back before letting fly. A moment later their patent leather shoes were pointed skyward, the back of their velvet jacket trailing behind as the swing arced upward, and their dark hair, perfectly coifed earlier, was getting windblown.

"Benji!" Emily called in annoyance, following them a few steps into the grass. She set her hands on her hips. "Focus!"

"I can't help it," Benji replied, almost singing in the spring air, knees bending to gain momentum. "I still like to swing!"

"This is why you suggested we start here, isn't it?"

Benji smiled. "This is my swing!" they sang boldly.

Emily stepped into the pit and grabbed the heavy chain supporting the mechanism.

"Hey! Get off my swing!"

"Seriously, Benj. There's no time for this. We've got to stay on track."

Benji raised one hand in supplication as the swing's momentum twisted it around Emily's grip. "I know. I know. But swinging always feels so magical. Don't you think? I've loved it since I was a kid."

Their tone made Emily feel like some kind of monster.

The three of them had a lot of ground to cover if they were going to find another baseball field, and they had no idea where to start. At least Benji had suggested this place — which was more than Emily had done. Emily had no idea what a good place for an alternate fairy ring might be. What did it matter why they picked it? Besides, since Benji was a litmus test of sorts, it made sense to start in places that made them feel good, didn't it?

"I'm sorry," she said. "I'd rather be playing baseball, you know?"

"Yeah. Me, too."

Together again, they returned to the path, one taking each side of Patsy, who proceeded to pitch her head gently backward and let her darkly painted eyes close into slits. With her all-black outfit complete with leotards, a billowing drape, and black-painted finger-nails, she looked like a wannabe witch about to totally summon up a demon.

Emily fidgeted. "How long is this supposed to take?"

"Quiet," Patsy whispered. "Everything is in the tools and tech-niques, but I have to concentrate, or it won't work. Keep your eyes peeled for anything that seems odd."

Emily rolled her eyes. Luckily, Patsy had already focused elsewhere.

With a silent sigh, Emily kept a lookout for sparks of fairy magic.

Birds tittered in the treetops.

Across the park, the three school-aged kids pointed at them, then laughed.

Marion Bulldogs, Emily thought, finding it hard to ignore their scorn. The kids were from the same high school that Callie McMasters had gone to.

The scent of the wind turned thick with a coppery odor Emily recalled immediately.

Fresh blood.

The Wild Hunt.

The pit of her stomach dropped like a hard sinker. Power from the boys' gazes washed across the park, their laughter filtered through the wind, and their askew glances sent a wave of anxiety strong enough to raise the hair on her arms.

She wrapped her fingers over the edgy surface of the Web Gem shard again, squeezing until it cut her, still disappointed to feel nothing from it.

The snarl of a car engine rumbled behind her. The sound of wheels grinding against concrete made her perk up like a meerkat on point. Movement in the street across the field caught her eye.

A silver flash in the sunlight. A car. A Mercedes.

Her blood froze. She thought she heard a deep, almost guttural sniff as if a beast was picking up her scent. In her pocket, the shard of the Web Gem flared warmly.

She took an instinctive step toward the nearby copse of trees.

"Is that...," Benji said, shading their eyes.

"McMasters. Yeah," Emily deadpanned. "That's him." Her pulse quickened and the sound of a drumbeat echoed from so far in the distance she couldn't make out the pattern. McMasters was following her. She knew that now. He was after her shard. Worse, he was getting more emboldened. She felt the presence of the Web Gem with him, now, too. Felt the pull of it against the shard.

McMasters' car slowed down as it approached the park entrance. It hesitated, then swung a wide path into the lot. When it parked, the Mercedes' lights went off.

Nervous energy rose in Emily's throat. The skin along her arm tingled.

Across the way, the three boys from Marion began to pad Emily's direction.

The shard grew cold enough in Emily's hand that she might have been holding a lump of ice.

"We've got to get out of here," Emily said.

"Right behind you," Benji said, all trace of their earlier brightness replaced with seriousness. They took Emily's elbow and pushed her deeper into the woods.

"We're not done," Patsy complained.

"No time to finish up," Benji said. "He's found us. Let's go."

To Patsy's credit, she tucked her rods inside the folds of her black outfit without further complaint. The three of them disappeared into the woods and ran through to the opposite side of the park, looping around as the boys chased them, to the smaller second lot where Benji had parked their car.

It was an older model Mini Cooper four-door Benji had bought with money they'd made working at a restaurant, painted metallic gold. It was all they could afford, but Benji liked it because it came with wings — they'd explained once — pointing to the company logo.

Chests heaving with exertion, they arrived at the car and piled in, Emily in the back.

Benji hit the ignition, and the little car roared to life.

Emily slammed the door behind her and Benji sped off, tires squealing on the asphalt.

The sensation of being tracked didn't fade.

When Benji whipped around to leave the park, they passed the main lot.

Fred McMasters stood beside the open Mercedes door, wearing his Ball and Glove jacket and scanning the now-empty park. As Benji's car raced away, his gaze tracked to Emily. Their eyes met, and for that ice-cold instant, Emily knew there was no escaping.

As Benji's Mini raced into the distance, McMasters scowled, then quickly got back inside his Mercedes.

"Where next?" Patsy said.

Emily stared at her for a moment too long, heart still pounding. "I don't know," she said. She was out of options. She knew that now more than she knew anything else. Worse, as she looked at Patsy holding on to the passenger's hand-pull as if her life depended on it, and at Benji, hunched over and twisting the steering wheel left and right as they drove, Emily's heart sank even further. All she'd succeed in by denying the inevitable was to bring her friends into danger. She couldn't ask any more of them. She had to do this alone.

The tang of the Wild Hunt covering McMasters was all she needed to know he wasn't ever going to stop, and the pull she felt on the Web Gem was all she needed to know that they were connected now. That he would always be able to find her.

She twisted to look out the back window and was beyond unsurprised to find McMasters' car appearing in the far distance.

The Mercedes would outrun Benji's Mini Cooper in a heartbeat.

"Pull over, Benji!" she yelled. "Let me out."

"Over my dead body!" Benji called over their shoulder, dark eyeliner drawing to a thin line as they peered into the rearview mirror. They pressed the accelerator, and the car's cabin rocked back and forth as the little car picked up more speed.

The Mini's tires squealed as Benji took a left into the Prairie View suburb.

A right on Crescent Hill and a left onto Bonaventure got them back out onto Main Street. McMasters was nowhere to be found.

"Whoo hoo!" Patsy yelped. "Good driving, Benji! You left him in the dust!"

"It's not going to last," Emily said.

"It'll last long enough," Benji said, taking a right at the red light so that they could keep moving.

"No, Benji. It won't." Her voice was dead now. Carrying enough certainty that Benji understood what she meant. "Stop the car and let me out, or I'm just going to jump."

Benji pursed their lips as if thinking. The Mini slowed, and Emily prepared to make the jump. Tuck and roll, that was what you were supposed to do when leaping from a moving vehicle, right? She tensed in readiness.

Instead of stopping, though, Benji calmly reached over and pushed a button. The child locks clicked into place.

"What the hell!" Emily yelled, pressing against the back seat as the car accelerated again.

"We're not leaving you behind."

As Benji spoke, McMasters showed up behind them.

"Damn!" Benji peeled out amid a billowing cloud of debris.

"Don't do this, Benji," Emily pleaded. "You'll never get away from McMasters. Let me out!" Frustrated, she pounded on the window glass.

McMasters drew nearer, and the Web Gem shard flared.

Emily pounded the glass again, trying to break it, but she couldn't hit hard enough.

The Mini's engine revved, and the smell of overheating metal flooded the cramped interior.

Benji's left turn was hard enough to fling her against the far door. The smell of burnt rubber was sharp and acidic.

She held on for the next right.

McMasters was gaining, though. Close enough she could see the Web Gem's magic glinting from his pupils. Then close enough to bump bumpers, and then pull beside them.

The Web Gem shard burned hard against her leg, illuminating them all.

A brighter companion to that flare filled the compartment of McMasters' Mercedes. They were talking to each other, Emily realized. The Web Gem and the shard. The essence of fairy magic was so strong Emily thought she might choke.

"Please, Benji!" Emily yelled, tears of anger welling.

But, as the magic bolt receded, she saw a new expression had come to Benji's face.

"What is it?" Patsy asked as Benji took a sharp enough right turn down an alleyway that they were free of McMasters for the space of a breath.

"I know where the ballpark is!" Benji called out as the Mini's engine over-revved. The car shot out of the alley and into the street. "Hold on!" Benji yanked the wheel left and nearly collided with McMasters as the two crossed angles again. The rattle of the Mini merged with the growl of the Mercedes.

A moment later, they were running free.

Benji turned again, but this time with a sense of certainty rather than the rush of being chased.

Panting for breath and relaxing her hold on the seats, Emily glanced over her shoulder to see the road behind them was clear. It wouldn't be that way for long, though. Not long before McMasters would find them.

Benji and Patsy seemed resigned, too. But it was clear they were going to push against her attempts to get them out of this. She might as well accept the fact her friends were as crazy as she was.

"How?" she said instead as Benji made another precise, intentional turn. "How do you know where the ballpark is?"

"The Web Gem," Benji said with a beatific smile. "It talked to me."

"Crap," she replied.

It wasn't the answer she wanted to hear because it said there was no way for her to save Benji now. Over their head or not, Benji was now Officially In Too Deep.

"He's not leaving us alone from now on. You know that, right, Benji? If nothing else, he'll catch us at the park."

"I know."

"What are we going to do when that happens?"

Benji's toothy grin cut into her. "We'll figure something out."

"All right," Patsy said. "Enough jibber-jabber. Where is this ballpark?"

Benji smiled. The engine roared.

"West side," they said. "Far west side."

They turned the Mini that way. A moment later, glancing through the rear windshield, Emily saw the grille of a Mercedes far down the road.

CHAPTER
TWENTY-NINE

The fading sunlight of late afternoon gleamed on the hood as Benji drove their car across the expansive parking lot of an abandoned strip mall. The concrete lot was deeply cracked and faded gray. After a half hour's cat and mouse with McMasters, the car's compartment felt stuffy and cramped even with the windows down.

Benji rolled slowly to where the lot looked over an empty, gnarled field, ringed by a broken line of oak and sycamore trees. Even sitting in the car, Emily could see the field was weedy, full of sawgrass, and clotted with brambles.

The car came to a lurching stop.

The engine gave overheated pings and snaps. The wind rasped over the open lot, blowing across the concrete pavement and out into the brambly field. Far away, behind them, boarded-up skeletons of shops and stores were in their freeze-frame moment of wasting away.

More important now: behind them the expanse was empty.

No McMasters.

The Mini being maneuverable, and Benji being more daring than their parents would like to know, they'd lost the man several minutes ago. In this quiet moment, Emily and her friends breathed a collective sigh to relax. Emily's shard of the Web Gem seemed spent, too. It lay quiet in her pocket as if it was dazed by the intensity of their chase. Emily would never think of the Wild Hunt the same way again. It was nice to have the respite, but even Patsy and Benji understood McMasters wasn't finished with them.

Emily gripped her mother's baseball, buried in the hoodie's front pocket, thinking that her only way out of this might be to throw a beanball at Callie's father on purpose and wondering if she had the guts to do it.

They didn't have much time.

Emily's thoughts went to the field before them. "Is this it?"

Benji unbuckled their seatbelt and got out of the car. They stood with the door as a barrier between them and the field as an unseasonably hot breeze whipped the velvet jacket they had sweated through. "Yeah. This is it."

Emily got out, too, joining Benji and then Patsy in shielding her eyes to assess the tree line and the field. Here, among the deterioration of the abandoned parking lot and strip mall, spring was bursting out like a long-caged animal. Not a pretty spring of flowers and buzzing bees, but a gnarled, tangled, wild spring full of thorns and muck. The grass was greening up, and new growth brought fresh scents from the trees, but dry husks of the past remained here, too. From the open field, the hot breeze gusted again, carrying dirt and dust and human detritus along with papery leaves. A dry, desiccated branch bounced against Emily's sneakers. She stepped back to let it go, then picked it up when it didn't budge. Her brows furrowed as she held its worm-eaten, gnarled roughness between her fingertips.

There was power here.

For the first time, if she was being honest with herself, Emily began to hold out real hope that a second fairy ring might be here.

"Come on," Benji said, crossing over the lumpy berm and picking their way over the gnarled roots of two thickly barked trees.

Emily followed. Patsy, too, drawing her copper rods from inside her jackets.

Emily kept her lips shut about Patsy and the rods. She didn't need dowsing to feel the energy here. Her hand gripped the dried wood as she passed through the line of tangled trees that had been growing wild in the decades since this side of town had been abandoned. A moment later, Emily stood beside Benji, who was stock-still, breathing in long, contemplative breaths as if they had been struck by something.

"Are you okay?" she said.

"Yeah," Benji replied, voice calm, but filled with wonder.

"Benji's right! This is it!" Patsy called with intense joy behind them. She stood at the edge of the open expanse, panting with her effort, copper rods pointed downward, sweat making her makeup run in a gauzy tangle that seemed only natural here. "I told you finding things was my superpower!"

Emily smiled.

The field was weedy, overgrown, and full of clumped dirt and patches of sawgrass that smelled fresh and powerful. If she looked closely enough, she could see the patterns she knew had been there a century before. Basepaths and foul areas. Out in the wild-seeded field, she saw the bump of a grassy knoll that had once been a pitcher's mound.

Emily stepped forward. The rustling leaves felt welcoming despite the grass's saw-toothed edges, so she continued, taking another tentative step, then another until she'd climbed the grassy mound and, gripping her mom's baseball, turned toward home plate to peer into a non-existent catcher who would be ready to flash a sign.

Her shoulders raised as she drew in a huge breath.

This field was full of ghosts. She felt them watching her as she trespassed into their forgotten domain.

Spectators milling along the sidelines, gawkers leaning up against the trunks of trees that had been removed years before, and women in chairs, chattering along the baselines where brush had reclaimed the space. She smelled cigars and the thick aromas of meat, pickles, and onion. Voices rose and fell, children running, adults laughing, oohing and aahing together as games played out. The breeze brought other chatter, too, voices coming through the haze of static like an old-timey song, the natural cadence of short-stops and other infielders chiding hitters and pushing pitchers.

A familiar sensation filled her — that instant of anticipation that comes in that split second between when a pitch has been thrown and when the batter reacts.

The crack of a bat startled her back to the moment.

Benji was right. This was it — the old field, built out beyond the city proper so Black people could play their baseball in peace. The sensation of isolation under the joy of the game rubbed her in uncomfortable ways, but there was baseball magic here, ground into the fabric of the place.

She couldn't help feeling stronger.

"We can play here," she said, stepping off the mound. "I'm sure of it. There's baseball magic here. If we can get a game up, I'm betting I'll be able to cross over."

The heavy crunch of tires on gravel was like a sudden flash.

In unison, they turned their heads to peer out to the parking lot.

"Crap," Emily said.

McMasters. His car stopped crosswise to Benji's Mini, blocking it in, though Benji could drive out into the rutted berm if they wanted to try it. McMasters got out of the car, still wearing his Ball and Glove jacket, then reached to pull the Web Gem from where he'd held it beside him. The shard in Emily's pocket gave a throb. The sweat from McMasters' exertion while driving glistened from his forehead.

"Well, well. Look what I found."

Emily gripped the baseball tighter, hearing her mom's calm whispering in the back of her mind. "Get in the car," she said to her friends. "He's only after me."

"She's right," McMasters said as he crossed into the field. "This is between me and little Ms. DeWitt here. No reason to get anyone else all tangled up, now, is there?" His brown eyes sparkled with carnivorous intent.

"We're not going anywhere," Patsy said.

Benji stepped toward McMasters.

McMasters presented the Web Gem. "Don't be a hero, little man. You won't like the result."

"I'm not a man," Benji said, holding their ground, feet parted, chin jutted forward. They ran their eyes over the trophy in McMasters's hands and let a scornful expression curl their lips.

McMasters openly scoffed at them.

Emily's grip went across the seams, and she realized that, yes, she most definitely could throw a beanball on purpose if the situation demanded it, and that a threat to her friends was a solid mark on the demanded-it side of the ledger.

Fastball, she thought, focusing on the shiny patch of McMasters' sweaty forehead.

High and hard.

"You can't win this one, kiddos. You know that, right? I've got all the power here. One thought and a little magic later, and I can have you all dancing a jig if I want."

The trophy gave a glint in the fading light. Emily's shard responded with a thin pulse.

"Don't be that idiot," Emily said, calling his bluff. "You're no fairy lord. And you didn't win the series, so that's not how it works, and you know it. If it was, we wouldn't be here. So, I'd say that you should back off before I put this baseball through your skull."

McMasters' smirk carried mournful undertones. "I was hoping to do this the easy way, but I guess you're all opting to make it harder on yourselves." He gripped the Web Gem and began to whisper to it.

A burning sensation crawled over her skin. Emily gritted her teeth against the energy of the Web Gem. She reared back to throw the baseball but found her muscles weren't coordinated enough to make it happen. Instead, she toppled over, face-planting into the old pitching mound. Serrated edges of the sawgrass cut into her cheek, and the smell of rich soil mixed with the tang of fairy magic filled her senses.

Maybe she'd been wrong. Maybe McMasters' belief in his control over the Web Gem was right.

Benji, too, seemed uncoordinated, but Patsy managed to throw one of her dowsing rods at McMasters, and the hard copper handle flashed in the Web Gem's light as it flipped, axe-like on its trajectory to impact the back of McMasters' head.

"Arrrhh!" McMasters winced.

The magic of the Web Gem faded enough that Emily made it to her hands and knees. She scrambled to reclaim her mother's base-ball, which had rolled off a distance when she tumbled.

"That's it," McMasters yelled, holding the Web Gem in one hand and cradling the back of his head with the other. His face grew flushed, and his expression twisted with anger. "You're going to regret this!"

"No, I don't think they will."

The voice came from the tree line behind them, and Emily twisted to see none other than Megan Moore standing there, phone up and recording.

Emily had never been happier to see the reporter in her life.

"What?" McMasters whirled. "You!"

"You really don't drive well, Mr. McMasters. I counted ten red lights you ran and three yards sodded by cutting corners. And that doesn't even count going the wrong way on a one-way street and doing what had to have been sixty-five in a school zone. All caught on video, of course. Dash cams for the win."

McMasters bared his teeth, and a genuine snarl rumbled in his throat. "I don't have time for this."

"I left you a message, Mr. McMasters," Megan said. "Several, in fact. I need an interview. It's a shame you made me trail you just to get it."

"I'll just take you, too," McMasters said. He brandished the Web Gem at her.

"Go ahead. But if you do, I'll have this whole video loaded onto my public stream before you can say assault, battery, and wanton endangerment."

Megan's gaze was as piercing as a fey lord's.

McMasters hesitated, clearly weighing his options and beginning to see the ramifications of her pushing that button. The Web Gem's glowing form shimmered in his hands.

The breeze swirled through the field, too hot for the tail end of February.

Emily thought she caught a flicker of movement, a wave of long-dead motion, from the true inhabitants of the field.

McMasters stood down. "I don't think that will be necessary now, will it? I'll be happy to give you an exclusive interview any time you want. Just contact my assistant and we'll set up a time when we can sit and talk awhile."

Megan held her finger over the send button. "You need to leave now, Mr. McMasters. Unless you want your entire afternoon's activity dropped out in public. And that goes for forever, too. Leave Emily and the rest of the Unicorns alone, or I go public."

McMasters glared.

Megan brought her finger closer to the screen. "Your choice," she said smugly. "I was hoping we could do it the easy way, though."

McMasters shrugged and drew a resigned breath.

Emily stood up. "Go on. You heard the journalist."

"This isn't over, Emily," he said. "You're dealing with stuff bigger than us."

"Like I don't know that."

McMasters pressed his lips together, then slipped away like a wolf with his tail between his legs. A moment later his Mercedes growled as he drove away.

Emily, Benji, Patsy, and Megan exchanged silent expressions, then all burst out speaking at once.

"Thanks," Emily said after everyone had taken a much-needed moment to laugh.

"No problem," Megan said. "If there's anything I hate more than an obnoxious asshole, it's a liar who weaponizes an interview."

"Yeah. I can see that."

Emily wasn't sure if she and Megan Moore could ever be best friends, but she was growing to appreciate the reporter. Megan was competitive and tenacious. Traits Emily had, too. But rather than using them on a baseball field, Megan used them on a dogged quest for the truth. Sometimes Emily didn't like that, because sometimes the truth hurt. But she could respect it. And in the end, it was probably for the best that the truth came out.

"All right, then," Benji said. "What's next? Are we going to rock this place, or what?"

Emily quirked a corner of her lip, then looked at Megan.

"You up for the scoop of a lifetime?"

The reporter's eyes flashed. "Tell me more."

Emily's quirk turned into a full-beamed, toothy smile as she turned to her teammates.

"Megan just bought us a bit of time, here. So, let's use it. Tomorrow night," Emily called. "Midnight. What do you say we get the Unicorns out here and make some baseball magic?"

"All right!" Benji gave a whoop.

Emily turned to Megan. "Bring your camera. You're not going to want to miss this."

CHAPTER

THIRTY

The time was late in the mortal realm as the Seelie King entered the pitch-dark offices of the building labeled MCMASTERS BALL AND GLOVE. Not that it mattered. His fairy magic meant it might as well have been midday. His bigger complaint was the mortal realm's smell — which was toxic to his sensibilities. Everything from the exhaust of cars to the odor of the asphalt they toiled over was acidic and harsh.

And this was just nighttime when everyone was asleep. He shuddered to consider what the place smelled like in the open light of the day.

The Seelie King came to the Ball and Glove's back entrance and pulled a baseball from the bag he'd carried across with him.

The ball gave a brief flash of pale gold.

He smiled and pressed it to the door, grinning wider after the magic worked and the lock clicked open.

Counter to the council's opinions, the Seelie King was no one's idiot.

He was also no plebe when it came to the use and sense of magic.

The Duke of the Silver Forest had not told him everything, but with an operation of the size it took to raid the Unseelie Queen, it wasn't difficult to discover the details.

No one knew where the Web Gem was. Now here was the duke, and his council members, telling him they were ready to acquire it and threatening him with subordinate roles.

That simply would not do.

He was the king.

It was time they found out what that meant.

He had doubled back after their meeting and found the store of baseball magic allotted to the duke in a locked storeroom. Being king still held privileges, though, even with such mutiny as the council was attempting. Opening the storeroom, he found, quite fittingly, piles of baseballs — each radiating the essence of magic so strongly it took his breath away.

The king had pushed as many handfuls as he could manage into the skins he'd looped through his belt.

Later, from the comfort of his own tower, and using one of the balls to scry along the path of the details he already knew, the Seelie King had found the truth. That the duke had spent the magic it required to traverse the gate and foolishly placed the Web Gem into the hands of an imbecile mortal. Or mostly mortal.

He understood McMasters had a bloodline that ran through the Seelie Court, but even just standing in the human's building was enough to let him know that trace was so faint as not to matter. The place was a disgrace. Boxy and barren of anything resembling character or taste.

The Web Gem was here, though.

Its pull had been picking at him even before he entered the premises, and just holding the baseball charged with the game's magic was confirmation. The Seelie King loved the game, and if that love had taught him anything, it was that baseball magic knows baseball magic. He let the ball guide him through the building until he came to the office labeled FRED MCMASTERS, PRESIDENT, AND CEO.

The Seelie King pressed the same magic-laden baseball he'd used to enter the building onto this locked door.

Once again, the ball's cover flared — this time with the opalescence that indicated magic lay here. The aroma of baking seams wafted upward. That much, at least, was pleasant.

The door clicked.

He stepped into the office, which was nicer than the store itself, though that wasn't saying much.

Not that any of it mattered to him.

Simply stepping into the room brought a surge of desire over him.

The Web Gem was in the man's safe, which he found behind a hideously done life-sized portrait of, the king assumed, the man himself.

Working the magic to finagle the combination was more complex than simply unlocking the doors, but the king bent himself to the task, and another baseball's worth of magic did the trick. Wiping a layer of nervous sweat from his upper lip, the Seelie King turned the lever on the safe and opened the door.

Crystalline blue light flooded from the compartment. He bent to examine his find.

There, in its full, gleaming splendor, was the trophy of his desire.

"What are you doing?"

The voice behind him was sharp.

The Seelie King whirled to find McMasters standing in the office doorway — confirming the portrait's identification.

McMasters eyed the king cautiously. "You're one of them," he said.

The king stood to his full, imposing height.

McMasters took a quarter step back, looking for the moment like he might bolt. He glanced at the Web Gem and seemed to think better. He was clearly in distress. "Did the duke send you? I can explain."

"Yes," the king said. "I think you should."

McMasters stammered for a moment, then seemed to catch his wind. "You see. Um. I figured out who ... through intensive footwork tracking down leads, that is ... I figured out who has the Web Gem shard. A girl, right? I used all my business clout to try to get her back to the duke through that portal under Unicorn Field, just like I promised. But she's been tricky, and now she's got friends helping her out. I've got her in my sights, though. That Web Gem of ours is great for that. To a degree, anyway. I can always see her when I try, but I've been afraid to take it outside into the public eye. I tried it today, but..." He trailed off with a shrug that spoke volumes.

"That's wise."

The king assessed the mortal fully, sensing a considerable degree of untruth to his blathering, but also sensing that it might be best to simply let the imbecile talk on. Could it be that a mortal had a piece of the Web Gem? A young woman, no less? No wonder things were going to hell so quickly. He should have guessed the Small Folk, with their strange views of sharing, would do something so brash as to defile the trophy.

"I promise it's just a matter of time now, though. I'm waiting for when she's properly alone. Once I get hold of the piece, I'll pass it right along."

"I see."

"Maybe you can help?"

The Seelie King brushed his hair back. "I'm sure I could. And who is this girl with the Web Gem shard?"

"A real brat. Emily DeWitt's her name."

His lips were almost impossible to restrain, but he managed to avoid giving a luxuriously wicked smile. "Emily DeWitt," he said, letting the name roll over his tongue, tasting the syllables and letting power shape itself around them. "Little Miss Em."

"What's that?"

"Nothing," the king said. Everything made sense, now. The Duke of the Silver Forest had the Web Gem, but with a piece missing, and without authorization as a true owner — like the Small Folk would be — the duke and his council would be unable to take advantage of the artifact's full power. So he'd given it to this mortal imbecile and charged him with finding the shard that would make it whole.

"And where is Emily DeWitt now?" the king said.

"That's what I was coming here to find out. I was hoping I could catch her alone."

"I see."

The king grabbed the Web Gem out of the safe. Just touching it was ecstasy.

"Show me the one named Emily DeWitt," he said.

The Web Gem flared, and heat radiated from the bag of magicked balls at the king's side.

Scintillating light filled the room.

An image formed.

"Do you know where that is?" the king asked.

McMasters' face twitched. "You betcha. But I can tell you she won't be alone there. She'll have all her bratty little friends around."

The king lifted one gracefully arched eyebrow. "And you believe this will be a problem for me because...?"

McMasters gave a smile that was at least half relief. "Got it," he said. "You're the boss, aren't you? Let's hop in the car and I'll get us over there lickety-split."

The king groaned.

An automobile drive. An unknown length of time spent encased in a moving cage of cold iron. He wondered how long he could hold his breath in this realm.

"All right," he said. "Let's go."

He tucked the damaged Web Gem into the crook of his arm and let McMasters lead them out into the parking lot.

CHAPTER

THIRTY-ONE

Dawn broke, and the myriad of tattered denizens of the Fairy Realm arrived at the practice field. Not only those who would play in the game, either. Lady Marne had brought her selkies and undines to spectate as she herself served as the umpire.

The cyclops who usually filled the role was currently made of stone.

Which was a microcosm of the reason they were gathering now. Make baseball magic, open the portal to the Real World, and use Emily DeWitt's piece of the Web Gem to set the Fairy Realm right again.

The entire Wild Hunt had shown up en masse. Callie was under no illusions that they had come to save Trace or the satyrs they'd lost. The Hunt leader had commanded they play, so here they were. It was behavior she understood because the Hunt was very much a live-and-let-live kind of organization. If a member of the Hunt — be they a slavering werewolf or one of those psychotic little Red Caps — showed weakness, it was up to them to get better or be left behind.

Still, though their ability to forget about Trace and move on was understandable, it was no less annoying.

On the more heartwarming side, the field was positively teeming with Small Folk. Essie had carried the plan of attack to Fennoc, and though she'd been all fired up to bully him into complying for the sake of her poor Greeven, Fennoc had agreed instantly.

"My brother is on the Field of Statues," he'd said. "As well as Twy and many others we Small Folk count as friends. And Miss Em is in danger. If the leader of the Wild Hunt and Lady Marne agree to play using the queen's plan, so will the Small Folk."

And play they would, even more than Fennoc had anticipated. Now every pixie, gnome, dryad, and faun for a hundred miles had to be here on the practice field, stretching, prancing, dancing, and otherwise getting themselves prepared to play whatever form of baseball they could.

Feeling admittedly a touch anxious about her part in the game, Callie watched the players warming up, which, given the on-again and off-again drizzle, was more difficult than it should have been. As a result, though, the field had greened up brilliantly and, when the sun occasionally broke through the clouds, it made a series of vivid rainbows.

It was Callie's blood the queen would use to open the portal. She didn't like getting stuck for simple blood tests, and this was like that feeling, amped to eleven. At least a blood test didn't entail the nurse twisting fairy magic into her DNA.

Little Essie sat on a mound of river rocks that had been stacked one on top of the other. Fennoc had claimed it for their dugout, and the team had scattered their stuff over the ground there.

Essie was warming up, too, already cheering. "*G – R – E – E – V – E – N!*" she called. "*M – I – S – S – E – M! Hit them hard, hit them long, let's go get that danged Web Gem!*"

To Essie's side stood the immaculately uniformed Fennoc, his traditional long blade of grass bending from his lower lip. There was a hardness in his eyes Callie had never seen there before. She wondered if he was thinking about his responsibility for the Web Gem and his distaste for the Fairy Realm leaders who had done him dirty. She hoped he didn't blame himself for it.

When he noticed her looking, he pulled his hat down over his eyes.

The Unseelie Queen sat farther down the third base line, the Designated Hitter still by her side. Callie doubted the queen would allow him out of her reach until she'd fully recovered from the Seelie attack, which, given the amount of effort she'd expended, could be a while.

Neither the queen nor her Designated Hitter would play today, but once enough of the baseball magic was gathered, the Designated Hitter would carry the queen into the fray so she could work her spell.

Callie suppressed a shiver at the thought, trying again not to think of the moment when she would let a drop of her blood fall into the evil fairy's hand until she had to.

She hefted her bat, feeling its excitement.

There was that, at least.

Lady Marne stepped onto the field. Though she'd agreed to the queen's scheme, she still cast a stormy glare at the fairy who had turned so many to stone. Even now Callie saw her glance in the direction of the Other Field and its Field of Statues.

In the early, dark hours of the morning, Callie had gone for one final visit to Trace. She'd found Lady Marne already there, kneeling in land-going form before the dual sculpture of centaur and faun — Trace and Maddoc. Callie had joined her, wordlessly, and the two of them had kept a silent vigil. She'd suspected the mermaid and the Small Folk manager's brother had been an item at one time or another — this made her think that maybe they still were.

Now, Lady Marne broke her glare at the queen and lifted two fingers to her lips. A shrill whistle pierced the morning air. "Play ball!"

Between the drizzle and the rainbows, the game progressed, and

Callie found herself finally able to put the rest of the world behind her.

For a moment, anyway.

It was the strangest game of baseball she'd ever played, fueled more by instinct than the written rules of the game.

One play included three Small Folk fairies, who were all playing left field, missing a fly ball and then relaying it back and forth to each other with such exuberance that no one seemed to care that three runs had been scored on the play.

At one point, Nash, the little gnome catcher, hit a ball that was almost a double, but the throw came in a little too early. Instead of sliding into the tag at the rock that marked the base, Nash stopped early and dove directly into the earth, digging a hole the instant he touched the ground. A moment later he emerged on the other side of the rock and coyly reached out to touch it.

"Safe!" Lady Marne called.

"He was out of the basepaths!" the slavering werewolf shortstop said, sniffing hard at the umpire.

Lady Marne lined up the two holes and the base. "I'd say he was right on the path. Safe!"

The game continued like that for long enough that time seemed to stand still.

The Hunt pulled a sneaky triple play by dipping the ball in a bag of blood and twisting off a bit of Hunt magic. Fennoc called a double steal, the wrong way, just for fun — then did it again, Izusa making it safely back to third by doing a cartwheeling maneuver, complete with a double twist and a landing that stuck exactly on the third base stone.

Callie, beginning to feel even closer to her bat, drilled a pair of homers.

The lumber crooned sweet nothings to her when she returned to the sidelines after the second.

She tried not to let its praise go to her head, but at the same time, she *was* a very good batswoman.

The Wild Hunt had scouted her for a reason.

The game continued until the sky grew darker, but still the Unseelie Queen had not indicated that the baseball magic they'd accumulated was enough to work her spell. She was lounging on a night-black blanket, looking smugly satisfied as her Designated Hitter spooned sweet honey custard into her mouth.

Callie came up to bat again. Mellica was on the mound, a softly glowing baseball in her mitt, her wings blurring as she held herself aloft so her toes barely brushed the dirt.

Callie raised her bat.

Now, she said to it. *When she's least expecting it.*

The bat shivered in anticipation.

The pitch came. Mellica's curveballs trailed purple sparkles after them, and when Callie smacked it straight on, the sparkles persisted in its new arc.

The ball struck the Unseelie Queen right in the face with a burst of violet embers.

Across the entire field, players and spectators let out a smattering of nervous giggles.

The queen screeched her fury, but Callie knew she was fine. And sure enough, when the queen rose to her feet, only a single, thin trickle of blood dripped from one nostril.

"Blood for blood, your Majesty," Callie called, emboldened by her success. Using her bat like a sophisticated walking cane, she strolled to the queen's little picnic spot. She indicated the translucent haze of baseball magic that covered the practice field.

"Seems like this ought to be enough to do your spell," she said. "Or do you need me to send another shot or two your way? I admit that's a lot more fun than I thought it would be."

The queen glared at her and waved Adrien away before he could blot her bleeding nose.

"This will be sufficient, mortal. Provided you keep your end of the bargain."

She slipped one hand into her billowing robes and produced a gleaming silver knife.

More drama queen than Unseelie Queen if you ask me, Callie thought. She gathered herself, though, and nodded curtly.

Together, she and the queen — with the help of her Designated Hitter — walked back to home plate.

This was it. The most dangerous thing Callie could do.

She didn't hesitate. Never breaking eye contact with the queen, she held one hand out over the plate.

Movement around her let her know others were edging closer. The Hunt leader came to stand at her shoulder. Lady Marne positioned herself between the plate and the mound, arms crossed. Fennoc came from the Small Folk's dugout with Essie perched on his shoulder.

The queen let out a huff. "So untrusting. I gave my word, did I not?"

"You also stole from us and turned our friends into statues," Callie said, unable to keep the snark from her tone. "I think they can come with us."

"Just try and keep us back," said Essie. She flung herself from Fennoc's shoulder and clambered up Callie's body. "I'm watching you until my Greeven's fixed."

The queen gave her a thin smile. Then, with snake-like quickness, she grabbed Callie's hand.

The knife drove into the pad of Callie's index finger, and she hissed with the pain. Somewhere inside her, the flight part of her fight-or-flight response kicked in. *Pull away,* it said. *Run! Hide!*

I will not run, Callie thought, clenching her teeth against the pain.

She watched as a single drop of crimson blood slid down her finger and fell onto home plate.

The queen let the knife fall, too. It clattered against the plate as she lifted her hands to the cloud of baseball magic.

She spoke her spell.

The baseball magic gathered with enough heft that it no longer seemed a translucent, ephemeral thing. The air grew thick with the odor of stale lightning and wet soil.

A jagged, shimmering slit appeared in the air over home plate, and Callie gasped as every single cell of her blood aligned towards it.

She felt him. Her dad.

The Web Gem was with him.

The slit rent open, and a maelstrom rose over the field.

With no time to steady herself, Callie — with Essie clinging to her shoulder — fell through the hole in the world.

CHAPTER

THIRTY-TWO

J ust past midnight, Emily stood on the old pitching mound, wearing her full Small Folk uniform and casting a nervous eye around the gathering of her friends and teammates.

The coordination it took to get everyone out to this forgotten field had been a bit of a madhouse, but Benji had pulled it off.

The Unicorns had worked on the field all afternoon and into the evening, leveling the worst clumps and clearing up the basepaths. The outfield would be a bit dicey, but it seemed safe enough. Emily was worried the infield would be a breeding ground for bad hops and twisted ankles, but Benji had worked to fill in what holes they could. Still, the field felt good to be on. Even Megan had helped. And, as midnight had drawn closer, the Unicorns brought every kind of light to the old field they could find, from camping flashlights to photographers' get-ups. Five cars were parked around the field, their high beams left on to blaze through openings in the tree line. Even the sky got in on it, bringing out a big, full moon that gave everything a sharp haze of dark indigo.

Jamal Douglass and Jake Nesbitt were in on the full details of the night's plan, as, of course, were Benji and Patsy. And Megan, too, whose demeanor seemed to oscillate between amused and enthralled as she watched preparations.

The rest were here for the party, which was fine by Emily, though she was still nervous about involving them in something that touched the Fairy Realm. Still, she needed baseball magic, and her failure with Benji at Unicorn Field told her she couldn't do this with less than a full team. With the truth coming out anyway, there was only so much she could do.

So, the more the merrier. Those not fully in the loop thought tonight was meant to be a bit of fun, a celebration of the start of spring training played on a field no one had known existed, or perhaps just a small bit of rebellion against the McMasters takeover of their home field. If anyone thought the requirement that Emily score three times was strange, they didn't say anything.

The night was warmer than it had been for weeks.

The sky was open, and the brightest stars drilled through the moonlight. A depth of trees spanned the third baseline and wrapped around to left field — lit occasionally by what Emily first thought might be the season's earliest fireflies. They came too often, though, and as she stood on the mound, waiting for Jamal to take his position at the plate, she flashed on the pixies, Mellica and Jessebel, and on Shady Marie, who would have adored the gnarled, ancient oak tree that grew behind home plate.

Emily transferred her mom's baseball from her baggy uniform pocket to her bare hand, just to feel the smoothness of its casing and the comforting ridges of its bright crimson seams.

Every crossing had a cost, she thought. Last time, when she worked with Callie to cross over, she'd had to give up her mom's ball, and only luck — or a trick of the baseball magic itself — had let it fall back into her hands again.

This time she had to be ready to say goodbye to it forever.

She breathed deeply, letting the warm night air linger in her lungs. Despite her nerves and her looming sense of loss, standing in the middle of this derelict old field felt marvelous.

The teams were ready, and a glance to the side let her see Megan was also poised, phone at the ready to document the activity of the evening.

Jamal stepped into the batter's box.

Behind her, her teammates chattered. Their secret game was getting ready to start.

Emily put the ball back in her pocket for safekeeping until later, then picked up the plain ball she'd dropped at her feet. She leaned in to get Jake's signal, feeling the flare of the Web Gem shard in her uniform's baggy back pocket.

Then she let loose a fastball right down the middle.

"Strike!" Jake called.

Without a formal umpire, everyone had agreed the catcher would call the pitches. This was merely a fun scrimmage, after all.

Jamal did not argue. Instead, he used his bat to knock non-existent dirt from his cleats, then stepped in again.

He hit her next pitch for a single into right field.

"Nice hit," she called to him as he took his lead. "Don't get used to it, okay?"

He gave her the Unicorn Salute, his index finger raised from his helmet.

The game progressed.

Jamal pitched for the opposition, and it was like his stuff had been amped. Emily smiled, remembering that Callie's coaching had focused on him at times last season. Now Jamal's play had risen to the level where the college coaches were starting to notice.

Jake was doing well, too, catching everything that made it to his catcher's mitt. Emily's money was on Jake Nesbitt catching for a major school next year.

But tonight, there was no discussion of scouts, no thought of colleges or professional baseball. Tonight, there was only pitching and catching, the sounds of baseballs popping into orbit, and the lovely arcs of swinging bats.

The crack of the bat sounded so beautiful out here in the dark. The voices of players merged into the nighttime and felt as natural as an owl's call in the distance.

Emily sat on the dewy grass as her team went to the sidelines in the seventh inning.

She would hit third.

Her hands wrapped around the handle of the bat she would use, and her breathing brought in the most gloriously scented air she had ever tasted.

This would be it. She could feel it. Emily had doubled and scored in the first inning. She'd grounded into the last out of the second inning but managed an inside-the-park homer in the fifth.

Around her, pressure built. As the game progressed, heat flashes came from the woods around them—flashes only she could see. She felt her mom's presence here, too, tied up in the baseball she'd handed over to Jamal at the start of this inning, but also somehow bigger. Her mom was in the air tonight. Emily felt her in the gentle breeze of nighttime and in the hushed rustle of leaves at the edge of her senses.

This was the moment.

She thought about Callie, and about Adrien.

It was time to break his curse for good, and time to get Callie out of the Fairy Realm if she needed to. It was time to make sure the Small Folk were all right.

"You good?" Benji said as they sat in the grass beside her.

"Yeah." Her gaze caught theirs.

"I don't want you doing this alone," Benji said.

Emily shook her head, understanding what Benji was saying. "No, Benji Amberman, you can't come with me. As much as I appreciate the thought, I couldn't deal with it if something bad happened to you there."

Benji put their hand on Emily's knee, a touch that seemed both urgent and intense. "I don't think you understand."

On the field, Jake stroked a single, and as he scooted down the first base line, Emily took in Benji's entire being. Their posture. Their expression. The way their arms bent and lay against their crossed-legged position.

"It's about your family," she said, thinking about them for the first time since they'd started this whole search.

"Yeah. Some, I guess. But mostly it's about me. I need to know who I am, Emily. I need to know where I come from."

On the mound, Jamal taunted Patsy as she stepped in to hit. Emily would be next.

Jamal's first pitch was a strike.

"All right," Emily said. As much as it scared her, she knew now it would be wrong of her to shut Benji out. And if there was one thing she'd learned in dealing with the Fairy Realm, it was to let people have their own truth. "If I score again, make sure you're at the plate when I get there."

Benji smiled. "Thank you."

Patsy popped out to the second baseman.

"Here we go," Emily said. She stood up and saw Megan Moore was ready. As if she wouldn't be, Emily thought. Tenacious people are always ready. They locked eyes as Emily took a practice swing to loosen up. Then she stepped to the plate.

THE MERCEDES ROLLED down the street, out to the west of town, to the area where the poor lived before it had gone back to seed. Until yesterday, McMasters hadn't been here in a long time, but he remembered the abandoned strip mall and its expansive, cracked parking lot.

A flood of adrenaline rolled over him as he saw the lighted field.

With his headlights off, he rolled the car to a stop.

He couldn't wait to see the kids' expressions when he rolled up with a full-blooded fairy lord in his back pocket. The DeWitt brat would be particularly delicious to watch. Truth was, she wasn't a better player than Callie had been. But she could have had it all if she'd just up and played ball with him. Now here she was, about to be shown what it means to play in the big leagues.

Even with the seat pushed back, the lord from the Fairy Realm beside him was too tall for the compartment. He hunched over to keep his head from hitting the ceiling and cradled the Web Gem in his lap.

"Here we are, bud. You can breathe again," McMasters said as he opened his door.

The lord got out so quickly that, despite his athletic grace, he nearly fell. As he clutched the Web Gem to his side, the trophy gave a blue and white flash. The smell of ozone filled the air around the Mercedes.

The sounds of baseball filtered over the parking lot. The glow of lights came from an open meadow across the way.

"There they are," McMasters said.

His passenger oriented himself in the direction McMasters pointed, then, jaw clenched, set out on a direct course.

"Hey, wait for me." McMasters slammed his door shut, then did the same on the passenger side before running to catch up.

The fairy lord was tall, though, and he walked with a brisk pace. Keeping up was not an easy task.

As EMILY STEPPED to the plate, the world closed in on her. There was only her and the baseball that Jamal held. Her mom's ball this time. The pitch came. In the distant haze of Everything Else, her chest rose and fell. The weight of the bat levered magically around her shoulders. Her body weight transferred majestically from her back foot to her front. Her torso twisted to drive power into the ball.

The crack of the bat was an intimate thing.

Her mom's ball rocketed into the air and disappeared into the trees beyond the outfield. A pang of loss struck Emily's heart as she ran the bases.

But now her surroundings reasserted themselves.

Baseball magic coalesced.

Cold lightning crackled over the woods, and a vortex formed, twisting in fairy space, pulling at Emily as she trotted. Power from her mom's baseball wove itself into the wind of that vortex, bringing the maelstrom to settle over home plate. The shard in her pocket grew warm, too. Too warm, Emily thought. Its vibration came in so low it made her stomach twist.

She rounded third, pressing on and ignoring the shock of her teammates, who were beginning to react to the signs of real magic happening around them.

Across the way, though, a new entity drew nearer.

Emily's heart froze. There, coming from the parking lot, was the Seelie King, his pale visage ablaze with triumph as he strode rapidly toward her — completely ignoring Mr. McMasters running hard to catch up to him.

What was the Seelie King doing here?

He had the Web Gem in one hand. Despite the darkness, Emily knew it was true. The Web Gem. It called to the shard in her pocket.

Homeplate pulsed with baseball magic as the vortex linked to it. Benji was there, too, cheering her on, oblivious to the threat stalking up from behind. Panicked now, Emily ran harder, sprinting as the Seelie King raised a hand that had already begun to gleam with the arcane light of magic. He was here to stop her. Emily was sure of that. She had to get to the plate, or she'd never be able to help Adrien or Callie.

The sound of his voice rose.

Three steps away. Then two.

Thunder rumbled, and the sound of splitting trees broke the air.

Benji grabbed Emily's shoulder as she braced for the tumble through the transfer gate.

"Stop there, Emily DeWitt," the Seelie King called as she started the final step that would bring her into contact with the plate.

Against her will, Emily froze.

"No!" she screamed. She struggled, fighting with mind, body, and soul against the Seelie King's hold.

But he had her. Her true name had fallen from his lips, and he had her.

An inch away, the gate opened.

She slid her eyes to Benji, clenching her teeth against the urge to beg them to go in for her, to save her friends where she could not. Because if there was one thing she knew was true as a perfect curveball, it was that the presence of the Seelie King here with the Web Gem in the Real World meant that things were horribly bad on the other side.

The Seelie King glided towards her, holding the Web Gem aloft. "You will give me the shard, Emily DeWitt."

The Web Gem swam in a scintillating current of wispy magic.

He held out his free hand.

"And you will give it to me now."

"Over our dead bodies."

Patsy stepped forward, bracing herself through the now gale force winds of the vortex as she clambered to home plate. She wasn't alone.

"You mess with one Unicorn, you mess with us all," said Jamal.

Emily looked around, and tears welled in her eyes. None of her teammates had run from the crackling magic or the threatening figure of the Seelie King. Every Unicorn stood around her, smacking fists into gloves or brandishing bats like clubs as the wind pulled at their hair and uniforms.

The Seelie King's lip curled in a sneer. "How quaint. But it's all for naught. I have the girl's true name. She will do as I command."

He twitched his long, thin fingers, and Emily's muscles itched to comply.

Then Patsy snickered. "Maybe not," she said. "Think fast, Em."

Fast as blinking, she whipped her hand out from behind her back and threw something at Emily.

Emily reacted on instinct. She was at home plate, and a pitch was coming her way. But since she had no bat, all she could do was hold out both hands to catch the ball.

She didn't even realize she'd broken the King's command and moved of her own will until the smooth, familiar leather of her mom's ball smacked against the meat of her palms.

Instantly, the Seelie King's hold on her melted away, and she breathed a shuddering sigh of relief. Just as her mom's ball had shed the Unseelie Queen's magic in that fateful game in the Fairy Realm last season, it was now breaking up the Seelie King's spell.

A new sense of wonder came over her at the realization of this deeper magic her memento held.

"How?" she croaked to Patsy. "I hit it into the trees. It was gone."

Patsy grinned into the wind and patted her hip, where a pair of copper rods poked out. "I may never leave home without these babies again."

The Seelie King let out a shriek of rage. "Emily DeWitt! Give me that shard now!"

Emily clenched her fingers around her mom's ball. "Nah, I don't think I will. I think I'm going to go rescue my friends, instead. C'mon, Benji."

Benji took her hand, and together they turned to face the open gate that still gaped over home plate.

In tandem, they stepped forward. But the gate shuddered and instead of opening wide it gave a shriek. A brilliant explosion of light blinded Emily and a wall of hot pressure clapped her in the face.

She gritted her teeth and willed herself not to take a step backward. She couldn't stop now. Not when she was so close.

But before she and Benji could leap into the portal, someone else tumbled out.

Many someones.

First came Adrien Thorn, falling forward and twisting his body so the Unseelie Queen would fall on him rather than the ground.

Next came Callie McMasters, with none other than little Essie clinging to her shoulder and a truly fantastic bat strapped to her back. Callie managed to stumble sideways quite athletically, avoiding tripping over Adrien and the queen.

Finally came the leader of the Wild Hunt, Lady Marne, and Fennoc, falling in a tangled, flailing pile in the knobby dirt before home plate.

The vortex closed shut with another momentous clap of thunder.

"Miss Em!" cried Essie, jumping down from Callie's shoulder. "Everything's gone mildew and mold in the Realm. We have to get the Web Gem back, or the Seelies will ruin everything, and my poor Greeven will be a statue forever!"

The howling winds had died the instant the gate closed. Now a ringing silence fell over the field as the members of the Unicorns gathered, watching events unfold with expressions of astonishment and wonder that grew as the seconds ticked by.

Megan Moore, of course, could barely decide where to point her phone camera.

Essie broke the silence, speaking in a cascading rush, again about the Seelie oppression, about the loss of baseball in the Realm, and about the Field of Statues.

"Statues?" Emily said, feeling a bit faint.

"Many of our friends are stricken," said Lady Marne as she brushed blades of grass and clods of dirt from her pearlescent legs. "'Twas the queen's doing, but since the Seelies stole her power along with ours, nothing will save them but the restoration of the Web Gem."

"Seelie King!" the Unseelie Queen said with a wavering voice as she lay sprawled in an undignified, most certainly not queenly position atop her Designated Hitter, who was gasping for breath. "Your Court's crimes must be answered for. You will taste the vengeance of the Unseelie Court this night."

"I have the Web Gem now, Unseelie Queen," the Seelie King said, holding it forward and ignoring the crowd. "I'm afraid you will have to go unavenged."

"You may have possession, but you do not have rightful owner-ship," said Fennoc, also brushing dirt from his jersey, but with an expression of no little dismay. "The Web Gem belongs to the Small Folk this season."

The Seelie King ignored him, turning his terrible face to Emily.

"I will have the shard!" he said, rushing at her. Magic built around the Web Gem in his hands.

Emily held her mom's baseball before her, feeling a protective power building around it but uncertain if it could stand against the strength of the Web Gem.

"Just try it," Callie said as she whipped the bat from her holster, stepped to the space between Emily and the king, and waggled it back and forth. "I dare you."

The king glanced warily at the humming bat barrel as it glinted in the coolness of the nighttime air. "Hunt Master, see to your charge," he said, though the conviction in his phrase was now lacking.

"We're on my home turf now," Callie said. "Be careful you don't bite off more than you can chew." She pursed her lips and cocked her head defiantly.

"Callie," Mr. McMasters said, stepping into the circle for the first time.

His appearance caused her to hesitate.

"Dad?"

Sensing her diversion, the king took a step toward Emily, but Callie bore down, stepping even more fully between them. "I should have known you were involved from the start. This whole thing reeks of bad business."

The king laughed. "Enough of this frivolity." He focused on the Unseelie Queen, who was now standing, though with significant effort. "It saddens me to see you consorting with such low folk. You of all people know the Web Gem must be made whole again. You know what will happen across the realm without its full presence."

"Then I'd say it would be better for you to give me your piece of the Web Gem," Emily said before the queen could answer, mocking the king by holding her hand forward, palm up. "I am Small Folk, after all. It belongs to us. And if what my friends say about the state of things in the Realm is true, you'd better hand it over quick."

"You have a better chance of getting the queen to give up her Designated Hitter than prying the Web Gem from my fingers."

Emily locked eyes with Adrien, who had now mostly caught his breath and was standing, propping his queen up against his side. For her part, the queen seemed bedraggled and frail, unable to bear her own weight. A sallow hollowness undercut her face and spoke of illness. The last time Emily'd seen the queen, she had been strong and formidable, even in defeat. The difference was startling.

The queen was vulnerable, Emily saw. There was no way she could weasel out of granting Emily any boon she asked for.

The shard in her pocket pulled at her insistently. She reached back and pulled it out.

As the piece appeared, a shock of power pulsed over the field so strongly that the entire audience took a step back. The shard's edges bit into her fingers. Its pull towards its proper place was so abrupt the shard nearly slid out of her grasp.

Sensing its power, Emily understood exactly how much effort Fennoc and the Small Folk must have gone through to get her share of the prize to her. She understood something else, too. After that effort, she could not afford to waste her boon on saving one person, no matter what she had promised.

She turned to the queen, who met her gaze boldly now, and she spoke in a trembling voice. "As I recall, this will give me one boon."

"Emily, no." It was Adrien who spoke.

Emily smiled so she wouldn't cry. "I know, Adrien. And I'm sorry to have to agree with you now, but I'm going to have to break that promise I made you. Bear it a little longer, will you?"

Relief danced in his eyes as he nodded.

Emily turned to the Seelie King and held up the shard as if it were a weapon.

The king recoiled. It was a slight motion, but it was enough.

"The shard allows me to ask for one boon from any fairy leader. Seelie King, for my boon I request that you hand your piece of the Web Gem over to me."

Her hair twisted in a sudden dust-up of power.

A fragrance thick like roses swelled up around her.

Then the king's voice rose through the mist, giving a thunderous laugh.

He was fighting her. She could feel it through the power of the Web Gem flaring between them. Her heart sank. She had the right to wield this power, but he had the bigger piece as well as all his natural Seelie magic.

The power broke off, and a crack of lightning sizzled to the ground between them. Emily fell back with a cry.

An oily chuckle slithered through the air. "Possession is nine-tenths of the law, isn't it, DeWitt?" said Mr. McMasters.

Scowling, Emily clambered to her feet.

"Don't be so obtuse," the queen said, her demeanor as snobbish as if she'd been asked to explain Court etiquette to McMasters. "One cannot use the Web Gem to ask for the Web Gem."

The Hunt leader came to stand before Emily, sniffing the air around her as if picking up a trail. "Things have degraded," he said, turning to the king. "If you do not give her the Web Gem, it will only get worse."

The king scoffed. "I will never submit to a mere mortal or one of the Small Folk. If I cannot have the Web Gem's power, then let it degrade."

"You're a bigger fool than I suspected," said the Unseelie Queen. "Even your courtiers respect the threat of the spiderkin."

The king bared his teeth at her. "Do not speak of my courtiers. They will get their just rewards in due time. As for the ancient arachnids, we have not seen their kind for centuries upon centuries. I doubt they care one silken thread for our squabbles. The Web Gem is *mine*."

Emily didn't know what these "spiderkin" were, nor did she want to. All she cared about was setting things right. But if she couldn't make the Seelie King grant her the boon she was due, what hope did she have of helping anyone?

She clenched her hand around the shard, feeling it bite into her flesh.

The faces of the kids who had been playing ball to help her create the baseball magic stared at her as if they were waiting for her to do something. The Unicorns were all here. Their wide mix of expressions said they were coming to realize that whatever was going on around their baseball club was quite real.

Seeing them here, and knowing she had brought them into the situation, made Emily sick to her stomach.

The Unseelie Queen laughed her sharpest socialite's laugh. "You think you know the Web Gem so well, foolish King of the Seelies? You forget I held it for more than a century, longer than you've had your crown, even. I know its secrets far better than an upstart like you."

The king glared at her, his knuckles pure white around the Web Gem. "Be silent."

"I will not. Miss Em, don't let him twist things in your mind so. Even divided, the Web Gem cannot be made to act against itself. But that doesn't mean you can't request a different boon."

Emily blinked at her, then looked down at her clenched fist. "A different boon."

But what would she ask for, if not the Web Gem itself? What would put the world — both the Fairy Realm and her Real World — to rights?

It was Benji who broke the silence. Their voice was quiet, but anyone who heard it couldn't help but lean in to listen.

"What about a baseball game?"

Emily stared. "A baseball game?"

"Winner takes all. Unicorns and whoever wants to join us versus the Seelies. After the game is over, Emily agrees to put the piece back, and the king here agrees that if we win, the Web Gem goes back to the Small Folk where it belongs."

"And if you lose?" the Seelie King said with a sneer.

Benji shrugged. "Then you get your trophy, I guess."

Emily considered her options. "A sporting deal," she said under her breath.

Benji put a hand on her shoulder. "We'll win," they said.

"I don't know, Benj. I don't want to get you all involved."

Benji laughed and waved an arm at the gathered Unicorns. "Everyone's already involved. And why not? Unicorn Field is inherently tied to the Realm. We've all got a right to understand that heritage. And we're good enough to play ball with anyone. We almost took state last year. With you, we're so much better."

"Yeah," Jamal said. "I plastered that pitch of yours earlier, Em. Don't tell me I can't play ball."

"We can do it," Patsy said.

But Emily had her doubts. She'd seen the Seelies. They were a very good team.

Callie cast a glare at her father, then holstered her bat. "I'm a Unicorn," she said. "So long as they'll have me."

"Once a Unicorn, always a Unicorn," Patsy said, giving the team salute.

"I, too, will be a Unicorn," the leader of the Hunt said, coming to stand beside Callie against the king. He acted as if he did not see Callie's surprised expression.

"I will be a water Unicorn," said Lady Marne. "My kelpies will drag you to the depths of every mud puddle in this field."

Fennoc stepped forward, his back straight and his beard quivering. "The Small Folk are Unicorns, just like Miss Em."

"And me!" shouted Essie. "I'll cheer the Unicorns until they grind you to dust, Seelie King!"

The king glared at each fairy who pledged, but said nothing. Behind him, Mr. McMasters shifted in obvious discomfort.

The Unseelie Queen nudged Adrien to bring her closer. As he did so, she lifted one pale hand.

"I am in no shape to play for any team. But to see your fine face rubbed in the dirt, O Seelie King? I offer the services of my own Designated Hitter to the Unicorns. Once a Unicorn, as the witchy girl said."

Adrien grinned fiercely up at the king.

"It's not happening," the king said. "I refuse to bow to this farce!"

"Oh, shut up, you blowhard," Emily said, raising the shard. She felt its power rise again, and now that the queen had pointed out the problem with her first request, the magic flowed easily in this attempt.

She spoke loud and clear, so everyone on the field heard her words. "I request the boon of a baseball game to be played here on this field, starting tomorrow at midnight. You bring your Seelies. I bring my peeps."

The king struggled, but Emily saw the truth of the queen's words in his efforts. He would capitulate because he had to.

"Winner," she said, "takes the Web Gem."

THE BIG GAME

CHAPTER
THIRTY-THREE

Under Benji's unrelenting pressure, Callie stayed at the Ambermans' place that day, snatching rest where she could and recuperating her strength with the aid of Mrs. Amberman's delicious cooking. As far as Callie could enjoy anything, it had been an amazing day.

News of the Fairy Realm seeping into the mortal world had set Benji's mother on fire. After hearing details, she'd flittered from place to place around the house, moving like she was drinking an endless flow of caffeine. "I knew it," she would whisper between whistling jaunty tunes. She riffled through pictures and touched a number of mementos scattered around the house. At each stop, she told Callie about this family legend or that.

"This was my mother's," she explained as she touched a crystalline marble the size of an egg. "She used to stare into it for hours. Said she could see things more clearly with it. And this," she said, staring at a sepia-toned picture on the wall, "was my great uncle Rassis. He was a remarkably good shortstop in his day. Outstanding with the glove and better than adequate with the bat."

Callie had nodded and made appreciative sounds — completely genuine — as she took another piece of chocolate babka.

Compared with what she had expected at her own home, it had been a joy.

Talking with Mrs. Amberman had made it easy to forget her own father, and to quiet her racing thoughts about Trace and the others in the Field of Statues, though the knowledge of their predicament never fully left her. The babka alone was enough to earn her a brief respite from thinking about what her future might be.

To be honest, Callie was worried.

Before all this happened, before fairies of any sort had come into her life, her future was clear. Play baseball, get a scholarship, and fight to make it to the pros.

Now, with hordes of fairies prying their way into the Real World like something out of a nightmare, Callie couldn't focus on those old dreams.

Tonight, her hometown would play host to the most powerful fairy lords as they played a game of baseball for the right to claim the Web Gem. Where would it stop? Was it such a leap to envision the Wild Hunt racing through neighborhoods on Midsummer Night? Or the Unseelie Queen promenading down Main Street on Samhain?

There wasn't enough chocolate babka in the world to ease that worry.

The sun had set, and the air was taking on a springtime chill. Despite the hours that remained until the midnight game time arrived, neither Benji nor Callie could sit still. Mrs. Amberman packed and repacked the boxes of sandwiches and soft drinks she was sending along — enough for the whole Unicorns team, muttering about making sure there were extra for the fey folk who would be joining them.

"I wish I could watch you play," she said, finally coming to sit on the sofa between Benji and Callie. Her cheeks glowed in that same familiar way that Benji's did.

"It would be too dangerous," Benji said. "Emily's right about that much."

"I know," she replied, a sadness in her eyes. The Amberman family understood the problems inherent in messing with the Fairy Realm. "But later, if we can, I would love to see it."

"I know, Ma," Benji replied with a tone that sent a wave of tangled emotion through Callie's entire body.

The Ambermans knew who they were. Their sense of self-awareness felt foreign to Callie.

Time ticked by in slow clumps.

Dinner was a strange, furtive, and yet warm affair, with both Mr. and Mrs. Amberman alternately casting worried glances at the clock and telling anecdotes about everything from Fairy Realm ancestry to annoyances at work.

Finally, after the dishes were cleared and both of Benji's parents had given Benji and Callie a tight hug each, Callie followed Benji out to their car.

She laid her bat across her lap and stared out the passenger window. The aura of discomfort radiating from the wood let Callie understand exactly how dangerous this moment could be.

Before they had disbanded last night both Callie and Emily had gathered up their Unicorn teammates to discuss the need for complete secrecy when it came to tonight's baseball game.

"I promise to tell you everything I can," Emily had said. "But right now I think it's best to wait. Because the little pieces of magic you've seen tonight are nowhere near what leaders like the Unseelie Queen and the Seelie King can do if they get riled up. Baseball magic and the Web Gem will keep them in check during the game — I *hope*, anyway, but we're playing with fire. I don't want to be responsible for having unleashed anything like that on our city — and I'm sure you don't either."

Callie had told them, in sharp, clipped tones, briefly about magic she had seen.

"You can't imagine what it's like to see someone you *care* about be turned to stone right before your eyes and to not be able to do anything about it."

She'd trailed off and let her audience fill in the gaps.

She hoped it would work.

The last thing they needed was to have a whole city show up to gawk.

But the thing was, for all she figured they could trust the Unicorns — who, according to Callie's Marion classmates, were nothing if not a bunch of goody-two-shoes — she had no idea how to predict what her father would do.

If he felt he was losing his advantage, would he call in the media? Or the cops? Or worse?

He had more than enough money to throw at his problems.

She felt more than a little pukey recalling the smarmy tone of his voice as he tried so oafishly to play dealmaker last night. It wasn't that her dad was *evil,* but he was so full of himself that he couldn't see certain things even when they were shoved directly into his face. Sometimes it added up to the same answer, though.

And there would be no changing him.

Callie saw that now.

Her jaws clenched tight, and her hands made fists around the bat handle. The smell of its rough-hewn woodgrain sent fresh energy surging through her veins. The feel of mud rubbed into a baseball was dry against her cheeks.

See the ball, hit the ball, the fairy wood whispered to her. *Simple solutions work for many problems.*

Callie sighed. As much as she'd relish hitting her dad upside the head, she knew he wouldn't be so simple a problem to solve.

Benji, also, was lost in thoughts. During the drive, the conversation between the two of them consisted of mostly grunts and sighs.

The tires bumped as Benji guided the car to the overgrown baseball field outside of town. Since they planned to use the headlights to help the game, Benji drove into the field and parked along the first baseline.

It was nearing darkness as they stepped onto the field. Spring insects were beginning their chants, and the smell of growing grass was thick.

Emily's car rolled up to the parking lot a short distance away. Her dad was driving.

Emily clambered out of the passenger seat. She was in her teal and blue Unicorns uniform this time, rather than the brown Small Folk kit. Seeing it brought Callie a sense of their old rivalry, now flavored with the spice of friendship.

Mr. DeWitt got out as well, hugged his daughter, then glanced Callie's way. He lifted one finger to the brim of his White Sox cap. "Play well," he said with a nod. Then he turned and walked to the fence line as if scoping out a good vantage point to watch the game from.

Not for the first time, Callie felt a small tinge of jealousy. Mr. DeWitt was a good dad.

Callie shouldered her bat. It whispered a soft sound that comforted her.

"Couldn't wait any longer, either?" Benji said to Emily as she approached.

"Getting my game face on," she replied.

Together, the three of them went to the field to find that, despite their promptness, they were not the first to arrive.

"Adrien," Callie said.

"Hi."

Wearing his Unseelie regalia — uniform, cleats, and hat — he was seated against the gnarled oak that grew behind home plate. The Unseelie Queen was there, too, still looking fatigued, but with enough strength to be sitting up on her own and picking sprigs of various weeds and wildflowers. With her feet tucked elegantly beneath her and her midnight black skirts laid out around her in the long grass, she looked, oddly, like both the innocent peasant girl and the wicked queen of common fairy tales.

And someone else was there, too. A girl, a stranger to Callie. She stood against another tree, a blue bicycle lying awkwardly on the ground by her feet as she tapped furiously at her phone. In the darkness, the bright light of the screen illuminated her face like a kid holding a flashlight up to tell a ghost story around a campfire. She was scowling.

"Hey, Megan," Emily said, sounding tired. "Figured you wouldn't be late."

Callie's footsteps whisked through the grass as the trio came to stand nearby.

The girl — Megan — glanced up from her phone, took in all three of them in one deeply assessing sweep, then lowered her eyes again. "Good news and bad news. I finished my article. Submitted it to the *Pattersonville Times*."

"And the bad news?" Benji said.

"Already rejected."

Emily made a dismayed sound. Benji gaped.

"But the exposé...," Emily said. Her eyes darted to Callie as if in apology. "How can we get the truth about Mr. McMasters out now?"

Callie swallowed the wave of nausea rising in her belly. They were trying to expose her father to the public. Of course, they were. Benji had filled her in on the details of what he'd been up to while she was trying to play baseball in the Fairy Realm.

It seemed their plan had run aground before it had even set sail, though.

Megan waved her hand as if shooing flies, continuing to type one-handed. "Not a problem," she said in a dismissive tone that was too obvious to be real. Even Callie could tell Megan was seething underneath that veneer of indifference. "I'm the best reporter Pattersonville West has turned out in years. I'm not giving up that easily. Mark my words, the *PT* is going to regret that choice. I'm already chasing the next scoop."

Callie looked to Adrien for a deeper explanation, but he merely shrugged. "Megan Moore is nothing if not persistent."

The three Unicorns shared a soft, uncomfortable laugh.

As if commanded by a force they did not understand, they all fell silent.

A force came over her, or a presence. The hair on the back of her neck stood up. She caught first Emily's gaze, then Benji's. Megan's furious typing paused.

At first, Callie thought it was the Seelies coming from the Fairy Realm early, but it wasn't that. The Seelies would wait until the last minute, she figured. All the better to make their opponents sweat. But there was *something* here. People, she thought. Sweet spices. The smell of a cigar, maybe.

Her bat grew warmer, and the faint echoes of voices played at the edge of her senses.

"What is it?" Callie said. She glared at the Unseelie Queen as if the queen were a child who'd brought a creepy crawly into the house.

But the queen gave a dismissing twist of her spindly fingers and went back to weaving her weeds into a tiara. "Don't look at me. I have no ties to whatever shades haunt your mortal world."

Beside her, sitting in the tangled roots of the dark oak tree, Adrien blew out a breath heavy enough to draw attention. He laid his head back against the gnarled bark and propped his elbows over his knees so that his long hands dangled loosely.

"What do you know?" Callie said.

"We used to call this place Dark Field," Adrien replied in an uncomfortably awkward tone. "It's where Black people — we called them negroes at the time — would play. They weren't welcome on Unicorn Field."

Callie's stomach dropped. Then she promptly chastised herself for being surprised. What's that? Small-town America? Mistreat Black people? Please.

Callie knew all the history. She'd read about Jackie Robinson, and she'd watched plenty of movies about the past. It still hadn't prepared her for standing in this place and feeling the remnants of the power of the people who'd made their own magic here filtering through the night.

Tuned in, though, she felt the presence of the crowd and the heat of the players. Somewhere, she heard a bat crack against a ball. Her own bat gave a soft hum in reply.

A final moment's silence settled over them.

Adrien stood up and dusted moss and soil from his Unseelie uniform.

"Not our finest moment," he said. He pulled his cap off his head, then reseated it and turned to the others. "We're going to need to play our best tonight," he said. "And I worry even that won't be enough."

"It likely won't," the queen said.

"What's that supposed to mean?" Callie replied. She whipped her bat around, limbering her muscles, already feeling better for the release of endorphins.

The queen twisted to face them. Her eyes flashed with enough vigor that Callie wondered what treacherous plan she was cooking up.

"The Seelie King has the Web Gem. Don't pretend he is going to play you straight up."

The four of them looked at each other. Megan typed ever onward.

Emily retrieved her shard of the Web Gem from her back pocket. It sat on her palm, looking like nothing more than a hunk of costume jewelry. She'd already spent her single boon. As soon as the Seelie King made good on it, the shard would return to the main body of the Web Gem.

The crunch of tires on grass approached. More Unicorns arriving.

"Well," she said. "At least we won't be facing him alone. Our friends are behind us."

The queen chuffed. "Good luck with that." She settled back into the knotted root system of the tree and returned to harvesting little bits of wild growth that were within reach.

Like the jaws of a wolf around her prey, something in Callie snapped.

"Says the woman who couldn't beat the Small Folk even when she was cheating. The Web Gem's going to make the Seelie King play, fair and square. So, what does he have that we don't? My dad? Like *he's* a catch. He hasn't played any sports since the stone age. We're going to win, your Unseelie Majesty. And we're going to win big." Her gaze whipped to Megan. "You can add that to your next article, reporter girl."

Megan tipped her head back to cast a wry smile at her. "I will."

Emily chuckled. "Right on," she said. "Enough doom and gloom. Game time is coming. Let's get ourselves loose and ready to go, all right?"

"All right," Benji said.

"Let's do it," said Adrien.

Callie twirled her bat like a baton.

"Game on," she said. "It's a great night for baseball. Let's make this happen."

CHAPTER

THIRTY-FOUR

Without time for the Unseelie Queen to concoct the magic they would need to open a portal again, the fairies who'd come to reclaim the Web Gem had chosen to stay overnight in the Real World. Only the Seelie King had flaunted his power by returning to the Fairy Realm to collect his players.

Stretching her arm, Emily watched from the pitcher's mound as — having spent the day hidden in a sheltered portion of the woods — the leader of the Wild Hunt emerged from the gnarled thicket past left field. Fennoc, with Essie riding on his shoulder, appeared a moment later. Lady Marne, still dripping from the creek bed Patsy had helped her find, came from the opposite direction.

They each looked worse for their day spent in this Real World of mortals.

On the leader, that dishevelment made the already feral glint in his eyes even that much more hair-raising. He reeked with such a strong odor of blood that Emily didn't want to ask him how he'd occupied his time.

Fennoc had dusted his uniform, but there was only so much that could be done about stains made of a day sleeping among the trees of this mortal world with no magic to keep things from getting messy and uncomfortable.

Lady Marne's iridescent scales sparkled with prismatic rainbows in the light of the parked cars lined up along the baselines, but Emily saw fatigue in her darkened eye sockets. It could not have been pleasant being alone in an unfamiliar trickle of water.

The Unicorns, too, arrived in a steady stream of one or two at a time, each stepping out of the darkness and into the sharply lit field as if they were as ephemeral as the ghosts that lingered here.

Jamal was the first to arrive, Jake the last.

At first, the Unicorns seemed hesitant around the fairy folk, as if they needed to confirm these new teammates were real, and that what had happened last night was *not* a figment of their collective imaginations. Lady Marne broke that tension like she would the surface of a still lake, however, joining Jamal's game of catch and then helping Patsy stretch out.

"I love what you've done with your eyes," the lady said of Patsy's night-black makeup.

Patsy smiled. "Would you like me to show you how?"

"I'd rather you teach me your swing. My hitting is my weakness."

"Deal!" Patsy said.

The Hunt leader simply ignored the cowed looks on the Unicorns' faces as, during batting practice, he barked out coaching tips, though occasionally Emily had to temper his ideas.

"I am not wrong!" he said through gritted teeth the second time she interrupted him.

"The game is different here than in the Fairy Realm," she told him. "Where you're from, pitches can do weird things when the magic gets to flying. But in the mortal world, there's no such thing as a 'blood-marked pitch.' My players can't hit as aggressively as you do."

"No blood marking? But then how do you throw a nose-breaker?"

Emily bit her lip to keep from laughing at the bewildered look on his wolf-like face. She turned instead to encourage Lizzy Rodriguez to try her warm-up pitch again.

As the evening proceeded, the warmups became a jovial affair that included banter and even, eventually, cautious cajoling between the fairies and the mortals. They were teammates, though. And after throwing baseballs with the fairy folk, the Unicorns seemed to grow into the idea that they were just baseball players, like all the rest of them were. The fairy leaders, likewise, took to the moment, the leader of the Wild Hunt yapping after each batting practice swing, and Lady Marne deflecting the attentions paid by the humans she played catch with.

The warmup included Fennoc hitting infield grounders.

"Fine scoop out there!" the faun called as Patsy reached a tough chopper he'd sent her way. "Nice throw!" he called to Jamal when he ranged to his left to grab a ball up the middle, then twisted to get a proper toss to first base.

It was hard for Emily not to smile at Fennoc as he worked with the team.

He was such a natural coach.

The team liked his steady banter and the pep he brought to infield practice.

Emily noted, also, that every one of her Unicorn teammates found a way to spend a few moments with little Essie, who radiated a boundless source of excitement and energy. "You'll get them!" she'd say to one. "Just have fun!" she'd encourage the next. "Wallop one for my Greeven!" she told Jake when he asked Essie to make his bat magic.

The night grew darker, and a sense of anticipation blanketed the field.

The stars emerged, gleaming through the light of the nearly full moon.

For a moment, there was only the sound of Megan Moore pecking her intrepid story into her phone.

The team was ready.

All they needed was an opponent.

"Where are these Seelies?" It was Jamal.

As if on cue, a flare of silver light flashed from centerfield, accompanied by an electric *whumpf*.

A pane of light shimmered in midair, lined by a darker frame that sparkled and snapped with emerald and sapphire flares. The sharp, sweet aroma of magic came flowing outward.

From the portal's center, players from the Fairy Realm began to arrive.

The Seelie King led the procession. Over his pristinely ultra-white Seelie Court uniform, he wore a heavy robe that draped down his shoulders to touch the grass behind him — woven of rich golden flax lined with white sable. His uniform gleamed in the harsh lighting. His baseball cap glimmered like it was gilded with sixteen-carat gold.

In the crook of his arm, he held the Web Gem, caressing it with regal, if not artificial, indifference.

Emily wondered if he realized how much it made him look like the Unseelie Queen of last season.

The rest of the team followed: a collection of satyrs, sprites, and other fairyland athletes who each outdid the other when it came to their decorum. They wore their uniforms primly, and each stepped forward with a sense of control that made their movements seem like a ritual. One by one, they took positions beside their teammates until they stood en masse, each focused forward onto the field and the Unicorns before them, some with bats slung over their shoulders, others with mitts pressed under their arms. As a collective, they looked smug, standing there with chests puffed out and shoulders thrown back like they were preparing for a team picture.

The last figure to step out of the gate was Mr. McMasters.

Or, at least, when Emily saw Callie's dad step out of the portal, she was shocked enough to assume he was the final member of the Seelie Court's entourage to arrive.

There was, however, one more member of the Seelie Court to arrive.

He seemed older than the rest. His hair was silver-gray, though the skin over his cheekbones was as smooth and beautiful as was usual for Fairy Realm highborn. Unlike the members of the Seelie Court baseball team, he wore a suit that included an overcoat of the darkest blue, trimmed with golden thread, sharply creased at the shoulders, and almost military in bearing. His trousers were also dark blue lined in gold, fitting tightly against legs that, despite the fairy's apparent age, were still honed and well-muscled. He paused briefly upon arriving, taking a moment to survey the grounds and then breathe in the air — motions that belied a certain familiarity with the place. His air was detached in the way of all royals, so much so that Emily thought the rest of the Seelie team may well bow or curtsey at his arrival.

They did not, but their lack of such civility did nothing to reduce the sense of power Emily felt coming from the fairy lord.

"The Duke of the Silver Forest," Adrien, who was standing beside Emily, whispered.

A glance to the sidelines showed the Unseelie Queen's eyes were slitted as the Seelie politician strode across the outfield grass, flanked on one side by the Seelie King and the other by Mr. McMasters.

"The Duke of the Silver Forest?" Emily muttered back. "Why is he here?"

Adrien shrugged. "Fairy politics is a tangled web."

"Don't condescend to me."

He winced. "Sorry, Em. Being back with the queen has me talking all Shakespearean again. If I knew what was going on, I'd tell you."

Emily didn't have time to accept any apologies, though. Her dad was striding in from the first base side where he'd been watching. His face was flushed with anger, and the vein in his forehead was visible for the first time Emily could ever remember. He was heading to cut McMasters off.

"What the hell do you think you're doing, Fred?" he called, his voice strained with barely controlled anger.

McMasters, unconcerned, let a slow smile spread across his face.

Unheeding of the Seelie players bristling behind their cohort, Emily's dad came on. "By god, Fred, you've got a lot to answer for. I won't stand for what you've done to my girl. If you think—"

"Dad!" Emily called in her firmest voice.

Her dad stopped.

She took a step his way, then paused, too. "Dad. I'm sorry, but I've got this. You can't help here."

He stood still for a moment. His fists clenched, then unclenched. He shot another look of dark fury at McMasters. Then, like air being slowly released from a balloon, his shoulders came down from around his ears. "All right, Emily." He retreated only one step, but that was enough.

Emily returned her focus to the oncoming Seelie representative.

The Duke of the Silver Forest stalked his way toward the infield until he stood before Emily.

"So. You are the notorious Miss Em," the duke said. "I've heard much of you, of course." His expression gave away nothing of whether his assessment of her matched those stories.

"I don't have the luxury of any such knowledge about you, Duke of the Silver Forest."

The duke's expression said he was indifferent.

"Your boon call compelled my king to participate in this game, Miss Em, so participate he will. But we are the Seelie Court, and, according to the Laws and Rightful Ways of our court, you cannot compel the rest of the team to play without our council's commitment."

Emily glared at his attempt to confuse her. "What does that mean?" She turned a pointed glare on the Seelie King. "He's the king, right? He puts out a royal decree or whatever, and everyone jumps to do what he says."

The duke clucked his tongue like a disappointed father. "That is not the Way Things Are. Our king has an important role to play in our court, yes, but he does not have carte blanche with our folk. That is what the council is for."

He smiled then, a not-nice smile that would have been right at home on Mr. McMasters' lips.

Emily could just bet he took great joy in using his council power precisely the way Emily had described the king might do.

He continued, pontificating now like a dramatic television lawyer.

"The Web Gem boon must be complied with to the extent that the Fairy Lord in question has the capacity to enact it," he said. "But only to that extent. My king will play, if such a game does, in fact, occur. If the game you requested *cannot* occur, then the agreement is void."

Emily's heart clenched. From behind her, she felt more than heard the gasps coming from Callie and the rest of her teammates. She felt the truth of the duke's statement in the hollow sensations that were coming through the shard of the Web Gem where it rested in her back pocket. Its power had been used up, the boon satisfied the moment the Seelie King had stepped onto the field ready to play. There was nothing she could do.

The duke's eyes glimmered.

Emily narrowed her eyes at him. "So, you're backing out?"

"I didn't say that," the duke said. "It happens that our council is intrigued with your proposal. We are a long-sighted governing body, and an incomplete Web Gem benefits no one in the long run. As such, we have an interest in entering into the game."

Relief fell over her.

"With a condition."

"Condition?"

"As the challenged party, the council claims the right to assign the official for this One Big Game."

"You want to bring your own umpire?"

The duke's lips curled into a comfortable grin.

The leader of the Hunt interrupted. "And if we don't accept?"

The Duke of the Silver Forest drew a resigned breath. "You have no place in this negotiation, Huntsman. Miss Em made her boon call, so it is Miss Em, and only Miss Em, who can make this decision." He turned back to Emily then, and his voice grew tight. "It would be a shame to have been so close to reunifying the Web Gem. But if that is your choice, then that is your choice."

"You're saying that if I don't agree with your umpire, you'll take your team and go home?"

The duke's response was a subtle change of expression that told her she had a decision to make.

As if considering his proposal, she tugged on the bill of her Unicorns cap. Then she looked at him sideways as she tapped non-existent dirt from her cleats.

There was only one choice to be made, and everyone knew it. They were going to play this game, no matter how the Seelies tried to weasel their way into the upper hand. She and her mishmash of a team were simply going to have to play the cleanest and best game in all of human history.

"I hope your umpire understands the rules as we play it here in the Real World."

The Duke of the Silver Forest glanced at Fennoc, then back to Emily. "Oh, believe me, Miss Em. Our umpire knows all about the rules." He cupped his hand and cast a glowing strand of magic into it, then released it toward center field, where once again a silvered flare of light flashed.

A moment passed.

Then a creature stepped from thin air. No gate opened to let it through; it simply stepped out of nothing and into reality.

Dark.

Spindly.

Eight legs bent at awkward angles to lift an almost robotic body so large that, at first, Emily didn't recognize the shape as that of a spider. Then she took in the features of the human torso that rose from that arachnid foundation. That human part of the thing the Seelies had chosen to be their umpire was bone pale against the shiny blackness of her abdomen and legs. Her long, blonde hair hung in matted chunks like clumps of straw, as pale as her shoulders and torso.

The spider woman paused, swaying to catch her bearings. The spinneret at the back of her bulbous abdomen spun a shadowy thin filament that attached her to the outfield grass.

The Unicorns players gasped, and Jamal gave an audible yip. Adrien gaped in silent confusion or awe — perhaps a bit of both. The Unseelie Queen's eyes drew down as if she was contemplating something, but Emily could tell the queen was stunned by this turn of events, too. On the first baseline, the Seelie King made a noise of disgust, but Mr. McMasters stared as if he looked upon a goddess. Even Megan stopped typing, though, after a dazed moment, she slowly lifted her phone to take a photo.

Only Callie seemed unfazed by the creature's arrival. She came to Emily's side, brandishing her scintillating bat as if it were a flaming sword. She met Emily's eye, then gave a wordless nod of readiness. That look helped settle the nausea that had twisted Emily's stomach, but only a little.

What kind of monster had the Duke of the Silver Forest set upon them?

"A spiderkin," said Fennoc, his stunned voice filling the tense space.

"Indeed, Small Folk," the duke replied. "You broke her toy. Now it's time you paid the price for your insolence."

"How did you find her?" Fennoc asked, now fidgeting, though fidgeting was too small of a word. Fennoc was an anxious mess. He had chewed his traditional grass stem to a nubbin, and his ears still twitched this way and that.

"That's hardly the right question," Emily snapped as she took in the new umpire, still getting her bearings just beyond the mound. A shiver of revulsion ran through her. "What *is* this spiderkin thing?"

Fennoc opened his mouth, but nothing other than a dry bleat came out.

"The spiderkin are an ancient people," the Unseelie Queen responded from her seat in the shadows. "Disappeared in the early ages of both the Fairy Realm and the mortal world, along with a slew of other Ancients." Her gaze glowered with a deep purple opalescence, and her voice was both smooth as butter and sharp as a knife.

"What other Ancients?"

"Dragons!" Fennoc blurted.

"Among others," the queen added. "The Spider Folk left with the true giants, the sphinx, and —" She paused for dramatic effect as her gaze fell over Emily's teammates. "—even unicorns. But the Arachnid Ancients were the most magical of them all. When they retreated from the Realm, they left the most powerful artifacts behind."

"The Web Gem," Emily said, feeling a rush of enlightenment. "The spiderkin made it?" She cast an awe-filled glance at the horrible thing standing on the field and tried to imagine such spindly appendages even touching something as wondrous as the Web Gem.

The queen's smile was so strong Emily could almost hear it slide over her lips.

"And I broke it!" Fennoc moaned, putting his head in his hands. "I never believed they would come back!"

"And yet they have," said the queen. "It will be a certain kind of pleasure to watch the Spider Queen take her justice, little faun."

Fennoc blanched under his thin fur. The tufts in his brows drooped.

Emily glared at the queen and felt heat rise to her cheeks. "Don't blame Fennoc. He was trying to do the right thing. Which is more than I can say for you. If I had half a mind, I'd tell your Designated Hitter to throw the game just to spite you. He could do that, couldn't he? You can make him play, but you can't make him do his best. That would be your worst nightmare, wouldn't it? The Seelies controlling

326

the Web Gem? Maybe I should tell him to throw the game unless you give him his freedom."

Emily glanced at Adrien, who was watching in carefully neutral silence.

"You don't know your friend so well, do you?" the queen said with a soft laugh.

Emily glared at the queen. Adrien would throw a game if it meant saving his friends. That was something that, even in the short time she'd been with Adrien Thorn, she'd come to admire about him. "I know he hates being under someone else's command, and I know he's already thrown himself on that grenade to keep someone else from suffering his fate."

The queen's reply was laden with sardonic threat. "He knows how much your friends will suffer if the Seelies win the Gem."

Emily turned back to Adrien, but he wasn't looking at her anymore. He was staring with narrowed eyes at the spiderkin umpire, assessing her the same way he'd sized up Emily when they'd faced each other as pitcher and batter during the previous Fairy Realm season. The sight made Emily's heart sink with understanding. Whether he loved baseball or not, Adrien had to play this game. And he would.

"You're a beast," she said through gritted teeth.

"I am who I am, Miss Em. And it would be best if you realize that I am a fairy queen who knows exactly who you are."

The threat inherent in that statement sent a chill down Emily's spine.

"Well," Callie called from the on-deck circle where she'd been both listening in and warming up. "As long as the Spider Ump doesn't keep me from clobbering the snot out of the king's pitches, I don't care who she is." She dropped a heavy workout bat and picked up her own. "I'm getting us that Web Gem so I can fix the Field of Statues for good. I gave my word on that."

Emily clenched her jaw.

Since she'd grown closer to Callie, Emily appreciated that she was one of the most driven people she knew, but sometimes that drive felt overpowering. Now, as Callie gave that massive bat of hers a trial swing, a smattering of that gung-ho energy settled over Emily.

Callie was right.

She'd already agreed to the game. There wasn't anything Emily could do now but follow Callie's advice.

"All right," she said, though no one else seemed convinced. "Let's do it."

Fully acclimated now, the spider umpire ran a hand through her hair, then scanned the players from each team. She smiled, revealing a pair of fangs that glistened with venom.

"Bassssseball," she hissed. "My favorite sssssport. Play. Play!"

When no one moved to obey, the spider woman's fangy smile turned into a dark frown of fury. She clapped her two human hands together. The sound was like thunder.

A wave of raw power swept over the field. Emily felt it grab hold of something deep inside her, something she might call her essence.

"I ssssaid, *play ball!*"

CHAPTER
THIRTY-FIVE

As the spider fey took her position behind the plate, Emily felt a clear power emanating from her — a power that fell over Emily's entire sense of being and tangled around her inner self. Emily took the mound, testing that aura. She shook her shoulders and tried to get comfortable with it. The umpire's presence was tied directly to the Web Gem and the now empty shard in her back pocket, as well as to the baseball magic she could already sense gathering in the air around the wild field.

By agreeing to the Duke of the Silver Forest's umpire, Emily had given the spiderkin an allotment of power over the game.

It was a peculiar kind of control, she thought.

She, along with all the other players, was free to play the game her own way, with her own athletic abilities and tactical decision-making. But it was like invisible strings tethered her to the field and to the game that was about to be played on it.

No matter how much leeway she had to play that game, Emily didn't care for the Spider Queen's constraints. She hated the intimate intensity of the umpire's assessing gaze. It made Emily feel like prey, like the spider woman was simply waiting for her to make one wrong move before pouncing.

She had to face it. The umpire gave her the heebie-jeebies.

As she peered in at Jake squatting behind the plate, she couldn't keep her gaze from flicking to the hulking spider woman sitting on her too-many haunches beyond him. She looked like Shelob fused with a mournful graveyard sculpture.

"You got this, Em!" Jake yelled out as Emily stood there, her pitching hand behind her back, the baseball rotating in her fingers. How was he not trying to claw out of his own skin with that massive thing hovering right over his shoulder?

Stop it, Emily told herself. *This is no time to get squeamish.*

This was it. The Big Game. The one for all the marbles — or rather, all the pieces of the Web Gem. And with the spider woman presiding as umpire, Emily and her ragtag team couldn't afford to play anything less than a pristine game.

All around her, the world felt too big and too alive.

The grass on the ancient field smelled robust. The dirt below it was rich and loamy.

She felt the place in her bones, too. The afterimages of players in the past flickered at the edge of her vision. The rumbling of a crowd seeped in from the edges of her hearing.

But when she squeezed her eyes shut and shook her head to clear it all out, she realized most of the noise was simply the voices of her Unicorn teammates shouting encouragement to her, just like Jake.

"Strike 'em out, Em," said Patsy from her place at first.

"Show those smug fairy lords who rules the field!" shouted Lizzy Rodriguez from right field.

Others added their pieces, until the field became a cacophony of affirmation, almost loud enough to drown out Essie's wild cheering.

They were great teammates, she realized. Just twenty-four hours ago, most of these kids had laughed at the idea of such magical creatures. They had all read those horrible articles Megan Moore had posted, of course, and Emily supposed it was human nature that they join in the snickers whenever Adrien passed by. But here they were now, sharing a field with the leader of the Wild Hunt and Lady Marne, and taking directions from Fennoc as if they'd always had a fastidious faun in their dugout.

Not only that, but they were ready to put up a united front against the Seelie Court, even if the haughty nobles had called a horrible spider monster to ump for them.

Emily set a grim smile on her face as the Seelies' leadoff hitter stepped to the plate.

The pristinely uniformed satyr waggled a piece of lumber the size of Connecticut, his tail flicking behind him in unison with his practice swings. He wore no batting helmet, as the curved horns coiling from his forehead looped around to give him protection.

Her heart pounded as Jake signaled a curveball.

That made sense.

She could throw it for a likely strike, and odds were the satyr was as nervous and hopped up about this game as she was. A breaking pitch on the first offering would catch him off guard.

After giving a nod to Jake, she rose and prepared to go into her windup.

"Halt!" the Seelie King called as he marched toward the umpire at home plate. "I protest!"

"What?" Emily said, stepping down from the mound.

The king waved the Unicorns' lineup card over his head. "This batting order is illegal."

"It is no such thing!" Fennoc called, bustling forward. He cautiously edged around the plate far enough to avoid the umpire's spindly reach.

"The rules expressly state that the Designated Hitter can only participate for the pitcher," the Seelie King said gruffly, pushing the lineup sheet toward the umpire. "This card includes both Miss Em and the Designated Hitter. Therefore, they must forfeit!"

The umpire focused prismatic eyes on the card.

"We're in the realm of mortals," Fennoc argued. "And as I understand, the Unicorns are ... um ..." he glanced at Emily, who had covered this rule with him before the game.

"We're a school team, Madame Umpire." Emily stepped in. A combative wave of annoyance crossed her thoughts, but she kept her tone polite. "The Unicorns play in a high school league, which means we play by high school rules. And our rulebook says the Designated Hitter can hit for anyone. In this case, he's hitting for Lizzy, our right fielder."

"That's absurd!" the king replied.

"No more absurd than the DH is to begin with," Emily countered, buoyed by the sense of her mother filling her. Mom had always hated the DH rule. *"If you can't hit, you can't play,"* Mom would yell when the topic came up.

A soft titter came from the gnarled oak backstop, where the Unseelie Queen lay amid her weedy flowers. "How like the Seelies to try to use the rules to wriggle their way out of a tight place."

Emily's anger flared, and, letting Mom's presence bolster her, she snapped at the king. "This was your plan all along, wasn't it? You don't want to play us straight up, so you bring in your own umpire and try to win with silly quibbles over rules you don't even understand. Well, you can't get away with that kind of dirty trick here. Just because you don't know the rules doesn't mean we're going to forfeit anything."

The spiderkin shifted her weight from her front legs to her back, as if preparing to pounce. "Ssshow me thisss rule."

Fennoc, prepared as only the best team manager could be, drew the high school rulebook Emily had given him earlier from his back pocket and held it forward for the umpire to see. "What Miss Em says is true."

The spiderkin leaned forward to examine the print with such focus that Emily thought the paper might burst into flames.

The power field around them warped.

Emily's throat grew tight. She realized then that, no matter how right she was, the only thing that mattered was what the umpire thought.

Tension quivered like a silken string.

"I allowsss it," the spiderkin said.

The Seelie King began to argue, but the umpire cut him off.

"I sssaid, I allowsss it. I want to see a bassseball game."

Fennoc gave a sharp nod of satisfaction and slid the rulebook back into his uniform pocket as he quickly returned to the Unicorns' side of the field. The king, defeated, slunk back to the Seelie bench, and Emily, breathing easier, climbed back to the top of the mound.

"Where were we?" she said.

"I think we were getting ready to strike out a Seelie," Jake said. He pulled the mask down and flashed a signal again.

The satyr gave an unimpressed grumble and took his stance.

Grunting, Emily let go of the pitch.

The satyr swung hard and connected.

Having timed it perfectly, he sent the ball rocketing in a line, out to right-center field, looking in the sharp lights like it might be a white comet.

Voices rose—celebration from the Seelies, dismay from the Unicorns—and the sound of his hooved feet pounding around the bases filled the space as the ball bounced in the outfield. The leader of the Hunt, who was playing center field, raced to catch it, but his dive came up short.

The ball bounced again, then disappeared into the darkness at the edge of the field.

A moment later, the satyr finished his dash around the bases and scored the game's first run.

One hitter, one run.

Emily kicked at the pitching rubber with enough force to leave her toes stinging.

"It's all right, lassie!" Fennoc called from the dugout. "The game is long."

"You'll get them!" Essie's high-pitched squeal came next.

That, at least, made Emily laugh to herself, which was good.

She tried to bear down, but the five pitches she gave the next hitter were mostly so far off the mark that she walked him.

The third hitter, a wiry elven woman, took her fastball directly to the white-uniformed shoulder. She made an exaggerated show of brushing the dirty mark from her sleeve as she strolled to first.

That brought up the cleanup man, who, of course, was the Seelie King.

"You're running out of places to put my teammates, Miss Em," he called out the obvious with an undertone of disdain as he shrugged off his cape and strode confidently to the plate.

Emily stood on the mound, feeling as alone as she'd ever felt.

That was the thing about pitching. When it was going well, she felt like she was a spider of her own kind, positioned in the middle of the field and connected to everything that moved. But when it wasn't going so well, being on the mound felt like she was alone on a pedestal raised for all to see, isolated in the middle of a green ocean.

She took a calming breath, but her nerves were still all over the place.

Emily stepped off the rubber to collect herself.

The king tapped his cleats with his bat. "That's all right. I'd be afraid to pitch to me, too."

His smug, too-casual tone focused her nerves. She'd had him in this position once before and, with a healthy dose of baseball magic and pure love of the game, had come out on top then.

Have fun, said her mother in her memory. *Play your best with a team you love.*

Emily shoved her mitt under her arm and got back on the mound.

"The last time I was afraid to pitch to you was never."

She pulled harder on the bill of her cap, then gazed up into the stars, thinking about her mom. "Thanks," she whispered.

A fastball later, she was up on the count. The king fouled off a second fastball and then chased a sweeping curve for strike three.

As the king all but stomped back to the dugout, Emily restrained herself from making a parting shot.

With runners at first and second and only one out, it was too early to gloat.

The next hitter stepped to the plate and blasted a scorching drive into the hole between shortstop and third base.

Emily was certain it would score at least one run, but then, out of nowhere, Benji Amberman leapt forward, stretched out, and, as their entire body pulsed with a golden glow, nabbed the shot in midair.

"Ouuut," said the umpire.

But Benji wasn't done yet. With uncanny quickness, they scrambled to their feet and, two steps later, tagged the runner who'd been on second, and who had taken off on contact.

"Ouuuuut!" said the umpire.

A double play!

Unassisted!

"Yes!" Emily called. "Great play, Benji!"

Just like that, they were out of the inning, down only one run after being in a much more dangerous position.

As she and Benji reached the dugout at the same moment, she clapped them on the back.

"You saved my bacon there."

"Well, it wasn't kosher," they replied with a mischievous glint. "Had to do something."

She laughed, but from the corner of her line of sight, she noted that the umpire had sat up further on her hind legs and was examining Benji as they stepped into the dugout together. Had the spider woman seen what Emily had seen — that Benji's dive had been extreme, that they had flown far and fast, farther and faster than a mortal human ought to be capable of unassisted by magic?

Magic that most definitely wasn't allowed according to the rules of high school baseball.

She didn't have a chance to caution her teammate, though. The dugout was alive with activity as the Unicorns and their fairy additions prepared to bat.

"Let's go!" Fennoc said, clapping. "Time to get some runs!"

The exciting buzz of pumped-up teammates filled the dugout, loud, but not so loud that it drowned out the mechanical rattling that came from the parking lot a short way from the field.

The entire team froze.

The soft crunch of tires on old asphalt filled the night.

Emily whirled to face the parking lot. It was a beaten-up rust bucket of a car. Late model of some kind, held together by dust and dirt that hadn't been cleaned away in a decade.

"Damn it," she grumbled. "What now?"

Despite every measure she and her team had taken to keep tonight's events a secret from the greater Pattersonville population, someone had found them.

The passenger's door squealed open, and that someone clambered out, revealing himself to be a skinny college-aged guy. Emily had never seen him before.

A slack-jawed expression of wonder showed on his face as he pushed a Cincinnati Reds cap up on his forehead. His jacket, however, bore a slightly out-of-date logo from one of the other high school teams. Bradford, she thought.

"Holy cows, Kenny, can you look at that? It's just like they said on the feed," he said. The kid driving got out, too, but the passenger was already tromping across the expanse to the field.

Callie stepped toward the kid. "What are you doing here?"

But the kid just held his phone out in front of him, taking pictures as he walked.

"Oh, my hells, man! I can't frickin' believe this," he called back to his friend. "Kenny? Can you frickin' believe this?"

When he reached the first base tree line, he shouldered in next to where Emily's bewildered dad had been sitting against a tree trunk, turned his back to the game, and held his phone up to snap a selfie.

"Aw, yeah." He reviewed the image. "That one's going straight on the InstaChat."

Emily's dad had risen to his feet by then.

"Hey, man," the kid continued as his friend finally caught up to him. "You ever think something as crazy as this would happen here in boring old Pattersonville?" He nudged Emily's dad with the point of his elbow in jocular solidarity. Then, he beamed at the Unicorns' dugout.

"What is all this?" Kenny, the driver said, voice full of something that might be awe or might be horrible confusion.

The passenger kid grinned straight at Emily, and at Adrien standing beside her, seemingly oblivious to the fact both of them were paralyzed in absolute horror.

Across the parking lot, another pair of headlights pulled in.

The Duke of the Silver Forest let out a soft, sinister chuckle. "Bringing in your fans, I see? Very clever."

"It's not clever at all," Emily said, fuming now that she had time to assess the situation. Her fists had clenched with involuntary rage. She turned to Megan, who was no longer sitting on the thick oak tree limb she'd been using as a good vantage point earlier. The reporter now stood tall and lanky in the darkness, the field lighting dancing off an expression of delight and anticipation. In her hand, the screen of her phone gave a cold glow.

"Megan?" Emily said, lowly. "What have you done?"

"Only what needed to be done," Megan said. "The people here need to see Adrien and the rest of you for the heroes you are. I've been posting all night. Come out and see the real Adrien Thorn take on his nemesis from the Fairy Realm. Support your hometown hero. You know? All the things that should have been said to begin with. And pictures to back it all up."

Her gaze went to a third car rolling into the lot.

Her expression grew a tinge of wonder.

"Post it and they will come," she whispered to herself with a delighted giggle.

Adrien groaned in pain. Color rose to darken his face in the shadows.

Megan spun back to smile pointedly at him. "You're welcome," she said.

"Welcome? Are you kidding me? I thought the queen was sadistic enough. This kind of attention is the last thing I need! How am I supposed to—"

"Give them a chance, Adrien. People love great comeback stories. Trust me, everyone's going to love you!"

Adrien threw his arms into the air. "I'm not a comeback! I'm a never-was!" He raised his glance to the parking lot to take in the kids walking toward the field. An expression of pure panic flushed his cheeks and glittered in his widened eyes. He took a hesitant step back, away from the would-be spectators, deeper into the ramshackle dugout. "I don't think I can do this."

"Yes, you can," Emily said.

Adrien blinked, looking like a startled deer at the strength of her voice.

Emily kept her tone firm. "You're right to be mad. And we'll have to deal with what Megan's done later. But there's a game to be won now, and the queen is right when she says you know what will happen to your friends if we lose. You can do this. You're going to do this. Just like we all are. Everyone on the team is behind you." She paused to tip her chin towards where Mr. McMasters was consulting with the Duke of the Silver Forest in furtive gestures. "There's more on the line than just the Web Gem. You feel it, too, right? If the Seelies get control of that artifact, who knows what they could do even here in the Real World?"

An awkward silence stretched out in the dugout.

Adrien stood still.

The Unicorn teammates came to his side.

"We got your back," Benji said.

"Once a Unicorn, always a Unicorn," Patsy added.

Jamal gave the salute, index finger to the bill of the cap.

The leader of the Hunt and Lady Marne closed ranks, too. Fennoc, calming for the first time since the spiderkin had arrived, waggled his faun ears. "Miss Em's got it right," he said. "The Small Folk may not have much, but we'll give it to help you through. And, my boy, you're not a never-was. You're an about-to-be."

Adrien let out a gasp of laughter that was just this side of a sob. Emily thought she saw a tear glistening, but Adrien blinked before it could drop. He drew in a chest-heaving breath.

"All right," Emily said, seeing that he was going to be okay for the moment. She clapped her hands. "Let's get to it. Unexpected audience or not, we've got a Web Gem to win."

As the team turned to their preparations with renewed vigor, Emily wheeled on Megan, barely able to keep her anger from exploding.

"Don't go thinking this is over, Megan Moore. I'll deal with you later."

CHAPTER
THIRTY-SIX

Callie took a knee and leaned into her bat beside Jake Nesbitt in the on-deck area.

The smell of the grass was thick in the evening, and the air felt alive. Around her, the sounds of baseball settled her nerves.

The Seelie King was finishing his warm-up tosses, and Jamal was getting ready to lead off.

Jake would be next, then Callie. If any of them got on, Adrien would clean up. The leader of the Wild Hunt would hit after that, then Emily.

The team had settled down, now, too. Or at least the situation on the field had, anyway. She glanced over her shoulder to see even more headlights nearing. A smattering of spectators stood at the tree line, mostly kids from the local schools yammering on about the "billy goats and strange creatures" in the field and other silly stuff. Their voices filled the empty spaces between the pop of baseballs hitting mitts and the chatter of infielders warming up. Their phones lit up, too, taking pictures and posting more.

Callie scowled at them.

"I can't wait to rip into Megan after this is all over," she muttered. It was one thing for someone like herself to go courting the Fairy Realm. She had negotiation experience, which was practically the mother tongue over there. These kids had no idea what they were stepping into.

"I think you're going to have to get in line," Jake said with a wry laugh.

Callie twisted the bat to loosen her wrists and felt its energy zing through her arms. She liked that. The bat's energy made her think of Trace, though, and remembering him being turned to stone in the Field of Statues made any excitement she might have felt fade quickly. She bit her teeth into the inside of her cheek and looked across the dugouts to where her father sat beside the Duke of the Silver Forest. The expression of pure smarm covering his face made her ill.

"Don't worry," she replied, fighting anger, "I think I can find a way to get to the front of that line."

Jake followed her gaze. "What's with your dad? One minute he's all about the Unicorns, the next..."

"I don't know."

"Maybe he's bipolar or something."

"That would explain a lot." Callie couldn't bring herself to care, though. "Not that it matters now."

"I'm sorry about that," Jake replied.

He stood up to start warmup swings as Jamal stepped into the batter's box. Jamal stood still in his stance, bat in position, waiting to try to time the Seelie King's first pitch.

Callie stood up, too, but rested on her bat handle like it was a cane. She couldn't help but feel her father's gaze. It prickled the hair at the back of her neck. She heard his voice inside her head, too. *You're the star, Callie. Get that straight in your head. You're the winner. All these other kids won't make it anywhere. But you, my little girl, you can make it. If you keep the right mindset, that is. If you leave these losers behind and make this team about yourself.*

That was his frame of mind when she was still the star player for the Marion High School Bulldogs. When she was first struggling with the whole thing with Emily and the Unicorns and before she'd been expelled for her apparent cheating. Which wasn't cheating, but go tell that to the Athletic Commission.

Her dad was the complete opposite of Emily's mindset.

And he knew all the tricks when it came to getting inside her head.

She could still recall her father yelling at her after she complained that no one on the Bulldogs liked her. "You don't need to like anyone, Callie, and nobody on that team needs to like you. Playing on a team just because they love you is a sign of weakness."

The first pitch was outside. Jamal let it pass.

A girl's voice rose above Essie's nonstop chants, cheering the umpire's call. "Go Unicorns!" the girl called through cupped hands.

Callie tried to ignore the crowd.

Focus, she said to herself. *Focus.*

It was a mantra she'd been saying all night, but especially in that first half inning when she'd been in left field. The Seelies had posted their third base coach deep enough that he could throw barbs at her with ease. It was a task the coach, a sharp-tongued elf of some kind, clearly excelled at.

"Your pitcher's quite horrible, isn't she?" the elf quipped after that first hit.

"I suppose you might well give up now and save yourself the embarrassment," he called after the walk.

"You must be a horrible pitcher yourself, Callie McMasters," came after Emily hit the batter. "I can't believe this is the best you've got."

In between he made fun of Jamal at shortstop, Benji at third, and Patsy at first.

"Not a drop of the baseball magic in the lot! Bunch of coattail-riding wannabes, aren't they? Can't see this lot helping you to the pros."

Callie had gritted her teeth and done her best to ignore the way his barbs slipped right beneath her skin.

Now, as Jamal made the first out by grounding to the shortstop, she smothered the sting of the barbs. She was a good player, and though her father wouldn't believe her, she'd found she played even better on a team that meant something to her. Something more than a path to future stardom, anyway.

That was something her dad and his Seelie pals would never understand.

Still, the sense of failure lingered like a cloud of sour cigarette smoke.

Jake went to the plate.

Callie swung her bat, trying to keep her mind on the here and now, but it didn't help much.

She'd caught the elf's use of her true name. Which meant her dad was up to his usual no good. Or that he'd simply been too stupid to shield her name from them. Either way, she knew it meant trouble wouldn't be far behind.

She hadn't responded to the elf's barbs, not even when he went that last step.

When Benji made that great diving stop, the third base coach had quipped only about Jamal.

"The kid just stood there, eh?" he said to Callie as she ran off the field. "Like he was made of stone or something! Ha! Like all your other friends! Ha!"

As if you have friends, she heard her father's voice in her head.

"Stop it!" she said aloud so strongly that Jake looked quizzically at her after taking a strike.

Sheepish embarrassment flushed her cheeks. "Sorry."

Jaw clenched tight, Callie swung the bat again. Its power whooshed through the air. The movement cleared her mind.

Lightsaber to the rescue, she thought, though the bat didn't glow so much as glinted. It would help her. She knew it would. The power of the ring under this field was even stronger than the one under

343

Unicorn Field. It was older and wilder for having lain abandoned so long. When she dialed into it, the bat squirmed with anticipation in her grip.

Whatever her father and the duke had up their sleeve, she couldn't let them win.

She couldn't let them get to her.

She needed to free Trace and the rest of her friends.

Jake, who had taken a pair of fastballs high and outside, then swung and missed a strike, hit the Seelie King's next pitch. Unfortunately, it was a popup, easily hauled in by the Seelie troll who played first base.

Callie gripped her bat. "I *am* a winner," she said to herself. "And I'm going to win this Web Gem. For Trace."

"Go get 'em!" Essie called, raising two clenched fists.

As Callie stepped towards the plate, a small roar from the crowd down the first baseline surprised her.

She glanced that way to see a set of Pattersonville West students had unraveled a hastily painted sign that read *Go Unicorns! We Love You Adrien Thorn The First!*

It was covered in rapidly shedding blue and teal glitter. There was even a remarkably well-done drawing of an older version of the Unicorns logo.

It made her smile.

Then she stepped up to the plate. She didn't flinch as the spider umpire shifted her too-long, too-many legs in the dirt behind her. She focused her attention on the Seelie King as he towered out there on the mound.

The extra car lights that the kids had left blazing to help visibility bathed the fairy lord in light — his white uniform danced with flashing highlights, and Callie couldn't decide if the dazzling flair was magically created or just dust motes catching the headlights.

Either way, he looked like a winner.

She dug in.

"All right, King-o," she quipped. "Let's see what you got."

The king smirked and, as he wound up, a hissing, chittering cacophony rose from the Seelie dugout.

The pitch came at her blazingly fast, but to Callie, focusing hard enough to keep the jeering voices of the Seelies at bay, it seemed to trundle towards her as if it had been thrown through molasses.

A moment later, Callie belted a drive high and so deep it was certainly going to get lost in the woods.

The bat fell from her fingers, but its power still thrummed through her as she pelted down the first base line, the first leg of her home run. *Look at me now,* she thought, baring her teeth at the Seelies. *I got your winner!*

She could feel their dismay as they watched the ball fly. Didn't they wish they'd signed her for their side? Well, let them just wait. She'd barely even begun to show them what she was capable of.

As she rounded first, one of the outfielders, a thin-boned deer girl with a set of small, delicate horns, sprinted through the overgrown grass of the outfield. Then, as her legs churned, she shifted her shape, soft doe-eyes becoming glittering compound jewels, gossamer dragonfly wings erupting from her shoulder blades. She took flight, rising through the nighttime darkness to snare the ball and bring it back inside the park.

"Shhhheeeessss out!" the umpire hissed.

Out? The word took a moment to penetrate through Callie's brain.

Then, as the meaning sunk in, anger flared. She couldn't be *out.* She'd hit a *homer.* Callie turned to race back to the plate. "She can't do that!"

The umpire rose up, easily twice Callie's height. She bared her fangs, and her scopulae braced as if ready for a fight.

Fennoc, seeing what was happening, raced out to the field, trying to get between Callie and the spiderkin umpire. He was too late, though.

"I sssssaid you were outtt," the umpire said coldly as Callie approached. "Innate ability. That'sss the rule."

"Not here it isn't!" She was as mad as she could ever remember being. Heat flushed her face. Static raged in her ears. She smashed her helmet to the ground as she came to stand chest to thorax with the umpire, unafraid of an over-large spider. She'd stomped on her fair share of the nasty things. She'd probably squished hundreds over her entire career running the bases.

"That's a crap call! A total crap call! That hit was out of the park! Everyone saw it, you saw it, the Seelies saw it—"

A white-hot sting struck Callie's shoulder. The force of the impact spun her halfway around. The pain of it left her gasping as she tumbled towards the ground, her hand lifting automatically to touch the thick, sticky thread the umpire had shot from her spinneret.

She never touched the dirt, though.

The umpire grabbed her up, spinning and twisting her until Callie was wrapped in a sticky cocoon of stinging silk.

The pain of whatever toxin the spiderkin secreted gave way to a creeping numbness that threatened to completely overcome Callie.

She fought against it with everything she had.

"Hey!" she yelled just before a warm glop of gooey paste plugged her mouth. It tasted as slimy and gross as it looked. She groaned as she wriggled against the spider woman's grip. She achieved nothing more than toppling to the ground on her side the moment the umpire woman dropped her.

"Your hitter is disqualified from further participation," the spiderkin said to Fennoc. With the clawed tip of one hairy leg, she pushed Callie's encapsulated form to one side. "Feel free to argue further if you would like to join her."

A shout rose from the Seelie dugout. "Go on, then, you old goat. Join your batter on the loser's bench!"

Fennoc froze, then bent backward to take in the full height of the umpire.

A drop of ichor dripped from the spider's fang.

"No, Madam Umpire," he said, casting a fearful eye on Callie. "I have nothing to add."

"Then play on," the umpire said.

As the Unicorns took the field, the umpire returned to her place behind the plate.

Callie, writhing against the painful numbness crawling over her entire body, found herself looking right into her father's eyes. Despite the field spanning between them, she had no trouble reading his disdain.

He held the look for a moment, then turned to speak to the duke, his daughter forgotten as easily as any other wannabe.

CHAPTER

THIRTY-SEVEN

T he inning was over. The Seelies were next up.

Off in the corner, Fennoc and Essie were working to cut Callie out of the umpire's sticky webbing. They weren't making much progress.

But, as the rest of the Unicorns raced to take their positions back on the field, Adrien remained on the bench, fighting a wave of anxiety that threatened to make him puke. The crowd of spectators had grown throughout the first inning and was now large enough that their cheering had become a dull throb pressing against Adrien's ears. His heart was likewise throbbing, a rapid pounding that made the churning of his stomach even worse.

He clenched his eyes shut and tried to pretend that Fennoc had not just come to him and explained that with Callie disqualified, the team was down a player.

They needed him in the field.

The pretending didn't work, though.

His hands were clammy around the thick leather of the mitt he held, his skin sticking to it as he flexed his fingers repetitively. Essie had handed it to him with a cheery "Go get 'em!" as soon as he'd stepped into the dugout. Trust the team brownie to know who needed what equipment and when.

Adrien felt the full extent of his predicament as he held the mitt, then heard the roar of the crowd after Fennoc announced the new lineup.

He couldn't be DH for Lizzy Rodriguez anymore.

Another wave of nausea engulfed him as he stared at the mitt. A deep breath did nothing to stave off his desperation. The air in the dugout smelled too much like dirt and sweat and leather — too much like baseball — to provide any relief.

He'd been able to psych himself up to play his role once again, to be the Designated Hitter he'd been for a century. The cause was good, and DHing was something he could do falling out of bed. But now...

His gaze went to the crowd.

Now ... in front of everyone, he was going to ruin everything.

Emily came to stand before him.

"Let's go," she said, tension in her voice. "We've got a game to win. Time to go warm up."

Adrien's fingers clamped tight around the glove so hard the leather squeaked. He opened his mouth twice before answering. "We've got a problem, Em."

"What's that?" She glanced down at the glove. "Do you throw left-handed or something? Essie can get you another glove."

"It's not that," Adrien said. Out on the field, Benji and Patsy were throwing back and forth to each other. Their motions were smooth and practiced. Like they'd been playing out in the field for years. Beyond them, a trio of Unicorn fans waved a sign with his name on it. The glitter they'd decorated it with flashed in the light of the headlights pointed at the field.

Emily called his attention back to their conversation. "Adrien, what's wrong?"

"It's just ... I never play the field. I haven't played a position in over a hundred years."

Emily rocked back on her heels as she took in this revelation. "Right. You've been the Designated Hitter."

"I don't know what I'm going to do if anything comes my way. Probably stand there like an idiot, and definitely make a fool of myself."

The sounds of the crowd swelled over them, and the prattle of the team warming up filled the empty spaces. Callie's unhappy grunts as she struggled against her bonds added punctuation to the moment. Adrien distracted himself from his feelings of inadequacy by watching the play of emotions on Emily's face. At least Emily understood what he meant. There was no way he could play the field without making an ass of himself, and Emily knew him well enough to understand exactly how devastating that would be for him.

He saw calculations run through her head.

So much was riding on this game.

They had to win it. She knew it, he knew it, the Seelies knew it. Not to mention the unexpected spectators they'd gained, here to see his big comeback thanks to Megan's meddling.

Now he would be the one to make them lose.

Her expression made him feel better. Emily understood. Maybe she would convince Fennoc and the team to play with only eight fielders? But then, like a special kind of completely not-fairy magic happening right before his eyes, he watched a new wave of emotion cross her expression. She smiled at him.

"Then this is a great opportunity for you, isn't it?"

Adrien looked up at her, bewilderment swirling through him. "Em," he said.

"Just going out there proves how much you care about the team. And who knows? Maybe you'll get to touch a baseball for once, right? During a game, anyway?"

"Emily," he said more firmly. "If the Seelies get runs because I can't field—"

"Don't worry about any of that, all right? I'll see what I can do to keep them from hitting it your way but don't worry about it. Just focus on having fun. Isn't that right, Essie?" she called the last over her shoulder.

Essie looked up from her handful of spiderwebs. "Have fun with a team you love!"

Adrien shook his head and cast a narrow glare over to where his queen sat against her tree trunk. She met his gaze with a possessive smile. "That's easy for you to say. You *do* love baseball. But for me, it's tainted."

"Hey," Emily said, putting a hand on his shoulder. "Seriously. Don't think about her. No matter what she's done to you, you're still you, Adrien. Whoever you want 'you' to be. And you're still a Unicorn, too. I dunno about anyone else, but I think you can be a 'you' who plays left field like a pro. I'm sure it's just like riding a bicycle, yeah?"

Adrien loved her enthusiasm. He really did. But he couldn't share it.

Still, it wasn't like he had any choice.

He shook his head and clutched the glove. He shoved his fears to the back of his mind, then pushed himself up from the bench, remembering Mrs. Rodriguez's coaching during his last audition. He didn't love the game like Emily did, but if he could turn it into another school play, he might make it through. "Fake it 'til you make it, right?" he said.

Emily grinned. "Atta boy. Look, I will try and keep stuff from coming your way. But if something does, just relax and let yourself have fun. I promise it helps."

"Yeah." He knew she was right, at least about the relaxing part. And as he walked out onto the field, he tried to shake himself out, tried to do that relaxing thing, rotating his arms and legs, feeling the stretch in muscles he hadn't used in over a century. And who knew? Maybe nothing would come his way? Maybe the Seelies wouldn't even see him as a disadvantage.

"Looks like we got a weak spot!" the Seelie third base coach bellowed when Adrien crossed the infield. "The queen's boy looks about as good in the outfield as a piece of fresh meat. Bet you can't catch a cold, right, *DH*?"

Adrien's stomach clenched.

But just as a new wave of despair grew inside him, a fresh cheer loud enough to blot out the Seelie coach swelled up from the crowd.

"Adrien Thorn! Adrien Thorn! Our boy's back home! Our boy's back home!"

He turned to the kids, slack-jawed.

Three of them were dancing at seeing him.

"Go, Adrien! Let's win it all this time!"

Adrien closed his eyes and let it wash over him, letting himself feel the discomfort of their attention. Then, carefully and deliberately, he made himself take on the role they'd come to see: Adrien Thorn, Unicorns Legend, Winner of the 1923 State Championship.

It didn't make the churning in his stomach lessen any.

What a way to learn I suffer from stage fright, he thought wryly as he turned to toss the clumsiest warm-up throws anyone ever had thrown to the Hunt leader in center field.

Across the field in the Seelie dugout, the Seelie King and his entire bench watched, clearly noting the awkward mechanism of his tosses, and just as clearly plotting for the best ways to hit baseballs his way.

It was going to be a long game.

ON THE UNICORNS' bench, Fennoc and Essie finally cut Callie out of the gooey spiderkin webs.

"I've ruined everything," Callie said.

"It's all right," Fennoc said, fussing. "We'll find a way to make do."

"But look at what's happening. Adrien looks like a lost kid out there. We'll never get Trace and the rest back now. Some hero I've been. I've let everyone down."

She sat on a rock and put her head into her hands.

"I can't believe I let them get to me that way."

Essie came to sit on her knee.

"Don't worry, Miss Rival," the brownie squeaked. "Everyone knows you didn't do it on purpose.

"I lost my head."

Across the field, her father sat smugly beside the Seelie King, arms crossed, and gaze leveled directly on hers. She shivered. Her dad had wanted her to come to his side. That was obvious now. Probably wanted her to follow in his footsteps at the Ball and Glove. Hell, he probably thought the umpire was right to toss her. Probably even helped.

A raw feeling washed over her then.

"That son of a..." She stifled the word she was about to use to describe her father. He had done this. She could tell it in the glint of his gaze. He had given them a few magic phrases that were guaranteed to get into her head, and the Seelies had bound them up into an ugly little spell of some kind. The truth throbbed in her mind. "He told them," she said. "My dad found a way to help the Seelie King cast a spell that made me pop off."

"That's cheating!" Essie squeaked.

"Tell that to Spider Ump."

Essie frowned. "With family like that, I'd rather have friends!"

"You can say that again." Callie swallowed hard. "I should have done better."

"At least you can join me in cheering for our team!"

"Like that's going to help."

"Hey!" Essie pushed back with sass. "Don't you tell me that I don't make a difference!"

Callie drew a resigned breath and watched the action on the field. "All right," Callie said. She didn't have anything left to do, besides picking spider silk out of her hair, anyway. "Teach me how to do a good cheer."

The inning started.

Adrien stood in left field like an awkward deer in a meadow, keeping alert as Emily faced the first Seelie batter. She threw two strikes in a row, then a ball. By that point, Adrien was a nervous mess.

Now, as Emily wound up again, a surge of fear tensed his entire body.

The crack of the bat came like a gunshot.

The ball flew his way.

A popup.

An easy catch. Or it would be, for anyone competent.

Adrien moved like some kind of malformed contraption. His arm thrust out, glove held open as every horrible what-if he'd ever thought raged through his mind. His legs moved in a proper run — but keeping the little speck of white in his sight as he ran without looking where he was going tripped him up.

He stumbled, and though he caught himself before he went down, he lost sight of the ball until it bounced in front of him, then ricocheted off the poorly timed stab of his glove. By the time he chased it down the runner was already rounding first. Adrien scooped the ball into his glove.

With a wrenching twist of his shoulder, he hurled the ball to Pash Kulpari, the Unicorns' second baseman. Pash had to step off the base to catch it, which let the runner get safe.

Shame coursed through Adrien as he slunk back to his place.

The sound of the Seelie dugout's belly laughs felt like ten thousand-pound dumbbells crushing his chest.

He couldn't have asked for an easier popup.

The runner should have been out. Instead, the Seelie elf was standing at second, shaking out his long blond hair from under his batting helmet, and chuckling as if it was the most obvious thing in the world that a pop fly to Adrien was an automatic double.

To his side, the Seelies' third base coach let out a mocking whistle loud enough Adrien couldn't fail to hear.

"So much for the Unicorns' legend, eh?" he said, slapping his thigh as if he was telling the best joke ever told. "Oldsters ought to be put out to pasture before they embarrass themselves and their team, I always say!"

Adrien couldn't shut the coach's words out. They were true, after all.

On the mound, Emily prepared to pitch again, which thankfully shut the hecklers up for a brief respite.

As Emily went into her windup, the night grew quiet enough that a thread of conversation from the Unicorns supporters behind left field caught Adrien's attention.

"Did you see the rocket he threw to second?" one voice said in awe.

"Yeah! It was crazy good. Like, wha-*pow!*"

"The guy's got a cannon for an arm!"

"Oh yeah. A1's still got it!"

What?

The dissonance between his memory of the play and what he was hearing now made his brain stall out. Was he hearing them right? The kids' voices were full of admiration. They liked something he'd done. The tone of the spectators' voices built a spreading sense of something new inside him. Something completely unlike the dread he'd wrestled as the inning began.

He remembered this feeling, this ebb and flow of playing in the field. Sure, he'd messed up the first catch, but hearing the voices, and sensing the grass, and feeling the tingle that still warmed his arm after throwing that ball — no, he thought to himself with a genuine smile — after throwing that rocket ... well, the feeling was still here, inside him.

The crack of a bat jolted him back to the moment. The ball was flying towards him again.

On complete reflex, he ran forward, eye on the tiny white sphere overhead. His legs moved with total coordination this time, and a sweeping rush of competence filled him.

He was going to catch this one.

It hooked, though, flying towards the parking lot, where one of the spectators — Adrien thought it might have been the first guy who'd shown up — rushed to chase it down.

"Foulsss ballsss!" called the umpire.

As he returned to his place once again, the third base coach cast a smirk his way. He said something, too, but Adrien did not hear it this time. Instead, he let himself sense the earth under his feet, smell the grass of the outfield around him, and hear the swell of excitement undulating through the crowd.

He focused on the infield. Not on Emily, but on the batter. He watched the sylph raise her bat once again and noted how she shifted her back foot in preparation. With the experience of a hundred years of batting, he recognized the tells of how she would move when the pitch came.

He knew she was, in fact, trying to hit towards him.

He'd watched hitters like this before, of course. But he'd mostly done it from the bench or the on-deck circle.

He'd forgotten just how engaging it was to watch it from the field. From a place where he could react to the incoming hit.

From a place where he could engage in the whole of the sport.

It was that exact moment when a sudden epiphany struck, so strong it left him gasping.

He did not hate baseball.

The truth was, that even if he moved on to something else, he could never really hate the game he'd grown up with.

He'd thought he'd hated baseball because of what the Unseelie Queen had turned it into, because of how she'd made him play the game. But that was wrong.

He hadn't *played* baseball since before he'd first tumbled into her clutches.

This game, this inning, was the first time since he'd hit that championship-winning home run.

Oblivious to the world shifting under her left fielder, Emily pitched. Curveball, coming in hot.

The sylph swung and connected. This time, she did not foul it.

The ball arced towards him, taunting, daring him to catch it.

And Adrien moved on reflex. The sound of the crowd gasping as the ball rose into the air fell into place around him. The grunt of his own voice seemed distant as he ran back, eyes on the ball, feeling a powerful bubble of joy expanding within him, completely aware of the space of the field around him. Nearing the tree line that would serve as a fence, he jumped at the place where he thought the ball should be, arm up, fingers spread.

It was a lucky catch.

He knew it even then.

A catch made partly of his own raw intuition, partly on the power of the voices cheering as the ball fell earthbound — chief among them coming from Callie McMasters. Adrien sensed her voice, amplified by the familiar tang of the fairy magic that had been imbued in that bat she now carried.

But a catch, no matter how lucky, is still a catch.

And when the ball landed in his mitt with a soft pop, that bubble he felt burst into a scintillating cloud of the most beautiful baseball magic he had ever tasted.

And, in the aftertaste of that burst of baseball magic, he twirled around and uncorked the absolute hardest throw he could make toward third base, where the Seelie runner was tagging up. The warm hide of the ball felt magnificent leaving his hand, and the rocket of a throw traveled over the field on a line that scored the night.

Benji held their glove in readiness, standing over third base as steadily as if no Seelie elf were barreling straight for them.

The elf dropped into a slide, sending a cloud of dust into the night air.

The ball slammed into Benji's glove.

"Sssafe," the umpire declared.

The crowd groaned. A pair of the more daring guys even booed.

The umpire raised herself onto her back legs. "Silencccce! I sssaid sssafe!"

Adrien, however, didn't feel the same disappointment. On the contrary, he felt the best he'd felt since the ages when he knew nothing of the Unseelie Queen, nothing of the Fairy Realm at all. When he was just a regular kid playing a regular game of baseball. A game he had always and would always love.

Around him, his teammates shouted encouragement to one another, while the other team's players talked up their batter. From the mound, Emily made a gesture that said, "Way to go!"

But, as he sauntered back to his position, Adrien felt an unraveling of the past tingling through the baseball glove he wore and through the baseball magic that he'd just created. Suddenly he had eyes only for the queen.

She was still where he'd left her at the base of the large tree by the dugout. But she was no longer lounging indolently.

She sat ramrod straight, a bloodless look of tight fear pulling at the lines of her face.

Yes, Adrien thought, holding the glove up where he could see it better and feeling more truth falling into place. *You should be afraid.*

That night, when she'd taken him from Unicorn Field, came to him, then.

Fully for the first time.

He'd played on that field for three seasons. He'd learned its every detail like he knew his own home. But in all that time, he'd never felt a truth like the one he'd felt just now — that on that day he'd fallen by accident upon the pulsing magic that lay underneath that field, just as it lay underneath this one out in the wild country, and as baseball flowed over the top of it, the magic had moved likewise.

Because, as he now realized, baseball *was* magic.

A magic that anyone could reach out and touch if only they could see it. Even if they'd simply felt it like he had those hundred years before.

The part of Adrien that knew he was in the here and now of the big game against the Seelies stayed there, but the rest of him looked back, feeling each of the hundred years that separated him from this memory of how he'd touched the magic that day. The way he'd pulled at a thread of it and wrapped it around his glove so he could feel the thrum of baseball magic directly during the play. He saw how his clumsy attempts had brought his existence to the attention of the Unseelie Queen, and he saw how she'd lain in wait for him, not unlike a spider herself, until the moment when she could snatch him up.

He saw how she had controlled him, not by controlling his play, but by cutting him off from the magic of it.

He smiled then, returning fully to the moment and staring still at the queen.

That was the power of her curse, he realized. That constraint was the thing that tied him to her.

And now, he'd found the magic again.

The queen's eyes narrowed. *You need me,* she seemed to say. *I made you what you are, Designated Hitter. If you want to win this game, you need my power.*

Not anymore, Adrien replied.

Holding his glove out, he reached out, grasping the baseball magic through the field, through the earth, and through the entirety of the game playing out around him, reading into the baseball magic that churned through the fairy ring below this old field.

The Unseelie Queen lurched forward, trying to stand despite her weakness.

Stop! You think you can be free of me? You'll never be free, Adrien Thorn!

Her use of his true name came laced with her power. He felt its sting but ignored it. Her tone was too shrill, he thought, too skewed by her fear.

Watch me, he said.

And, as he'd tried to do a hundred years before, he pulled up a thread of the baseball magic and wrapped it around the leather of his glove, weaving it through the fingers and into the webbing.

Unlike a hundred years ago, though, this time, he knew something of how magic worked, and this time he didn't fumble the job.

When he was finished, he held the glove up so the soft, golden glow of it spilled both onto the field around him and over all of himself. He felt it pulsing and shifting, felt the glove grow warm.

This is my glove, he thought, holding it up through the light. *It proves I've got a field position. I can play the whole game now, and I remember why I've always loved baseball. Because baseball is magic, and magic is freedom.*

Adrien faced the queen then.

I'm your Designated Hitter no longer, Unseelie Queen.

A weight lifted from his shoulders, and he felt as if he were hovering an inch above the ground. Across the field, below the tree, the Unseelie Queen slumped as if in a faint.

In the distance of the infield, the Seelies' third batter, perhaps wise to Adrien's new power, grounded out to Patsy at first. Patsy stepped on the base, then whipped a stellar throw to Jake at home in time to catch the elf runner.

With that, the top of the inning was over.

The Unicorns filed into the dugout to prepare for their turn at bat.

But before he joined his teammates, Adrien took a moment to breathe the outfield air and taste the open freedom on the night breeze.

Then he turned to face the kids who had been dancing at his arrival.

We Love You Adrien Thorn the First sparkled from the glitter sign.

Welcome home, Adrien Thorn! read another sign, shaken by a pair of older guys wearing Unicorns jackets. Adrien recognized faces amongst the crowd: fellow classmates who had snickered at him in the halls a few weeks ago, teachers who'd praised his schoolwork, Mrs. Rodriguez standing near the front, cheering as hard as anyone else.

Except for one person.

"Al! Al! Over here!"

Sydney, hopping up and down with unconstrained excitement, and beyond him, Aunt Peg and Uncle Gary, smiling their pride so hard their cheeks must ache.

They'd come to see him play and to cheer him on.

Him.

The real Adrien Thorn. Not the normal, modern kid he'd pretended to be. They'd accepted him either way, though. All of them had. No matter who he wanted to be, they'd always accept him. More than any baseball magic, their acceptance made him free.

The knowledge made him laugh, loud and bright. In a move so familiar it might have been only yesterday that he'd last done it, he brought his hand up to the bill of his cap and pointed one finger upwards.

As one, the crowd returned the Unicorn Salute to him.

Only then did Adrien turn and jog toward the dugout.

He couldn't wait to go up to bat, for real, for the first time in a hundred years.

THIRTY-EIGHT

I nnings spooled out into the night like a strange ritual, simultaneously crawling and flying by in a jumble of highs and lows. Emily could tell her teammates' experiences were similar.

Hitting for the first time since his time in the Fairy Realm, Adrien took his frustrations out. His towering blast was so deep that not even the flying fairy in left field could flag it down.

But no one else managed to make it home, and the Seelies got another run the following inning. The Unicorns were down 2-1.

Despite his earlier catch, it seemed clear the Seelies were magicking everything they could to make balls they hit head toward Adrien. And it was paying off. Emily was delighted to see Adrien find his groove alongside his new freedom, but a century of rust just does not disappear on the turn of a spell. Having Adrien in the field was a real problem. Despite his athleticism, with Seelie magic countering baseball magic, he could not catch much. And when Emily waved the Huntsman over to protect him, that left too much of the field for Lizzie to cover. The Seelies were crafty about it, though, focusing on spells that extended players' skills beyond where they seemed natural, but not so far as to break the "innate ability" rules that baseball in the Fairy Realm was so heavily founded upon.

The best idea was to strike the Seelies out.

Easier said than done, though. For all the Seelies' moral faults, they were good hitters.

The Unicorns weren't without their own good players, though. Two innings later, when Benji led off with a double, the glimmering wake they left as they ran brought cheers of delight from the spectators. The expression on Benji's face as they dusted off their uniform was enough to make Emily forget their dire situation. The measured pulse of Benji's glow led Emily to think her friend was learning to control it, though, which gave her pause.

She had not wanted to bring the rest of them into this, but now, with the throngs of the city's Unicorns fans gathered here to cheer for them, that fear had come out to the open.

What was in store for the city next worried her, but when the Seelies broke through for three runs in the fourth she realized this was not the time to dwell on it.

The Unicorns came to bat again, and a bunt, a single, and a walk later, Emily drilled a triple down the right field line that scored three runs.

Seelies: five runs to four. The game was heading to the last innings.

Things were getting serious.

"We can do this, guys," Emily said, addressing the now ragged, but determined-looking team in the dugout. "I know we can."

She got a bunch of thumbs up and a smattering of grunts in agreement, and the team picked themselves up to take the field once again.

Adrien dropped a fly ball the next inning, though, and the Seelies scored two more runs. The Unicorns got one back when the Hunt leader singled, stole second base, and raced home on a ground ball, but they were losing ground. Emily tried not to focus on how bleak their outlook was becoming.

It's not over 'til it's over, she told herself.

"We can't let the Seelie King have his way!" Essie said, pressing her clenched fists into her eyes. "I can't stand even the thought of it!"

Emily couldn't stand the thought of it, either. In fact, if she had to face the Seelie King one more time, she thought she might hurl. Which was bothersome, as she trudged out to the mound for the last inning, only to find the Seelie King waiting.

"What do you want?" she snapped.

"Perhaps you might rethink your proposition," the king said. "Give up now, and I promise to go easy on your Small Folk friends."

"Go easy?"

"They will simply serve, rather than pay any deeper price."

"Go away," Emily said. She had no energy to play games of fairy politics. He was only trying to distract her, anyway.

As she warmed up, though, the king's offer rang in her head. If the Web Gem was lost, the Small Folk would pay a large price. Perhaps she should have taken it.

No.

The Small Folk were due their freedom.

She focused on the hitter.

The first batter drove a liner right at Adrien. He didn't catch it, but at least it thudded off his chest rather than bouncing out into the darkness of the outfield. The runner finished with a double. Then he stole third and scored on a grounder that Benji stopped but could only make a play at first.

Emily struck out the king, though, and thanks to a nice scoop by Patsy, they held the Seelie Court scoreless for the rest of the inning.

Three runs down. Three outs remaining.

A sense of foreboding settled over the field.

Clouds rolled in and the wind gusted up, rattling with dust and debris.

The air had that electric feeling of impending rain, but with more than five innings in the books, Emily knew the game would be complete either way.

"All right!" she called. "We need runs and we need them now!"

Benji would lead off, then would come second base Pash Kulpari. That would bring up the top of the order: Jamal and Jake.

Unfortunately, Lizzy, who was not a strong hitter, was batting in Callie's spot.

Then—if they could get that far—would be Adrien, the Huntsman, and Emily.

It looked even more bleak when Benji hit a grounder that the first baseman played without a throw.

Pash followed with a bouncer to the shortstop, but just as the usually sure-handed elf in the field bent to pick it, the ball took a wicked hop, and Pash was safe!

"That'll do 'er, folks!" Fennoc said. "One out, runner on first!"

"It's a sign!" Essie sang.

Emily began to feel a trickle of hope, and when Jamal drilled a solid single into the outfield and Pash made third, that trickle grew to a full river.

"One out, two on!" Fennoc called gleefully, rubbing his hands together as Jake went to the plate. "Send one a long way and we're right back in this one, Jake-y my kiddo!"

Energy coursed through the bench.

Could it happen? Could late-inning heroics snatch this victory from the jaws of defeat?

The Seelie King frowned as Jake took practice swings. "We'll end this right here," he said.

Jake took a ball, then a strike.

He swung at the king's third pitch, hitting it on a line – but right at the king, who managed to snare it in self-defense. Jamal was lucky to get back to first in time to avoid being picked off, which would have ended the game.

Instead, there were two outs.

And now came Lizzy, looking timid and defenseless in the on-deck circle.

Fennoc put his stubby arm around her shoulder and walked her to the plate. "Make your stance low. Take a couple of pitches," he whispered. "The king's looking a little winded out there. He's going to be anxious to get this over with. Let's see if you can draw a free pass."

Lizzie nodded, and indeed the king's first two pitches were off the plate.

The next two were strikes, though. Then a third ball.

With the count full, Benji stood up and went to the on-deck area as if to chat with Adrien, the expression on their face filled with such an odd mix of nonchalance and trickery that Emily found herself watching them as the Seelie King wound up.

As the king delivered his next pitch, Benji released a golden pulse so intense that the king's balance was thrown off. The ball skipped ten feet before the plate.

"Ball foursss!" the umpire said.

Lizzie, delighted, skipped down to first base. Jamal moved to second. With Pash at third, the bases were full.

The king ripped his cap off his head. "They can't do that!"

"Innate ability," the umpire called. "I allowsss it."

"Innate ability? That's a human. They have no innate ability!"

The spiderkin rose on her haunches, and once again prepared her spinnerets. "And yet, Sssseelie Kingling, I rulesss innate ability."

The king's cheeks reddened, but he huffed and returned to the mound.

Three-run deficit. Two outs. Bases full.

And the next hitter was Adrien Thorn, the boy who had made a name for himself as the Unseelie Queen's Designated Hitter. A home run would win it. Even a base hit would bring up the Huntsman, who was nearly as dangerous.

Adrien waggled his bat. "Let's see what you've got, King of the Seelies."

The first pitch was right down the middle.

Adrien swung.

It was, Emily could objectively say, one of the smoothest, sweetest swings she had ever seen.

The bat contacted with a sound of pure perfection, and Emily thought her heart might jump from her chest as the ball rose, flying high and far, disappearing into the nighttime darkness. Around her, as the fielders turned to give chase, the Unicorn bench came to their feet in full voice. The spectators gave a throaty cry.

They were going to win!

The Web Gem was going to be Fennoc's again!

But the night had grown damp, and the air heavy. This time it was the center fielder who, with a massive race, snared the ball just as it might otherwise have disappeared into the dark woods.

"Out!" the umpire called.

And that was it. The game was over.

The crowd quieted. The air left the field.

The Seelie King pumped his fist and jumped up and down — as did the rest of the Seelie team as they gathered, pounding themselves on the backs and flashing in magical exuberance.

In the distance, the Duke of the Silver Forest was radiant.

The Unseelie Queen dour.

Cries of despair came from Essie, and Fennoc merely sat stoically grieving, a limp sprig of grass dangling from his mouth. A string of sour invectives poured from Callie's lips. Across the way, Mr. McMasters' grin stretched maniacally over his face.

Emily felt the shard in her back pocket vibrate. When she put her hand back to feel for it, the shard was gone. At the same moment, the Web Gem flared with opalescent blues and pinks.

"You had your chance, Miss Em!" the king said as he nearly danced to grab up the Web Gem. "Now you and your Small Folk will pay the true price!"

CHAPTER

THIRTY-NINE

The Duke of the Silver Forest appeared beside the Seelie King and tried to wrest the trophy away. The king fought him, grunting with the effort of yanking the artifact to his chest. "By baseball rights, the Web Gem is mine to control."

The duke pulled equally hard. "The council has decided that Seelie ownership of the Web Gem is too important to leave in one hand. So it will fall to us."

To Emily, their quibbling sounded like distant crows fighting over some shiny trinket. A horrified numbness was settling over her, making it hard to care much about the outcome of their pettiness.

They'd lost. She'd lost.

Despite everything, the Web Gem had fallen into the hands of their enemies.

Swallowing against the thickness in her throat, she turned to her teammates. "I'm sorry. I thought we could fix everything if we worked together. I guess … I guess I chose a poor boon call."

"You are allsss wrong," a voice said over the din.

The spiderkin umpire levered her body up and down in a mesmerizing movement that was remarkably effective in gaining attention. "The Web Gem doesss not belong to any of the courtsss or housssesss excccept as granted by the ssspiderkin."

The Duke of the Silver Forest stepped forward, though he did not relinquish his hold on the Web Gem. "But we made an agreement, Madame Umpire."

"Oh, yesss — but you negotiated over an artifact neither of you owned." She turned her bone-colored gaze at the duke. "The Ssseelie acquisssition of the Web Gem was made under nefariousss pretenssses to begin with. As rightful creator of this artifact of power, I choose to grant you no ownersssship due to this game."

"What?" the Seelie king said, fist clenching so tightly over the base of the trophy that his hand turned as white as his uniform.

Emily's heart gave a lurch of sickening hope. Did that mean...?

Fennoc's little ears perked up. "The Web Gem is ours again?"

"No," the spiderkin umpire said. "The Web Gem is intact once again. But it wasss the Sssmall Folk who desssecrated the artifact. I will not returnsss it to you."

"I don't understand," Emily said. "If neither the Seelies nor the Small Folk control the Web Gem, who does?"

"The next true victorsss in the Fairy Ssseriesss. Until that point, the artifact will remain in the hands of someonesss trussstworthy."

The night grew silent, and for a moment Emily thought she could feel the sun under the horizon as it crawled closer to bringing a new day.

The spiderkin umpire held out her hand, gesturing for the Web Gem. An invisible pulse of power moved through the air, and the current took on the acrid scent of old magic.

The Seelie King hesitated, then, with a glance toward the Duke, complied.

The spider-woman raised the Web Gem to her eyes and smiled a wide-lipped smile at it. "Ahhh," she said. "Ssstill so lovely."

The hope that had squeezed Emily's heart a moment ago turned to an uncertain fear. What sort of creature would this spider thing consider trustworthy?

Callie stepped into the circle, one hand gripping her bat. "What about our friends who've been turned to statues? Will you save them?"

The spider-woman blinked at her, a blank look on her pale face as if she couldn't quite recall who this girl was, despite having wrapped her in webbing a few innings ago.

"The waysss of the Fairy Realm are as varied as the magic within each denizen," she finally said. "I have no hold over your friendsss."

Callie clutched the bat so hard her knuckles went white. "Sounds like you're passing the buck."

"Take care of your tone, mortal. You have no call over us, and I can promise my fangs are more painful than my threads."

"Good try, Callie," Emily whispered as the spider woman turned away. Callie's anxious face reflected the churning within Emily.

The spider-woman shuffled over the infield, her spindly legs piercing the dirt as she walked until she came to a stop right in front of Benji Amberman.

Benji swallowed visibly as she held the Web Gem out to them.

"To you, I assign the safekeeping of our artifact."

Benji? Emily thought in disbelief.

"Me?" Benji said, grasping the trophy out of instinct. Their cheeks paled, then flushed, and they looked like they'd just lost a game of hot potato.

At their touch, the Web Gem glowed with a golden light that matched their familiar fairy-kin flare. "What am I supposed to do with it?"

The spiderkin umpire's haunted smile was colored with an odd mix of sympathy, joy, and compassion. "Do notsss fear, my little sssspiderling. Your truth willsss win through."

"What does that mean?"

Her grin deepened, and she scuttled backward to give herself space. "My command is made," she said. Her arms rose, and a golden pulse the same as Benji's, though stronger, flared over the field.

Then she was gone.

The Seelies stood together, still stunned.

The Unicorns and fairy lords, too, seemed stymied.

"That's it, then," the Unseelie Queen, now fully recovered, cackled as she stood under her own power. "The foibles and fates of the spiderkin are strange, indeed. But we play the Fall Season. To the winner goes the spoils."

"What about our friends?" Callie said again, striding forward with her bat. "You made them what they are. You need to fix it."

"Be as angry as you dare, Miss Rival. I have no power to do that now. The only way you'll get your friends back is to deal with the eventual owner of the Web Gem. Which, with my Designated Hitter…" She started towards Adrien, thin fingers reaching to stroke his uniformed shoulder.

Adrien wrenched his arm away. "Your curse is broken, your majesty. I'm never playing for you again."

The queen narrowed her eyes, but let him step away. "We'll see about that, now, won't we?" Her voice was slippery with implications.

"You won't win the Gem either way, Queen," the Seelie King said between gritted teeth.

The Duke of the Silver Forest cast a thin glare at his king. "Just so. Our manager will not fail again," he added, with an accentuation that said it was as much a threat as a statement.

Essie's voice squeaked from Fennoc's shoulder. "We won last season fair and square! We'll do it again!"

"Enough with this senseless posing!" the duke said, whirling to point at Benji. "You! Spider child! It's time we returned to our homes. The Web Gem must likewise return to the Realm. So you come with us."

He snapped his fingers, and the silvery portal the Seelies had arrived via reappeared over the field.

Benji stood stock-still, both hands still clamped around the trophy, eyes wide as dinner plates, but their jaw was clenched tight. "Uh, I don't think I'm going with you."

The duke's eyes narrowed. "The Web Gem belongs in the Fairy Realm."

"Ha!" laughed the queen. "Says the fairy lord who stashed it here in the first place? Now you think you can sneak it into your domain before anyone else has a chance to win it? What other imbecile attempts do you mean to make? Or do you not feel this child's power? They're no bumbling pawn like the first fool you twisted around your will. Attempt to manipulate them at your own risk."

Behind the duke, Mr. McMasters made a sound of deep insult. Everyone ignored him.

The duke grimaced but lowered the imperious arm he'd held out to Benji. "As you say. And the Web Gem, Queen? Will you tolerate it remaining outside the Fairy Realm?"

The queen gave a delicate shrug. "I will put my faith in the spiderkin."

"Maneuvering yourself for victory already, O queen?" said the duke. "Very well. We shall see how it plays out for you. Until the Fall Season."

A moment later, the Seelies traversed their portal in tightly disciplined rank and file.

"Us, too," the Huntsman said, weary from the game. "Come along, Mistress Cal. There's training to be done before Fall."

"With half our team still stone? I'd rather stay here and belt some sense into the queen, or at least some magic out of her."

The leader peered sharply her way. "You are still under contract. We will have our day on the field."

Callie slumped, clearly defeated.

Emily sighed. She was suddenly so tired, and, just as suddenly, less certain about the future than she had ever been.

She'd lost the shard.

The queen, who seemed recovered now, was back to her normal dangerous self.

Callie was still going to be stuck in the Fairy Realm, losing precious time for any possible career in the colleges or pros. And now her Small Folk friends were in just as much danger as ever. And that was before adding in the fact that a big chunk of the team, Maddoc, Greeven, and Twy, were all calcified.

How could any of the lesser houses of the Fairy Realm stand up against the Seelies and the Unseelies, the only two teams who, if Callie had told her properly, didn't have members standing on that Field of Statues?

Emily looked at Benji, then in turn at Jake, Jamal, Patsy, Lizzy, and Pash.

She'd gotten her Unicorns into something she should never have gotten them into. Benji in particular, she thought as they clutched the Web Gem with an awkwardness that seemed so foreign to their usual self-assured demeanor.

Her friend had certainly gotten what they wanted but with a typical fairy-trick twist. Now they knew exactly what their heritage was: dark and full of spiders. It was going to be a lot to handle. She worried about what that kind of knowledge would do to Benji.

But as she watched them turning the trophy over in wonder, some of that familiar self-assurance leached back into their posture. It made an idea spark in her mind.

"Hey, Benji. Can't you use the Web Gem to un-statue everyone?"

A moment of pregnant silence stretched out as Benji met her eyes.

"Oh my god, yes! You can fix this!" Callie exclaimed, stepping up to face Benji. "You can use the Web Gem to release everyone from the stone."

"I — uh." Benji swallowed hard and examined the Web Gem as if it might be an Oracle. "Yeah. Maybe. I mean. Yeah, I can at least try."

As the remaining crowd watched with bated breath, Benji adjusted their hold on the Web Gem and frowned in concentration.

The fairy lords hovered nearby in anticipation.

Benji's golden glow rose around them, and a trilling sound like a flute on the wind filled the field. A quick cyclone of wind blew the

Unicorns cap from their head. Emily tried to ignore the sensation of tiny spiders crawling up her legs.

"I see it!" Benji gasped, throwing back their head. "I see it! Everything is—"

They cut off abruptly, and, as their eyes rolled back, their knees buckled.

Standing right in front of Benji, Callie was the first to rush to grab them, but Emily and Adrien weren't far behind. Together, the three of them supported Benji as they came back to themself.

"What did you see?" Callie asked, her hope almost too overpowering. "Did you see how to undo the spell?"

Benji shook their head. "I can't do it, Callie. I'm not like you. I can't work any magic with this thing. I'm only a caretaker."

Dismay threatened to choke Emily. "So, there's no way to save everyone?"

"That's not what they said," Adrien murmured, peering inquisitively at Benji. "Already getting the hang of talking like a fairy lord, eh, Benji?"

Benji flashed a quick grin, already recovering. "There's a way. I don't think I can use magic with the Web Gem, but I can see it. All of it, as well as the ways it all connects. Like a web, you know? It's like things vibrate when they touch one another, and I can read those."

They took a deep breath and looked at Callie.

"I saw how *you* can save everyone."

"Me?" Callie gaped.

"All three of you. The baseball magic put itself literally in your hands this season, didn't it?"

Adrien got it first.

"My glove," he said, lifting it so they could see it still faintly glowing on his hand.

Callie nodded. "My bat."

Emily looked between her three friends, uncertain. Then, her gaze caught on someone standing beyond them, still part of the crowd of spectators.

Dad.

He didn't say anything, didn't come over to stand with her. But she could hear his voice in his expression. *You're all grown up, Em. Your mother would be so proud.*

"Right," she said, feeling in her pocket. "My mom's baseball."

A flare pulsed from Benji. "They're all charmed in some way or another, aren't they? One bat, one ball, one glove?"

Emily felt a spike of hope again. "As different as the magic within each denizen," she said, quoting the Spider Queen.

"How much more varied can you get?" Callie said, her voice full of awe.

"It will take a trip back to the Fairy Realm," Adrien said. "But that would be worth it."

"Let's do it," Emily said. "If we can set Maddoc and the rest free, I say we do it."

A voice rang out from the shadows.

"I'm coming, too," Megan Moore said as she marched up to them — her cheeks highlighted with the fading glow of her phone, which had been recording everything.

Emily was already shaking her head. "No way. The last thing we need is a reporter in the Fairy Realm." Emily might have a newfound respect for Megan's reporting, but the girl had pulled one too many publicity stunts tonight. The idea of Megan Moore in the Fairy Realm made her want to break out in hives.

"Yeah," Callie said, agreeing with Emily. "The Fairy Realm is too dangerous. Besides, we just want to get in and get out. Extra baggage would just slow us down."

Megan gave no ground. "Extra baggage or not. This is the biggest story in Pattersonville history, so there's no way I'm going to miss it."

Even Benji was frowning. "I don't think it's a good idea, Megan. Callie's right, it's going to be super dangerous. I can't do anything to protect you over there."

Megan's face was set, and she put her hands on her hips, taking as strong a pose as any champion scolder.

"I think she should come," said Adrien.

Emily gaped at him. "What? Adrien!"

He shrugged, but something sparkled behind his nonchalance. "Didn't you say she's been working on this case for years? I think she deserves to see how it ends. Besides..." He paused, flicking his eyes towards the reporter. A warmth came into his expression as he continued. "You may not be very happy with her intervention tonight, but without it, I never would have been able to get my glove. And without that..."

He shrugged again, sheepish this time. All around them, the Unicorns spectators cheered.

"Yeah, Adrien!" a voice rang out over the open field.

"Welcome home!" another called.

Adrien grinned at them and gave the Unicorn Salute. Then he turned back to their little group and put his arm around Megan.

"She's kind of the one who made this final rescue possible, you know?"

To her credit, Megan managed to cloak her astonishment in rapid fashion.

Emily couldn't help but notice that she did not step away from Adrien's encircling arm after he was done talking.

A sense of amused resignation came over Emily.

The baseball gave a warm glow in her hand, and she knew Adrien was right.

"All right," she said. "Megan comes too. So, let's do it."

THE UNSEELIE QUEEN, Lady Marne, and the Huntsman combined their powers with the residual baseball magic that hung over the field, and a moment later, as the remaining fans cheered them on, Emily, Callie, Adrien, and Megan joined with the fairy lords to step through the portal.

As Benji, clutching the Web Gem in the crook of their arm,

watched them go, a strange wistfulness filled their heart. They pushed it out of their mind, though, and instead focused on the field and the crowd that was now dissipating into the final dark of night. Soon enough, only the Unicorns remained. Benji expected they, too, would depart now, but each seemed to be unwilling to leave the old field behind.

"That was amazing," Lizzy said.

"It was," Jamal replied, his gaze falling again over the place where the shortstop would position himself. "It was the greatest game I've ever been a part of."

"Hey, Benj. I want to play," Jake said.

"What's that?" Benji said.

"The Fairy Series. I want to play."

"Ha," Benji replied immediately. "That would be funny." But the Web Gem seemed to light up as they thought about it.

"Could you imagine if we won?" Patsy said, gazing dreamily up at the lightening sky.

"I'm serious," Jake said. "They said they're going to play for the Web Gem. That thing has some sort of influence over the fairy ring under Unicorn Field, right? That's our home." He put his hand on his chest in emphasis. "So, I want to play, too."

"I don't think they'd let us," Benji said.

"It was fun playing on a team with Essie," Lizzy said. "Maybe we could join them?"

"Be careful what you ask for, Lizzy. See what happened to Adrien?"

"Well, I still think it would be worth a try," Jake said. "Unicorns should get some say in how Unicorn Field gets used."

The field grew quiet, then. To the east, the sky was growing lighter in earnest.

"I guess it's time to go home," Pash said.

"Yeah," Jamal said, though it was clear none of them really wanted to.

They walked away, though, each of them holding thoughts in

their heads, and Benji feeling the Web Gem's energy as it seeped into their hands and warmed their arms against the cool night.

Jake's idea gnawed at them.

Could they do it? Could the Unicorns play in the Fairy Realm series? Could the Web Gem and the vision of the magic it had given Benji allow them to, as it were, pull some strings? Jake was right: The Unicorns should have the right to influence how the magic of their own field worked.

Their baseball cleats scrabbled on the asphalt parking lot, scattering their ruminations.

They let out a jaw-cracking yawn, beginning to crash after the long night. They wondered what their parents would think of the Web Gem.

"Hope the car batteries aren't all too dead to start," Jake said. "Otherwise it'll be a long walk home."

Benji held up the Web Gem. "Maybe this thing does a mean jumpstart?"

They all laughed.

A few moments later, the field stood alone and empty, echoing once again with the silence of baseball played, and games won and lost.

EPILOGUE

Adrien shivered as a cool breeze passed over what had once been the Field of Statues, but was now, once again, simply the Other Field.

The space around him was awash with joyous feelings. Friends laughed and cried as they hugged one another. Fairies who'd been motionless stone just moments before jumped and danced about the field for the sake of moving. Even the stands were populated, and getting more full, as word of the broken spell rippled through the Fairy Realm. Somehow — Adrien suspected the Hag Sisters — game day refreshments had been conjured in. Their light, sweet aroma wafted over the festivities.

Adrien breathed it all in.

Freedom.

The glove on his hand still tingled with the residue of the counterspell he had worked alongside Emily and Callie. And though Emily now stood smiling fiercely with her Small Folk friends, and Callie was busy trading amusingly shy smiles with a large centaur, Adrien felt his connection to them still pulsing strong.

Besides, he had his own company. Megan stood beside him, her phone whipping from one camera angle to the next so rapidly she couldn't possibly be getting anything but blurry shots.

"I don't know which fairy is the most amazing," she said breathlessly as she snapped a picture of Maddoc slapping a tearful Fennoc on the back. "How am I ever going to be able to pick just one to feature in my article?"

His silence made her look up at him.

"What?" she said.

"You light up when you're working on a story," Adrien said. "Did you know that?"

Megan's lips twisted as if she was annoyed at him, but her cheeks flushed hard enough that the freckled side stood out. Adrien decided he liked that, too.

"I'm serious, Adrien. It's a real problem."

For an instant, Adrien saw a gap of uncertainty in her gaze. For her bravado, he could see she was still feeling her way through this story and wasn't sure where it was going to come out. It was an image that made him like her even more. "Don't worry. I've seen your work. You'll figure it out."

She paused her photography to meet his eyes. "I think it has to be one with a mix of beauty and darkness. The people of Pattersonville need to know what they're dealing with, both good and bad. I don't want anyone else to go through what you did, Adrien, or those other kids that have fallen through the Fairy Rings over the years. I got a scary shot of the Unseelie Queen right as she was whooshing herself away in that black cloud of hers. I think that's the one. Look."

She tipped her phone so he could see the screen and swiped with an expertise Adrien still could only dream of. He'd never get the hang of smartphones, no matter how much time he spent in the mortal world.

With a touch of indulgence, Adrien glanced at the screen.

The image she showed him made his lungs squeeze in a sudden burst of fear, which melted into a hazy wonder. Megan had worked a magic all of her own and had managed to capture not only the dramatic moment when the Unseelie Queen had departed in a swirl of black smoke right before Adrien, Emily, and Callie had undone the statue spell, but also the true face of the Unseelie Queen, the one Adrien had known over the hundred years of his captivity. Darkness burned in her eyes. Malice dripped along the curves of her face.

It was as intensely beautiful as it was terrifying.

"Wow," he said. He knew he was staring at Megan now, a bit breathless. "I think you're spot on. Everyone should see this picture."

"Oh, they will," Megan said with a grin. "I'm thinking magazines. Full glossy photos, slick columns of text. It'll be a sweet debut, exclusive inside scoop on the Fairy Realm."

Adrien chuckled. There was the confident, tenacious Megan Moore he was used to. "I'm thinking that maybe I should give you that interview after all," he said.

"Oh yeah?" She halted and gave him a mischievous sideways grin that also served to make her eyes sparkle. "You think an exclusive interview with Pattersonville West High School's most up-and-coming Thespian will give this article the oomph it needs?"

She gave him a playful nudge with her elbow.

He didn't try to stifle the warm swell of happiness her little joke evoked in him. She was right. Without the queen's threats hanging over him anymore, he could be whoever he chose to be, whether that be a baseball player, groundskeeper, actor, or all three at once. Even better, thanks to Megan's work in getting his truth out to the greater population, he could do it all as himself.

He could make friends, now, beyond just those who knew his secret.

"Well," he said. "Fairies are known to have a weak spot for the Bard."

"I bet Shakespeare would have had a killer curveball."

"He'd've played shortstop, for sure."

"And dashed out a sonnet while he waited to go up to bat."

"All the world's a stadium," Adrien said, and the truth of the statement resonated with the baseball magic swirling through him and around him.

He had a feeling the upcoming season, both here in the Fairy Realm and back home in the real world, was going to be something really special. And he wouldn't miss joining in for anything.

Thespian or not, he was a Unicorn, after all.

Always.

ABOUT BRIGID COLLINS

Brigid Collins is a fantasy and science fiction writer living in Nevada.

Her fantasy series *The Songbird River Chronicles* and *Winter's Consort*, her fun middle grade hijinks series *The Sugimori Sisters*, and her dark fairy tale novella *Thorn and Thimble* are available wherever books are sold. Her short stories have appeared in Fiction River, Feyland Tales, and Mercedes Lackey's Valdemar anthologies.

Sign up for her newsletter at www.brigidcollinsbooks.com/newsletter-sign-up/ and get a free copy of *Strength & Chaos, Mischief & Poise: Four Cat Tales*, exclusively available to her subscribers!

Website: https://brigidcollinsbooks.com

Also by Brigid Collins

About Ron Collins

Ron Collins is a best-selling Science Fiction and Dark Fantasy author who writes across the spectrum of speculative fiction. You can find his work at all major online retailers.

His short fiction has received a Writers of the Future prize and a CompuServe HOMer Award. His short story "The White Game" was nominated for the Short Mystery Fiction Society's 2016 Derringer Award.

He holds a degree in Mechanical Engineering, and has worked to develop avionics systems, electronics, and information technology before chucking it all to write full-time.

Website: https://www.typosphere.com

Get Free Books!
Ron's Reader List: Newsletter: http://typosphere.com/newsletter

ALSO BY RON COLLINS

<u>Novels</u>

Stealing the Sun (9 books)

Saga of the God-Touched Mage (8 books)

The PEBA Diaries (2 books)

The Knight Deception

Wakers

Home Run Enchanted (with Brigid Collins)

<u>Collections</u>

Tomorrow in All the Worlds

Picasso's Cat & Other Stories

Five Magics

Collins Creek (3 volumes)

<u>Nonfiction</u>

On Writing (And Reading!) Short

On Creating (And Celebrating!) Characters

<u>Poetry</u>

Five Seven Five

ACKNOWLEDGMENTS

The authors would like to thank Sharon Bass, who is a beta reader extraordinaire, and Lisa Collins, wife, mom, and most excellent last reader.

Insert standard disclaimers: All errors are our fault.

All right, who are we kidding. If there's anything wrong in this book, you can pretty much take it to the bank that it's Ron's fault. [grin!]

Thanks also to the Kickstarter people who backed *Home Run Enchanted*, the first book in this series. Without you, book 2 may not have happened!

www.ingramcontent.com/pod-product-compliance
Lightning Source LLC
Chambersburg PA
CBHW020121070726
47497CB00020B/317